The *Italian Flame*

ROSANNA LEY

The Italian Flame

QUERCUS

First published in Great Britain in 2025 by

QUERCUS

Quercus Editions Ltd
Carmelite House
50 Victoria Embankment
London EC4Y 0DZ

An Hachette UK company

The authorized representative in the EEA is Hachette Ireland,
8 Castlecourt Centre, Dublin 15, D15 XTP3, Ireland (email: info@hbgi.ie)

A CIP catalogue record for this book is available
from the British Library

HB ISBN 978 1 52942 773 8
TPB ISBN 978 1 52942 774 5
EBOOK ISBN 978 1 52942 776 9

1

Typeset by CC Book Production
Printed and bound in Great Britain by Clays Ltd, Elcograf S.p.A.

Papers used by Quercus are from well-managed forests and other responsible sources.

For Maria Donovan

It is so still and transcendent, the cypress trees poise like flames of forgotten darkness, that should have been blown out at the end of the summer.

D. H. Lawrence

CHAPTER I

Marilyn

1965

It was a warm, sunny day in July and Marilyn was sketching on Burton Beach.

There was a certain place, a nook, in which she could stretch out her legs, have her back to Burton Cliff and see the coastline snaking effortlessly past Cliff End and Burton Mere all the way to Portland. The shore in front of her was a mixture of sand and the small pea-pebbles of Chesil Beach, the rolling waves beyond steaming in as if they intended to take over the world. She watched them frothing over the stones in perfect arcs of foam which dissolved into the air, were absorbed into the sand, and then were gone – while the tide drew back, rushed forward, inexorably, wave after wave. Somehow, it was this she must capture on her page.

At the shoreline, two children were playing in the shallows and Marilyn had sketched them too, in silhouette, searching for the loose, cheerful movement of their young bodies, the elasticity of their limbs as they ran into the sea, jumped, shrieked, then streaked out again, holding hands and laughing with delight. It was a challenge – to somehow find the careless-ness, the joy, the lack of inhibition, simply through the lines of the pencil and the delicate shading on paper. Later, though, with watercolours, the curl of the brush, the flow of the paint might help her.

As Marilyn continued to sketch, someone else wandered into the frame, as people always would do, down by the water's edge. Marilyn narrowed her eyes so that he became less real, more of a moving blur than a man, as she followed his progress. He was walking barefoot, scuffing at the pebbly sand, allowing the water to lap over his toes, pausing to watch the waves.

Should she include him? Marilyn put her head to one side and considered his worth. It seemed a shame not to. He looked interesting and was clearly not from around here, and yet she sensed he had an affinity with the sea. He was young – about her own age, she supposed – of medium height, and his dark curly hair was damp and seemed to gleam in the sunlight. He was wearing baggy shorts and a T-shirt, once red perhaps, but now faded to a light rose. He walked with a slow and relaxed gait, swinging his sandals in his hand, as though he was con-fident, as though he had no particular place to go.

Marilyn glanced at her watch. She had thirty minutes of her lunch break left and the hotel was only a five-minute sprint away. There was time. She squinted towards him and made a few strokes. It was difficult, though, because he was walking out of the frame and up the beach. In fact, she realised, he was walking towards her – and quite purposefully now – so perhaps he had twigged what she was doing and was coming over to object.

She just had time to turn the page of her sketchbook before

he was upon her. She blinked up at him. He had dark eyes and a full mouth – he was, in fact, good-looking, she saw – and he didn't seem like the objecting type. But he didn't say a word and so Marilyn gave a little nod.

He nodded back.

Hmm. She definitely hadn't seen him before. He was unshaven and his skin was a rich olive, his eyes a dark brown. Was he Spanish perhaps? Or French?

He lifted his free hand. 'Hi,' he said (with an accent, she noted) and smiled.

Gosh, thought Marilyn. That was some smile. 'Hi,' she replied.

He pointed to her sketchbook. 'You . . . ?' He mimed drawing.

'Draw? Yes.' She'd always drawn, always painted. It wasn't even anything she thought about much – she'd just done it. She smiled back at him. He obviously didn't speak much English. And he probably wouldn't mind appearing in her sketch; people mostly didn't – she supposed it was flattering.

'I see?' He sat down beside her with that easy confidence she'd noted earlier.

'Sure.' Marilyn flipped over the page.

'Ah, good,' he said. 'Very good, yes.' And he stared at the drawing for much longer than people usually did. Sometimes it would be a cursory glance, sometimes a smile of approval (often a fake one, Marilyn suspected), most often a non-committal nod, or if it was her boss, he would tell her to put that thing away and find something useful to do. But that was one of the advantages of working on the reception desk at the Cliff Hotel – Marilyn could observe the comings and goings and, if she wasn't too busy, she could draw them too.

3

Once, she had hoped to be a professional artist – in some capacity, at least. But her parents had given the idea of art school short shrift. 'Drawing's just a hobby. If you'll take my advice, you'll train for something practical,' her no-nonsense mother had told her. 'Look at Glenda – she'll always have her secretarial training to fall back on.'

That was how it was, Marilyn thought now. A secretary or a mother . . . But increasingly, there were other choices, and she knew her chance would come. If her parents wouldn't help her, she would save until she had enough to train for something she really wanted to do. And in the meantime . . . Since Marilyn still lived at home, since she must make a financial contribution, she had drifted into this job at the hotel instead and, almost to her surprise, was still here several years later. It was easier sometimes, Marilyn had found, to drift through life. But she was only twenty-five; something exciting would surely happen to her soon.

'Are you Spanish?' she asked the young man now sitting next to her, stretching out his legs beside her own in a way that was strangely intimate.

He shook his head. 'Again?'

'Try again?' She laughed. 'Okay, French then?'

'No . . .'

Come to think about it, he looked a bit Roman, Marilyn decided. In profile, his nose was definitely aquiline. 'Italian,' she concluded.

'*Si, si.*' He looked disproportionately delighted that she'd got it right, considering it was her third guess. 'Yes,' he said.

'And why are you here in Dorset?' Because he couldn't live here. If he lived here, surely he would speak better English? And surely she would know about it?

4

Marilyn wished more people from overseas came to West Dorset; she would love the chance to talk to them about wherever it was they came from, learn more about the world and maybe decide where she would travel to – when she got the opportunity or when the exciting thing she was waiting for actually happened. But so far, Dorset had remained depressingly British.

He frowned. Clearly, he didn't understand.

'Why . . .' Marilyn gave an exaggerated spread of the hands, accompanied by raised eyebrows. 'You.' She pointed at him. 'Here?' She gestured to the beach, then swept her arm around to encompass the entire area. She hadn't expected to be doing *this* at lunchtime, she found herself thinking. It was different. And it was quite fun.

'Ah.' He nodded enthusiastically, said something in Italian, then, 'I work in Bristol.'

'Now?'

'Not now.'

'Right.' Marilyn felt they were getting somewhere. 'You were working in Bristol,' she said. 'And now . . . ?'

'Now I come here.' He grinned.

They continued like this for another ten minutes. Marilyn explained that she lived nearby and worked in the hotel. She turned to point; the building was visible, white and looming on the cliff to the west of their position on the beach. He told her that his work – building work; here he mimed brick-laying and decorating rather vividly, she thought – had finished earlier than expected (he'd been laid off, she assumed) and so he had come to Dorset for a few weeks to take a look around.

'To see the world,' he added.

Marilyn laughed at the idea that West Dorset was in any way 'the world' and he nodded as if he understood.

'But it is beautiful,' he said, and she had to agree. It was her home and she loved it, despite her longing to get away from it sometimes.

'Tell me about Italy,' she urged.

And as he began to speak, she watched him, wishing she could draw him as he talked – half in Italian, half in English – about his home town, a dreamy and passionate look in his dark eyes.

Eventually, she could resist it no longer. 'May I?' she asked him, and she pulled her sketchbook back onto her lap and tried to capture the essence of this unexpected and attractive stranger on paper in just a few quick strokes of her pencil.

He laughed and watched her and talked some more. Marilyn could listen to his voice all day – it seemed to contain everything she longed for. It was soft and had a lilting rhythm that was like a song; it was different, sexy, exotic even. She could close her eyes and simply float off into another world, she decided.

'It is good,' he said when she'd finished the sketch. He looked surprised. 'It is me.'

She laughed again, ripped out the page – although slightly reluctantly since she'd quite like to keep it – and offered it to him. 'Do you want it?'

'Oh, yes, *si si*.' He took it almost reverentially. 'Thank you.'

Their eyes met. Marilyn found it hard to look away, until a thought struck. She glanced down at her watch and jumped to her feet. 'Oh my Lord, I'm late.'

She swept her pencils and sketchbook into her shoulder bag. 'I must go. *Pronto*.' She looked at him and they both laughed this time.

'Okay.' He too got to his feet, still carefully holding the sketch she had given him.

Marilyn smiled and sprinted towards the cliff path. To her delight, he didn't hesitate – he went with her.

'But your name?' he puffed as they ran. 'What is it, please?'

'Marilyn.' She too was out of breath.

'Marilyn.' He seemed to taste it on his tongue. He gave the last syllable a long, delicious length with another vowel at the end – *linnne*. 'I see you again, yes?' He glanced across at her.

The wind was in her hair and the sound of the sea roared in her ears. They were climbing the cliff path now and the grassy sandstone was soft underfoot. Marilyn came to a sudden decision. 'Yes!' she shouted into the wind.

She stopped a little way up the path by the low wooden gate that led up to the Cliff Hotel and he stopped with her. 'There is a dance,' she said. She added a quick mime. 'Tonight. At the village hall. I could see you there?'

He had his head to one side regarding her intently. Marilyn wasn't sure if he had even understood what she'd said. 'Yes,' he said. 'Tonight.'

She nodded, unlatched the gate. 'See you later then,' she called. And ran.

CHAPTER 2

Lily

2018

Lily rang the doorbell. She had a key, but she hadn't told her mother she was coming and she didn't want to just barge in. Her mother wouldn't like it, she knew.

As she waited, half listening for her mother's step on the stairs, her voice wafting down the hall, Lily looked around her. The front garden was more unruly than usual – though that had been her father's area of concern rather than her mother's – and she noticed a general air of neglect: the windows clearly hadn't been washed for a while and white paint was flaking from the wooden frames, although in the flower bed a few early daffodils were putting on a cheery face at least.

Lily hadn't been back here for months. Since her father's death two years ago, it hadn't felt like home – how could it? She and her mother spoke on the phone from time to time, but it was always a brief and awkward conversation and Lily tended to be relieved when it ended. Visiting . . . well, that was even worse.

Lily peered through the glass in the front door but couldn't see much beyond the oatmeal carpet. She rang the doorbell for a second time. She supposed that home was now Hackney since she lived there. Only . . . She sighed. Hackney had never really seemed like home either. And would she even be living there in a month's time, now that Cate was moving out?

As for Jack's suggestion . . . Lily had told him she would think about it, but really, she didn't need to. And besides, she had other more pressing things to consider. Such as why Auntie Glenda had been so determined that Lily should visit her mother, and why she needed to come right away.

'I know you two have had your differences,' Glenda had said.

Her aunt didn't know the half of it, thought Lily.

'But you need to get yourself down here to see her, love.'

Lily frowned. 'Why the sudden urgency?'

But Glenda refused to say.

Her mother had told Lily she was fine the last time they'd spoken. So, what was the problem? Lily supposed that her mother must be having one of her dramas. She sighed again.

And where was she? Should Lily let herself in? Or maybe phone her instead? Lily felt pulled back into childhood. Nowadays, she liked to think of herself as decisive. In her work, she was firm; she was good at telling people financial truths about their businesses which they didn't always want to hear. But when it came to her mother, Lily reverted to dither mode.

Now that she was about to ring the doorbell a third time, though, she heard a shuffling in the hall. It couldn't be her mother. Her mother didn't shuffle. And then the door slowly opened.

'Mum?' Lily stared at her and her mother stared back. Her face was gaunt, her blue-grey eyes dimmed and confused.

9

'Mum?' Lily was shocked; she couldn't hide it. Her mother looked as if she'd had all the life sucked out of her.

'Lily!' At least she seemed pleased to see her. She even smiled. 'You didn't tell me . . .' She glanced down at Lily's weekend case. 'You're staying for a few days? How lovely.' Even her voice had changed. It sounded dry and brackish, and she was hanging on to the door frame as if she needed the support.

'Mum.' Lily touched her arm, loosened her mother's hold on the door frame, took her hand. Her mother's skin looked wrinkled, old and pale with a bluish tinge as if it hadn't seen sunlight for a while. When had she last held her hand? Lily had no idea. And she'd never seen her look like this. Her mother seemed so frail and she wasn't wearing a scrap of make-up, which was unusual in itself. 'What is it? What's wrong?'

'Oh, I'm just tired.' She slipped her hand from Lily's grasp. It felt both evasive and insubstantial; her mother had lost weight, there was nothing to her. 'Come in, darling. It's cold out there.'

'Yes.' Although it wasn't, not really. It had been very mild for February.

Lily picked up her case and followed her mother inside. The house smelt different too. It used to smell of cooking (Lily's father had been a keen amateur chef) and it used to smell homely. Now, it smelt medicinal and harsh and the central heating was on so high that Lily could barely breathe.

You should get yourself here to see her, Glenda had told her on the phone.

And now Lily could see why.

Once inside, her mother went back to bed. That was a shock. The bed was downstairs in the living room and Lily stared at it, this piece of further evidence. Someone had brought it in,

10

her mother told her, waving her hand as if it was of no importance either way. It was a proper hospital-type bed, which was useful, no doubt, but seemed profoundly depressing to Lily. Presumably, her mother couldn't even manage the stairs.

And then, when Lily sat beside her, not knowing where to go or what to do, her mother told Lily that she had cancer. Actually, she was dying, she said.

The bald statement seemed impossible to take in. Lily stared at her, confused, speechless. They had never been close, but now Father was gone, there was only Lily. Apart from Auntie Glenda, of course. How could her mother have not told her she was so very ill?

'I don't understand,' she heard herself saying.

Her mother closed her eyes for a moment as if it was all too much. And then she spoke again.

She'd undergone courses of both chemo and radiotherapy, she told Lily in a weak but matter-of-fact voice that was also horribly new. Glenda had taken her to the hospital for these. Lily's aunt had been very good, apparently. Her mother spent most of the day in bed now, she said; it was easier that way.

Easier . . . Hesitantly, Lily reached out to stroke her mother's hair from her face. Her hair had always been fair and shining, though latterly showing streaks of grey, but now it was sparse, brittle and dry to the touch. This too was painful; Lily could hardly look at it. She took her hand away.

'Why didn't you tell me?' She felt hurt and angry. And in these circumstances she didn't know what to do with either emotion. 'I only spoke to Glenda last week. Why didn't she say?'

A soft sigh. 'I asked her not to.'

'But why?' Again, Lily felt shut out. Again, she felt that

11

familiar sense of rejection. Even when her mother was dying, she didn't want her near . . . Lily gritted her teeth. But this wasn't a time for being self-absorbed, she reminded herself. She reached for the glass of water on the bedside table and offered her mother a sip from the straw.

'There was no point,' her mother said. 'I didn't want to worry you, didn't want to make you feel you had to come rushing back to Dorset.'

Was that it? Had she been thinking of Lily after all? 'But you need looking after.' Lily felt helpless. It was all-consuming. Everything she'd been worrying about before was inconsequential compared with this.

'People come in.' Her mother was getting tired now, Lily could tell. 'They want to move me to a hospice.'

Did that mean that time was short? Lily swallowed the lump in her throat. 'And you, Mum? Where do you want to be?'

But she did not reply. Perhaps she couldn't. Perhaps it was just too much effort.

Lily too remained silent now. She was trying to compute everything. She was trying to match this weak and frail woman, this dying woman, with the mother who had whisked around the house as if she always had somewhere more important to be, something more important to do – which quite often meant escaping to her art studio in the garden and a painting she was working on at the time.

Once, Lily had craved her attention. But at some point, she had given up. It wasn't so bad. She'd had her father and he adored her – she counted herself lucky for that. But when he died . . . Lily shifted in her seat. She still found it hard to think of. When he died from a sudden and severe stroke, her mother had crumbled. She spent more time in her studio than

12

ever and Lily hadn't been able to get through to her at all. But she didn't paint a thing.

Lily had tried her best to support her. But it was as if only her mother was allowed to grieve. Lily's grief — that dark and bottomless pit that could open up anytime day or night and suck her in — was given no importance, no acknowledgement, nowhere to go. Perhaps she and her mother should have grown closer, but in fact, his death caused them to drift even further apart. They grew cooler towards one another as they became more distant, as if Lily's father had been their anchor, and without him they were unmoored, free to go their separate ways. He was the one who had made them work as a family, Lily realised. Without him, they didn't seem to belong together at all.

After his death, Lily had stayed here at home for a while. She and her mother had circled around one another, awkwardly, like the rivals they had always been. Her mother drank; Lily went for long walks on the grass-topped ginger cliffs of West Bay and Hive. They argued too and eventually Lily had packed her bags and gone to Hackney to move in with her friend Cate, also from Dorset. Lily worked freelance as a financial business consultant and accountant and there was more work for her in London. It would be a new start with fewer reminders of what she had lost — and there was no reason to stay.

Now, while her mother slept, Lily prowled around the house. Her own bedroom was as empty and impersonal as she'd left it; she could sleep there. Her parents' bedroom was frozen in time, as if her mother had just walked out of the room one morning: bed unmade, the lid off a jar of loose powder on her dressing table, curtains half drawn. Even her mother's nightie was draped over the foot of the bed, where she might have

13

carelessly thrown it that same morning. The room smelt of her mother's perfume – Chanel No 5. What had happened on that day? Lily wondered. What had her mother been feeling? Would she have known that she would never come back up here again?

Lily phoned her aunt, who lived nearby. 'I'm here,' she said. 'Auntie Glenda? Why didn't you tell me she was so ill?'

'I promised her.' She heard her aunt's intake of breath. 'But you're there now, love. How is she?'

'In pain. Exhausted. Asleep.'

'She only has a short time left, Lily,' her aunt said. 'Can you help?'

Lily thought of the flat in Hackney. She had to be gone in a few weeks. She thought of Jack and how he was waiting for the decision she'd already made but had failed to tell him. She thought of her mother and how it had always been between them. And she thought of her father and what he would have wanted. 'I'll stay,' she said. 'If she doesn't want to go into a hospice, I'll stay here with her, until . . .' Her voice broke. Saying it out loud was hard. It made it real.

'Good girl.' Lily heard the relief in her aunt's voice. 'I know things haven't always been easy between you. And God knows, since your father passed away, she's been away with the fairies even more than ever. But she needs you, love.'

'Yes.' Her aunt was right. However difficult things had been between them, whatever resentments Lily still harboured, however separate and distant they had become, she was still her mother.

CHAPTER 3

Marilyn

1965

He was already at the village hall when Marilyn arrived at the dance, standing near to the door, looking dark, brooding and interesting. Marilyn felt the skip of excitement. And she didn't even know his name.

'Hi,' she greeted him. He looked even better than he had on the beach. He was wearing navy trousers and a crisp open-necked white cotton shirt with a dark blazer, and his wild curly hair had been brushed back and tamed.

'Marilyn.' And without any hint of self-consciousness, he bent to kiss her on both cheeks.

Instantly, she was charmed. She had never been kissed that way before and she liked it. He smelt of something clean and citrussy. His lips were warm and she could feel the intimate graze of stubble on her skin. He hadn't shaved then, she found herself thinking. And she was glad.

The band, who were dressed smartly in suits and ties, lived

locally and were regulars at the weekly dance. They had been good on beat music and now had moved into pop, playing songs made famous by The Beatles, The Dave Clark Five and others, doing their little moves as they sang and played guitar.

To Marilyn's relief, her Italian stranger liked to dance and she did too.

'You haven't told me your name,' she said at the end of the first song. It was a twist, a number by Chubby Checker designed to get everyone on the dance floor. Already they were both slightly out of breath. The hall was buzzing with noise and she had to lean in close in order to be heard.

He frowned.

She indicated herself. 'Marilyn.' And pointed at him. 'You?'

He smiled. 'Bruno.'

'Bruno,' she repeated.

The band started playing once more. It was a slower song and, with no hesitation, he took her in his arms. It felt good. It felt right. It was exactly where Marilyn wanted to be.

They spent the entire evening together and this had never happened to Marilyn before either. Other boys she knew tried to claim a dance – including Tom, who she was friendly with because they both worked at the hotel – but Marilyn didn't want them. She only wanted this handsome Italian stranger. She couldn't take her eyes off him and it seemed to be the same for Bruno. His steady gaze pulled her towards him like a magnet. Plus, he was a great dancer – whatever the song, he had a natural rhythm and none of the inhibitions she'd seen from a lot of the men around here.

The band moved seamlessly from one song to another and there was barely chance to catch breath, let alone talk in between. But when the band took a break, he went to fetch them glasses of lemonade, and they took their drinks outside to get some air. If dancing with this man was intoxicating, then the breaks were a sweet relief. They talked – in the mix of mime and simple English that they'd used on the beach – and she found out that, like her, Bruno lived by the sea and that he had a sister and lots of other relatives from the sound of it. 'Family – it is big in Italy,' he told her.

Marilyn thought of the small terraced house where she lived with her parents, her sister Glenda, Glenda's husband Ted and their toddler. 'It's pretty big in England too,' she told him. 'Or at least it is where we come from.'

And then, the band started up again. They glanced at one another and drifted back inside, drawn by the music, by the compulsive beat, by the chance to feel the heat of the other's body once again. He smiled as he led her to the dance floor and as they danced, they moved in sync, in what seemed to Marilyn to be a natural harmony. She felt that she could dance like this for ever.

Marilyn glanced shyly up at him. This man, this gorgeous Italian man, seemed to represent everything different that she'd ever ached for. There was a spark between them, a connection when he looked into her eyes, when he touched her arm, when he held her close and she breathed in the scent of the clean citrus mingled with the male smell of him. It was a revelation.

By the end of the evening, he was no longer a stranger. They had danced away most of the night and talked away the rest of it and Marilyn had come to realise that if English should fail them, there was another language they could both share and understand.

It passed through the hands, the feet; it was in the brush of their bare arms. It glimmered within a smile, the breath of laughter, a certain look in the eye, a whisper. After he walked her home, when he kissed her under the lamplight outside her parents' house, Marilyn didn't want whatever was happening between them ever to end. She felt so drawn to him; already she felt she knew him better than any man she'd ever met.

And that was just the beginning . . .

Over the next two weeks, Marilyn met up with Bruno in every free minute of her time. They went for long walks from Burton Beach along the cliff path, past the coastguard station to Cliff End and on towards the fringes of reeds around the Mere where sea campion and sea kale with creamy white flowers grew in clumps out of the pebbles. Here, they were alone, apart from the occasional fisherman who paid them no mind. And they shared picnics on the stony beach or in the grassy meadows still full of buttercups – hunks of bread and cheese with tomatoes, which they ate while feeling the warmth of the summer sun on their faces and bare arms and legs, and listening to the joyful skylarks above.

She drew him – often – and sometimes she ripped out the page of her sketchbook and gave the drawing to him. Sometimes not. But she could never capture him, she felt, not entirely. They talked incessantly in their strange broken language, they walked for miles hand in hand, to West Bexington and back, and they swam – not on busy Burton Beach or at West Bay, but in more deserted spots along the way where he would lift her out of the water and she would hold on to his shoulders and twine her legs around his waist, skin to skin. He kissed her with salty lips while Marilyn twisted her fingers through his damp curly hair.

They made their arrangements to meet and, if he needed to, he could come to the hotel. Marilyn knew her parents wouldn't approve. *What's wrong with the lads round here?* That was what they would say.

During this time, the passion simmered between them like a slow fire. She knew that he respected her; he did not ask for more. But Marilyn recognised his desire and she too wanted it. She was hungry for all of him.

It was very warm that July – summer was in full thrall. They often walked on the beach in the evenings too, and one time, they met after Marilyn's evening shift. It was late, the sky was soft and dark, lit only by a waning half-moon, and they strolled slowly eastwards along the gentle cliff path until they were quite sure that they were alone.

As one, they sank down onto a grassy mound. He held her close and she clung to him. His kisses seemed more urgent tonight. Or maybe it was the soft, delicate moonlight, the sigh of the reeds nearby, the soft rush of the sea back and forward, in her ears, in her head, echoing the pull of her heart, it seemed.

Marilyn undid the buttons of his shirt, slowly, one by one.

'Marilyn.' His voice was husky.

'I want to be with you,' she said. 'I want to be with you properly. Now.' She looked at him expectantly. She knew he would understand.

'You are sure?' he asked her. His hands were on her waist.

'More than I've ever been in my entire life,' she told him.

She wasn't an immature young girl – Marilyn was twenty-five and there had been two others before Bruno.

The first was a boy she'd grown up with and experimented with when they were only sixteen – a fumbling encounter that turned out to finish their relationship before it had properly begun. The second, though, she was a little ashamed of. Two summers ago, a man had been staying at the hotel. He was a salesman and he knew the right lines to say. He'd flattered her into bed — Marilyn could see that now — and she'd later found out that he was married. (Of course, he was; what had she been thinking?)

There had been other, more casual boyfriends, but they hadn't lasted long either. So you could say her love life had been something of a disappointment so far. Until now. Marilyn had always believed that somewhere, there was something more for her — and now she thought she knew exactly what it was.

Bruno looked worried. 'I have nothing,' he said, patting his pockets as if a packet of condoms might suddenly appear.

Marilyn shrugged. At this moment in time, she couldn't give a damn. She just wanted him, that was all.

'I take care,' he told her solemnly.

'Okay,' she said. She trusted him. He was the only person in her world who meant anything to her right now. Somehow, he had come to mean it all.

They made love on that grassy mound sheltered by the slender, rustling reeds. It was magical. He was gentle, tender and passionate. And that's when he told her he loved her. Marilyn knew it already, though — she'd seen it in his eyes, heard it in the lilting rhythm of his words, felt it in the space between them that they always had to fill . . . And she knew already that she loved him too.

They were the best days of Marilyn's life. Talking, walking, swimming, making love . . . But she knew that one day, it would end.

One afternoon, she went to meet him on the beach. He was sitting disconsolately chucking pebbles into the sea, his dark brows drawn together in a frown.

'Don't be sad,' she told him as she sat beside him on the stones.

He reached for her hand, kissed her gently on the lips. 'I am not sad,' he said. 'Not now you are here.'

'But you must leave soon? Is that it?' And when he frowned again. 'You must go back to Italy?' He had talked so little about his family, about his life there. Their love had kept them in a bubble; it had sheltered them from reality. But she knew that he *had* a life there. She had always known that he would not stay for ever.

'*Si.*' He twirled a strand of her hair around his finger. 'But I come back.'

'For me?' She'd hardly dared hope. Marilyn had imagined there might be a girl waiting for him at home; she sensed this was the case. But she also knew that what they had, it was maybe once in a lifetime. It was special.

'For you,' he agreed. 'I work, I gather money . . .'

'Save,' she said.

'Save,' he agreed. 'And I come back. For you.'

Marilyn rested her head against his shoulder. 'How long before you come back?' she murmured. She counted the weeks (or more probably months, she guessed) on her fingers and held her hand up to show him. 'One month, two, three, four?'

'Maybe longer,' he said.

'Longer?' Her spirits dipped. That was a very long time.

He put his arm around her. 'I come back,' he said again. 'And I write to you, yes?'

'Yes,' she nodded. Her parents would see the letters and they wouldn't like it, but they would have to know eventually. Marilyn knew that with time, she could make them understand.

From his pocket, he pulled a small package. He unwrapped it.

'What is it?'

Bruno pulled it free. It was an orange stone — a gemstone, she supposed — shaped like a tiny pyramid with horizontal lines etched into it. As it caught the sunlight, it shone like a flame.

'I have no ring,' he said. 'But this stone — she is special to me . . . She is mined in Italy. She is from the air.' He gestured. 'And from the heart.'

'It's beautiful,' she breathed. The colour was deep and ancient. She had never seen a gemstone like it before.

'It is for you, Marilyn. For the good luck. For the . . .' — he frowned — 'hope?'

'Is that what it represents? Hope? And the element of air?'

He nodded, gesticulated between them both. She saw the frustration in his eyes and knew that he wanted to say more but lacked the means.

'It is to keep you . . .' — he sighed as again he searched for the right word — 'safe.'

'Thank you.' She kissed the stone. She already loved this Italian flame. And who needed a ring? This was the most romantic gesture she could ever have imagined.

'Will you wait, Marilyn?' he asked her. 'Will you wait for me, my love?'

'I'll wait for as long as it takes, Bruno,' she assured him. Because he was her future, she knew. 'Even if it takes for ever, I will be here.'

CHAPTER 4

Lily

2018

The next day, when Glenda came round to see her sister, Lily took a break to go to the beach. She'd practically lived there as a child. She wandered down to the shore, taking a moment to watch the waves, to remember . . . Being here in Dorset again was strange, like going back in time. But everything had changed.

After a few minutes she turned back and began to make her way up the steep pathway of the cliff. She needed to walk; to try to recover her sense of equilibrium. Because everything had indeed changed, and not just the awful deterioration of her mother's health, which had shocked Lily to the core. There had been more rockfalls since her last visit: two huge piles of ginger rubble at the base of the cliff had spread out onto the sandy beach and were slowly being swallowed up by the sea. Erosion, she thought. Loss. Always loss. Loss was the hardest part.

As she climbed the cliff, Lily relished the feel of the fresh air on her skin. There was nothing quite like a sea breeze. She looked around her. It was too early for the wildflowers – purple thrift and gangly daisies would bloom here in in the spring – but at least the grass had an end-of-winter freshness after rain and some weak and hesitant sunshine.

Despite what she had found when she arrived, despite her mother's illness and how hard that was, it felt good to be here. This was a surprise. Despite everything, she found Dorset soothing after the hurly-burly of London. She must have bonded with the landscape when she was a girl – taken it for granted, she supposed, but bonded with it much more than she had realised.

But there was something else she must do today. Lily pulled her mobile out of her pocket and called Jack. It would be a difficult conversation, but better to do it sooner rather than later, she thought, what with everything else that she now had to think about. 'Hey.'

'Hey.' He sounded upbeat, but then Jack usually did.

They hadn't been together very long and had drifted into a relationship – mainly, Lily suspected, because Jack was a close friend of Travis's and Lily was equally close to Cate. A foursome built on convenience, she supposed. Jack was fun, but even before he made his suggestion, she'd already been wondering how she could extricate herself from the relation-ship without upsetting anyone. She'd come to believe that Jack might want more from her than she was willing to give, and now she was certain.

Lily sat down on a bench to focus on the call. 'Jack . . .' She was about to tell him about her mother, about what she'd found when she arrived in Dorset, but he gave her no chance, he was already on it.

'Have you made up your mind, Lily?' he asked her. 'I know it's a bit soon, but . . .'

Oh dear. She should have told him straightaway, but he'd taken her by surprise. It had never been a realistic option for Lily. Yes, it was too soon, but that wasn't the reason she wouldn't be moving in with him.

'With Cate moving in to Travis's place, surely it's the ideal solution?' he added. 'And I've got loads of space.'

Lily sighed. She would have to let him down gently. 'I'm not looking for a serious relationship, Jack,' she said. 'I'm sorry.'

'It doesn't have to be serious.'

But it would be. Moving in with Jack would solve the problem of where to live, but Lily shuddered to think how many other problems it would create. She valued her independence. And besides, Jack was good company and a nice guy, but he wasn't *her* nice guy. She had to face it – he wasn't even close.

'You have to move out of your flat, don't you?'

'Uh, yes, I do.'

He laughed uncertainly. 'So, we could at least give it a try.'

'I'm sorry, Jack,' she said again. 'I don't think it's a good idea.'

'But when you get back from Dorset . . .'

'I'm not coming back,' Lily said. She thought of her mother – but she didn't want to talk about that now. 'At least not for a while.'

Nearby, in a field bordering the cliff path, nonchalant-looking sheep chewed the grass, some early new-born lambs gambolling among them, leaping and bounding in that way that only lambs could. Below the golden cliffs, the water was smooth as silver. 'I'm staying here for a while, Jack,' Lily said. 'That's what I called to tell you.'

25

'I see.' He was silent for a moment. 'It feels like you're saying goodbye. Have I been dumped for Dorset?'

She had to laugh then, but at least she knew he wouldn't be suffering with a broken heart – it was early days for both of them. 'Not really,' she said. 'But I seem to be at a bit of a crossroads.'

'Okay.' He let out a sigh. 'Big shame, but I can take it. Stay in touch, Lily. Let me know how you're getting on.'

'I will.'

Maybe she would and maybe she wouldn't . . . He had let her off lightly, she realised, as she ended the call. She hadn't told him about her mother and she'd never told him about her childhood either. She hadn't confided in Jack much at all. Which said a lot, when you came to think of it.

As she continued her tramp over the cliff, heading now for Freshwater Beach where the River Bride pooled and found a way through the shingle bank in order to flow in a stream into the sea, Lily settled into the rhythm of walking. She counted her paces too, in groups of four, which had always been calming and helped her breathe more steadily. She needed to be calm and steady in order to deal with what had been waiting for her here at home.

As a child she'd always counted things; she couldn't remember a time when she hadn't. Her stuffed animals, lined up on top of the bed; the number of tiny outfits Barbie possessed; even the number of peas on her plate at dinner time. She couldn't help it. It had seemed impossible to curb the impulse. And then there were the dreams . . .

Lily forged on towards the highest point of the cliff. To her right in the distance, and beyond the river which ran parallel to the cliff at this point, were the buildings of Burton Bradstock, the church tower and thatched roofs as familiar to her as her own skin.

That was the thing about coming home: it brought your childhood back in full force. Those dreams had been nightmares really, she supposed, and for a while she'd had them almost every night. In the dreams, she couldn't stop counting and she'd wake up weeping because there was no end to it, only the certainty of infinity. Not that she'd known much about infinity back then; she only knew that numbers seemed to go on for ever.

It was her father who had talked her down from those dreams. 'You don't have to keep on counting, my darling,' he had said to her. 'You can let it go. You can stop.'

It hadn't been easy. But the dreams had faded, even though numbers had continued to be Lily's thing – in a good way – as time went on. Her father had listened as she'd talked about them – their shapes, their patterns – long before she fully understood how they could be used. They just made sense to Lily, though she couldn't really explain why. They were another language, she soon realised, and it was a language that Lily was inexplicably drawn to.

It was different now. Since then, Lily had learnt how versatile and useful numbers could be. They could mean so much. They could represent quantities, measure properties and describe patterns. They could be used to create mathematical models and to predict outcomes. Although Lily now worked with numbers almost every day of her life, they had never ceased to fascinate her, and she had never lost that early sense of wonder.

Back then, though, her mother thought that she was crazy. Her father, however, started teaching her mental arithmetic even before she learnt to read. That, she reflected, as she reached the top of the cliff, was just one of the differences between them.

Lily looked down at the landscape of her childhood, at the golden beach and the waves curling in to shore. Her mother had never been easy. Even so, Lily knew what she had to do next. She had to make her mother's last few months on this earth as painless and pleasant as possible. However hard that might be, Lily had to find a way.

CHAPTER 5

Marilyn

1965

Marilyn waited. It wasn't something she'd ever been good at doing and she wasn't good at it now. She worked, she mooched around the beach going to all the places she'd gone with Bruno, as the gap he'd left in her life grew ever wider. She drew, she painted and she waited. She had no address for him. He had hers. He was supposed to write first – that was what they'd agreed. How long before a letter might come? She counted the days.

When Marilyn missed her first period, she barely registered the fact. It was still busy at the hotel in the height of the summer and she'd never taken much notice of her dates.

When she missed her second period, she thought, *Hang on, it's been a while since* . . . and she did a rapid calculation. Had she even had a period since Bruno left?

Summer blues slipped into the grey and yellow skies of autumn and Marilyn was almost surprised to see the coppery tones in the leaves on the trees, the burnished conkers on the ground wrapped in their spiky coats, the grass on the cliff flat and muddy from the rain. There were few summer visitors now. She felt tired and nauseous – not just in the mornings but at other random times of the day – and she became adept at covering it up, at strolling almost nonchalantly to the bathroom and silently retching. No one noticed – there was too much going on at home. And still she waited.

By the end of October, she knew for sure. They had been careful, of course. But maybe once or twice they had not been quite so careful, had got carried away. It hadn't seemed to matter too much back then. But it mattered now.

Marilyn veered between pretending nothing was wrong and pure panic. With every day that went by, she thought, *He'll write tomorrow. He must write tomorrow.* Only he never did. What could be taking him so long? Marilyn wasn't showing yet, but she soon would. It had been three months now since he'd left and she hadn't heard a thing. Her heart was still with him, her soul still trusted him, but she was scared.

Perhaps if she could write to *him*? But how could she find out where he lived? The only clue she had was that he had stayed at Mrs Briggs' B & B. Might she know? At the hotel they kept a guest ledger that required a home address, so it could be the same at the B & B. If Marilyn could only get word to Bruno, she felt that somehow everything would be all right.

She went round there the following day. Mrs Briggs was a dour woman who rarely had a smile for anyone, but Marilyn was desperate.

'Yes?' the landlady snapped when she opened the door and saw Marilyn standing there.

Marilyn knew she should have rehearsed what to say. 'It's about Bruno,' she began.

'Who?'

'Bruno. He stayed with you in July – for three weeks.' She must remember him, surely?

The woman's eyes narrowed. 'What of him?'

'I need his address,' Marilyn blurted. 'That is, he gave it to me and I lost it and now I don't have any way of getting in contact with him.'

'Oh, don't you now?' She looked Marilyn up and down.

Marilyn blushed. The woman's expression was making her feel cheap. She knew something. At least she knew that they had been together, even if she couldn't know the rest of it. But Marilyn wouldn't be ashamed of what they had. How could she be? She straightened her back. 'So, I was wondering if you could give it to me?' she asked.

The woman sniffed. 'There is such a thing as confidentiality,' she said. 'My guests expect it. I couldn't possibly let them down. This is a respectable establishment, you know.'

'He would want me to have it.' Marilyn spoke in a rush.

'Then why didn't he tell you it himself?'

'He meant to, but—' Marilyn immediately realised her blunder. She hadn't even been able to stick to her story. 'It's important,' she said.

'Important, is it?' The woman stared at her – yes, again, as if she knew. And her gaze was triumphant.

Marilyn stood her ground. 'Yes.'

The woman smiled thinly. 'Then I'm sorry to disappoint you,' she said, 'but I don't have it.'

'You don't have it?' Should she believe her? This had been Marilyn's one hope.

'I don't have it,' she repeated.

'But in the guest book . . .' Marilyn hesitated. She didn't like the woman but she could hardly call her a liar.

'The young man merely wrote Italy.' She shrugged. 'But if he wants to get in touch with you . . .' – the inference was clear – 'I'm sure that he will do. Goodbye.' And she shut the door in Marilyn's face.

Marilyn stood on the doorstep. What now? Bruno hadn't even told her the name of the town he lived in. What hope did she have of getting a message to him? But surely he would write soon? He had to. Marilyn put her hand to her belly. She didn't know how long she could keep it quiet.

Glenda sussed it soon afterwards. Marilyn had been trying to vomit quietly in the bathroom and her sister had practically beaten the door down.

'What's going on with you?' she hissed when Marilyn opened it.

Marilyn turned to look in the bathroom mirror and saw her own white and terrified face staring back at her. It was obvious, she knew.

'Bloody Nora,' said Glenda. 'You're not . . . are you?'

Marilyn eyed her warily. 'Yes,' she said. 'I think I must be.' She hung her head.

'You little idiot.' But Glenda took Marilyn in her arms, held her close as she sobbed her heart out, and Marilyn felt just a bit better now that somebody else knew.

'There,' said Glenda. 'Accidents happen. And not just to you, you know.'

No, but this was small consolation.

'It was that Italian, I suppose?' Glenda asked. She was the only one at home who had known about Bruno.

Marilyn nodded. 'I love him,' she said uselessly. Because that was immaterial now. Bruno still hadn't written to her and almost four months had gone by. She knew what that meant. She had made a very big mistake.

'And no one knows?'

'No one knows.'

Glenda let out a sigh. 'So you're what . . . four months gone?'

Marilyn nodded miserably.

'Have you tried to . . . you know?' she said.

'What?' She was her older sister. She had two children of her own now. Marilyn just wanted Glenda to tell her what to do.

'Have you tried to get rid of it?' Glenda whispered.

'No.' But the thought of getting rid of their baby – that hurt. And wouldn't it be too late now?

'You have to try.' Glenda seemed very sure. 'Well, you can't actually have it, can you? I mean, does he even know? And where is he?' She looked around the bathroom as if Bruno might suddenly materialise from the airing cupboard.

'But he said he'd come back.' Marilyn was floundering. 'He said he'd write.'

'And has he?' Glenda stood, hands on hips.

'Not yet, but—'

'That's crazy talk.' Glenda shook her head. 'He clearly isn't coming back – not in time to look after you anyway. And if he hasn't written, well . . .' Her voice trailed. She looked at Marilyn with pity.

'Well, what?' Marilyn bridled.

'Well, he's probably not going to.' Glenda sighed. 'You've always been such a dreamer, Marilyn. When are you going to realise? That's what it's like for us women.'

'What do you mean?' Marilyn had never thought of her

sister as wise, but now she seemed to know everything and Marilyn felt very ignorant indeed.

'They get what they want, don't they? Men. While we get left with the baby.' Glenda looked pointedly at Marilyn's belly. 'Literally.'

'But . . .' It wasn't like that. That's what Marilyn wanted to say. He wasn't like that. But she had to admit, right now, that was what it looked like. Even so . . . 'I don't want to get rid of it.' She stood up straighter.

Glenda clicked her tongue. 'You haven't thought it through.'

'I have.' Because she had thought of nothing else. 'And—'

'What do you think Mum and Dad will say?' Glenda's eyes were wide. 'My God, Marilyn, they'll go bonkers!'

Marilyn supposed that she was right. She groaned at the thought.

'Here's what we'll do.' Glenda leant closer. 'And if we do it right, no one will be any the wiser.'

Marilyn didn't want to do any of it but she was desperate by now.

But they hadn't done it right, or at least, nothing worked. They tried a scalding bath, which took Marilyn's breath (but nothing else) away. They tried castor oil, which made her sick, and they tried gin sneaked from a dusty bottle in the sideboard. It tasted foul and Marilyn was violently sick again. But she remained as pregnant as ever. Even Glenda had run out of ideas.

'You'll have to tell them,' she said eventually. 'They'll see for themselves soon enough.' She eyed Marilyn's waistline. 'Everyone will see soon enough.'

★

At first, Marilyn couldn't do it. Glenda was busy with work and with her family, so she didn't push it either, although she did give Marilyn long significant looks from time to time and muttered, 'What are you waiting for? Christmas?' whenever they were alone.

October had already barged noisily into November with harsh winds and rain, and now the days grew shorter and colder as the great gales attacked and eroded the coastline. Soon it was too windy and cold to spend time on the beach. The people who lived here in West Dorset retreated into their homes with their comforting Agas or woodburning stoves and the beaches were near deserted apart from the regular dog walkers and fossil hunters.

And so, November passed in a blur of waiting and hoping. If he would only write to her, somehow things might become bearable again. Marilyn was always first to get the post. But there was nothing. What could be taking him so long? Her smocks and loose-fitting coat wouldn't hide her expanding belly for ever.

Marilyn put it off for as long as she could. In the end, she told her mother when she was making their tea – as if the grilled herrings might prove something of a distraction.

'I need to tell you something, Mum,' she began.

Her mother pulled out the grill and began turning the herrings. 'Don't tell me you're in trouble at work?' she said.

If only . . . 'It's worse than that,' Marilyn said.

Her mother shoved the grill pan back under the heat. She turned around. 'You've not lost your job?'

'No. I'm . . .' How could she say it? The words were impossible. 'I don't know what to do, Mum.' And she burst into tears.

Her mother stared at her. 'What is it? What's happened?'

But Marilyn still couldn't say it. She couldn't stop crying.

35

Her mother wiped her hands on her apron and came closer, herrings forgotten. 'For heaven's sake, girl,' she said. 'It can't be that bad. It—'

'She's pregnant.' Glenda came into the kitchen. She sent Marilyn a sympathetic glance.

'What?'

'It's true,' Marilyn managed to stutter.

'Pregnant?' As predicted, Marilyn's mother looked furious. 'Pregnant?'

She seemed lost for any other words. She stared at Marilyn, shook her head, marched over to the cooker and pulled the herrings out from under the grill where they were already blackened from the heat. She seemed torn between needing to tend to them and coming back to Marilyn. 'How could you?' She looked back at Marilyn. 'Who was it? How could you?'

'His name's Bruno,' Marilyn told her. She glanced across at Glenda, who rolled her eyes, made another sympathetic face and left the room. Marilyn didn't blame her for getting out of the firing line. She would too if she could.

'Bruno? Bruno, you say?' Her mother started flicking bits of blackened skin from the herrings. She frowned. 'Bruno?' She gave his name such a withering tone that Marilyn rocked back on her heels. 'He's not from round here then, I take it?'

'No.'

'The shame,' her mother muttered. 'How could you?' And she turned to look at Marilyn once again – as if she no longer knew her, Marilyn thought.

There was nothing Marilyn could say in her defence. All she could do was watch her mother resuscitate the herrings, while turning back to stare at Marilyn as if she could not possibly be any daughter of hers, repeating it over and over. 'The shame.'

36

And, 'How could you?' She kept saying that, tutting and shaking her head, until Marilyn wanted to scream.

'He's in Italy,' Marilyn told her mother.

'Oh, that's helpful.'

'But he'll come back for me.' Marilyn thought of the fiery gemstone. Hope, he had said. Air and the heart. Weren't they as good as engaged?

'Don't be so stupid, Marilyn.' Her mother sounded like Glenda now.

'But—'

'You listen to me, my girl.' And finally, her mother left the herrings and came over to where Marilyn was standing by the door. Her mother grasped her by the arm so tightly that it hurt. Marilyn realised that somehow in what had happened to her, in what she had allowed to happen to her, she had lost her voice, her right to reply. 'You're stupid for getting pregnant and you're stupid if you think he's ever coming back.'

'You're wrong,' Marilyn whispered. Though it was getting harder and harder to believe. She told her mother about the gemstone. 'It's to keep me safe,' she explained.

'Well, that didn't work then, did it?' Her mother's lips were pursed into a thin line of disapproval. 'You're even more of a fool than I thought, if you believe all that silly romantic non-sense. Don't you know that real life is built on practicalities? Not pretty words and poetry.'

Marilyn flinched. She felt a surge of protectiveness towards this, her unborn child. 'The baby—' she began.

Her mother glared at her. 'You can't keep it, can you? Where would you live for starters?'

'But couldn't I stay here?' Marilyn wailed. 'Me and the baby, I mean? Glenda and Ted are here, and—'

37

'Glenda and Ted are married,' her mother snapped. 'There's no spare room here anyway. And no spare money either. If you can't think of the rest of us, then for God's sake think of the child.'

The child . . . the child . . . Marilyn put her hands on her belly. What sort of an upbringing would he or she have if she kept it? What was Marilyn bringing their child into? If they were right and Bruno wasn't coming back, then Marilyn would be a single parent and her child would be illegitimate. Marilyn still had a job – just – but who was going to look after the baby? Not her mother by the sound of it. And how would they manage for money? There was no spare cash in this house, she knew that was true. Not enough anyway, to feed and clothe another child.

'What can I do?' she asked her mother. Marilyn needed her help. She needed her support. She couldn't do any of this alone.

'How far gone are you?' Her mother was frowning again.

'Five months, I think.'

'You should have told me before.' Her mother sighed.

'I know. I was waiting for him to write. I . . .' What more could she say?

'You're not the first girl to get herself into this situation.' Her mother seemed to soften slightly, though she didn't take her in her arms as Marilyn wanted her to. 'And you won't be the last.' She gave her one last sorrowful look. 'Leave it to me.'

And so Marilyn did.

Meanwhile, the hotel was getting ready for its Christmas visitors. The casual staff had been let go at the end of the season, but Marilyn's position was permanent. That was something.

It was her mother who talked to the hotel manager after Christmas and persuaded him that giving Marilyn three months off from mid-February would be beneficial for them both. He grumbled a bit because Easter was early that year and there was no way Marilyn would be back for that, but her mother said that it couldn't be helped and that Marilyn would make up for it when she returned in May. It was her mother who arranged things with the social worker and the C of E mother and baby home in Sussex and with a distant aunt who lived nearby. But it was her father who took her there in February, stony-faced and silent.

Valentine's Day. The irony was not lost on Marilyn. She had not quite given up on him, despite all evidence to the contrary. And still, she looked for a card that was never going to come.

The cover story was that the distant aunt needed some help in her guest house while she was recovering from an operation, and the entire family was sworn to secrecy.

As for Marilyn, she did what she was told. In part, she was relieved to be away from the oppressive atmosphere in the family home, and at least where she was going there would be others in the same boat, others who would understand. As for the fact that she would be giving her child up for adoption . . . She felt she had no choice. Perhaps they were all right in assuming that Bruno had never intended to return for her. Perhaps she had been a fool to believe him. It didn't look as if he would ever write to her. It didn't look as if he was ever coming back.

Which left Marilyn feeling alone and angry. She didn't think she would ever trust a man again. How could he have deceived her like that? How could he have let her think that he loved her? How could he have used her and discarded her and left her so terribly alone?

CHAPTER 6

Lily

2018

Lily was working on some accounts at the dining table, glancing across every few minutes at her mother, asleep in the bed, occasionally shifting slightly, or letting out a small gasp or a soft groan. It was difficult to concentrate. Lily was trying to keep her freelance work to a minimum, so that she had more time to care for her mother, but sometimes work was also a welcome distraction from just sitting beside her and thinking.

Lily hoped she wasn't in pain. The doctor had assured her this wasn't the case, but who really knew? And was she even asleep? From time to time, Lily got up, went over, smoothed wisps of her mother's hair from her forehead. And as she watched her, she was unable to stop herself from thinking of how it had always been.

It was the contrast that shocked her the most. From the mother who never had time to spare, who dashed around, who seemed to live on a slightly different plane, never quite with them, never quite there . . . to this. An elderly lady, trapped in her bed, barely moving, waiting to die.

Sometimes, Lily actually couldn't bear it. When her mother's eyes were open, Lily talked to her, she smiled, she made her as comfortable as she could. And when her mother's eyes were closed, she left the room and she cried.

She wasn't crying for the imminent loss of her mother even, Lily supposed – because she'd never had her, not really. Perhaps she was crying for what might have been.

Glenda came through from the kitchen with two mugs of tea. 'You need to take a break, love,' she said. She had been amazing; Lily was so grateful to have her here. She called in every day, sat with her sister, tidied up, made tea, and persuaded Lily to take a bit of time out.

'I'm fine.' Lily broke off from her work. 'But thanks. You're a marvel.'

Glenda pulled a face. 'I know what it's like. My Ted . . .'

Lily nodded. Her uncle had been ill for more than two years before he finally passed away and Glenda had been his primary carer. Lily wished she had thought more about helping her aunt when she was still living in Dorset. But she had been much younger then, and selfish too, she supposed.

'Why not take your tea into the garden, love?' Glenda glanced out of the window. 'It's a bright day.' She went to sit by the bed. 'I'll sit with her for half an hour.' And then when Lily hesitated, 'Go on now.'

Lily did as she was told. She stood in the back doorway and breathed in the fresh early-spring air. No matter how much she opened the windows, the medicinal smell, the smell of illness, lingered, and it was a relief to escape it, if only for a short time.

She took a few steps into the garden. Something would

41

have to be done to tidy it up a bit – it had run wild. Another task to add to the list, she thought. The first perennials were trying to push through, but the weeds had taken over their patch and the grass was more like a meadow. It was rather nice, she thought, with bright buttercups and dandelions scattered among the tall grasses. But it would take a while to make everything presentable again.

There was such a lot to do . . . Lily closed her eyes for a moment and lifted her face to feel the warmth of the March sunshine. She held her mug of tea cradled in her hands. Not just work – she was setting her alarm for six a.m. every day so that she could get a few things done before the morning properly began – and not just the house. But her mother . . . It was the constant watching, she supposed. The constant worry, the burden of care.

Her mobile rang and, seeing it was Cate, Lily answered it. They'd already talked about Jack, and Lily's decision not to move in with him. Thankfully, Cate didn't blame her in the least, which was a relief. She was sad to lose the perfect foursome, Cate had told her, but she'd never thought Jack was quite the right fit. Who might be the right fit, her friend didn't speculate on.

'Hi.' Cate's voice was warm. 'Is it an okay time?'

'Definitely.' It was good to hear her, even though she was a reminder of a life that seemed a long way from Lily's reach right now. 'How are things?'

'Oh, things here are pretty good,' Cate said.

Lily knew she'd be busy sorting out her stuff and getting ready to move to Travis's. She would be happy and excited and yet her friend had still found time to call her.

'But more to the point, how are you, my lovely? And how's your mum?'

Lily sighed. 'She sleeps a lot of the time,' she said. 'I don't know how much longer . . .' Her voice trailed. She wasn't even sure what she was going to say. How much longer before her mother passed away? Or how much longer Lily could go on?

'Oh, Lily.'

'Yeah, I know.' Lily felt the tears surfacing again. Sympathy. That always started her off.

'But you're managing?' Cate was trying to sound bright and positive and Lily loved her for that. She was a good friend and Lily would miss living with her.

She sniffed. 'Yes,' she said. 'Of course.'

'And you would tell me . . . ?'

'Tell you?' Lily took a sip of her tea. Auntie Glenda always made it milky, but that was a comfort right now.

'If you need me,' Cate said. 'I could be there in a few hours. I've got a bit of holiday left, and I could always work away from the office.'

'You're an angel,' Lily told her. 'But my aunt's here helping out. And really, I'm fine.'

'Okay.' Cate hesitated. 'But I mean it. Anytime. All right?'

'Yes. Thanks, Cate.'

'Take care, Lily. Talk soon.' And she was gone.

'Lily?' Auntie Glenda was standing in the doorway.

'Yes?' Lily jumped. 'Is she okay? Has something—' Every moment, she thought. That was probably the worst part. At every moment, Lily was half expecting her mother to die.

'She's saying your name, love.' Glenda's eyes shone with sympathy and unshed tears.

'I'll come in.'

But by the time Lily had sat down by the bed, her mother was drifting again, in the state of half waking, half sleeping that she'd been in almost constantly during the past few days. It wouldn't be long, the doctor had told them. It could happen any time.

'Mum?' she said. 'Mum?'

And was it her imagination, or did her mother try to reach out for her? Lily took her hand. 'I'm here,' she whispered.

'Darling,' she said.

Darling? Lily hardly dared breathe. 'Mum? What is it? Are you comfortable? Can I get you some water?'

'There's something . . .' Her eyes flickered open – blue-grey, faded, with . . . surely an expression of regret?

'Yes?' Lily felt the faintest of squeezes, so faint it was hardly there. But her mother's eyes had closed once more.

Lily sat beside her for a while longer, holding her hand, hoping she might be aware of it.

'I'll be off then, love. See you tomorrow.' Glenda touched Lily's shoulder and was gone.

And still Lily sat there, holding her mother's hand and waiting.

CHAPTER 7

Marilyn

1966

The mother and baby home was not what Marilyn had been expecting. Instead of some new pre-fabricated building that looked like a modern hospital, it was a huge Victorian house – although it did have a medical ward within it. 'It'll save you going to the local hospital,' her aunt told her when they visited the place together for her interview. Interview? Marilyn had assumed everything had already been arranged. She even had her suitcase with her. If they wouldn't take her, what would she do then?

She was interviewed by the Matron, which was scary – the woman had a disapproving shape to her mouth, and she talked about the necessity to do chores as if they were some sort of penance for Marilyn's bad behaviour. She also wanted to know about Marilyn's background, her family, and she asked about the 'father' as if Bruno must be some kind of alien species. Marilyn was rather old, she said, to have got herself into this sort of trouble; most of their girls were teenagers. But lessons, she concluded crisply, could be learnt at any age.

Marilyn couldn't help but agree. She'd learnt her lesson all right, and Matron could rest assured, there was no way on earth that Marilyn would be stupid enough to trust a man again.

The rules of the place were simple, Matron told her. Visiting was on Saturdays (Marilyn supposed that her aunt would come; she hoped so anyway – she had a feeling she'd appreciate seeing a familiar face), church was on Sundays, and routine was for every day. Chores before free time was the order of each day.

'Any questions?' she asked when she was done.

'Can I go out?' Marilyn asked. 'For a walk, I mean? Is it allowed?'

Matron's expression relaxed – just slightly. 'This isn't a prison, my dear,' she said. 'We're not living in the Dark Ages.'

'So . . . ?'

'Of course you may go out.' She leant forwards. 'Fresh air and exercise are good for you. And good for baby too.' She glanced pointedly at Marilyn's left hand.

Marilyn hadn't wanted to wear it. Her mother had thrust it into her palm just before she'd left. A cheap wedding ring – from Woolworths, she supposed – which only increased her sense of shame. It gleamed dully, fooling no one.

'But wear your duffel coat when you venture out,' Matron advised. 'It's still rather chilly.'

A duffel coat, a wedding ring . . . What point was there in pretending? Marilyn looked around the room. Everyone who lived around here would know what sort of a place this was and they would all have made their own judgements.

'I'll show you and your aunt around.' Matron got to her feet.

Marilyn trailed after her. There was a big shared bathroom,

and a common room full of tables and chairs with girls in various stages of pregnancy sitting knitting or sewing. Marilyn smiled at them doubtfully. What were they like, these girls? They all seemed very young. Had they experienced anything like she had? Were they all unmarried? Were all their babies to be adopted? Marilyn shivered. She supposed so.

There was a communal kitchen and a dormitory. And the nursery . . . Half the cots were already occupied by sleeping babies and Marilyn would have liked to linger there, but Matron whisked them straight out again. 'We don't encourage too much contact,' she informed Marilyn's aunt as if Marilyn wasn't even there. 'Although all the girls are expected to look after the practical needs of their own child, of course.'

Marilyn wished she could run away. But there was nowhere to run to.

And so, straightaway, she moved into the home with the small case she'd brought with her, and her aunt left, looking relieved to be gone. 'Don't worry, dear,' she said as she walked out of the door. 'When it comes to it, you'll be in the best possible hands.'

By 'it' Marilyn supposed she meant the birth. She had no idea what to expect and as she got talking to the other girls over the following days, she realised that none of them did either. There were a few girls who had already given birth, but they didn't say very much about it either, apart from a dark *you'll find out for yourself when the time comes.* Despite being a fair bit older than most of them – but equally naive, she found herself thinking – Marilyn got along well enough with the other residents. After all, she thought, everyone was in the same boat, they all had to make the best of it.

So Marilyn did her chores every morning like all the

47

rest – cleaning mostly: scrubbing the steps, dusting the hallway and polishing the banisters and the chests of drawers. She went for a walk in the afternoon – head down, talking to no one – and then she sat with the other girls chatting and making up their baby boxes, knitting matinee jackets and crocheting little baby bonnets.

It was grim. Those boxes were destined to leave with their babies . . . But Marilyn wouldn't think of that now. Knitting was a suitable activity for this surreal time, she decided. Unlike drawing and painting, it was mindless; it allowed her to feel numb.

On Saturdays, her aunt visited, made awkward conversation about family news and the weather, and on Sundays all the girls – pregnant girls and new mothers alike – were frog-marched to church, where they sat in the back pew. 'So we can't pollute anyone with our shame,' a girl called Hilary whispered to Marilyn. Hilary had already given birth to a boy, but she'd be losing him next week, she informed Marilyn with a bitter smile.

When Marilyn's waters broke, when she was taken into the labour rooms, when her baby was finally born after a kind of pain Marilyn had never imagined, she experienced a maelstrom of emotions. It was as if she'd never truly been alive until this moment. She felt grief, she felt loss, she felt shame and she felt a euphoria that took her breath away. They swirled, one around the other, these emotions, streaking together – rather like her watercolours, she couldn't help thinking – until Marilyn wasn't sure what she felt or thought, because it had all blurred into one.

She knew she loved her, though.

Almost immediately, her child was whisked away and out of sight. Marilyn panicked, let out a little cry.

'It's just to do the routine checks,' a nurse assured her. 'She'll be back.'

And she was. Back for feeding and back for bathing and nappy changing. The rest of the time her baby stayed in the nursery with all the others and it wasn't easy to sneak in there for a cuddle. Marilyn did, though, whenever she could, and even this small act of resistance cheered her. She also made feeding last as long as she dared.

When she looked into her daughter's eyes, when she stroked her hair and held her to her breast, she saw Bruno, and although this made Marilyn sad, it was somehow beautiful too. Because perhaps something had happened to him? Perhaps he was ill? Perhaps he needed her? Perhaps he hadn't got in touch because he couldn't? And so, perhaps this wasn't truly the end?

Her thoughts stayed close to the father of her child. What if Bruno were to write or return to Dorset while she was here in Sussex? Would anyone even tell her – or tell him where she was? And what if he returned after the adoption? What would he say when he learnt that she had given their baby away? She couldn't dwell on that thought, though – the guilt was too overwhelming.

'How long will we stay in here for?' she asked the social worker who visited her soon after the birth. She didn't seem to be there to give Marilyn any options – if, that is, there even were any. She was businesslike – she dealt with all the admin, she told Marilyn.

'We?' The woman raised an eyebrow. 'Haven't you been told?' She sighed, as if she was too busy for any of this. 'It's six weeks after the birth, those are the rules. Adoptive parents will be found – there's no reason why not – and you'll be free to get on with your life.'

'Why six weeks?' It was such a short time. It seemed so cruel.

But the woman just shrugged. Maybe it was so that no one could say there had been a forced or traumatic parting. Maybe it gave them time to find those adoptive parents, for babies to be weaned from their mothers. Maybe if they waited any longer . . . mothers would become too attached.

It would be laughable, Marilyn thought, if it weren't so tragic. She'd been attached to her baby daughter from the moment she knew she existed and she felt she would remain attached for ever. But the child would be taken anyway and Marilyn knew that, alone, she could do nothing to stop that.

And so, while she fed her and bathed her and changed her, Marilyn stared at her. She committed her daughter's face, her movements, her early smiles (which apparently weren't smiles at all) to memory. But what if Marilyn were ever to forget? When her aunt visited the following Saturday, she begged her to find someone to take a photograph of her baby daughter. If she had a photograph, she could at least look at her sometimes, and not just in her mind's eye.

'I'm not sure that's a good idea,' her aunt said. 'Far better to put it behind you now, dear. It's no use to brood.'

'Please,' Marilyn sobbed. 'It will be all I have of her.'

'You should have thought of that before.' The aunt tutted. And she would not relent.

So, Marilyn picked up her sketchbook and her pencils which she had brought with her, because she couldn't not, and in stolen moments, whenever she had the chance, she drew her child. She captured the contours of her face, the blue innocence of her eyes, the wisps of soft black hair and the look of her that was Bruno's look.

She would call her Josephine, she decided, and she whispered

50

the name into her daughter's ear, and wrote it on the back of the drawing. She would keep it for ever. For Marilyn, Josephine would never be gone.

Eventually, though, the time came when Josephine was to be taken away. Marilyn supposed that suitable adoptive parents had been found, but no one seemed to want to tell her anything — not Matron, not her aunt, not the social worker who had presumably arranged it all. She was given a few minutes alone with her, though. She dressed Josephine in her best outfit, complete with an oyster-pink matinee jacket, and she stroked the wisps of dark hair from her sweet face. But there was no chance for a prolonged goodbye — just a kiss on her soft baby brow, a last chance to breathe in the scent of her.

'You must leave her now,' the Matron told her, and she led Marilyn from the nursery. Marilyn remained dry-eyed — she felt as if all her tears had been shed, as if something inside her had turned to stone. And within an hour, Josephine was gone.

And now Marilyn too must leave, go back to Dorset, somehow pick up the threads of her life and make them into something that had meaning. She could go back to her parents' house, her home; she could resume her old job. She could sketch and she could paint. She must take the emptiness inside her and she must try to fill it. It seemed like an impossible task.

'You should be pleased,' her aunt told her. 'You should be relieved. You're young and now you're free again. You'll get over this, you know.'

But she was wrong. Marilyn wasn't relieved at all. Because nothing was as it had been. Everything was broken. And for once in her life, she had no wish to be free.

CHAPTER 8

Marilyn

2018

How long had she slept for? Marilyn had no idea — that was how it was these days. And Lily . . . Had she imagined her here? Thoughts, memories, old hopes . . . they were so mixed up that it was hard to tell which were reality, which were dreams.

She felt an ache, a stiffness — in her shoulders, her back — that she couldn't shake off. She could barely sit up unaided. Marilyn wasn't sure how she had got to be so old, how she could be dying. Neither did she understand how life could go by so fast when each day would pass so slowly. When you were young, you never thought about time running out — there was always a tomorrow.

And sometimes now it seemed to Marilyn that she was twenty-five again, for she could feel that girl still burning with life just under her skin. Images in her mind shifted and swayed. Time evaporated; years dissolved like the spray of the waves on the beach and there was Marilyn, young again, sketching and still dreaming of the life that lay ahead.

Ah . . . Marilyn remembered. The love that would change everything. Because that was how it was when she met him. She saw it so clearly. He was her future. She knew he would change her life for ever. *Hmph.* Angry with herself now – so often since then, she had felt angry with herself – she attempted to clench a fist but she was too weak . . . Her hand trembled with the effort. *Hopeless. Hopeless.*

Well, she might have thought Bruno would be her future, but before too long, he was her past. And that was what made her so angry. Marilyn had believed in him. She had believed in him and in love. She had held her hopes, her dreams in the palm of this same hand and back then she had been strong enough to close her fingers around them and hold them tight.

When Marilyn returned to Dorset after the adoption, there wasn't really anyone she could talk to about it. Glenda was always too busy. And now, she was pregnant again, which was another bitter irony, even though her sister had cried when she told her the news and asked her if Marilyn was upset, if she was cross with her. No, Marilyn told her, because what was the point of that? As for Marilyn's parents, her mother didn't seem to want to understand what she had gone through, and her father was still pretending it had never happened.

One day, Marilyn was sitting at the reception desk, lost in a world of her own. Things were quiet at the hotel today. This afternoon everybody would be watching England play Germany in the World Cup final and she would watch it too on the television in the back room, even though she had little heart for it.

She'd been looking at the hotel notice board where they kept letters and postcards sent to them from appreciative guests from both the UK and abroad. Some of their visitors had come from

Europe – there was one postcard that always caught her eye, which showed a sea as blue as the deepest sapphire, a line of houses, a church and a castle on a hill, and it always made her think of Bruno. She didn't really know why. Because it showed another place, another world, she supposed. And wherever he was, he was lost to her now.

'Marilyn.' Her friend Tom, who did maintenance work at the hotel, was there, standing patiently in front of her. 'Have you got the key to room four? I need to repair the window.'

'Oh, yes, hang on.' Marilyn reached up to get it from the hooks behind her.

He took the key from her hand, hesitated.

'Was there anything else, Tom?'

'Will you be watching the match later, Marilyn?'

She gave a little shrug. 'I suppose so.'

Still, he didn't leave the reception area.

'Tom?' She frowned. 'What is it? Are you okay?'

'Oh, I'm fine.' He smiled at her and with that smile Marilyn felt just a little bit warmer. 'Just . . . if you ever need to talk . . . well, you know where I am.'

'Thanks.'

Tom already knew about Bruno. She'd told him about the adoption too, when he'd caught her weeping in the hotel grounds one afternoon, and it didn't seem to change his opinion of her. He was a good man, and the fact that he was there for Marilyn, as a colleague at the hotel, a friend and a confidant too, made her feel a lot better.

Marilyn watched him walk away. She'd always known he had feelings for her, and she'd taken those feelings for granted back in the day, knowing he wasn't exciting enough for her, knowing he wasn't the man she was looking for. But . . .

54

Things change.

Tom was always around, he never judged her, he never asked for more.

Dear Tom, she thought now. He had remained stoic until the end.

They started dating two years after Josephine's birth, when Marilyn had finally accepted that Bruno was never going to contact her again. Those hopes and dreams she had held on to so tightly . . . she let them go on the same day she ripped up all the drawings she had made of him, all the sketches she had treasured during the long days of waiting, the images she had gazed at and held dear.

Like Marilyn, Tom had waited. He seemed to understand that it would take her a long time before she trusted a man again. He was gentle. He never pressurised her. And with Tom it was as different to Bruno as it could be. Their relationship was comfortable; Marilyn felt safe. There wasn't the passion she'd shared with Bruno, but where had that got her? Tom was steady, he was reliable, he adored her. Excitement, she came to realise, was transitory. You couldn't pin it down. It was a bubble. It wasn't lasting and it wasn't enough to build a life, or even a hope or a dream on.

It turned out that Tom was good at saving money too. In time, he left the hotel and started his own business, and it did well. Pretty soon, he employed other men to do building work, and most of his days were spent in the office, talking to customers on the phone, or overseeing the jobs, organising the men. And Marilyn continued to draw and to paint. Oh, how she painted. But she still worked as a receptionist at the Cliff

Hotel. Tom told her she should go to art school, that it wasn't too late. But for Marilyn, it was too late.

Was she still looking for something? She would deny it. Some things, they would never be found.

By the time Tom asked Marilyn to marry him, he had enough money to put down on a house. She'd told him she didn't want a family; she told him that part of her had died. She had her sister's children, she said. She'd grown close to them – she often took them out and helped her sister when she could.

Tom didn't seem to mind. He could offer her love, security and a home, he told her, and in that home, she could be herself, she could have as much space as she needed. So, of course Marilyn said yes. Could Tom save her? He had certainly tried. And Marilyn had loved him, of that she was certain. It was a different kind of love from the one that she'd thought she shared with Bruno, but surely it would be enough?

There were times when she still thought of Bruno, times when she even wondered about trying to contact him, just to find out how he was, where he was, just to see the image of his face . . . But Marilyn had torn up that image – literally. He had let her down when she most needed him and besides, it would not be fair on Tom.

And then there was Lily. It had been a surprise to find herself pregnant, because they had always taken precautions. Both her daughters had begun life as accidents – which was unfair on them, she knew. Marilyn had not wanted Lily, but it mattered to Tom. After everything he had done for her, how could she deny him?

But then, of course, how could the pregnancy, the birth experience not bring up traumatic memories? Those painful memories that Marilyn had worked so hard to suppress. And after Lily's birth – that too, had been a sad and difficult time. But Tom was happy and her parents were delighted too and so . . .

Now, Marilyn tried to focus. Yes, Lily had come to the house, she knew. She had stood on the doorstep – Marilyn hadn't been quite so low at that point, though it had been an effort to pull herself out of the bed that had been installed downstairs in order to answer the door – and then Lily had come inside. Marilyn didn't deserve it. But Lily was here; she had stayed here, talking gently, bringing Marilyn water and soup, sometimes even holding her hand.

If life offered more than one pathway – and of course, it did, as everyone knew – then Marilyn knew she had gone wrong, badly wrong. She often looked at the drawing she had made when she was in the mother and baby home in Sussex and she kept it close always. The daughter she had lost was a constant shadow; she thought of her every day, of how she would have changed, of what she might look like now. She could not let her go. Was Josephine happy? Was she loved? Marilyn would never really know. They say time healed – Tom had often told her this – but it hadn't been that way for Marilyn. For Marilyn, sometimes it seemed that time had only increased the pain of the loss she'd suffered.

Losing Josephine had left her feeling incomplete. Would Josephine ever contact her? She had longed for it and at the same time she'd been terrified of the thought. Because surely her first daughter would never forgive Marilyn for giving her away?

Marilyn had tried to take refuge in her painting, because it was her painting that had always defined her, she felt. Without her art, she was no different from the next woman. Without her art, who was she? Who must she be? But perhaps she had tried too hard. Perhaps she simply wasn't good enough. Perhaps there had been no refuge, only a place of loneliness, where she had cut herself off from those she loved, from those she should have made time for. That was it then. Try as she might to find release . . . it was never there to be found.

Lily was never a shadow. She was a real and demanding child, following her mother around, wanting this, wanting that. Wanting to be loved. A solitary tear crept from Marilyn's eye and stayed poised and motionless for a second before she felt it slip to her cheek.

But how could she let herself love her, when Marilyn's first daughter had not been allowed to know her mother's love? Marilyn sighed. Sometimes she felt overwhelmed by the guilt, the anger, the shame . . . Those emotions had built a brittle shell around the softness of her heart. She wasn't open to that kind of love; all her maternal urges had been dragged out of her.

And Tom, dear Tom, who knew he had never been Marilyn's first choice, her soulmate, her one and only. He understood that so well. So, he had done all he could do. He had gathered that little girl into his waiting arms and given her all his love. He had become her everything, so that Marilyn could be free — from fear, from love, from all that had the power to hurt her.

Now, she would laugh, if she were able. Free from those things? Free from living, more like it.

And so, could Marilyn tell her daughter Lily all her hopes and fears, all the reasons she had never felt whole? Could she explain her guilt, her inability to give love? Perhaps. Perhaps if she had more time. And perhaps Lily might forgive her for not wanting her, for not being the mother Lily deserved. Because

58

Marilyn didn't think she was ever meant to be a mother after all.

But she loved Lily. It had happened almost without her knowing and then she had realised that in fact the love had always been there. Of course she loved Lily. How could she not?

Marilyn shifted in her bed. She saw now that Lily was at the dining table typing, and she sensed her casting careful glances Marilyn's way. Marilyn kept her eyes closed. With Lily here, the guilt grew heavier. And yet somewhere inside, she was glad.

She tried to sit up. Tom was gone now, of course. It was his strength she missed more than anything; she had needed it to lean on and she wasn't sure she could stand alone. She had kept his things and that helped a little. But now she must think of Lily, their daughter. She had not done right by her. There was something she must do, something she must say. But she was dizzy. Dizzy with the past that had in its way finished her. The room, the furniture, seemed to close in and Marilyn felt herself unable to breathe.

'Mum? Are you okay?' Lily was at her bedside now, she knew. 'Are you comfortable?' she asked. 'Can I get you some water?'

'Darling.' Marilyn thought she said that to her. She thought she held her hand. 'There's something . . .' Because really, she must tell her. Really, she should know.

'What is it, Mum?'

Marilyn had looked for her elusive sense of self and she had been unable to find it somehow. But now perhaps, to Lily, she could at least try to explain.

CHAPTER 9

Lily

2018

How should you feel when you lose a parent you have never been close to?

Lily was packing books into boxes. They had been her father's books, but her mother had kept them. It seemed to Lily that she'd kept everything – his gardening boots still stood in the porch; his wax jacket still hung on the hook by the door. Lily wasn't sure what this meant. Her mother had loved her father, of course. Lily had seen with her own eyes how she had suffered when he was gone. But as time passed . . . Had she still needed his presence perhaps? Was it that she couldn't bear to lose the feel of him?

In two years, her mother hadn't got rid of a thing. And now they were both gone, and it was up to Lily to clear out their past.

Regret, Lily supposed, was what she felt the most. Regret that she and her mother had never really bonded, never shared what mothers and daughters were supposed to share, and now they never would. There had been moments in the days before she died when Lily had felt close to her, and she wanted to imagine that her mother had felt that too. But perhaps it was wishful thinking. Lily sighed. If *she* ever had a daughter . . .

On the lowest shelf, she came upon some books from her childhood. She smiled fondly. *When We Were Very Young*, *Winnie the Pooh* . . . And she remembered her father's Winnie the Pooh voice: 'You never can tell with bees.' She couldn't part with that one, for sure. There were just too many memories.

Would Lily ever have children? She thought of what she'd said to Jack about not wanting to get serious. She'd dated, she'd had boyfriends, but she'd always focused more on her career. Or maybe she just hadn't met the right man? She placed the book carefully in the 'to keep' box. She was only thirty-four – there was time.

Lily sighed. The last weeks with her mother had been exhausting, but Lily was so glad that she'd come here. She had cared for her mother as best she could until the end, and it had brought them closer, Lily was certain of that.

What had her mother been thinking of in her last hours? Lily wondered. There had been clues . . . Had she too felt regret as Lily sat by her bedside and held her hand? A few times, it had seemed so. Lily was sure she'd been trying to tell her something and her Aunt Glenda had confirmed it. The expression on her mother's face, the tremor in her voice when she called her 'darling' . . . Lily had to hold on to that. Perhaps if she'd come sooner, there would have been more? But maybe even then it would have been too late.

She taped up another box of books, wondering if she could donate them to the phone-box library in the village. Or the local care home maybe? Someone somewhere would appreciate them, she was sure.

Darling . . . Had the distance between Lily and her mother been partly her own fault? As a child, had she naturally been drawn into her father's orbit and away from her mother's? Perhaps. And, she reminded herself, her mother had always been fragile; she had often needed to be protected from real life – Lily's father had taught her that. She'd had her anxieties, Lily knew. Some people weren't cut out for parenthood (perhaps Lily was one of them?). Some people were vulnerable.

As the days had crept by, as her mother became more and more dependent on Lily, as she was dying . . . and now, as Lily dealt with the ghastly business of sorting the house and contents, of considering what to do next . . . Lily knew that she had to stay strong. But now, both her parents were gone. And Lily felt lonelier than she ever had before.

But she mustn't brood. She started on another box. Books, vases, ornaments . . . there was so much stuff. She packed methodically, in bubble wrap, choosing only one tall green vase to keep for herself. Every springtime, in her childhood, her mother had filled it with daffodils, and Lily had continued the tradition in these past weeks, hoping their bright faces could bring her mother a little cheer in her final days. It wasn't much, but it was something. And she would continue to do it in the years to come, Lily decided. She'd do it and she'd think of her – the mother who had always been so far away.

'What will you do?' her Aunt Glenda had asked her yesterday when she came over to help Lily pack up some of the kitchen things. 'Sell the house?'

'Yes, I'll have to.' Lily loved her family home, but it was too big for one, even if she decided to stay here in Dorset. From the proceeds, she'd buy herself a flat somewhere. It was ironic, she thought, that when she came here just over a month ago, she'd been worrying about the prospect of becoming homeless, and now . . . well, now, she had a legacy. Her parents had never been wealthy, but they had paid off the mortgage on their home, and house prices in Dorset were on the up.

Lily had been putting it off, but now she decided to tackle her parents' bedroom. She walked up the stairs, paused in the doorway, stepped inside. The room still smelt faintly of Chanel No 5. The classic scent was so typical of her mother's taste; she'd rather wear no scent at all than cheap perfume. Quite rightly, Lily thought, so perhaps she was her mother's daughter, after all?

She opened the wardrobe door – his and hers, it was all still here – and started pulling out the clothes, sorting and folding. It wasn't easy, especially with her father's things. Clothes were so personal and they brought back images of the person wearing them, but Lily closed her mind to that as much as she could; she just needed to get it done. Glenda had come up here yesterday to see if she wanted anything, but she hadn't taken much. As for Lily, she kept one soft blue cardigan of her mother's and a red corduroy shirt of her father's. It was enough.

Next, the bed. Lily removed the bedding. Perhaps she should try to sell this lovely old wooden sleigh bed? She lifted the corner of the mattress. It was high quality and seemed in good condition; the slats were all intact. Maybe she'd get someone to come over and give her a price for all the furniture in the house? Because, after all, what would she do with it? It wouldn't belong in the kind of flat that Lily would ever buy.

Something wedged in the wooden slats caught Lily's eye and she peered closer. It looked like an envelope, with some fabric trapped next to it – from an old sheet perhaps? She up-ended the mattress onto its side. It was a large envelope, she could see that now. And next to it, a small fabric pouch. Weird, she thought. Had someone – her mother or her father – hidden something here?

The envelope was held in place by a worn piece of Sellotape. She pulled it off. The pouch was tied around the slat with a ribbon. She untied it.

Lily opened the envelope. She caught her breath. Inside was a drawing of a baby. A girl? Maybe. But Lily knew immediately it wasn't a drawing of her. This baby had dark hair while Lily as a newborn had been blonde. Who then? The baby's expression was solemn. Dressed in a simple nightgown, he or she was lying in a pram which had been loosely sketched in behind. Lily knew instinctively that her mother had drawn it. It wasn't her style – she had mostly painted flowers and fluid landscapes in watercolours – but Lily knew it nevertheless. The baby was very young. And Lily imagined she could feel the love that had gone into the strokes of the pen.

She stared at the baby's face. It had been drawn in pre-cise detail – the wide-open eyes and delicate lashes, the tiny nostrils, the soft downy cheeks. She frowned. She turned the drawing over. One word was written on the back in her mother's flowing script. *Josephine.*

'Josephine,' murmured Lily. Who was Josephine? And why would her mother have hidden a drawing of a baby? One obvious answer immediately sprang to mind, but . . . ? Her mother? It seemed highly unlikely.

She opened the fabric pouch carefully. Inside was a small gemstone unlike any she had seen before. It was shaped like a tiny pyramid with delicate horizontal striations and it was

64

a very dense orange, almost the colour of amber. It seemed so old, as if it had been buried for generations in the rock or under the sea. Lily ran her fingertips over it, feeling the contrast of the rough and the smooth. What was the significance of this stone? Why had her mother (or her father? Although this seemed less likely) kept it under their mattress? And who on earth was Josephine?

CHAPTER 10

Lily

2018

The following day, Lily went round to Auntie Glenda's. She had some questions to ask – questions that had been churning around in her head all night – and they were questions that must be asked face to face. Her aunt had always been direct and honest and she and Lily's mother had always been close, so Lily hoped that Glenda would be able to answer them.

She waited until they had exchanged chit-chat about today's weather (still mild for this time of year) and discussed how Lily was getting on at the house (so much stuff, Auntie Glenda, I'm drowning in it). And until Glenda had made coffee and sat down opposite her.

Now, Lily had her full attention. 'Who,' she asked, 'is Josephine?' It was better, she felt, to come straight to the point.

'Oh my.' Glenda wrapped her hands around her coffee cup. 'Did your mother talk to you? She did say . . .'

'No.' But perhaps Lily had been right. Had her mother

wanted to tell her something, but not known how to begin? '*What* did she say?'

Glenda sighed. 'That she hadn't done right. That she needed to explain to you.'

Lily bowed her head for a moment. She hadn't been mistaken then. Her mother had wanted to talk to her.

'Did you find something at the house, my dear?' Glenda still seemed cautious. Lily supposed that strictly speaking it wasn't her aunt's secret to reveal.

Lily put her tote bag on the table and retrieved the envelope containing the drawing. 'This,' she said.

'Ah.' Glenda took it from her, sighed, smiled, turned it over just as Lily had, read the name. 'I see,' she said. 'She kept it then.'

'Under the mattress.'

Glenda nodded. 'I'm not surprised,' she said. 'You can never fully move on from these things, can you?'

'From what things exactly?' Though Lily could guess.

'I said to her she should have told you a long time ago. There's no shame in it — not these days at any rate.'

'This was my mother's baby?' Lily had guessed, of course, that she must be. Why else would she have hidden the drawing? Why else would she have kept it so close?

'Yes.' Glenda sipped her coffee. 'I don't see why you shouldn't know the whole truth, especially now that she's gone. And like I say, I think she intended to tell you herself anyway.' A shadow passed over her face. 'Josephine was adopted, back in the mid-sixties, just a month or so after her birth.'

Oh my goodness . . . So it was true. She had a sister. Lily absorbed this. She'd always wanted a sister — or a brother, come to that. Someone to play with, share secrets with, grow

67

up with. This sister would be almost twenty years older than her then. But what had happened to Josephine?

'Why didn't she ever tell me before?' she said out loud. It was such an important thing, and didn't Lily have a right to know?

'Perhaps she did still feel ashamed,' Glenda said. 'Perhaps it was too painful for her. She showed me this drawing when she first came back here after her baby was born, after Josephine was adopted. But as time went on . . . she never wanted to talk about her. And your mother could be quite secretive, you know.'

Lily did. Sometimes, growing up, it had felt as if her mother had built a wall around herself. In that wall was a narrow gate, and there were very few people she would let through. Lily, unfortunately, had never been one of them.

'Was Josephine my father's child too?' Lily asked her aunt.

'No.' Her aunt shook her head.

No, she wouldn't have been. Otherwise, presumably she wouldn't have been adopted. Half-sister then. It made no difference. 'What happened, Auntie Glenda?' she asked. 'Will you tell me the story?' Her mother's story, she thought. How Lily longed to hear it, longed to understand.

Glenda pushed a plate of biscuits towards Lily and took one herself. She bit into it, chewed thoughtfully and then nodded, as if she'd confirmed her decision. 'I'll tell you everything I know,' she said. 'It can't do any harm. Not now.'

Lily waited. Would this help explain some aspects of her mother's character that had always been a mystery to her? Would it explain the distance between them? She couldn't really see how.

'Your mother met someone,' Glenda said. 'An Italian chap. They fell in love. It was the nineteen sixties.' She shrugged, leaving the rest unsaid, though Lily could imagine some of it for herself. Obviously, it was before her father had come on the scene. Her mother was dreamy and artistic; she might easily have fallen for someone who seemed different – and romantic, no doubt.

'But they hadn't been together long when he had to go back to Italy – to sort things out with his family, apparently, I don't know. Anyway, he asked your mother to wait for him.'

Lily nodded. *Oh dear*, she thought. 'But he never came back?'

'He never came back.' Glenda let the weight of this settle between them. 'I was surprised,' she added. 'You wouldn't normally be surprised at that, I suppose. It's a story as old as the hills, isn't it? He goes back home, reality sets in. He gets with one of his own kind.' She caught Lily's eye. 'That was how it was in those days anyhow, love.'

'So why were you surprised?' Lily wondered.

'Just because those two . . .' She gazed into the mid-distance past Lily's shoulder. 'They really were like love's young dream.' Again, she glanced at Lily. 'At the time, I mean.'

'I see.' Lily wasn't offended in the least. But she wanted to know more. From her bag, she took the little gemstone from the fabric pouch and held it carefully in the palm of her hand. She was so curious about this.

Glenda gave a nod of recognition. 'Oh, yes, he gave her that. I remember, she showed it to me. A talisman, I suppose. So, she kept that too?'

Lily nodded. 'It was with the drawing.' She put the gemstone back in the pouch and took a sip of her coffee. 'And then what happened?' she asked.

Glenda shrugged. 'Ah, well, then your mother discovered she was pregnant.'

'Right. God.' Lily could only imagine how difficult that must have been for her. Especially back then.

'Exactly.' Glenda helped herself to another biscuit and again pushed the plate towards Lily. 'She didn't know who to turn to. She tried to get rid of it – that sounds harsh, but there are ways, as I'm sure you know, my dear – and she expected lover boy to turn up any day to rescue her. But he didn't. And in the end . . .'

'She had the baby.'

Glenda broke her biscuit in half and took a bite. 'In those days, girls were under a lot of pressure,' she said after a few moments. 'Marilyn admitted to me that she was expecting, but what could I do? I had my hands full with my own toddler by then. We all lived at home . . .' She sighed. 'I've always thought I should have done more to help her. I fell pregnant again myself just before the adoption, and it felt as if I was rubbing salt into Marilyn's wound – she was so heartbroken. Should I even have tried to persuade Ted that we should adopt Marilyn's baby? It would have kept the child in the family, at least. I don't think he would have gone for the idea, and as for our parents . . .' She shook her head. 'It seemed impossible. But I've always felt bad about it, you know.'

'I'm sure you did all you could.' Lily was getting the picture. It was, she reminded herself, a very different world back then. 'And how did my grandparents react?' she asked her aunt. They had died when Lily was young and she'd never got to know them as well as she would have liked to. But this must have been quite the bombshell.

'Badly,' Glenda said. 'Your mother wanted to keep the baby, but our parents were in a tricky position. It would have been frowned upon. Marilyn – and the child – wouldn't have had an easy time of it from people around here. The house was already full, there was no father for the baby and no spare money. Our parents didn't want to be unkind, but we all knew adoption was the best thing all round.'

Best for who, though? Lily wondered.

'So, Marilyn was sent off to a mother and baby home in Sussex, under the pretext of staying with a relative to help her out in her guest house, and that was it.'

'It must have been so awful for her,' Lily murmured. What a nightmare. Her mother had never been the most maternal type, but perhaps this was one of the reasons why. And as for Lily's grandparents . . . they had always seemed practical and certainly kind enough – at least to Lily. But they had never been exactly warm and loving. She couldn't remember them ever showing her much affection other than giving her a dry kiss on the cheek. Had they given Lily's mother any emotional support back then? From what Glenda was saying, she suspected not.

'It took a long time for your mother to get over it,' Glenda admitted. 'And like I said, I'm not sure that she ever did – not properly.'

Lily absorbed this. If her mother had never got over it, that might explain a lot.

'I did feel awful afterwards.' Glenda shook her head as if she didn't really want to remember. 'When she came back – late spring of nineteen sixty-six it would have been – Marilyn just seemed so lost.'

Lily thought about this. It was as if her aunt was describing an entirely different woman. But she wasn't. This was Glenda's sister, Lily's mother . . . *Lost*.

'But life goes on, doesn't it?' Glenda continued. 'She knew

71

your father already by then. They both worked at the hotel, they were friends. But he'd always had a thing for her, I think. And when the other chap never came back . . .'

Lily pictured her mother waiting for her lover at the water's edge. The story was getting sadder all the time. 'So Mum never heard from him again?'

'No.' Glenda shook her head. Once again, she turned the drawing over. 'As you can see, she called the baby Josephine. Josephine was adopted and after quite a long while, your mother moved on – to Tom, to you.' She took Lily's hand. 'But don't worry, my dear. She loved your father – and she loved you.'

'Mmm.' Lily supposed that she was right. But how had her mother felt about the adoption years later? *Had* she ever really got over it? Had she always wondered about Josephine? 'I would love to try and get in touch with her,' she said. 'With Josephine.'

Glenda patted Lily's hand before she let it go. 'I understand how you feel.' And her faded blue eyes were kind. 'She's family, isn't she? But you know, it's usually the person who has been adopted who gets to choose whether or not to contact her birth parents. Josephine – wherever she is now – would have been given the details of her adoption when she was eighteen. She could have got in touch if she wanted to – with her mother, even with you.'

Lily considered. 'Perhaps she did get in touch with Mum?' Though she couldn't imagine this somehow.

'I think Marilyn would have told me,' Glenda said, confirming her feelings.

'So, I'll never be able to find her?' Lily sighed. 'I wouldn't even be able to find out her surname, I suppose.' And her adoptive parents would probably have changed her first name anyway . . . It seemed hopeless.

But Glenda was looking thoughtful. 'Now, there I might be able to help you,' she said.

'Oh?' Lily felt a jolt of excitement.

'Her adoptive parents wrote to your mother one time,' Glenda said. 'When Josephine was about three years old.'

'Really?' That surely was a sign that they were good people and Lily was glad. 'To let her know how Josephine was doing, you mean?'

'Yes, I suppose so. To thank her. And to tell her they were moving back to Italy. I think the letter must have been forwarded by the adoption agency, I'm not sure.'

'Italy?' Lily thought of her mother's Italian lover. Was that a coincidence, or . . . ?

'I know.' Glenda nodded. 'In those days I believe they tried to match adoptees with their background,' she said. 'Marilyn may well have told them that Josephine's father was Italian and so although his name wouldn't have been on the birth certificate, Josephine was matched with a similar couple – the woman was English, I think, and he was Italian.'

'Do you think Mum kept the letter?' Lily had gone through most of the paperwork and certainly hadn't found anything like that.

'She tore it up right in front of me.' Glenda clicked her tongue. 'Said there was no reason to keep it. And I suppose there wasn't, not really. There was no address or anything.'

How Lily wished that her mother hadn't destroyed it. There might have been some clue. Perhaps she was angry that the couple had contacted her. Perhaps it made it even harder for

73

her mother to forget . . . But whatever she'd felt, Lily would never know.

'Can you remember anything else about it?' she asked her aunt.

'Just that it said they were going back to run the family café because his parents were retiring, and that Josephine would be brought up in Italy.'

'They kept the name Josephine then?'

'Yes, they did.'

'But surely you don't remember the surname of the couple after all these years?' Lily asked her.

Glenda looked into the distance. 'Yes. I do remember it, because at the time I thought it was such a parody of justice, you know, them having Marilyn's baby and Marilyn . . . Well, it was before she and your father were married. And before she had you, Lily, of course.'

Lily frowned. 'Parody of justice?'

'Yes, because that was the name,' Glenda said. 'I never forget a name, you know. It was Parodi. Parody but with an i.'

'Josephine Parodi . . .' Lily repeated.

'Not that it will help you,' Glenda said. 'It's probably a common enough name. There must be thousands of people named Parodi in Italy. And I don't even know what area of Italy his family came from. Or even her adoptive father's first name. But still . . .'

Lily got to her feet. She had a name. It was a start. And the little fizz of excitement inside her had not gone away. 'It's got to be worth a try,' she said.

CHAPTER II

Lily

2018

Secret lives, thought Lily, as she switched on her laptop. So many people must have them. Past secrets, hidden in people's minds and hearts, that they chose not to share for whatever reason. Lily's father had known about Josephine, according to Glenda. Glenda knew; probably her husband as well. Lily's grandparents too . . . But Lily's mother had put her secret in the past, and since then, it seemed, she had never gone there.

She must have thought about her older daughter, though. There was the drawing after all . . . Lily glanced at it, now propped on the dining-room window sill; she'd hoped it would provide her with inspiration during her search. The soft wisps of dark hair, the impossible knowingness of the baby's eyes . . . What had Lily's mother been thinking of when she sketched her daughter that day? The love that she felt? The imminent loss?

And later . . . Had she wanted to meet her? She must surely

have wanted to find out what had happened to Josephine? Had that, Lily wondered, been a sadness in her mother's life that she had never been able to come to terms with? She suspected so. Lily opened the search engine. There was so much she would like to know. But where to start?

She put three words into Google – the three words that she knew as fact, if Glenda was correct. *Parodi. Café. Italy.* She would see what came up.

Two cafés appeared on the first page of her search results – both in Italy, both called Caffè Parodi. Of course, Lily wasn't certain that was the name of the *caffè*, but it was the family surname if Glenda was correct, and it was the husband who was Italian and whose parents had run the *caffè*, so it seemed a good starting place. Besides, it was pretty much all she had.

The first was in Alessandria. Lily got up the website, trawled through menus and pictures. What would Josephine even look like now? But there was no mention of staff names and it seemed a big place; not quite what she'd envisaged. But then again, what did she know?

The second one in Novi Ligure seemed more likely, but again there were no staff names listed. Should she email them? Maybe. This one was a possibility, though there could be plenty of others on future pages. Or maybe the *caffè* wouldn't have a website at all – that was assuming that the family still even owned it and that it was called Caffè Parodi in the first place . . .

She found a decalcification product for coffee machines called Parodi and Parodi and, interestingly, a Bernadette Parodi who had appeared in *Bake Off Italiana*. There was another *caffè* in Milan, plenty of material about Parodi cigars, and several individuals named Parodi. But although she scrolled down a number of pages and went down a few fascinating but totally irrelevant rabbit holes, she found no mention of a Josephine.

Lily glanced at her watch. She couldn't believe how much time had passed. She made herself some coffee and returned to her laptop to answer some work-related emails. Looking for a long-lost half-sister was definitely not going to be easy and she decided to pace herself. In the afternoon, she went for a walk, did some more packing and sorting and it wasn't until the evening that she started her search again.

She would have to use all her powers of logic, she thought grimly. This time, she looked for Josephine Parodi on social media sites, but there was no joy. There were only a few, all too young and living in Canada, America and France respectively. Perhaps Josephine wasn't a social media type of person. Or perhaps . . . She was probably married, Lily realised, which meant she might not even be called Parodi any more. Oh dear, that was an added complication Lily hadn't even considered until now. Although, if she could locate one of Josephine's adoptive parents, she reasoned, she might be able to contact Josephine through them?

It wasn't ideal, but . . . Lily called Glenda. 'Can you remember the first name of either of the Parodis? The couple who adopted Josephine?' she asked her aunt. She supposed that it would have been written on that letter when they signed off. They might feature on a café website, or even on social media.

Her aunt seemed to be pondering. 'I'm sorry, my dear,' she said after few moments. 'It was a long time ago. I really can't recall.'

Lily felt a dip of disappointment. But her aunt had done brilliantly even remembering as much as she had, she reminded herself. 'Never mind,' she told Glenda. 'Thanks, anyway.'

Back on the laptop, she continued scrolling. It might be worth emailing all the cafés named Parodi, she thought, to ask if there was a Josephine there, or if they knew of a Josephine Parodi. It sounded desperate, but what other options did she have? Contacting a mother and baby home which probably didn't even exist any more?

She tried another tack. She put *Parodi, Italian surname* into her search box. *Parodi* had a coat of arms and a two-fold origin, she soon learnt. It was a locational name, the dweller at the sign of the finch – apparently a Middle Ages thing. Hmm. Not overwhelmingly helpful.

And then she had a breakthrough. Her *Parodi* surname search revealed a map of Italy with differently coloured sections, and surnames printed by size according to their popularity in each region. And there was *Parodi*, almost exclusively in Liguria, the region of the Italian Riviera with Genoa at its centre, stretching along the curve of the coastline, the second most common surname of the entire region.

Wow. Lily did a solo high five. This was a major clue. She thought of the Caffè Parodi in Novi Ligure. It seemed even more likely now. Although . . . Lily sat up straighter. It was getting late, but she couldn't stop now. It seemed almost certain that the Parodis would have lived somewhere in Liguria. She sent off an email to the *caffè* in Novi Ligure asking them if they were aware of any Josephine Parodi with connections to their business, and then added Liguria to her original search words and scrolled through the results.

Ah. She found another Caffè Parodi and clicked on the website. This one was simpler. There was a picture of a most beautiful landscape: a pink bell tower outlined against a blue-green sea and azure sky, and red-roofed houses with clambering

78

red and purple bougainvillea and dusky olive trees beyond. *Caffè Parodi, Perlarosa, Liguria*, she read. It was probably worth emailing this place too.

Lily clicked on to the contact page – there was a phone number and an email address and she froze, her fingers poised above the keyboard as she read the contact name. Josefine Parodi. Could it possibly be her? The spelling was different, but this would be the Italian version of the name. There was no picture – that would be way too much to hope for – so she couldn't estimate this Josefine's age or possible physical similarities . . . She glanced up again at her mother's sketch. 'Is this you?' she whispered.

The name was right. Lily felt the thrill of excitement. But how popular was the name Josefine in Italy anyway? She had no idea. Still, this was Josefine Parodi and this was a *caffè* in Liguria, Italy. It seemed a definite possibility that this Josefine was her Josephine. So what next? Lily's approach would have to be sensitive, she knew. Josefine had a British adoptive mother, so she'd presumably speak English. Lily hesitated. It was best to email her, she decided. To call her out of the blue wasn't a good idea – she might freak out completely and Lily didn't want that.

It was hard to know what to say in the email, though. This was a big deal – or it could be. Lily didn't want to shock or upset her, or even frighten her off. She must remember that Josephine had not tried to contact her birth mother, and that this Josefine Parodi might not be her anyway. Lily didn't want to say too much or too little. And how much did her Josephine even know about her own past? It was a tricky one.

Dear Josefine, she wrote. I am getting in touch because I think we may be related. I would love to discuss this with you. Please contact me. Lily.

And then she waited. She waited for days, then the days stretched into a week and more. The first *caffè* in Novi Ligure had written back long ago denying any knowledge of a Josefine. But from Josefine Parodi in Perlarosa, Lily didn't hear a thing. She wrote twice more, but there was no reply. Perhaps Josefine never checked her email or had changed the address? Was now the time to try and call her? Lily felt her stomach churn at the prospect, but she had to do something.

The first time she called, Lily listened to the ring tone, trying to control her nerves. What should she say? She would be calm and careful, she decided. She wouldn't blurt anything out that could be off-putting or upsetting. Perhaps she'd ask Josefine if she had any British relatives? That would be a good starting point.

Lily let the ring tone go on and on until it cut off with no voicemail. She wasn't sure whether she felt more relieved or disappointed. She tried again later that day, and then again at different times in the following few days. But although the phone rang on and on, no one picked up. Perhaps the *caffè* had closed down? Or maybe Josefine was no longer there?

The funeral came and went. Lily had mixed emotions. She was grieving, yes – this was the woman who had given birth to her, this was her mother, and so of course she was sad. But what made her even sadder was the waste, the loss of a love that had never even made itself felt. Finding out about Josephine had made her feel differently about everything. There had been another side to her mother, she realised, one that she had never known.

As friends and relatives came to pay their respects, as they stood chatting in Glenda's house after the funeral service, where Lily and her aunt had prepared a simple buffet, Lily found herself wondering, did this person know about Josephine? Did this one? Would anyone know more than her aunt Glenda? Lily doubted it and she certainly wasn't about to ask any of them. But it was sad that these people hadn't known her mother either, not really.

In the past weeks, Lily had been making the house presentable and now it had been put up for sale. She had spent some time going through her mother's paintings – there were so many and it was hard to know what to do with them – and in the end, she had chosen her favourite three and given others away to Glenda and a few other relatives and friends. She would decide what to do with the rest later. Lily had inherited a small sum of money too – her parents' savings – which was already lodged in her bank account and now, she had to make a decision.

Lily phoned Aunt Glenda. She had kept her up to speed with what she had discovered so far.

'I've decided what to do,' she told her aunt when she answered the phone. 'I'm going there.'

'Where, my dear?' Glenda enquired mildly. 'Back to London, do you mean?'

'To Liguria,' Lily said. 'I'll start off in Perlarosa at the Caffè Parodi and I'll go on from there. I could do with a holiday anyway. And I haven't got too much work on at the moment.' Though Lily wasn't sure why she was justifying it to Glenda or to herself. She could do as she liked, and what she most wanted to do was go to Italy and look for her half-sister.

Would that journey help her find out more about the mother she never really knew? Perhaps not, but she felt she had to do it anyhow. And the idea of finding a sibling who had been kept a secret was irresistible. She could afford it now, Lily reminded herself sadly. It might not lead her to Josephine, but it was an adventure at least, and she'd never forgive herself if she didn't try.

'Oh my goodness,' said Glenda. 'That's terribly exciting. But are you sure this is a good idea, Lily?'

'Yes, I am.' Though Lily knew she sounded more confident than she actually felt. How might Josephine feel about having been adopted? Abandoned? Resentful? Perhaps so. But wasn't it somehow Lily's duty to try and resolve things, to try and find out the truth? It was a risk, because who knew what she might discover? It might be something she'd rather not know or have to think about. But nothing ventured, nothing gained, as her father used to say.

She glanced again at the drawing, at Josephine. 'I think it's the best idea I've had for a long time.'

CHAPTER 12

Lily

2018

It wasn't an easy journey. The emotional turmoil was continuing to build. Lily had never done this sort of thing before – of course she hadn't. And then there were the practicalities.

From Pisa Airport she took a shuttle to the railway station and then a train to La Spezia. From there, she eventually found the right bus to take her to Lerici where she was spending the night, before she would have to take another bus to the small village of Perlarosa. Phew. The journey certainly gave her time to think. Could this Josefine Parodi be her sister? What were the odds? How would Lily feel if this wasn't the right woman? And how would she feel if she was?

Lily was glad of the rest in Lerici; it gave her a half-decent night's sleep, a delicious *spaghetti vongole* dish of pasta and clams that evening, a first glimpse of the famous Bay of Poets – which was all deep turquoise sea, cobbled piazzas and tall, narrow and colourful houses. And the chance to muster her courage for the

83

day ahead. She'd made the decision to come here. Now, she just had to get on with it. Otherwise, she would never know . . .

It was a bright end-of-March day, chilly to start with, before the clear sky deepened into spring blue. Lily repacked the few things she'd needed for the previous night into her case, and then trundled it down the steps from the pink and red old town, tucked under Lerici's dominating grey castle by the port.

In Piazza Garibaldi, she ordered coffee and a *cornetto alla crema* – this seemed to be the breakfast of choice for most – bought a ticket from the *tabacchi* and waited for the bus. Something was making her feel shaky – the hit of caffeine perhaps? Or maybe the prospect of meeting her half-sister at last. If it was even her. *Josefine* . . .

She whispered the name to herself. How many Josefines were running a café in Italy? Probably quite a few. But how many of those caffès were owned by someone named Parodi? Not many, she hoped. And besides, this Josefine was the only one she'd found.

On the bus, her case safely stowed in the luggage compartment at the front, she drank in the landscape greedily as the road wound upwards past stately villas and dry-stone walls, gifting Lily tantalising glimpses through the umbrella pines, olive groves and bamboo of the little beaches half-hidden below and the deeply sapphire sea.

The bus dropped her on the outskirts of the village of Perlarosa. Lily pulled her case down with her. *Wow* . . . She looked around. The sheer beauty of the place made her catch her breath. And the colours – the blues, the pinks, the reds – were so intense and overwhelming that she had the strangest of feelings, as if she wanted to hug Perlarosa close and never

84

let it go. Lily blinked. She was surprised at herself. She'd never had such an emotional reaction to a place before.

She took a few steps down the road, wheeling her case behind her. The village ahead seemed to be balanced on the cliff itself. It was a cluster of pink houses and red roofs, of hazy green olive trees, fig and oleander, of paving and cobbles and a tall, stone church gazing beatifically down at her, the sea shimmering invitingly way below.

Lily stopped and stared. She really hadn't been expecting this.

She tore her eyes away from the view. First, she must locate her B & B and then she could explore. She checked her phone and saw that it was on this main road (Lily suspected there weren't many roads in Perlarosa) back a bit from where she was standing, so she retraced her steps, and there it was, almost opposite where she now stood. It was a tall villa with a dark pink facade, green shutters and little black wrought-iron balconies, set in a garden full of palms and olives behind a stone wall. A very good start, she decided. She took a deep breath and made her way over towards the steps that led up to the front door.

Her hostess was welcoming. '*Si, si,*' she said. 'Come in. *Prego.* Welcome.' The room was ready and here was bottled water, she told her, and a tiny bottle of Prosecco chilling in the fridge.

'*Grazie, Signora.*' Lily would have to practise her Italian, which was limited, to say the least.

Hopefully, Josefine would indeed speak English – whether she was *the* Josefine or not. Because it would be hard enough to express what she wanted to say even in her own language and this was a big thing to lay on somebody. *Hello, I'm your long-lost sister. How are you doing?* just wasn't going to cut it.

Lily would need to do this gradually, carefully, sensitively. She sighed. And even more than before, the enormity of the task ahead, the gamble she'd taken, the pure craziness of coming out here alone with no guarantees, hit her deep in the gut. But then again . . . She smiled. Perlarosa *was* beautiful.

In less than an hour, Lily had unpacked her things, got changed and set off to look around the village. She wouldn't even consult her phone for directions, she decided. She'd explore this place the old-fashioned way. Discover it for herself. Somewhere here was the Caffè Parodi. Somewhere here was Josefine.

As she walked down the street, passing more colourful houses and gardens full of fig trees and pomegranate, Lily absorbed the spring fragrance of leafiness and fresh growth. *Heaven* . . . She breathed in more deeply, sure that she could hear the sound of the waves carried on the soft breeze. Opposite the stone church was the most perfect *belvedere*, a walled viewpoint looking out towards the ocean. She went up the steps and noticed the stone plaque on the wall. *Belvedere Eoa Rainusso*, she read on the inscription – an Italian *poetessa*, no less.

Oh my . . . She rested her hands on the railings and gazed out to sea. Beyond the olive and tamarisk trees, past the blue jasmine and red-roofed houses, she could also see the faded pink bell tower of a church standing on the promontory, dusky and gorgeous. Lily recognised it from the Caffè Parodi website, but it was even more luscious in real life, she decided. Out to sea were two islands – she'd look at a map later and find out their names. They were surrounded by the dense glimmering green-blue of the sea. The Bay of Poets, she thought. Little wonder that Shelley, Byron and D. H. Lawrence had wanted to spend so much of their time here. This landscape must have been quite an inspiration.

She walked on, past a bright orange house with green shutters on the corner, a little greengrocer's shop displaying delicious-looking fruit – sleek aubergines and vivid red tomatoes – a man selling plants from the back of a blue van, a pharmacy and a dress shop. There was a bar, but definitely not the caffè she was looking for.

A couple of minutes later, she came to a paved square, or more of an oblong, if you were going to be mathematical and pedantic – which she wasn't, not today. It was probably the main square, she guessed, since there were some people milling around and sitting in the shade on the benches under the ilex oak trees. She couldn't spot the name of the piazza, but there were a couple of pastel-painted houses on one side, along with a *tabacchi* and some lush palms and succulents in big stone planters. There was also another bar, and a couple of restaurants and caffès with tables outside.

Lily felt a dip of nerves. Was this Piazza Figoli? Surely the caffè must be here? She took a breath, braced herself. Then scanned them, one by one. No, no, and then all of a sudden there it was. Caffè Parodi.

She stood motionless. What now? Lily gave herself a little shake. *Go in, of course.* After all, she'd come all this way . . .

CHAPTER 13

Lily

2018

The *caffè* was old-fashioned and quirky. The *terrazzo* flooring inside extended out onto the small courtyard, which was strung with fairy lights and tangled with pink bougainvillea and shared the same breathtaking view of the pink bell tower and the sea with the belvedere just up the road. Lily paused for a moment before she crossed the threshold.

She blinked. It wasn't quite what she'd expected. Mismatched chairs were crowded around mismatched tables, the wooden beams above were hung with pots, pans and old weighing scales, bare light bulbs dangled from the ceiling and the walls were painted bright purple. Books were crammed into two wooden bookcases in the corners, and lanterns stood precariously on top of glass cabinets full of plates and glasses. Pictures – a variety of landscapes and abstracts – decorated each wall, in another corner a large television was thankfully not switched on, and a couple of ancient transistor radios stood on a shelf nearby. The side wall was completely taken up by a deep counter full of pastries, *focaccia* and other delicious-looking temptations. Apart from that one detail, it was unlike any café Lily had ever seen.

A few people sat at tables eating pastries and drinking coffee. And on the far side, a woman wearing a blue and white apron, her dark hair pinned in a knot at the nape of her neck, was clearing plates and cups onto a tray quickly and efficiently, talking meanwhile in rapid Italian that Lily had no hope of understanding, to a man on a nearby corner table. He was around the same age as the woman – who was around the right age (early fifties, Lily had calculated) to be the right Josefine. He looked weathered and interesting and he had, Lily saw, a nice smile.

But it was the woman she was most interested in. Lily stilled. Could this be her? She thought of her mother's drawing. It was impossible to tell. And the woman had her back to her. But there were no other waitresses in sight. Did she run this place alone?

As Lily stood there, taking it all in, the man seemed to notice her and he must have said something to the woman who might be Josefine, because she picked up her tray and swung around.

Lily gazed at her. She had been thinking so much about her, wondering what she might look like . . . and although admittedly the woman looked nothing like Lily, even so, there was something . . . What was it?

She was tallish, maybe five foot eight, with strong features – high cheekbones, a wide mouth – and she was still in her prime. She definitely looked Italian. But there was something in the tilt of her head, in the lightness of her eyes – were they grey or blue? Lily couldn't tell from this distance. Something that reminded Lily of her mother. She hoped she wasn't imagining it; how she hoped that this was—

'*Prego*,' the woman was saying. Unlike the man she'd been talking to, she wasn't smiling. She glanced curiously at Lily, no doubt wondering why she was staring quite so hard.

'Oh . . .' Just as Lily was debating whether to apologise or take a step forward and introduce herself, the woman gestured to an empty table, raised an eyebrow in enquiry. She didn't exactly seem the friendly type. And she looked, thought Lily, as if she did not suffer fools gladly.

'*Grazie*.' Lily sat down. *Pull yourself together*, she told herself, one of her mother's old sayings that continued to haunt her. *Get a grip*.

The woman who might be Josefine nodded, took the tray over to the counter and returned with a notepad and pen. Once again, she raised an eyebrow. *We put up with you tourists*, her expression seemed to say. *But don't think you are important to us in the least*.

'*Buongiorno*,' Lily managed.

The woman looked faintly surprised. '*Buongiorno*.' Though she sounded grudging. She nodded, tapped her pen on the notepad.

Lily got the hint. She was clearly busy. She had a *caffè* to run, of course she did. But how on earth was Lily ever going to talk to her? This wasn't an auspicious start.

'*Un cappuccino, per favore*,' she said haltingly. She had heard that Italians laughed at the '*per favore*' thing, that they didn't themselves use this level of politeness when they were ordering food or drinks; it labelled you as a tourist. But what did it matter? Lily couldn't speak Italian and there was no point in pretending she wasn't an English visitor.

'You want coffee, yes? Coming right up.' And the waitress sashayed away, with the faintest of eye-rolls towards the smiling man in the corner.

Hmm. Of course she would speak English. Even if she were not the right Josefine, this was a *caffè* that clearly catered for many international tourists as well as locals. But she wasn't the most approachable. Lily would have to work hard to find a way in.

A few minutes later, the woman reappeared with a cup of foaming coffee. She put it down in front of Lily, but did not make eye contact.

'*Grazie*,' said Lily. And then quickly, before she could walk away, 'Excuse me. I was wondering . . . Are you Josefine Parodi?'

The woman's eyes narrowed. They were definitely blue-grey. She put her hands on her hips. 'Who wants to know?' She made a move back towards the counter.

'My name's Lily Knight.' Lily saw her register this and knew it meant something to her. She pushed on. 'I wrote you an email.'

But Josefine had recovered herself now. 'I have no time for email,' she said, and just like that, in a swish of her blue and white apron, she was gone.

After this, it seemed to Lily that she avoided Lily's table. She retreated behind the counter to prepare snacks and make coffee, which she whisked onto people's tables before promptly withdrawing again.

Lily sipped her coffee and watched her. So, what had she discovered so far? From the woman's reaction – not to mention the blue-grey eyes – she reckoned she might have found her Josefine; which was both exciting and also, given the woman's reaction, rather disappointing. Because something else was very clear. Josefine did not want to even talk to her.

Lily pulled a notebook out of her bag. If Josefine didn't want to talk to her, then Lily would have to convince her otherwise. She hadn't come all the way here to give up at the first setback.

Josefine, she wrote. *I'm sorry to turn up like this. But I've come a long way to see you. I think we might be related. If so, I have a drawing made of you when you were a baby and I so want to talk to you. This is my number.* She wrote it down. *Please call.*

She went to the counter to pay for her coffee. Josefine was still refusing to look at her and Lily knew it was pointless to push it at this point. So, she slid the note across the counter. 'Please read it,' she said. 'Please call me.'

Josefine eyed the note as if it might burn her but made no move to pick it up.

What more could she do? Lily walked out of the *caffè* into the glorious sunshine and lifted her face up to the sun. Despite this unsatisfactory first encounter, adrenaline was coursing through her. She grinned. Because she believed that she had found her. Against all the odds, she had found Josefine. And now she just had to hope that Josefine would agree to talk to her.

CHAPTER 14

Lily

2018

Lily wasn't sure what to do with herself for the rest of the day. She'd booked herself into the B & B for a week, thinking this would give her a chance to spend some quality time with Josefine, if it was her, before going home. But since Josefine didn't want to talk to Lily . . . She gazed down the street. Perlarosa was beautiful, but it was a tiny hamlet. So, what next?

Still, the sun was shining, so Lily returned to the B & B up the road, picked up a few things and made her way back to the Piazza Figoli. Josefine was out of sight. Maybe she'd call, maybe she wouldn't. But while she was waiting, Lily could explore the rest of the village. She had a book to occupy her. She had plenty to think about. And surely there had to be a beach?

From the piazza, the road – Via della Pace, she read, inscribed on the stone wall – led naturally round to a narrower street lined with pink and yellow houses, with plants hanging from wrought-iron balconies and washing strung high above. It was leading downhill, this street that was more like an alleyway – *caruggi*, she thought they were called, these traditional tiny walkways creating labyrinths in the old towns of Liguria.

Lily guessed they'd been built like this to keep the streets and houses cool in summer, but it was a strange, almost surreal feeling, being surrounded so closely by these tall skinny houses. The ground was uneven; she could smell the damp, dusty stone mingling with the scents of the plants and the flowers in terracotta pots next to great wooden doorways and black iron window grilles. And if she reached out to touch, the paint would flake in her fingers.

At the end of the street, Lily turned a corner. Facing her was a pink and grey wall – that of the church with the dusky facade that she'd spotted earlier, she realised. *Church of St Giorgio*, she read on a sign at the entrance. She stepped inside. The floor was of grey and white marble, and for an Italian church, the interior was plain and simple: it was pale yellow with stone pillars and arches and lovely swooping architectural lines.

The church was empty, except for one man sitting at the front, his head bowed. He didn't look up as Lily entered; in fact, he seemed oblivious to her arrival. But she could sense the sadness in him even from a distance, from the bow of his neck and the stoop of his shoulders as he sat in the wooden pew.

Lily hesitated. Should she leave? He seemed distressed and perhaps wanted to be alone. Lily certainly didn't want to intrude.

But just as she was about to turn and go, the man got up from the pew, almost stumbling, as if suddenly desperate to leave the church. Lily couldn't help staring at him. He was in his late thirties or thereabouts, she guessed. And he had a hunted look about him. His thick dark hair, raven-black, was sticking up at all angles from his head as if he'd been raking his fingers through it all morning. He was dressed in blue working overalls, streaked with black and dusty with a faint glitter, his face was lean, his cheekbones harsh and prominent, and as he came closer, she could see that his eyes were very dark and very sad.

She didn't belong here. She was intruding on his grief or silent contemplation or prayer or whatever he was doing, and so Lily quickly looked away. But already, he'd seen her. He paused. Stared at her so intently that she felt uncomfortable, and just like Josefine, he didn't smile.

Lily fidgeted, unsure whether to go or stay, whether to speak or remain silent. What was the rule here? In Dorset, you tended to greet people you didn't know when you came across them on a clifftop or in an almost-deserted church. In London, you generally didn't. She compromised on a small nod of acknowledgement.

He hesitated, seemed about to speak and then nodded back at her.

Lily exhaled. That was probably right then. It felt slightly strange to be alone in a church in Italy with a grief-stricken man dressed in a glittery boilersuit, but then again, this whole journey was strange.

Head down, as if keen to avoid further eye contact, he strode to the door, turned left and skittered off down the alleyway. Hmm. Lily had a feeling that although Perlarosa was small, it might contain more than its fair share of what her mother would have called 'characters'. And since the place wasn't highly populated, it was likely that during her time here she would meet them all.

*

95

Later in the afternoon, she walked back towards the Piazza Figoli and the Caffè Parodi, lingering for a moment outside, trying to catch a glimpse of Josefine. Had she thought about things while Lily had been sitting on the rocks enjoying the early April sun and exploring the village? Josefine had never been far from Lily's thoughts, but despite looking at her phone a hundred times, there had been no message. Lily's half-sister – for it surely must be her – was clearly determined not to make this easy.

The *caffè* was still open – Josefine worked long hours then – and Lily could see her wiping down the surface of one of the mismatched tables. Should she go in? She didn't want to be a nuisance; she didn't want Josefine to think she was some kind of stalker . . . But she had to do something.

Josefine, however, looked up as if sensing her scrutiny.

Lily made a motion. *Can I come in?*

Josefine moved her head – so slightly that it was almost nothing, but to Lily it was enough. She stepped inside. There were still a few customers, but it was quieter than before, and as she looked over at the counter, Lily saw that the supply of pastries was much depleted. It felt as if the *caffè* might be about to close, and sure enough, even as she stood there, a couple of people made a move to go and Josefine closed the door behind them, turning the 'open' sign over with a snap.

She looked tired, Lily thought. There was a light bruising under her blue-grey eyes and her expression was weary.

She motioned for Lily to sit at a table by the counter and she sat down opposite. Lily didn't say a word – she didn't want to say the wrong thing. It was better, she decided, to let Josefine lead the way.

Josefine laid her palms flat on the table in front of her. Lily could see, just from looking at her hands, that she was used to hard work. And she noted a wedding ring too. Was she married to the smiley man from earlier? For some reason, Lily didn't think so.

'You have wasted your time coming here,' Josefine said in perfect English.

Lily stared at her. 'But—'

'I am sorry,' Josefine continued. 'But I will explain.'

Lily waited.

'I do not want to talk to you.'

Lily absorbed her words. That was certainly telling it straight, she thought. 'But you are Josefine Parodi? You are . . . ?'

'Yes,' she said. 'I am.'

'And you were adopted? Your mother was British?'

'So I understand.' She was very cool. 'But I did not answer your email. I did not encourage you to come.'

This was true. Even so, Lily was stunned, hurt and, yes, angry. And it was hardly an explanation. She'd expected a potentially tricky and sensitive conversation. She had not expected this. 'But I'm here now,' she said staunchly.

'You are here now,' Josefine agreed. 'But it makes no difference.'

'Why not?' If Josefine had been told that she was adopted, then Lily simply couldn't believe that she didn't feel as Lily did, that she wouldn't be as excited as Lily was – about having a half-sister, about getting to know her. And wouldn't she have questions about her birth mother? Didn't she want to know anything?

'I think I am your half-sister,' she said. 'My mother's child was adopted by a couple named Parodi who came to Italy around nineteen sixty-nine in order to take over the running of the family *caffè*.'

Josefine nodded.

Lily couldn't understand her complete lack of enthusiasm. 'Was that you? Can you tell me – is your birthday in early May? And were you born in the mid-sixties?'

Josefine acknowledged this with the slightest of nods. 'Yes, that is me,' she said. 'Nineteen sixty-six. You are right.'

'Then—'

'I am sorry,' Josefine said again. She really looked so world-weary. Lily wondered if anything else had happened to make her react this way.

'Our mother—'

'*Your* mother.' Her expression was inscrutable now.

Lily took a deep breath. 'Yes.' Of course, it was different for Josefine. Their mother had not been able to keep her, not been able to give her a home. Lily wanted to tell her what she knew about that time, what her aunt had told her, about how difficult it must have been for their mother. She wanted to tell her that their mother had kept the drawing she'd made of Josefine under her mattress; that she must have thought about her every day. But she sensed this wasn't the right time; Josefine wouldn't be open to it. In fact, it seemed she wasn't open to anything.

'You're right.' Lily kept her voice low although they were now practically alone in the *caffè*. 'I don't know how it was for you – being adopted, I mean.' What had happened to her adoptive parents anyway? They didn't seem to be part of the Caffè Parodi, at least they weren't here today. And Josefine had that look about her, as if she might be running things single-handedly. 'What was your childhood like?' she asked. 'Was it a happy one? Can you at least tell me that?' It was something she guessed her mother would have worried about, and something that concerned Lily too.

Josefine gave her a hard look. *What is it to you?* she seemed to say.

But Lily wanted to know. It *was* something to her. She cared. 'I'm your sister,' she said. Now that she had met her, she felt it even more. 'And I came a long way to find you.'

Josefine sighed and gave another little nod. 'Happy enough.'

'And are you happy now?'

'Now?' Josefine looked down.

It seemed to Lily that her presence was almost too much for Josefine. But why? Didn't she realise that Lily wasn't trying to take anything from her? The opposite was true. She might even be able to offer support if Josefine should need it – although that was presumptive of her, she supposed.

Josefine shrugged as if her happiness was of no relevance to anything. 'Lily,' she said, 'I am trying to explain to you.' She looked sad now, almost as sad as that man in the church had earlier.

'What?' Lily was baffled. 'What are you trying to explain?'

'You must understand this,' said Josefine. 'Not every person who has been adopted wants to be found.'

CHAPTER 15

Lily

2018

Lily tried to get her head around this new development. 'You didn't want me to find you?' she echoed.

She thought of how happy she'd been when she made her discoveries. First, that she had a half-sister, and second, that Josefine might be here in Perlarosa and that Lily might meet her. The story around Josefine's birth was sad, of course – and not just for Josefine. But Lily had a sibling. A sister. They could meet. Of course they'd get on. Despite their different upbringings and the fact that Lily was a fair bit younger than Josefine, they'd be two peas in a pod. Perhaps Josefine too would love numbers? She might even have had weird number-linked dreams when she was a girl? Imagine that! Or perhaps she'd be the arty one, the yin to Lily's yang? Maybe Josefine would have children – highly likely after all – and so Lily might even be an auntie?

She hadn't let herself go any further than this. She'd known she was getting a bit carried away.

Now, though, it turned out that Josefine hadn't even wanted Lily to find her, which was why she'd never replied to the email. This was a scenario that Lily hadn't allowed herself to dwell on – otherwise, she might never have come here.

'Not you,' Josefine said. She smoothed her dark hair from her face and gave a little sigh. 'I didn't even know about *you*.'

Ah. No, of course she didn't. Even so, she probably hadn't wanted to be found by anyone. 'Sorry.' Lily stumbled to her feet. 'I'm an idiot. I never thought . . .' – she forced herself to look Josefine in the eye – 'that you wouldn't want to meet me.' And she let out a choked little laugh.

Josefine reached out and gently placed her hand on Lily's arm. Lily looked down at her sister's hand and noted again the wedding band. But there was no evidence of children around. She looked up. Josefine's eyes had softened.

Lily hesitated.

'Stay.' Josefine got to her feet. 'I do not mean to upset you,' she said. 'It was a shock. *You* were a shock. But please stay.'

Lily sat down again. Josefine retreated into a back room behind the counter and, after a few moments, she reappeared with a bottle of wine and two glasses.

'I think we need a drink,' she said.

Lily gave a little smile. 'Good idea.' She could tell that Josefine was still wary, but the atmosphere had lightened somewhat and Lily felt her shoulders relax. It seemed that her sister was prepared to talk to her at least.

Josefine opened the bottle with a deft twist of the corkscrew and splashed white wine into two glasses. 'Vermentino.' She pushed one towards Lily and raised her own glass in what seemed, from her expression, to be a sardonic toast.

To sisters, Lily thought, but she refrained from saying it out

101

loud. Although, one day, perhaps . . . She sipped her wine, which was light and delicious and made her feel a bit calmer.

'Tell me how you found me,' Josefine said to Lily as she sat down. 'Why now?'

Lily took a deep breath. 'I never knew about you before,' she said. This was difficult. There was so much to tell. 'And then . . . Our mother died recently,' she told her. She had no idea how Josefine might respond to this news. Could you truly grieve for someone you had never met? Probably, yes, but that would depend on what you felt for them. From her reaction so far, she guessed that Josefine wouldn't shed any tears.

Sure enough, she bowed her head, but when she looked up, her eyes were dry. 'I am sorry,' she said.

'Sorry that you never knew her?' The first few sips of Vermentino had also made Lily bold.

'In a way, perhaps,' Josefine conceded. 'But you must understand, she has never been in my life and so very rarely in my thoughts.'

Lily wondered how true this really was. Because surely everyone must have an emotional link to their parents whether they knew them or not? Your mother had given birth to you; she had been the first person to nurture you, to hold you. It must mean something. Although if, like Josefine, you were never going to be able to meet them, then perhaps it would be yet another reason not to rake over difficult emotions. You would wonder, wouldn't you, why your mother had ever let you go?

'And so, I am sorrier for you,' Josefine continued. 'Her daughter.'

Josefine was her daughter too, but Lily let that pass. She took another sip of wine. 'We weren't close,' she told her. 'In some

102

ways, I never really knew her either. Not properly.' Although Lily was not insensitive and she knew, of course, that while she'd had the chance, Josefine hadn't been given a chance at all.

Josefine raised an eyebrow. 'But you must have known that she loved you?' The words were stark.

'Sometimes I wasn't sure.' Lily had to be honest. She recalled her mother's final word as she was dying. *Darling* . . . 'But I suppose that in her way, she did.'

Lily thought of how it had been growing up. Her mother flitting in and out of the house, eager to escape to her studio. Whatever her mother had been doing, Lily always heard it and always felt it . . . That small sigh of relief. Because her mother was glad, Lily knew, to escape the chores, the house, Lily . . . Glad to escape from her family and be by herself, in her studio, painting. How could you feel close, growing up, to someone who always wanted to get away from you?

And then . . . Lily picked up her glass, took another sip of her wine. Her mother would come back hours later, a new brightness in her eyes, determined to do something with her family. Something fun! Maybe she felt guilty for neglecting them? Maybe she'd only just remembered they existed? Anyway, whatever demon had been seething around inside had been temporarily exorcised and now she was free to be with them. But sometimes they were no longer there – they'd gone out or Lily was in bed. Sometimes, it was just too late.

Lily took another gulp of her wine. 'She was a creative spirit,' she said – lamely, she felt. But there was a lot to say and she couldn't say it all.

'A creative spirit?' Josefine refilled both their glasses. Her voice was polite, as if she was only making small talk rather than discovering the truth about her own mother.

'She was an artist,' Lily told Josefine.

'A successful one?' Josefine asked.

'Not really.' Lily felt a small prod of betrayal. 'She painted in watercolours,' she said. Sad and fluid, beautiful, dripping watercolours. 'And she did sell a few pieces every now and then.' But Lily had the sense that selling her work had not been so important to her mother. She just needed to be doing it. Perhaps it had taken her away from her own thoughts — who knew?

Josefine took a long, slow sip of her wine; as for Lily — she knew that she was drinking too fast. She was getting maudlin, whereas Josefine was showing almost no emotion. This wasn't how Lily had envisaged their first meeting at all.

'Anyway . . .' She groped in her bag. 'After she died, I was clearing out the house and I found this . . .' Carefully, she took the drawing out of its yellowing envelope.

Josefine stared at it.

'It's you.'

Frowning, she picked it up. 'Really?' She turned it over, read what was written on the back.

'Her handwriting,' Lily said, though Josefine hadn't asked. She sat back in her chair. 'So you see, she must have cared.'

'Cared?' Once again, Josefine topped up both their glasses.

'About you.' She was very hard to get through to. 'To keep your picture, I mean.'

Josefine put her head on one side as if considering the evidence. She placed the drawing back on the table between them and took a swig of her wine. 'But not enough to keep me.'

'Oh, but—'

Josefine raised her hand. 'I do not want to talk about it, Lily,' she said. 'Or her. If you do not mind. I just wondered how you had found me, that is all.'

Lily was silent. She could understand why Josefine felt this way. Her sister knew nothing of their mother's situation and circumstances at the time of her birth – although hopefully Lily could communicate something of what had happened at some point. No matter how happy Josefine's adoption might have been, she must always have felt rejected by her birth mother. If Lily wanted to gain her trust, if she wanted to get to know her, to build a relationship with her sister, she must honour those feelings. You couldn't change long-held opinions and emotions overnight.

'And then?' Josefine prompted. 'After you found the drawing?'

'I talked to my aunt.' Josefine's aunt too. 'Mum's sister, Glenda.'

'She knew about me?' Josefine was watching her over the rim of her glass.

'Oh, yes. And she knew your parents' surname – they wrote Mum a letter, just before you all moved back to Italy.' Without that, Josefine would have been much harder to find.

'Ah.' Josefine swirled her wine around in her glass. 'It was the name then? Parodi? I see.'

'Yes, it led me to Liguria and then to the *caffè*.'

'Hmm.' Josefine stretched, looked out of the window and seemed to come to a decision. 'It has been a long day. Time, it is moving on. I need to eat something and go to bed. I have an early start in the morning.' She pulled a face. 'Every morning.'

Lily realised that they'd drunk the whole bottle of wine and that she was not only tipsy but also hungry and exhausted. 'I should get something to eat too.' She smiled – hesitantly at first, but, to her relief, Josefine smiled back.

'You scared me,' Josefine said.

105

'I did?' Lily was confused.

'Bringing the past through the door.' Josefine got to her feet.

'But may I come again?' Lily asked. 'Can we talk some more?' Because there was so much she wanted to say, so many things she'd like to know. How much had her parents told Josefine about her adoption? About their mother? And what kind of life did Josefine have now? She seemed to be running the *caffè* on her own. So what had happened to her adoptive parents? Her husband?

Lily felt the indecision. Josefine wasn't the kind to give much away. She really did remind Lily of their mother – cool on the outside. But what was on the inside? As yet, she had no clue.

'You could come tomorrow around seven,' said Josefine. 'I will cook dinner.'

'I'd love to.' Lily beamed at her. 'Thank you.'

Josefine half frowned. 'But it does not change the way I feel,' she warned.

Lily felt brave enough after the wine to take a risk. 'So, there's nothing you're curious about?' She followed Josefine to the door.

Josefine opened it, leaning on to the door as if she could do with the support.

'Just one thing.' Once again, Josefine fixed her with that steady look.

'Yes?' Lily waited.

Something flickered in Josefine's blue-grey eyes. Some long-ago hurt perhaps? A loss that could never be resolved? 'What was her name?' she asked.

'Marilyn.'

'Marilyn.' She whispered the name, gave a little nod, and slowly she closed the door.

CHAPTER 16

Josefine

2018

The *caffè* was busy the next morning and Josefine barely had
time even to think until almost midday when Angelo came in
for his usual espresso and sandwich. It wasn't lunch. Twelve
noon was far too early for lunch, but Angelo had been up since
five a.m. baking, so things were different for him. At seven
a.m. he delivered the pastries, bread and *focaccia* and for years
that was how it had been. But lately, in the past six months
perhaps – and Josefine didn't want to dwell on those six months
for other reasons – he'd become a friend. They rarely saw one
another outside the *caffè*, but most days he called in and, if it
was quiet, they got chatting as friends do.

'Another coffee, Angelo?' Josefine asked him now as she
bustled past with a tray full of cups and plates.

'*Si*, why not?' He put down his newspaper. 'Do you have
time to join me?'

'Just for a few minutes.' Josefine set the cups and plates down on the counter. She could do with relaxing for a moment or two. She should get help, Angelo often told her, but it was hard enough to manage as it was. Another person's wage — even part-time — would be tricky to find.

She cleared the crockery and made two coffees, serving a few other people in between. Angelo wouldn't mind waiting, she knew.

It was several minutes later when she finally brought the coffees over to his table and sat down opposite him, exhaling loudly as she did so. 'Ouf.'

'Tired?'

She nodded. Angelo was a good man, an understanding man. Life had dealt him a cruel blow, but he remained stoic and cheerful and Josefine admired him for that. 'You?'

'I am okay. Hoping for some good news for a change.' He tapped the newspaper. 'And thinking about what to cook for dinner tonight. You know, a man's work, it is never done.'

'Ha!' He wasn't even joking. Not only was Angelo an expert baker, but since his wife's death from a rare heart condition two years ago, he was also bringing up his daughter Sienna alone.

Josefine was temporarily distracted by the sight of Lily walking by outside.

She looked in and gave a cheery wave. Josefine lifted her arm in response. A weak effort, she decided. She had better summon up more enthusiasm before tonight.

'Oh hoh.' Angelo leant forwards. 'Is that not the mystery young woman from yesterday?'

'Mmm.' The second Josefine had seen her the day before, she'd had a bad feeling. It was something about the way she was looking at Josefine. Immediately, she had felt hunted.

'So, who is she?' Angelo had lowered his voice.

'You do not want to know.' Josefine drank her shot of espresso in one. That was better. Every morning, with each cup of coffee, she felt a little more able to cope.

'Ah, but I do,' said Angelo. 'The mystery — it is most intriguing.'

Josefine sighed. Although why not tell him? It did not have to be a secret. And in this town, everyone knew everything about everyone else anyway. She leant closer. 'You know I am adopted?'

'Of course, yes.' He patted her hand. He was such a kind man. It was rare, certainly in Josefine's limited experience, for a man to have such emotional intelligence.

'*Allora*. Well, it turns out that she . . .' — Josefine nodded towards the piazza where Lily had just passed by; she lowered her voice as she leant in closer — 'is my half-sister.'

Angelo whistled loudly and several people turned round to stare.

'Shh.' She glared at him. It did not have to be a secret but there was no reason to tell the whole of Perlarosa this very minute. 'Keep your whistling down, will you, please?'

'But she is much younger than you, Josi,' Angelo pointed out.

'I am aware of that,' she snapped. Lily had not mentioned her age but Josefine put her at mid-thirties. Not far off twenty years younger then. *Allora*, Lily could almost be her daughter . . . But Josefine threw away this thought as soon as it appeared.

Angelo was now fanning himself with the newspaper as if the excitement was all too much. 'And she came here to meet you, this sister of yours?'

'From England. *Si*.'

'Wow!'

109

'Why, "wow"?' Josefine asked crossly. Perhaps she had been mistaken about his emotional intelligence after all.

'Because, well . . .' He spread his hands. 'Sorry, Josi, but that is quite something.'

'Hmm.' Though she supposed it was. Which was why she had drunk a bottle of Vermentino with Lily last night. And why she had invited her to eat with her tonight. *Mamma mia*. What had she been thinking?

Once again, Angelo leant closer. As always, he smelt of bread, *focaccia* and rosemary. It was very comforting.

'And how do you feel about that?' he asked.

'About what?' Though she knew.

'About her turning up like that. Just walking into your *caffè*?' Angelo seemed more enthusiastic about it than Josefine, that was for sure.

She shrugged. 'What is it to me?'

'Josi . . .'

'What?'

'Come on now.' His dark eyes were twinkling. She could tell he was enjoying this. 'You cannot fool me.'

'And I cannot understand why she has come all the way here.' Josefine was truly baffled. Had Lily been propelled into coming by her mother's death? Or by finding that drawing she had shown Josefine? Hearing about the death of her birth mother had hit her, she had to admit. One moment, Josefine's birth mother had been tucked away in the recesses of her mind, because that was where Josefine had put her, rarely allowing her to emerge into the light of Josefine's day . . . The next moment she was out there, real as anything. And then the next moment she was dead – without Josefine even having the chance to see her, know her, blame her. Josefine had absorbed the shock, but

110

it had been a shock nevertheless. And the drawing . . . *Allora*, she would not think of that now.

Angelo was watching her closely. 'Because you are family?' His voice was serious now.

'Pff.' Josefine brushed this thought away with a swipe of the tea towel she had slung over her shoulder. Family were the people you had grown up with, was that not so? Or so one would think . . . *Basta*. Enough, she told herself.

She got to her feet. 'And now, I must be getting on.' She tucked a strand of hair back into place in the knot at the nape of her neck and glanced back at Angelo. 'But how is Sienna today?' It was important, she felt, to change the subject at this point.

'Sienna, she is fine, yes. Enjoying school, the usual, you know.' Angelo sipped his coffee, looked speculatively across at her. 'But back to this sister of yours – she arrived completely out of the blue, you say?' He seemed determined not to let the subject drop.

'She emailed,' Josefine admitted. 'But I did not answer.'

'Josi!' He clicked his tongue. 'So rude of you.'

'I was too busy,' she retorted. 'You know how it is. There is always so much to do.'

The email had been the first shock. After all these years . . . Josefine had been under the impression that if an adopted person did not want to be found, then they certainly could avoid it.

Her parents had told her many years ago that she was adopted. She also knew that if she wanted to, she could try to get in touch with her birth mother – that was her right. But why would she want to? What was she (*Marilyn*, she thought to herself) to do with Josefine? Nothing. She had chosen to

111

give Josefine away and in so doing had relinquished all rights to . . . well, to love, she supposed. And where there was no love, what was there to connect them? DNA? That certainly hadn't been enough for Josefine.

And so, when she received the email, and after all this time, *allora*, it had been simpler to ignore it, because then it would go away.

Only it hadn't. And now, of course, she knew that her birth mother – the woman she'd always told herself she never wanted to meet – was dead.

'I know. I know.' Angelo was patting her hand. 'I understand. It was difficult for you. You were busy.'

'I never thought . . .' Why would a woman who had enjoyed the childhood that should also have been Josefine's, the privileges that should have been Josefine's, bother to come all this way to see her? She did not even know her. And they were not sisters, not really. Half-sisters, that was all they were – and hardly even that since they had never met and because of the obvious age difference between them. 'Why has she come?'

'Because she wanted to find you, of course,' he said. 'It is a special thing to find a sister you never knew you had, *no*? Do you not agree, Josi?'

Angelo really had no idea. 'It is nothing to me,' she said. Had she not managed perfectly well all her life without? But *a sister*, he had said.

'Pah!' He clearly wasn't convinced. 'Who are you trying to fool? Her? Yourself?'

Josefine remained silent. He wasn't expecting an answer to that, surely?

Angelo leant back in his chair, surveying her in a manner that made her feel uncomfortable. She sometimes sensed that

112

he knew her rather too well – which was her own fault, since she had let him in.

'You are suspicious,' he said. 'You want to be left alone. So, what? You will not talk to her? You will remain stubborn. Is that it?'

'I have talked to her already,' she shot back.

'Oh, you have?' He was smiling again now, damn him.

'She came by when I was about to close yesterday.' Josefine decided not to tell him about the Vermentino. It would only give him more ammunition. Angelo was her friend, but that didn't mean it was any of his business.

'And what did you find out?' he asked. 'It must have been interesting at least? Or . . . ?' He cast a shrewd glance her way. 'Did she upset you, Josi, is that it?'

She shook her head. 'No, nothing like that.'

'Then?'

'I found out almost nothing,' she admitted. Apart from the fact that her birth mother had died. Apart from the fact that she would never know her, never find out why. 'And I do not need to know anything,' she said. 'It is the past. It is gone. I have had the life I have had. There is no use in brooding over things that could have been different.' Josefine herself would have been different. And she certainly would not have been standing here talking to Angelo in the Caffè Parodi.

Angelo nodded. He seemed to understand. 'But you know, Josi, would it not be good to find out more?'

'Good?' It felt dangerous to Josefine. It was easier not to know, not to feel. Look at what happened when she had allowed herself to feel. Her adoptive parents, Gianni and her birth mother too, of course – they had all left her.

'It might help, you know,' Angelo said gently as if he knew all this.

'How could it?' she asked, of herself as much as him.

He shrugged. 'I do not know. Help you understand? Help you forgive?'

Abruptly, Josefine turned away. She smoothed down her blue and white apron. 'I must get on.' And she meant it this time. He had gone too far. She should not have told him any of it.

Angelo was still watching her. She had always thought him an interesting rather than a good-looking man. His face was craggy like the rocks on the Ligurian coast, but it was also a trustworthy face. 'Did you like her?' he asked. 'Your sister, I mean? Did you feel a connection?'

Josefine began clearing the table. Really, he would not let this drop. He might be trustworthy but right now he was beginning to get on her nerves. 'What does that have to do with anything?'

And Angelo, damn him, was smiling again.

But yes, she thought, she had liked her, she had felt drawn to her, almost against her will. And Lily had come a long way to find her, it was true. It seemed churlish to send her away with nothing. Josefine moved away from the table. 'She is coming over later,' she said over her shoulder. 'For dinner.'

'Ah, and she is nothing to you, hmm?' He made a big point of unfolding the newspaper and burying his head in it. 'Good. I am glad.'

Josefine sighed. She was half dreading it. She would make her asparagus risotto, she decided. It was the right time of year. 'Risotto,' she called back to Angelo.

'Huh?'

114

'For your dinner tonight.'

'Ah, risotto,' he said. 'Yes, why not? Good idea. Thank you, Josi.'

'*Prego*,' she said.

CHAPTER 17

Lily

2018

As she walked under the ilex trees and through the piazza, past the Caffè Parodi, Lily spotted Josefine and waved. It gave her a bit of a glow just seeing her. She was sitting at a table with that smiley and interesting-looking man Lily had spotted the day before, and although she didn't look exactly overjoyed to see Lily again so soon, at least she gave a gesture of acknowledgement.

She wouldn't go in there now, though, Lily decided. She didn't want to get too intense. And, heigh-ho, she would be seeing her tonight. Tonight would be a chance for Lily to get to know her older sister better – if Josefine would let her.

Turning into the little street that led to the church, she passed the greengrocer's, where some people were clustering, buying fruit and vegetables that gleamed seductively in the sunshine. Lily paused to admire what was on show – fruit and veg in the Mediterranean were always deeper in colour, always bigger and definitely more inviting. She raised her head and was conscious of the warmth on her face. It must be all this gorgeous Mediterranean sunshine, she supposed.

Lily moved on. She felt for Josefine. Lily had turned up here with a bombshell – no wonder her sister was in shock. Maybe in time she would be ready to know more, but until then, Lily would tread carefully when it came to the past.

She wandered down the narrow alleyway, absorbing the scents of old stone, brewing coffee and rosemary *focaccia* emanating from the houses of rust, faded yellow and pink. And she came once again to the dusky sixteenth-century church of St Giorgio where she had encountered the sad-looking man in the boilersuit the day before.

On the belvedere, just beyond the church and the Soto-ria gallery with the mosaic stone floor, which she'd explored yesterday, she paused for a few minutes, looking down at the sea. It was wilder today, responding to the fresh spring breeze, crashing joyfully onto the rocks below. Lily allowed her gaze to drift . . . She admired a pale-pink house festooned with pots and flowers which stood beside the tiny slipway of a harbour. Little wooden fishing boats of blue and white and yellow and red had been dragged up and out of the tide, and left to lie in the sun. They wouldn't be welcoming any millionaires' yachts or motor cruisers in this harbour – there simply wasn't room. Lily paused as she surveyed the scene. It was only her second day, but already she felt that she was getting to know Perlarosa.

She took the street that led down to the harbour and a small piazza. This street too was lined with boats, some smartly painted, others somewhat the worse for wear. One advantage of having streets too steep and narrow for cars was that there were plenty of parking spaces for the little wooden boats. She smiled. They were delightful; this village was about as far away from the streets of Hackney as it was possible to get, and she was enjoying the experience of being here even more than she'd expected.

On her right, as Lily walked down the street, she noticed a small grey stone building, tucked in front of the bigger houses of dark pink and yellow positioned behind. It looked different from its neighbours; it seemed to be some kind of a shop. She went over to investigate. It was more of a workshop, from what she could see, but sure enough, a few pieces of jewellery were displayed in the dusty window.

She peered in. She could see a tiny, delicately scalloped silver trinket box, an engraved, coral silver bracelet and beside this, a silver ring in the shape of a bird – a falcon maybe. A jeweller then? A silversmith? It was quite an unusual sight for a small place like this, but on the other hand, Perlarosa was just the sort of village she could imagine would attract creative people, with so much history, colour and beauty all around.

Lily had a thought. She had shown Josefine the drawing Marilyn had done of her as a baby (though Josefine had not seemed to want to keep it; at least not yet). But she had entirely forgotten to mention the other thing she'd found – the gemstone. Lily hadn't been able to identify it, but . . . She glanced at the coral bracelet. Maybe the silversmith could?

She took the little pouch out of her bag, loosened the drawstrings, tipped the bag and let the gemstone rest in her palm. The ancient amber pyramid glowed and seemed to blink in the sun like a flame, a little piece of fire. Lily closed her hand gently around it. She could ask, at least. Before she could change her mind, she gave a little tap on the workshop door, because it seemed rude not to, and walked in.

The workshop was small but she saw at once that it was full of equipment and machinery. The silversmith himself was sitting on a high stool at a workbench shaped a bit like a horseshoe with some sort of leather hammock draped under it – to collect the silver filings perhaps. He wore protective goggles and clothing and his dark head was bent; he was entirely focused on whatever he was working on. Further along the workbench was a black metal vice and wooden boxes and terracotta jars crammed with tools. Lily had no idea what they all were, but she could identify a rack of saws, a jarful of files, hammers and other wooden-handled tools, and different-sized pliers hanging on a rack above. In one corner was some sort of blowtorch with an oxygen tank that reminded her of the science laboratory at school and in another was a sink next to a simple hob on which sat a large crockpot and a coffee maker. A bucket of sand and a fire blanket were positioned nearby.

Lily hesitated to interrupt him. But it did seem to be a shop, and she was a potential customer, so . . . '*Buongiorno*,' she said softly.

He looked up, abruptly, as if he hadn't even heard her come in. He put down the little hammer he had been using and pulled off his protective goggles.

'Oh.' It was the raven-haired man she'd seen in the church the day before, the man who had seemed so grief-stricken. He was wearing the same boilersuit and Lily realised why it had seemed to glitter.

He looked taken aback. He must recognise her too. Should she apologise for disturbing him yesterday? A few awkward seconds of silence elapsed.

'*Buongiorno*,' he said finally in a gruff voice. He got to his feet, uncurling from the stool as if he had been crouched there for hours. '*Si?*'

Lily took an uncertain step forward although there wasn't really anywhere to go. The floor was made up of plain flagstones, the small-paned shop window let in the majority of the light, although he was using the beam from an angle-poise lamp for his work, and there was no actual furniture in the small workroom apart from the stool he was sitting on and one other. She glanced at the espresso maker on the hob. Where did the silversmith go to drink his coffee and relax? 'Do you speak English?' she asked tentatively.

He nodded, gave a little shrug.

That was a relief. 'I'm sorry to disturb you.' She pointed at the piece he'd been working on when she came in. She couldn't see what it was, just that it was silver and that he had been hammering it.

Another shrug. Clearly not the most talkative then. Or was he annoyed at being interrupted? She supposed that silversmithing required close concentration, but also, the silver would have to be melted, wouldn't it? Hence the blowtorch, she supposed. And if he was hammering silver, then maybe it would get too hard if he was interrupted? Even so . . . Lily repressed a sigh. Was it her imagination, or did everyone here in Perlarosa seem a little, well, difficult?

'I wondered . . .' – she unclasped her palm so that he could see the gemstone – 'if you happen to know what this is?'

He glanced at it warily. He seemed suspicious, though of what, Lily had no idea. But at least he didn't appear to be as consumed with sadness as he had been when she saw him in the church yesterday. She placed the gemstone on the work counter within reach.

He picked the amber pyramid up with a pair of tweezers and placed it on a piece of white cloth. Then, rather to her surprise, he tenderly ran his fingertip along the striations, plucked an old-fashioned eye-glass from a tray of tools in front of him and leant forwards to examine it.

Lily took a step closer. She felt protective of the stone, weirdly, although the silversmith seemed to know what he was doing. She waited, watching him.

He had a typical Italian profile. High cheekbones, an aquiline nose, sensitive mouth . . . He wasn't unattractive, she decided, even dressed as he was. Though he was rather serious, intense and, yes, she had to say, unfriendly. Maybe they didn't much like tourists in Perlarosa? Not that she was exactly a tourist since she'd come here to find her sister, but he wouldn't know that, of course. And she understood. West Dorset had been a lovely place to grow up in, but although tourism was an important part of many people's livelihoods, she knew only too well that most locals breathed a sigh of relief when the visitors went home and they had their landscape back to themselves again.

'Anatase,' he announced at last. 'A good specimen. Large with interesting markings.'

'Right.' She pulled her phone from her bag and made a note of how she thought it might be spelt. 'And can you tell me where it could be from?'

'I am not a geologist.' He pushed the piece of fabric back to her along the counter. His words were brusque, but Lily thought she could detect at least a spark of warmth in his dark eyes.

'Sorry.'

'For that, you must consult Google.' He looked pointedly at her phone, which she was still holding.

121

'Yes, of course.' Would he ask her how the stone had come into her possession? Probably not – why should he be interested?

He sat back on the stool, turned his attention once again to the piece he was working on, clearly expecting her to leave the premises. He picked up his protective goggles. In a few seconds she would lose him again.

'What if . . .' she began. She'd had an idea.

He paused, turned to her, raised an enquiring eyebrow.

'What if I wanted to make it into a piece of jewellery?'

He put his head to one side. 'You?' he asked. 'Or me?'

Was he trying to be funny? If so, it was dry, because he still hadn't cracked a smile. 'You,' she said. 'A pendant, for example?'

Supposing she did that for Josefine, wouldn't that be a nice idea? It would be a unique piece of jewellery. The gemstone was striking and unusual and she could imagine it with a silver setting and chain. It must mean something too. It was presumably part of Josefine's history, and it would also show her sister that *she* meant something, that Lily cared. 'Would it be possible?'

He sighed – didn't he want the work then, was that it? – but picked the gemstone up again anyway, this time feeling its weight in the palm of his hand, maybe taking another look at its shape, its colour. 'Most things, they are possible,' he said.

'So, could you do it?' The philosophising silversmith, she thought to herself. Who knew?

'*Si*.' He frowned. 'I could make a setting for the stone. Design a claw to hold it.' He pulled out a glass drawer from a chest under the far side of the counter. 'And the chain? Which kind you want?'

Lily took a step closer. Various silver chains were laid out on a navy-blue velvet cushion, each one attached to a roll. She supposed that it made no sense for a silversmith to make his own chains – such a delicate and fiddly job would take for ever. Carefully, she looked through them, taking her time, aware of the silversmith close beside her, of his breath which she was sure she could feel at the back of her neck.

She selected a chain that was not too delicate (Josefine did not strike her as a very delicate person) but also not too heavy. 'This one?' she asked.

'Three-millimetre rope chain,' he replied.

'How much would it cost?' she asked.

He shrugged. Which by now was hardly a surprise. But if he didn't know, who did?

'Approximately,' she persevered.

He named a figure. 'Approximately,' he added.

It was extravagant, but within her budget. And worth it, she felt. 'Okay,' she said.

He frowned. 'It is for you?'

'No.' Lily considered telling him it was for Josefine from the Caffè Parodi but it was probably best to keep that quiet for the moment, especially if she wanted it to be a surprise. Not that the silversmith seemed much of a gossip – the opposite, in fact – but you never could tell. 'It's for a friend,' she said.

'Ah.' His brow cleared. 'Not for you – then, okay.'

It was Lily's turn to frown. Why wouldn't she be entitled to have a pendant made for herself if she wanted to? 'Why is that?' she asked him.

He eyed her speculatively. Lily felt her cheeks burn under the scrutiny.

'This one, it is wrong for you,' he said at last. He picked up a different chain, much smaller. 'A cable chain,' he said. 'Oval. Two-point-three millimetre. Still strong but more delicate. More this, for you,' he said.

Lily knew that she was still blushing, damn it. 'How long will it take to make?' she asked, to cover her confusion.

Once again, he shrugged.

Lily was feeling a little irritated by now. She was a paying customer. Couldn't he be a bit more helpful? 'I'm only here for a week,' she said.

He looked up at her again, held her gaze. 'I could do it in a week,' he said.

Almost as if he was saying something quite different, Lily thought. He was infuriating, but attractive too. She shook this from her head. 'But will you?' She felt she was beginning to get the hang of this conversation.

He considered. 'Yes,' he said at last. 'I will.'

'Thank you.' She waited for him to give her some sort of receipt or at least take her name and phone number, but clearly this wasn't how he operated. Instead, he dismissed her with another nod, picked up his goggles and his tools and continued with his work, Josefine's gemstone lying unattended on the counter.

Could she just leave it with him? It was precious after all, and she was only the messenger, not the rightful owner. Lily hesitated. But she supposed it would be all right. Despite his brusque manner, there was something about the silversmith that seemed trustworthy.

'Thank you,' she said again and opened the door.

Outside, the spring sunshine immediately warmed her after

the coolness of the workshop. But still, she looked back at the little grey building, thought of the silversmith and their first meeting in the church and wondered for a moment just what it was that had made that man so sad.

CHAPTER 18

Josefine

2018

Josefine let Lily in at the *caffè* door and led the way upstairs into the apartment she had shared first with her parents and her brother, and then Gianni. Now, though, she lived here alone. It was nothing grand – the wooden furniture was old and scratched and the armchairs were a bit lumpy these days – but it was clean and it was home. Besides, she spent little enough time up here, what with the *caffè* and all. But how would her visitor see it? Josefine couldn't imagine how different it might be to what Lily was used to.

Lily had brought a bottle of wine – another Vermentino she noted, rather more expensive than the first – and chocolates and flowers.

'Sorry it's a bit over the top,' she said. 'I couldn't decide what to bring.'

Josefine kept a straight face. 'So, you brought it all.' They both laughed and this released some of the tension Josefine was feeling. She wasn't concerned about the risotto; it was the prospective conversation that worried her more.

Lily went over to the window to admire the view and Josefine took the opportunity to observe her – this younger sister who had appeared from nowhere after all these years. Lily was wearing jeans, trainers and a close-fitting shirt. She was smaller than Josefine, slight of build and mid-height with fair, wispy hair and rather extraordinary dark brown eyes. Josefine found herself wondering which bits came from their mother and stopped herself before she could go further.

'It's beautiful.' Lily turned to face her. 'Perlarosa, I mean. What an amazing place to live.'

Josefine shrugged. 'It is Perlarosa.' Because when you'd never known anywhere else . . . She had been told that her first few years had been spent in the UK, but that time was so far away that it felt barely real. 'And you?' she asked. 'Where do you live?' This seemed polite; it felt like safe ground.

Lily smiled as if she recognised this. 'I was living in London,' she said.

'Was?'

'I moved back to Dorset when Mum was poorly . . .' Her voice tailed off as if she wasn't sure how much to say.

Josefine didn't want to dwell on their mother's ill health, didn't intend to dwell on the fact that she would never meet her now. She hadn't expected to, but neither had she contemplated the alternative.

'Dorset,' she echoed. She savoured the sound of the word. It should mean something to her, she supposed. It sounded familiar – although how could it be? That was not where she and her parents had lived after her adoption. They had been in Hampshire, in the New Forest, although Josefine did not remember it. There were photos, though, of toddler Josefine tottering over moorland clothed in heather, of tiny Josefine standing beside a very tall pine tree with red bark, of New Forest ponies wandering freely across heathland and narrow country lanes. Apparently, they came close enough to be stroked, and sometimes, if she looked very hard at one of those photographs, Josefine could almost smell the dryness of that heathland, almost feel the soft, matted mane of that New Forest pony.

'Hive Beach.' Lily rummaged in her bag and produced her phone. She scrolled through some photos, passed the phone to Josefine.

'Strange name,' Josefine commented. Although come to think of it, the place had the look of a beehive with its golden serrated cliffs. A blue-green tide was rolling in, foaming over a ginger shingle beach. 'But it looks like a pretty place.'

'Oh, it is.' Lily put her phone away and Josefine busied herself fetching glasses and opening the wine. She poured out two generous measures.

Lily lifted her glass and seemed to hesitate. 'To our meeting,' she said at last.

What else could Josefine say? 'To our meeting,' she replied. She met Lily's gaze and allowed herself to smile. Because Angelo was right. She was her sister and she had come a long way. Soon, Lily would be back in England and this was not so awful after all.

They chatted for a while – Lily seemed as keen as Josefine to keep things light – and then Josefine went into the kitchen to check the risotto, which was quietly bubbling in the pan and done already. 'Sit down,' she called. She fetched the bowls and dished out. 'It is only risotto,' she told Lily, although actually she was proud of her asparagus risotto; it was her favourite signature dish.

'It looks delicious.'

Josefine laughed. 'Wait till you taste it.' They were dancing around one another, she realised. How long before Lily told her another thing she'd rather not hear?

Lily scooped up a forkful. 'Mmm, it's very good.' She took a sip of her wine. 'I hope you don't mind . . .' she began.

Uh-oh. Josefine took a large slug of the Vermentino, which was also very good. Here they were already.

'But I noticed your wedding ring . . .'

'Ah.' Josefine looked down at it. It was so familiar. And yet – what was it doing on her finger after all that had happened?

'And I wondered, are you married?'

'No,' she said. 'That is, we separated some months ago.' *Certo*, she could say more, but she did not want this woman to become a confidante, sister or no.

'Oh, I'm sorry.' Lily took another forkful. 'I didn't mean to pry.'

Josefine shrugged. 'As for me, I am not sorry,' she said, though she still wasn't sure how true this was. When you had been with someone for as long as she had been with Gianni . . . When you had been through what they had been through, it seemed almost inevitable that they would part rather than have to live through it any longer. And yet . . . how could you bear to live without the familiarity of their presence?

'Right.' Lily took another deep breath. 'Do you have any children?' she asked.

Josefine let several seconds pass before she answered this question. It was a black hole and she didn't want to fall in. 'No,' she said at last. 'It did not happen for us.' And there it was, encapsulated in a single sentence, everything that had gone wrong for them – the root of it all.

Lily nodded, clearly not sure whether she should be commiserating with her or not. *Please don't*, Josefine thought. She didn't think she could bear it. She drank more wine. It was an easier option.

'And your parents?' Lily was clearly struggling now.

Josefine should help her, she knew, but the ground, it was so rocky, that she hesitated to even begin. 'They left Italy,' she said.

'Oh, I see.'

But she didn't, of course she didn't. How could she?

'Um, where did they go then? Not back to the UK?' Lily was toying with her glass of wine, not drinking as fast as she had the other night, Josefine noticed. Whereas Josefine, she would have to fetch another bottle from the fridge very soon.

'To Australia,' she told her.

'Australia?' Lily's brown eyes widened.

Yes, that is a long way away, Josefine thought. And yes, it had been a surprise. 'My brother lives there,' she said, hopefully with no bitterness on show. 'At least I should say, of course, my adoptive brother.'

What was an adoptive brother anyway? Less than a half-brother but also more, because she had grown up with him after all. But much, much less than a blood brother. She and Dario had never been close.

'He has a family of his own now,' she told Lily, as if that explained everything. Which it sort of did. Josefine's children – if she'd had them – would never have had such a strong bloodline.

Lily made a little 'o' sign with her mouth. Was Josefine not telling her what she wanted to hear? *Allora*. Well, perhaps she shouldn't have come.

'Your parents went on to have a child of their own then?' Lily froze, her wine glass halfway to her lips. 'Sorry, that was insensitive. I mean—'

'Yes, they did.' Josefine interrupted her. It had been, they told her, the most wonderful gift, the greatest surprise, by far the best thing that had ever happened to them in their entire lives. *Where does that leave me?* she had wondered.

She had worked hard at school, tried her best to please them. And she did please them; they loved her – of course they loved her. They even told her that they were glad to have a daughter. But Dario . . . Whatever he did, he radiated a brighter sunshine. So when he met an Australian girl, when he took a year out to go travelling, when he moved to Australia to be with her, to marry her, when they had not one but two perfect children, then of course Josefine's parents would want to go out there too.

'And so, you took over the *caffè*?' Lily had finished her risotto and her first glass of wine.

Josefine topped her up, went to fetch that second bottle, offered her more food.

Lily shook her head. 'Thank you,' she said. 'That was so good.'

'*Prego*. You are welcome.' Josefine nodded. 'And so, I took over the *caffè*,' she agreed. She sat down at the table again.

Perhaps it had been the guilt that made them give it to her? Perhaps they felt they had no choice? In fact, Josefine had worked in the *caffè* ever since she was a girl. Her brother hadn't been much interested; he couldn't wait to move away from Perlarosa. But Josefine . . . Well, she had always loved the feeling

131

of home. And she was grateful that they had at least given her this place, whatever their reasons. It was a living, though a hard living, and it was somewhere to live too. That hadn't been so important when she was with Gianni, but anyway, they had moved here to save money and now . . . It was something at least to call her own.

'It must have been very difficult for you,' Lily said.

How much did she understand? Josefine wondered. But *non importa*. What did it matter? At least her eyes were kind. 'It was not easy,' she agreed. She poured herself more wine. She was drinking too much, but she didn't care. She shrugged. 'It is their life. I have the *caffè*, my friends. It is not so bad.'

'Good.' And to Josefine's surprise, Lily put a hand over hers. It felt warm and she had to admit that it was a comfort. 'And it must be nice to be independent? You can do what you like now – with the *caffè*, I mean.'

That was true, although Josefine hadn't seen it quite like that before. Lily's hand was still on hers. 'And you?' she asked, to hide her confusion. Because the touch of her hand . . . it seemed like more than kindness. It seemed to suggest, well, some sort of solidarity. As if Lily was very much on her side.

'I'm not married.' Lily took her hand back at last to pick up her glass of wine. 'No children either. And . . .' – she pulled a face – 'as of a couple of months ago, no boyfriend.'

'And your father?' Josefine asked carefully. Lily had not mentioned him yet and she did not know the situation.

Lily shook her head and, in that small gesture, Josefine could see how close they had been. 'He died a few years ago.'

'I am sorry.' They were quiet for a few moments.

'What about the boyfriend?' Josefine asked. 'Did you mind about losing him? Are you sad? Was it a mutual decision?' It was funny, she thought. She had girlfriends, but they rarely had these kinds of conversations. Her old schoolfriends had either left Perlarosa, met someone, got married and had kids, or stayed nearby and done the same. Plus, Josefine was always busy. She didn't have much time for friends.

'A bit sad,' Lily admitted. 'But it wasn't working. He wanted more than I wanted to give. So, it was more my decision, I suppose.' She gave a little shrug.

'Hmm.' Josefine finished the last of her risotto.

She got to her feet and took the bowls into the kitchen. It had gone quite well, she thought, considering, and she was surprised at how late it was already. She came back to the window that looked down on the square. It was getting dark and the night-time, the moonlight, always drew her. Josefine didn't have blinds or curtains; when it was warm enough, she liked to have the windows open to catch the evening air.

As if from afar, she heard Lily telling her again how delicious the risotto had been, how good it was to meet her, to talk to her, how grateful she was that Josefine had invited her here tonight.

And down on the street below, she saw her emerge from the darkening shadows – Carlotta Barbieri strutting across the piazza as if she owned it.

'*Merda*,' she muttered.

'What is it?' Lily had got up and was by her side.

'*Dio santo . . .*' Josefine let out another curse. She was shaking with anger. *Brazen*, she thought. How could she be so brazen to come here, to walk around, to display herself like this?

'Josefine?'

Josefine pulled off her wedding ring – with some difficulty; it had been on her finger a long time – and flung it out of the

133

open window into the night. She didn't hear it land. Maybe it had landed in an ilex tree – who cared?

'You are right,' she said, though Lily hadn't spoken. 'Why wear a wedding ring when I am no longer married? What is wrong with me? Do I think he will suddenly come crawling back to me, the *bastardo*? Why should he? And if he did, why would I want him?'

And without considering what she was doing at all, she threw herself into Lily's arms and she wept.

CHAPTER 19

Lily

2018

The following day, Lily was once again standing on the belvedere by the pink church, looking out to sea. It had come to hold an allure for her; she loved the feel of having the heart of the hamlet at her back, as she gazed ahead across the ocean to the islands she'd noticed before, lying out to sea in the mid-distance. She'd looked them up online earlier this morning, wanting to get more of a hold on her immediate surroundings, and discovered that the larger island was Portovenere and the smaller, Palmaria, was its natural park. How enticing . . . And only a boat ride away.

Lily let her thoughts settle. Last night had held its surprises, not least when Josefine had unexpectedly launched herself into Lily's arms. Lily had been astonished, yes, but also hugely gratified. Not that she wanted Josefine to be upset – the opposite was true – but she had felt honoured that she'd been the one Josefine had turned to. Or was that because she'd been the only one there at the time? Lily looked over to her right, towards the harbour, the slipway and the little bar tucked away behind. Perhaps. But she had learnt something of Josefine's life, and she had also felt a deepening of the connection between the two of them. She just hoped it didn't exist only in her imagination.

From here she could see the other church too – the stone church higher up, back near her B & B – and in the distance the wooded mountains. She turned around. St Giorgio loomed behind her, the flushed paint flaking to reveal the grey-stone underbelly beneath, the pink bell tower standing like a determined forefinger against the backdrop of the deep blue sky. As if in response to her scrutiny, the bells began to toll, ancient and loud as thunder, making the very ground she was standing on vibrate. Three bells, she counted. That was an awful lot of sound.

She turned back to the ocean. Last night, she had been determined not to drink too much, to retain control, and apart from a few awkward silences, the evening had been going very well. Until Josefine had flung her wedding ring from the window, that was. Lily smiled to herself. A bit melodramatic of her perhaps. But it had been a powerful gesture, and one that had made Lily more intrigued by Josefine than ever.

There had been a woman in the piazza below – apparently the one who had prompted Josefine's outburst – but Lily had only caught a glimpse of her in the evening shadows as she passed under the ilex trees. Who was she? From Josefine's reaction, it seemed a safe bet that she'd had something to do with the break-up of her sister's marriage. But what had happened and where was Josefine's husband now? Lily shook her head. Despite weeping as if her heart would break, Josefine had refused to say any more about it. Lily must respect that choice – or maybe she would find out for herself, though she had no idea how.

Taking the steps down from the belvedere, Lily decided to head left around the promontory by the side of the grey crumbling stone of St Giorgio. There had been a few more clues regarding Josefine's history, though. She had said they'd had no children. Did that mean she and her husband hadn't wanted them? From her slightly wistful expression and the way she'd said it, Lily suspected that this wasn't the case. And if they had wanted them . . . Or if only Josefine had wanted them . . . Lily stopped in her tracks. Well then, that could certainly be a huge source of unhappiness. And how would it make Josefine feel about her own birth mother, the woman who had given her away?

Lily walked further around the little promenade. To her right, rusty grey railings divided the pathway from the high rocks and the water fizzing below, and to her left, more buildings seemed to be perched precariously on the steep cliff, their balconies literally hanging over the edge. Lily recaptured the train of her thoughts. No wonder then if Josefine felt bitterness, even anger, towards the woman who had rejected what she, Josefine, most longed for.

Pausing by a seat that had been carved into the rock, Lily sat down gingerly. The rock was around her and above her and it made the little seat seem like a bolthole; a retreat from the world. She settled further into the nook. Most of her thinking was supposition, of course. But it seemed clear that not only had Josefine been the victim of a good deal of abandonment in her life, but also that this wasn't the only disappointment she'd suffered.

137

The scent of herbs – wild dill or fennel perhaps, from the clumps of plants growing in the crevices of the rock nearby – drifted in the air, mingling with the ozone rising from the sea below. Lily breathed in deeply. With a cushion, she could stay here for hours . . .

Down on the rocks some distance away, a man was fishing. He was wearing a cap and had his back to Lily, but he seemed to give off an air of tranquillity. She supposed it was a calming activity – until a fish came along and you had to be more proactive. She gave a little shiver. She'd gone fishing with her father just once and hated it – watching the poor fish wriggle on the line, fighting for its life, gasping for breath. No thanks. She was happier just sitting on a rock looking out to sea, without any potential death in the offing.

Her phone rang. She glanced at the screen. It was Auntie Glenda phoning on WhatsApp. She answered. 'Hello, Auntie, how are you?'

'Oh, I'm fine, thanks, love.'

It was good to hear her aunt's rich, warm voice, Lily realised; an echo from home.

'But more to the point, how are *you*, Lily? And have you found her yet?'

Glenda always did cut straight to the chase. 'Yes, I have.' Lily smiled.

She knew how excited Glenda had been about this trip of Lily's, despite her misgivings. Understandably as Josefine was her niece and family was important to Glenda.

'Ooh.' Glenda's voice changed. 'And? What's she like?'

Lily chuckled, thinking of the ring-throwing incident. 'She's interesting,' she said. 'I think she's had quite a difficult life. I like her.'

'What does she look like?' Glenda was obviously keen to know more. 'Does she look anything like your mother?'

Lily noticed the break in her aunt's voice. 'There is something,' she said gently. 'Her eyes . . . they're the exact same shade of blue-grey.'

'Ah.' Lily felt her absorb this information. 'And in character? Or is it too early to say?'

'Well . . .' Lily's mother had certainly been emotional – Lily remembered many tears being shed, usually when a painting hadn't gone well, someone had been too critical of her work or there was a particularly sad item on the news. But she could also be hard – difficult to get through to, seemingly frosty and unfeeling. Lily sensed that in Josefine too. 'A bit,' she said. 'I'll have more idea when I get to know her better.' Because Lily hoped that she would get to know her better. And perhaps that frostiness was just Josefine's armour – to stop her from getting too hurt by the callous world outside. Lily frowned. So perhaps it had been her mother's armour too? Hmm. Lily had never considered this before.

'Does she seem more Italian than British, would you say?' Glenda was asking. 'Dark? Vivacious? Volatile?'

'Potentially all of those, yes,' Lily told her.

'Will you send me a photo?'

Well now . . . 'I hope to,' Lily said, 'at some point. It's just that . . .' They hadn't quite got to that point yet.

'What? What did she say when you turned up? Goodness me. It must have been quite a shock?'

'She's wary of me,' Lily admitted. 'And who can blame her?'

'Hmm.' Glenda seemed to be processing this. Lily knew that her aunt had seen a lot of *Long Lost Family* episodes on TV, and

139

she guessed that not many of these showed adopted children who *didn't* want to be found.

'Give her time, love,' Glenda advised. 'It's a lot to take in.'

'Oh, I will.' Only, would a week be long enough?

Lily was still gazing towards the high rocks where the man was fishing. The view beyond him was intoxicating; the water was green and almost translucent, frothing against the rocks, sparking in the sunshine. She got to her feet, pulled herself out of the hidey-hole and continued down the little promenade path. Tamarisks and cacti were growing out of the fissures in the rocks, along with the herbs and prickly pear. When she looked up, she could see the crumbling facade of what looked like a little chapel high on the cliff above.

'It's just a question of being patient,' Glenda was saying. 'Let her come to you. She must be curious, after all.'

'Mmm.' Lily supposed she was right. Only Josefine had shown very little curiosity so far – the opposite, in fact.

As she drew a bit closer, the fisherman turned around. Lily drew breath and it must have been more like a gasp because Glenda caught it. She was still ridiculously perceptive even when she was out of sight and many, many miles away.

'What is it? Are you all right, love?' she asked.

'Yes. Yes, I am.' The fisherman was, in fact, the silversmith. That was twice now she hadn't recognised him, twice he'd taken her by surprise.

The silversmith saw her. Lily stopped walking. He was wearing faded blue jeans today, with a loose shirt over a T-shirt. And these, admittedly ordinary, clothes made him look very different. He fixed her with that intent look of his that was almost a glare (how she could have ever thought him tranquil was beyond her) and he didn't look away.

140

Lily swallowed. For some reason, she wished she wasn't on her phone – it made her look more like a tourist than ever. He was the sort of man, she guessed, who scorned mobile phones, disliked the power they had over people, the fact that they had become the main way many people organised and controlled their lives. Even Lily thought the same, at least to some degree. She wasn't ruled by hers, though. She could switch her mobile off for whole hours at a time.

She felt a mad urge to climb down over the rocks and go and talk to him. Perhaps she would ask him about the pendant and whether or not he'd started the job? She'd looked up the gemstone last night and once she'd worked out the spelling by process of elimination, she'd discovered that anatase could be blue or amber and that it had been found in several different places, including Liguria, Italy – in the mountains behind Genoa to be exact. Which, weirdly, wasn't all that far from here. Perhaps she could tell him that?

Lily realised that Glenda was still rattling on, talking to herself by now. 'I'm sorry,' she told her aunt. 'I have to go. Talk later, okay?'

She shoved her mobile into her bag. The silversmith was still watching her but he hadn't waved or given any acknowledgement. Instinctively, she took a step forwards.

Then she noticed another figure. Someone else was walking towards the silversmith from the opposite direction along the flat rocks below. It was a woman, and as Lily watched, she heard her shout to him, though she couldn't make out what she was saying.

He heard her, turned round to face her. His body language changed dramatically. He put his hands on his hips. He shouted something back to her and she let out a torrent of rapid Italian in response. The silversmith jumped off the higher rocks, moving towards her on the flatter bit below, and she stopped, folded her arms and waited.

Open-mouthed, Lily watched the scene unfold. Obviously, they were having a row. They were both angry, but while she was letting rip, he was standing back, raising his hands defensively now, almost turning away from the confrontation. And obviously they knew each other well – very well.

As the two of them stood there – her yelling at him, he batting away her words – Lily suddenly realised something else. *My God*, she thought. Surely this was the same woman down in the piazza last night, who had reduced Josefine to tears? And there was something about the way she was standing, squarely, her feet apart, her body centred . . .

Now was clearly not the time to ask him about the pendant. Lily's head was even more full of questions than before, but none of them were about jewellery. Swiftly, not wanting to witness whatever it was that she was witnessing, Lily walked back the way she had come.

Because if this was the same woman who had upset Josefine, maybe even the woman who had broken up Josefine's marriage . . . then who was the silversmith and just what was going on in this village?

CHAPTER 20

Camogli, Italy, 2018

It is spring and he looks out to sea as he sits under the arches, where he sometimes meets his friends early evenings for a chat, perhaps a game of cards, maybe a beer. The undemanding companionship of old friends – that is a pleasant part of life, no? And he enjoys the sound of the pounding waves; he feels the vibration in his very soul.

He leans forwards, resting his arm on the rocky ledge beside him, chin cupped in his hand, taking it all in as if he has never seen it before. The view is of the beach by the pale-stoned church and bell tower of Santa Maria Assunta. Every year, that bell tower loses a bit of its pink paint, flaking away the days, months and seasons, but the clock remains true and the bell always rings on the hour and on the half. That is important. It is a note of regularity and dependence that he cherishes.

There are a few special places where he likes to sit and think, and they are all close to the sea. Hardly surprising really. He grew up hearing about the struggles and triumphs that his male ancestors had experienced on the sea, grew up listening to the tide and swimming in the waves.

Later, it became his living too. Si, si . . . it is his life and he never tires of it because, unlike most things, the ocean changes constantly. With the weather, with the seasons, with the sun and the moon and the stars. With each day that passes.

In the sea, in the shallows, a father and son are playing volleyball. The progression of the game makes him smile. The son is beginning to stretch the boundaries. He hits the ball fast and hard to a spot beyond where his father stands, a spot where his father will receive the splash and be forced to swim in order to retrieve the ball. The father remonstrates, with a laugh at first, then a groan, then by doing exactly the same thing back to the boy. Hah.

It is a macho game, he realises. A battle — almost a test perhaps. Typical of the way sons are with fathers and fathers are with sons. One sets a boundary, the other challenges and moves beyond, the other matches, the other moves further. That is how it must go.

He thinks of his own two sons — grown up now, both married, Stefano with a young boy of his own. Did he play that game with Stefano and Michele? Probably. He chuckles. Perhaps he should ask them what they think about it, eh?

On his left, the promenade runs on, the tall houses of yellow, rust and green, the Bagni — the old Lido, now a pizzeria — the bars, the ristorantes, gelateria. Life, which has come to include tourism. Eugh. He leans back and shakes his head. Even so. The locals complain, but they need them: these people that fill their beaches with their multi-coloured swimsuits, towels and parasols.

For a moment he closes his eyes to block them out and instead, he thinks of his own father, long gone now, a man with a fiery temper matched only by that of his wife Eugenia, his mother. He chuckles at a memory — the sight of his mother, hands on hips, complaining about Papa being late for dinner or coming in with muddy shoes or not being around to discipline his children and leaving everything to her. He can't

144

remember which it was, only that his father said the wrong thing in response and Mama promptly threw his dinner at the wall. He and his sister were dumbfounded. They stared . . . at the pasta sticking to the paintwork, at the splodge of ragu sauce trickling delicately towards the floor. What would happen? What would their mother do next? Who was going to clear up the mess?

Mama looked at Papa and he looked back at her. They both looked at the pasta sauce on the wall. And then they laughed – bent over, clutching each other, great spasms of uncontrollable hilarity – and he let out a sigh of relief.

He sighs now too, as he relives the scene in his mind. In moments, his parents were in each other's arms. It was just the way they were. Certo, *he and his father also played out that game of testing boundaries – for a while at least. And mostly, it seemed nothing like a game.*

As a boy, he was so sure of what to do. Such confidence, he had. How certain he was of what the world held for him and the place he held in it. He was proud. He turned his back on what his family wanted for him and he walked away. But they were right. With a wisdom born of years and experience, they were right. And yet . . .

He opens his eyes once again and looks further out to sea, to the thick navy line of the horizon. He pulls his hands through his hair – lucky you still have some, old man, *his friends say, though of course now it is as white as the feathers of a dove. Why does he feel dissatisfied then? Why does his life feel not quite complete?*

Just because I am an old man, he thinks. An old man in his dotage pestered by an overactive imagination. An imagination that grips him sometimes at night and makes him wake in a cold sweat. Something that always was missing . . . He shakes his head. Fool, *he thinks. Fool for ever thinking something was missing; fool for thinking there*

145

could be more. He grips hold of the ledge once again with calloused hands that once rowed out all weathers, mended nets and washed cold fish in winter. No wonder then. Everyone should be taught that they can never have it all.

CHAPTER 21

Josefine

2018

Josefine was nervous as she walked towards the Marina Bar. How long had it been since she had gone out to any bar?

She'd been talking to Angelo in the *caffè* this morning as usual, skating over various topics as usual, getting up to serve various customers and sitting down again – as usual – when he said something that wasn't usual at all.

'Josefine, I was thinking . . .'

'*Si?*' Angelo so rarely used her full name that she was immediately suspicious.

'That it would be nice to go for a drink sometime, *no?*'

'What?' Her attention moved from a couple about to ask for the bill, to the man sitting opposite her. 'What are you saying?'

He spread his hands. 'Nothing. Just that. A drink. The two of us. What is so strange about that?'

Everything, in Josefine's opinion. Number one, she almost never went out for drinks. Number two, she had never been

147

out socially with Angelo. Number three, he had a young daughter. She could go on.

'What about Sienna?' She chose this question from all the other questions buzzing through her brain, hoping it would cover up the awkwardness that had suddenly made itself felt between her and Angelo.

He shrugged. 'Paola will watch out for her.'

Josefine narrowed her eyes. Okay, so the neighbour would watch out for her. But . . . 'Why?' she asked.

He leant back in his chair, not answering straightaway.

Out of the corner of her eye, Josefine saw the couple gesture to her, asking for the bill. She pretended she hadn't noticed.

'When was the last time you went out for a drink, Josi?'

'I have no idea.'

'Exactly.'

Hmm. 'And your point is?'

'You should get out more, that is all I am saying.' He moved the bottle of balsamic to one side and then back again to its original position. Was he nervous then?

'You think?'

'*Si, si.*' He warmed to his theme. 'You are stuck in this place all day, are you not?' He waved his arms around to encompass the *caffè*. 'It is a dull life, if that is all you do.'

She glared at him. 'Perhaps I should be the judge of that, Angelo.' He was right, *certo*, but it was *her* life.

'It is all work.'

'*Si, si.*' And?

'You need to get out, have more fun.'

'And you are going to give me fun?' She snorted in disbelief.

He laughed and immediately the atmosphere between them was easy again. 'I can try,' he said. 'But maybe we can just talk?'

148

Josefine got to her feet. She couldn't ignore the customer any longer.

'Without you having to rush off every two seconds,' he added.

'It is not a date then?' she asked warily when she got back to his table. 'You are not going to go all crazy on me, Angelo?'

He sighed. 'I promise not to go crazy.'

Allora, then, why not? she thought. Maybe he was right. Maybe she should get out more. Her social life had narrowed down to this morning chat between her and Angelo. She valued it, but it wasn't much, as social lives went. But everything was such a struggle since her parents had left. Josefine was always so tired by the time she'd finished up here and she tended to work a seven-day week, but really, that was no excuse. She certainly wasn't so old and decrepit that she couldn't have a quick shower after work and find some energy from somewhere.

'Where were you thinking of?' she asked him.

He grinned, knowing already he had won. 'Two options,' he said. 'We could just have a quiet drink at the Marina Bar, or, if you want to go further afield, we could go into Lerici, why not?'

What he really meant, of course, was that if she didn't want to see anyone, they could go into Lerici. And by 'anyone' he meant Gianni and Carlotta. There weren't many bars in Perlarosa, so seeing them was a strong possibility.

'It does not matter if I see him,' she said quietly. 'You know it is over between us. It has been over for months.' God knows, he came back often enough at first, trying to talk her round. But Josefine believed a marriage could not recover from that sort of betrayal, and if she were honest, even the betrayal itself was more a signal of all the other things that were wrong. It

149

was just that they had not admitted it – either to themselves or to one another.

'I know.' Angelo patted her arm. He was the one she had confided in. He knew it all – at least everything she had acknowledged to herself. 'And in this town, you cannot hide from him for ever.'

This was true. They both still lived in Perlarosa. It was inevitable then that she would run into both of them from time to time – unless she became a total recluse, that was. She thought ruefully of the way she'd thrown her wedding ring out of the window. Perhaps she shouldn't have been so impulsive? It might not have any sentimental value – she wouldn't allow it to have was the truth – but it could be worth something. The gesture – it had been symbolic, she supposed. And besides that, it had felt good.

'Okay then,' Josefine said.

'*Va bene.*' Angelo drained his espresso. 'I will meet you at the Marina Bar at seven then, *si?*'

'*Sì.*' She held up her forefinger. 'But only one drink, Angelo. Remember we both have to get up early in the morning, yes?'

He held up his hands in surrender. 'How could I forget? But, okay, if you insist. One drink – or maybe two.'

Before Josefine could respond, he glanced away, smiling at someone who had just come into the *caffè*. Who was he so happy to see? Josefine turned. It was Lily.

She gave a little half-wave and came over hesitantly, unsure of her welcome, Josefine supposed.

'Lily, *ciao.*' Josefine was feeling expansive now. It must be the prospect of the rising star of her new social life . . .

She got up to kiss her on the cheek – she was her sister after all – and last night it had been comforting to cry in her arms, even though Josefine had been unwilling to tell Lily the whole story. She was a little embarrassed, though. *Allora* . . . Too much wine, and then the sight of that woman in the piazza . . . It had been too much. It brought it all back – the shame, the humiliation.

Both Angelo and Lily looked surprised at the affectionate gesture. Angelo recovered first. 'Please, join us.' He gestured to the unoccupied chair to one side of him.

'Oh, well, I was just on my way to—' But Lily broke off. 'Okay, thanks.' And sat.

'Coffee?' Josefine was already moving away to get it.

'Thanks.'

When Josefine returned, the two of them were deep in conversation and it was almost half an hour before she had the chance to return again to the table. What on earth could they be talking about for so long? She hoped Angelo wasn't being indiscreet.

'I thought you were leaving,' she said to him.

He gave a little shrug. 'Yes, I must be on my way.' But still, he made no move to go. He gave Lily what seemed to be an encouraging smile.

'Josefine, I was wondering if you were likely to be taking any time off in the next few days?' Lily asked her.

Josefine sat down. It was good to get the weight off her feet for a moment or two. 'I do not think so, no,' she said. Had Angelo put her up to this? 'I am quieter in the winter, but as you can see, right now there are people and when there are people . . .' – she shrugged – 'I must open the *caffè*.'

'It is a shame, though,' Angelo put in, 'when Lily is here for such a short time.'

Josefine raised an eyebrow and gave him one of her looks.

'I was hoping we could spend some time together,' Lily went on.

'Yes, but—'

'Or maybe we could get dinner somewhere? My treat.'

'An excellent idea.' Angelo nodded his approval.

Asked out twice in less than an hour . . . Josefine felt quite taken aback. '*Va bene*,' she said. 'That would be . . .' She hesitated. What would it be? Risky? After all, Lily would want to talk family. 'Very nice,' she said. She liked her. Lily had gone to a lot of trouble to find her and none of what had happened in the past was Lily's fault. So far, Lily had respected Josefine's wishes not to be bombarded with information about her birth mother and there was no reason for that to change.

'Brilliant.' Lily beamed.

'But not tonight.' Angelo wagged his finger. 'Josefine is spoken for tonight.'

Lily laughed. 'Tomorrow night then?'

Josefine got to her feet to serve another customer. 'Tomorrow,' she agreed. It was little enough. She owed Lily that much. And it would be very pleasant not to have to cook for a change.

Angelo finally left the *caffè*, returning to the bakery, she supposed; Lily too went on her way, and Josefine spent the rest of the day worrying about what would happen tonight if she ran into her ex-husband.

Now, Josefine walked through the little piazza towards the bar. This piazza backed by green-shuttered houses wasn't only home to the bar and the harbour; it was also where all the important meetings and fairs of Perlarosa were held. Her own *caffè* was near the entrance to the village but Piazza della

152

Marina with its stone-arched washhouses and slipway, brightly coloured fishing boats and cream parasols was the heart.

Some people were sitting outside on the terrace, but it was chilly and most had gone inside. She walked into the bar. It was buzzing and Josefine was immediately glad she had come. She'd forgotten – the excitement of anticipation, the getting ready, the spray of perfume, a bold lipstick, the wondering if anything unexpected might happen.

Music was playing – an old pop song that made her want to kick off her shoes and dance. Ah, but it had been a long time. The bar was full. People were chatting and laughing and, yes, having fun. She looked around for Angelo. Hopefully he wouldn't be late.

But the first person she saw sitting on a bar stool, a bottle of red wine in front of him and a glass in his hand, was Gianni. For a moment she wanted to walk straight out again. But, no. She straightened her back. He had to be faced. And so, instead, she walked right up to him.

'*Buona sera*, Gianni,' she said.

CHAPTER 22

Josefine

2018

Gianni almost fell off the bar stool. '*Ciao*, Fina,' he said, recovering fast. 'Drink?'

Josefine was aware that the surprise had given her the upper hand. 'I am meeting someone,' she said primly. Bracing herself, she looked around. 'Are you here with—'

'No.'

No, of course he wasn't, otherwise he wouldn't have offered her a drink. Was he still with her, though? Josefine guessed so. 'How are you?' she asked. He looked older, thinner even, and this gave her some small satisfaction. But how strange it was, she thought, that they could meet and be so polite, like almost-strangers.

'Oh, well . . .' He looked away, then back to her, then away again, opening his mouth like a fish. In fact, Gianni seemed much more uncomfortable than she, and it hadn't been a difficult question.

'Is something wrong?' He had looked like this before – that same expression in his eyes. He wasn't what you would call a good-looking man but his face was open and pleasant – which meant that when you knew him as well as Josefine knew him, you realised immediately when something was up, when he had done something he felt guilty about. Which was how she had found out, of course.

'Where have you been?' she had asked him back then when she saw it, when she almost knew for sure. And then, as his dark eyes clouded. 'Gianni?'

'I did not mean for it to happen,' he had blurted. 'I did not mean to get into it. I was an idiot. I had too much to drink. She kept laughing. She kept flirting. She was always there.'

It had poured out of him like lava from a volcano – an eruption of excuses – and Josefine knew that in some ways he was relieved to offload it: the guilt, the knowledge, the secrecy. Gianni wasn't a natural liar; he never had been. Josefine had always been able to read him. She almost found herself feeling sorry for him.

'Who kept laughing?' Josefine asked. 'Who was always there?' Her voice was steady.

'But at least she was not always on at me.' He rallied. Gianni had never been a pushover. 'At least everything was not always wrong.'

'Who, Gianni?'

'She made me feel like a man again.' A shrug.

Josefine felt bad then. She thought of how she used to love him. He was strong, capable. He looked after her. It didn't matter that he could not see into her soul – how often can a man see into a woman's soul? And would it be a good thing anyway? Because then perhaps women would lose one of their natural advantages . . . What mattered was that he loved her.

155

He had pursued her relentlessly when they were young, and for Josefine, not used to being the favoured one, this had been seductive. He was an easy choice; this man who she could lean on, who she could easily understand, whose love was so openly declared. Her parents, too, seemed happy about the match. Gianni lived in the village so Josefine would stay there too. She would run the *caffè*, he would see to the maintenance, everyone would be happy.

Josefine was already in her thirties when they decided that the time was right to try for a baby. They weren't concerned at first when nothing happened. She was still young enough, there was time. And besides, there was the *caffè*, always the *caffè* to occupy her, even while her parents were still here. But as time went on and Josefine got older . . .

She and Gianni sought advice; they waited, they hoped. They had tests, but it seemed there was no reason for her not to conceive. They made love when they were supposed to make love and in the best possible position. But their relationship – it became regimented. As the years slipped by, life was all about wanting a child and little else. Josefine grew desperate. And so, when that child did not come along, life then was different. Life was a disappointment. Gianni was a disappointment. She and Gianni both passed fifty. And love . . . Somehow, Josefine realised, love had drifted away.

What an irony, Josefine thought, that her birth mother had fallen pregnant so easily with a baby she did not even want. Josefine's adoptive parents had gone through a similar experience of childlessness, of course. But they had reached out, they had adopted Josefine and then been able to have one of their own. They had survived. Not so Gianni and Josefine. She would never have considered adoption; and besides, by the time they stopped trying, it was much too late.

'Who is it, Gianni?' Josefine had asked again. He had been going to the Marina Bar more and more often, to meet with his friends, drink beer, play cards. He had been coming home later and later and, if Josefine was honest, it had been a relief. She had felt more comfortable alone, with no one else around to make demands or say the wrong thing.

But stupidly, she had never thought . . .

'Carlotta,' he said.

'Carlotta?' She didn't even know a Carlotta.

'Carlotta Barbieri. She is Nico's sister-in-law.'

'Nico,' she said. One of Gianni's closest friends. She knew now who Carlotta was, because she had seen Nico talking to a woman she didn't know in the piazza one day. 'So, you are having an affair with this Carlotta then, is that it?' It was so cheap, so tawdry. And the woman must be a decade younger than Gianni. Josefine felt that she couldn't bear it.

He hung his head. 'It is not an affair. It is nothing. I never meant . . .' and off he went again.

'*Allora*, then you should pack your things and go to her.' Josefine turned around. She felt furious, ashamed, humiliated. She didn't know what else, but she was sure there was more. One thing she did know: she didn't want to listen to Gianni's excuses any longer. He was her husband. He had betrayed her. That was all she needed to know.

Of course, that hadn't been the end of it. Gianni had pleaded, she had been firm. He left then he came back. At first, he came back frequently – so often that Josefine found herself half waiting for him; his excuses and entreaties became part of her day. Then one day, several weeks ago now, he stopped.

It had been a shock. Josefine assumed that he'd simply given up trying. But seeing him now in the Marina Bar, seeing that look on his face, she wondered if there was more.

'Who are you meeting?' Gianni asked her now, instead of answering her question, which was vintage Gianni, *certo*.

'Josi.' On cue, Angelo appeared, a comforting presence at her shoulder. 'Sorry I am late. Sienna had a tricky bit of homework and—' He stopped. 'Oh, hello, Gianni.'

Gianni glared from one to the other of them. And perhaps he felt at a disadvantage because he got up from the bar stool and stood, legs slightly apart, hands by his sides. 'Why are you two going for a drink together?' he asked.

Privately, Josefine had asked herself the same question. But 'Why not?' She bristled. 'And what business is it of yours anyway?'

Gianni nodded glumly. 'Yes, yes, you are right,' he said. 'But, Fina, I need to—' There was an expression of urgency on his face now.

'Need to what?' she asked.

'Do you two need a few minutes?' Angelo took a step away.

'Yes,' said Gianni.

'No,' said Josefine at the same moment. She took Angelo's arm. 'Whatever it is, it can wait.'

Angelo looked different tonight. For a start, his dark salt-and-pepper hair was neatly combed. Josefine was used to seeing him in his work clothes, which were often as not daubed in flour. Tonight, though, he was wearing navy jeans and a smart shirt open at the neck and he smelt appealing too – not his usual comforting daytime smell of baking bread and rosemary, but some sort of woody cologne.

158

She remained conscious, however, of Gianni at the bar, looking over from time to time, while she and Angelo sat at a corner table chatting. Gianni looked morose and he was drinking too fast, she noted, as he drained the last of the bottle of wine into his glass. After about half an hour, he paid the barman, got to his feet and pulled on his jacket. He glanced across at Josefine and she quickly looked away.

Through the window, she watched him leaving, though, trudging across the piazza. Going home to Carlotta, she supposed. And what had he wanted to talk to her about? Whatever it was, she thought, she would find out soon enough.

'Does it make you sad, Josi?' Angelo's voice was gentle. 'Seeing Gianni? Remembering?'

She nodded, brought her attention back to him. 'A bit,' she admitted. 'But it is easy to remember the good times and forget the bad, *no*?'

'*Si, si,*' he agreed. 'You are right, of course.'

And Josefine was reminded that however bad things had been for her, they had been so much worse for Angelo.

After Gianni's departure, the atmosphere lightened and they continued to chat about this and that. But when they had finished their second drink, Josefine suggested that they call it a night. There was work tomorrow and it was best to break herself in gently to her blossoming social life, she thought.

'Did you have fun?' Angelo teased as he walked her home. The moon was half-full and casting its cool and shimmery spotlight on the inky sea below.

'I did not stop laughing all night,' Josefine confirmed with a wink, as they took the street that led away from the seafront and back towards the piazza. The tall houses were quieter now, many of the windows were dark and the washing had been taken from the balcony lines.

But despite seeing Gianni and experiencing mixed emotions which were not altogether pleasant, Josefine had enjoyed the evening. It had been a nice break away from the *caffè* and she always liked Angelo's easy company – all the more so this evening since there had been far fewer interruptions than usual.

'Thank you,' she said, relenting, and gave his arm a squeeze. 'It was lovely.'

'Well, *allora*, you know you could get out and have even more fun,' he said. 'If you got in some help, took some time off, made some changes.'

Josefine harrumphed. Changes . . . She'd seen too many changes already in these past few months. She wasn't sure she was ready for more. And besides, the man had no idea. 'I will let you come in and balance the books then,' she said.

'Ah.' As they turned left, his hand brushed against hers, but she did not take his arm, although it might have been comforting to do so. 'I may not be able to help you there, but I know a person who can.'

'Oh, yes? And where have you magicked them from, Angelo?' They were almost in the piazza now and Josefine realised that she was not quite ready for the evening to end.

He shot her a triumphant look. 'It is your sister.'

'Lily?'

'The very same.'

Abruptly, she stopped walking. 'I do not understand you.'

He spread his hands as he turned to face her. 'You know what Lily does for a living, *si*?'

Josefine frowned. She realised that she had not asked her. In fact, she had asked Lily very little about her life in England.

She supposed she'd been so reluctant to hear about the rest of it – Lily's family, her own birth mother . . . 'No, I do not.'

'She is an accountant. And not just an accountant – she works with businesses to find ways they can improve, become more financially viable, that kind of thing.'

'I see.' Josefine felt a grudging admiration. It sounded creative and interesting – and clever too.

They continued walking, side by side. Josefine was glad of the darkness under the canopy of the ilex trees, although the lanterns were lit in the piazza. *Lily* . . . she thought. But perhaps she, Josefine, might also have travelled in a completely different direction if she'd had a different start in life? Who knew? Not that she had ever wanted to study. And running the *caffè* had seemed the natural progression – almost the only choice perhaps? Not that she didn't enjoy it – or would do, if it wasn't quite such hard work.

But how did Angelo even know this about Lily? Had they been discussing Josefine and the *caffè* behind her back? She sneaked a glance at him as they walked on. He looked innocent enough, but she could not read Angelo the way she could read Gianni. Angelo always had a few surprises up his sleeve.

'But that is no help,' she said. 'She is only here for a few days.' Which was another reason why Josefine must take care not to let her get too close. What was the point, when she would soon be gone? Josefine had experienced enough abandonment in her life already; she did not need more. 'And anyway, why should she help me?' Josefine hadn't exactly welcomed her with open arms.

'Because you are her sister?'

They had arrived at the *caffè*. Angelo hung back slightly and seemed to be waiting for something. Her reply? Josefine wasn't sure that she was ready to give it.

161

'*Grazie*, Angelo.' Was it her imagination, or had the atmosphere between them changed?

But as per normal, he kissed her on both cheeks and grinned. '*Prego*. It is no problem. And maybe think about it at least?'

'Oh, I will.' Josefine pulled her key out of her bag. She might mention it to Lily tomorrow night, but then again, she might not.

Angelo moved away with a wave and Josefine felt herself relax. With relief? At least, she thought that's what it was she was feeling.

'And next time . . .' he called.

'Next time?'

'Next time, we have dinner. Out of town.'

Josefine smiled. She put her key in the lock. '*Va bene*,' she said. 'Okay.'

CHAPTER 23

Lily

2018

Lily had planned the evening carefully. She'd booked a restaurant situated between the hamlet of neighbouring Fiascherino and the town of Lerici, on the other side of the peninsula. And she had put some photos she had brought with her to Italy in her bag.

According to the woman in Perlarosa's tourist information office, Fiascherino was even smaller than its neighbour and, like Perlarosa, it clung to the coast. It was possible to walk there; it really wasn't far through the olive groves and pines, she told Lily. But it was a walk best kept for daylight hours, Lily reckoned, and so she organised a taxi to pick the two of them up at the top of the village.

'Did you have a nice evening with Angelo?' Lily asked Josefine when they were settled at their table, inside the restaurant and beside a large picture window. From here they had the most perfect viewpoint of the glorious Bay of Poets. The sea

163

was calm and glassy, glistening smooth and blue beyond the pines and scrubland. Lily could see paths leading through this, down the steep rocky cliff to the sea and to the gentle arc of a sheltered sandy beach where there were a few yachts and other boats, some people still swimming and paddle-boarding as the sun dipped lower and the sky took on tinges of pink and yellow.

'Nice enough.' Josefine looked up from studying the menu. She had changed into black trousers and a long-sleeved black shirt and Lily was glad she too had kept it quite casual.

'I was wondering. You and Angelo. Are you . . . ?' Lily wasn't quite sure how to ask this. They looked like a couple in some ways, but in other ways definitely not. She hoped it wasn't another subject that was off limits.

'He is just a friend.' But Josefine smiled, so presumably she didn't mind the intrusion.

'Ah.' And they exchanged a look which seemed knowing on Josefine's part and which only made Lily wonder even more.

'Angelo – he is trying to make me get out and about a bit more.' Josefine rolled her eyes. 'He thinks that the *caffè* – it should not be my whole life.'

'And is it? Your whole life, I mean?' Lily leaned forwards. The *caffè* had a lovely buzz to it and Josefine obviously worked hard. But . . . It seemed a shame not to have any life outside it.

Josefine shrugged. 'Only because it has to be,' she said.

'Because there's just you to keep it going?' Lily was cautious. She felt that with Josefine, she had to prod in order to find out anything. But she also guessed that if she prodded too hard, then Josefine would retreat and she'd learn nothing at all.

'And because it helps me forget.' She said it so quietly and so matter-of-factly that Lily was reluctant to pursue the subject – at least for now.

164

'Then Angelo is a good friend,' Lily said instead.

'He is.'

They both paused as the waiter brought their wine. Lily tried it and nodded her approval. He poured them both a glass.

'*Grazie*. Thank you.' Lily raised hers in a toast. 'And friendship is an excellent thing.'

She thought of Cate. They had spoken this morning and apparently everything was going well in London. Cate had moved in with Travis. 'And we're still speaking,' she added. 'I'm keeping all your stuff in the spare room. And it can stay there for as long as you want.'

'Thanks, Cate.' Lily was grateful. She hadn't had time since her mother's death to properly move her things out of London, and since then . . . well, she'd been in Italy and preoccupied. 'I'll come and collect everything as soon as I get back,' she promised. What there was of it. She'd moved to Hackney with very little and hadn't collected much since then. 'And what about Jack?' she asked her friend. She still felt a little guilty about that.

'Oh, he's fine. Don't worry, Lily. He's started seeing one of his work colleagues. She's okay, I quite like her. But she's not you.'

Lily was relieved. One less thing for her to worry about, she thought. Although right now London seemed so far away, it might as well be a different world.

Now, Josefine clinked her glass against Lily's. 'To friendship. Always so much more reliable than love.'

After they'd ordered, Josefine sat back in her seat and seemed to be regarding Lily closely. Lily wondered what she was thinking, how she measured up to Josefine's expectations as a sister, even though it was all so new. Had Josefine ever wondered if she had a sibling and what he or she might be like?

Josefine took a sip of her wine. 'Angelo said that you are an accountant,' she remarked, seemingly out of the blue.

Lily blinked at her in surprise. 'Sort of,' she said. 'I studied business and accountancy, and now I do a mixture of both. Freelance. Helping businesses become more . . .' – she paused – 'financially and personally rewarding, I suppose.'

'That must be . . .' – Josefine too was hesitant – 'interesting?'

Lily smiled. 'It can be.' It was nice that Josefine was asking. 'I definitely enjoy aspects of my job,' she admitted.

'Such as?'

'I like people.' Though in her job, people could also be difficult. Many did not like the idea of change. 'And numbers.'

'Numbers?' Josefine seemed intrigued. She leant in closer.

'I've always been obsessed with numbers,' Lily confessed. 'They're incredibly versatile and useful.'

Josefine laughed. 'I suppose they are.' She pulled a face. 'But as for me – I was never good with numbers at school.'

Lily sipped her wine. How different they were, after all. 'A lot of people say that, though,' she said. 'I reckon some people have got a sort of number blindness. But think how much we need them.' To Lily, numbers and the patterns they could make was endlessly fascinating, but she knew most other people didn't share her opinion.

'Hmm. I suppose you're right.'

And Josefine was clearly one of them. Lily could tell she wasn't convinced. She laughed too. 'They can even help us understand and predict the world around us,' she said.

'You think so?'

'I know so.' Okay, it was something she was passionate about, but Lily could see she was pushing a lost cause as far as her sister was concerned. If people didn't get numbers, then they didn't get why they were so amazing.

Josefine smiled. 'I can see why you wanted to work with numbers then,' she said.

'Plus, I like the idea of making things work,' Lily added, smiling back at her.

'Businesses?'

'Mainly, yes.' Lily considered. 'I'm not a creative,' she told Josefine. 'I know my limitations. Creative people possess vision – they have the initial idea and the energy to start the business. But they're not always so good at making things work financially.'

'Which is where you come in?'

'Uh-huh.' Lily wondered why she was asking. Was she just making conversation or . . . 'Is it the *caffè*?' she guessed.

'Oh, I get by.' Josefine remained breezy. She smiled at the waitress who had brought their first course of *calamari in zimino* with crusty bread. '*Grazie*,' she said. 'Thank you very much.'

'*Grazie*,' Lily echoed. And then to Josefine, 'Well, if you ever need any help . . .' She let the offer hang as she took a bite of the squid dish. The *calamari* had been cooked with a green vegetable – probably a variety of spinach – and was delicious.

Josefine toyed with a piece of *calamari* before placing it in her mouth. She chewed thoughtfully. 'Mmm,' she said, after a moment. 'The balance of the tomato and the wine – it is good.' She put down her fork. 'But would you have the time?' she asked Lily. 'Before you go back, I mean?'

'I mostly work from home.' Lily sensed a chink in Josefine's armour. She took another forkful of the squiddy-spinachy starter. 'But I could stay here a bit longer. If you wanted me to, I mean?' It would be simple enough to change her flights.

And what was waiting for her back in the UK? The daunting prospect of selling the family home, sorting out the rest of her parents' stuff, deciding what to do and where to go next. Extending her holiday and doing a bit of work while she was here sounded far more appealing – not to mention getting the opportunity to spend more time with Josefine, of course.

Josefine sighed. She picked up her fork again and took another mouthful, bit into the crunchy bread. She swallowed and drank more wine. 'I do not know, Lily,' she said at last. 'To be honest, I am not sure what to do.'

Was that an opening? Lily took a deep breath. 'Have things been hard?' she asked softly. Perhaps Josefine too had reached some kind of crossroads and needed to make a decision about the future?

For a few moments, Josefine didn't reply. Instead, she gazed out towards the sea – which was deepening into navy as the sun sank into the horizon – as if the Bay of Poets could give her some clue. She tucked a strand of dark hair behind one ear. Lily was used to seeing it up in a chignon, but tonight, Josefine wore it loose and it made her sister seem softer somehow.

She refocused on Lily. 'I told you my husband and I had separated,' she said.

'Yes.' Lily waited. Up until now, Josefine had taken care not to divulge much about her personal life, leaving Lily to guess the missing pieces.

'He had an affair.'

'Oh, I'm sorry—'

Josefine stopped her with a lift of the hand. 'I do not blame him,' she said in her low voice. 'Things between us were bad before that. Very bad.' She ate some more of the *calamari* and nodded for emphasis.

'I see.' Lily was struck by her honesty. It would be so easy to use the affair against him and take the moral high ground, but Josefine seemed to understand his motives. Lily thought of the silversmith down by the rocks yesterday, quietly fishing, turning to face her, staring; of the woman, Carlotta, walking over the beach towards him. Carlotta had to be involved in the break-up of Josefine's marriage – Lily had already guessed that much. So. Could the silversmith actually be Josefine's ex-husband? She had to know.

'What does he do for a living?' she asked. 'Your ex-husband, I mean.'

Josefine seemed surprised by the question; it probably seemed quite random. She shrugged. 'Gianni is a builder,' she said. 'What of it?' And she took a piece of bread to mop up the remainder of her starter.

'Oh, I just wondered.' A builder. It wasn't him then. Lily felt a wave of relief pass through her. Not that it made any difference to her, but . . .

The waitress came to remove their plates.

Lily waited for her to move away again. 'And you wanted children?' Because Josefine hadn't really told her this before, just that it hadn't happened for them, and now, Lily wondered if this was at least part of the reason why things had become so bad between them.

'At first, no. I was busy with the *caffè*. We thought there was plenty of time. And then later . . .' Her voice trailed and when she looked at Lily across the table, Lily recognised the unspoken longing, the pain in her eyes. So that was how it was. Her heart went out to her sister once again.

'Would you take him back?' Lily asked her.

169

'No.' Josefine tossed back the rest of the wine in her glass and Lily topped them both up. That was very definite.

'You don't love him?' she asked.

'Not any more, no.' Josefine lifted her glass as if making another more sardonic toast. 'No,' she said again, more sadly. 'I do not.'

Hmm. But Lily saw that it was more complicated than that for Josefine. What Gianni had done represented yet another rejection. She put a hand on her sister's. 'I'm sorry,' she said again.

Josefine didn't take her hand away. 'For what?' she said. 'Gianni?'

'For that, yes. But also . . .' Lily had to say it. She couldn't waste this opportunity. 'Also, for the fact that our mother had to give you up.'

Now, Josefine did pull her hand away. 'Had to?' Her blue-grey eyes suddenly seemed cold.

She reminded Lily so much of their mother in that moment. She hadn't been the best parent in the world. She had been selfish, even uncaring at times. But nevertheless, Lily felt she owed it to her, now that she had found Josefine, to explain, to tell Josefine how it had been, at least as far as she knew.

'Yes.' Lily ploughed on. 'She was young. She was alone. Her family wouldn't help her. In those days it was next to impossible to keep a baby unless your family supported you.' She spoke in a rush, trying to get it all out before Josefine stopped listening.

Josefine frowned. '*Is* that how it was?'

'Yes. I'm sure that's how it was.'

'And you do not think she might have found a way – to keep me, I mean?'

'I think she was desperate,' Lily said. She thought of what Glenda had told her. 'I think that she wanted to keep you. But I don't think there was a way.'

'But you were not there, Lily,' Josefine said.

'True.' And how would Lily feel if it had been her who had been given up for adoption? And yet . . . Hadn't Lily too been rejected by her birth mother, albeit in a different way? Lily had always assumed that her parents had tried for a baby for a long time, before her mother became pregnant with her. But when she thought of how her mother had been with her, almost as if she resented Lily's presence sometimes, it made her wonder. Had her mother wanted her? Had her parents wanted her? Or was it Lily who had been the accident when, in fact, Josefine had been the wanted one? It wasn't a particularly comforting thought. And yet perhaps this was all part of Lily's journey of discovery? Finding out her mother's story, finding Josefine, realising the impact certain events had made – on Lily, on Josefine, and on their mother.

'And so . . .' Josefine regarded her. 'How do you know?'

A good point. But . . . 'I spoke to Auntie Glenda,' Lily reminded her. 'She was there. She was her sister. She knew exactly how it was for our mother.'

Josefine looked up. 'And Glenda? Did she not support her?'

'Her life wasn't easy either,' Lily said. Although her aunt had admitted she felt bad for not doing more. 'She probably would have helped out, but she was newly married and had a little one of her own. They were all living at the family home and not very well off. It must have been hard for everyone.'

Josefine put her head to one side; she seemed to be considering this. 'Did your grandparents disapprove? Had Marilyn brought disgrace to the family?'

171

Lily shrugged. 'Apparently so.' Times were so different then. Even in the mid-sixties a girl who found herself in the family way, as they used to call it, could expect very little help or understanding; Josefine must know that as well as Lily did.

The waiter brought their main course and a pause in their conversation. Josefine was having tuna – *tonno alla Genovese* to be precise – which was cooked with onions, mushrooms and cherry tomatoes. Lily had chosen *Buridda*, which Josefine had told her was a Ligurian seafood stew traditionally cooked with olive oil, pine nuts and capers. She peered at it. It seemed to include lots of vegetables too – she could see celery, mushrooms and artichokes – and also the seafood, including anchovies. She sniffed. It certainly smelt good.

Josefine took a mouthful of tuna and gave an approving nod.

Lily tried the stew. It tasted as good as it looked and smelt. Really, the food here in Liguria was a revelation.

Josefine took another mouthful. She swallowed. 'And my father?' she asked.

'He was Italian.'

'Really? *Mamma mia.*' Josefine shook her head in surprise. 'My parents – they did not tell me that.' She frowned. 'But how did they meet?'

'He came to Dorset apparently. And they fell in love,' she added for good measure, remembering what Glenda had said on the subject.

'Hmm.'

Lily knew what she was thinking. Circumstances had made Josefine somewhat of a cynic on the subject of love. And perhaps she was right. But Lily wondered if Josefine was aware of the number of questions she was asking – rather a lot, for someone who hadn't wanted to know anything about the circumstances surrounding her birth.

'And what was he doing in Dorset?' Josefine helped herself to more wine and refilled Lily's glass while she was at it.

Lily continued to tuck into her seafood stew. It was rich and hearty and she hoped she would have enough room for it all. 'He was a construction worker, Glenda thinks. She reckons he was working on a building site in Bristol or somewhere close by, and then he got laid off. She's not completely sure.'

'A builder?' Josefine was absorbing every detail, Lily could tell. Perhaps she was also thinking of Gianni? It was a coincidence, of course, though it made Lily wonder about her mother, her sister, and their choices.

'And then?' Josefine asked. 'What happened when Marilyn got pregnant?'

Ah. Lily chose her words carefully. 'He went back to Italy before she found out,' she told her.

'And never came back?'

'And never came back.'

'Could she not have written to him?' Josefine seemed to be asking herself as much as Lily.

'I suppose she didn't have his address.' Though Lily was hazy about this part of the story. And who knew how much their mother had even told her sister Glenda? There could be bits of the story that only their mother knew; or that only Josefine's father knew, for that matter.

Josefine pushed away her plate. 'It must have been difficult for her,' she conceded at last. 'I can see that.'

'Yes, it must.' Lily took another forkful of fish and vegetables. 'I'm not sure she ever got over it. I'm wondering now . . .' She paused. It was hard to explain. 'It's as if I'm only just

173

discovering who she really was,' she said. 'Maybe that's why she was so . . . tricky. So closed in. As if she was afraid . . .' She shrugged. 'I don't know. Of something.'

Josefine was listening intently. 'But what about *your* father?' she asked. 'Did Marilyn not love him? They were happily married for many years, *no*?'

Lily had thought about this quite a bit. 'He was her rock,' she told Josefine. She picked up her glass and swirled the wine around. 'She needed him. He gave her what she wanted. And yes, I think she loved him.' She met Josefine's gaze. 'Because there are different sorts of love, aren't there?'

Josefine nodded and they were silent for a few moments while Lily finished what remained of her seafood stew and Josefine poured more wine. She put the bottle back on the table with the air of someone who had come to a decision. 'Do you have any photos, Lily?' she asked. 'Of Marilyn?'

'Yes, I do.' And Lily smiled. Because she had been so hoping she might ask.

CHAPTER 24

Lily

2018

Lily pushed her bowl to one side and took the folder of photos from her bag. She passed it over; watched as Josefine opened it, as she began leafing through the photographs.

The first was in glossy black and white, blurred, with worn edges, and showed their mother as a toddler playing in someone's garden.

'This is her?' Josefine asked.

'This is her.' It was a hot day, there was a tin bath filled with water nearby and she was wearing a checked swimsuit and a big floppy hat, screwing up her eyes in the sun as she gazed towards whoever was taking the photo – her father probably.

Lily was watching Josefine. She smiled as she lingered over that one. It was an adorable photo; Lily hadn't been able to resist including it.

The next was a rather demure school photograph where their mother was clearly trying not to laugh. It made Josefine chuckle and Lily laughed with her. And the next showed their mother as a teenager looking up from her sketchbook, caught by surprise, her fingers holding a pencil and her eyes still holding that dreamy expression that Lily remembered so well.

'She often looked like that,' she told Josefine. It was why she'd picked it – her mother's creativity had been such a big slice of her life. In part, her mother's painting had drawn her away from Lily. She loved this photo, though – if you looked closely, you could see that the sketch was of Hive Beach, near the family home. Lily could recognise the high grass-topped cliffs and bank of shingle, even though this photo too was in black and white, taken in the late 1950s perhaps.

'This was where she lived her whole life,' she told Josefine. 'In the village, near the beach.'

Josefine seemed to like it too, for she lingered even more over this one, a thoughtful expression on her face. 'It looks . . .' she said slowly after a while, '. . . like such a beautiful place.'

'It is,' Lily assured her. She gazed down at the shadowy Bay of Poets, at the trees, the hills, the moon in the darkening sky. This too, she thought. This too was such a beautiful place.

In the next photograph, still in black and white, their mother was standing stiff and upright outside the Cliff Hotel.

'This is the hotel where she worked,' Lily told Josefine. 'She was there for a long time, on the front desk, managing the bookings.'

'A seaside hotel?' Josefine glanced back at the previous picture.

'Up on the cliff,' Lily confirmed.

The picture was important in so many ways: this was where their mother had been working when she met Josefine's father – and Lily's father too, because he used to do building maintenance there. She was probably in her early to mid-twenties in this photo and Lily wondered who had taken it, and whether she had met him yet – Josefine's father. She could even be pregnant already, Lily supposed. And what about those two men in her mother's life? Had they ever met?

Lily guessed that before her parents' marriage, her mother wouldn't have owned a camera, so there weren't many photographs of this period available. But she had done her best, poring over the old albums before she came, deciding which ones to have reprinted, to take to Josefine.

Then came the photo of her parents' wedding, in colour now, Lily's father looking at her mother with unmistakeable adoration in his eyes and joy in his smile. Lily had hesitated over this one, not wanting to hurt Josefine by showing her the life their mother had made with a man who wasn't Josefine's father, but on the other hand . . . she looked happy here, and so it was an important photograph to include.

'You look like her.' Josefine glanced up at Lily.

'Yes, I do, a bit.' They were both fair, although Lily's eyes were dark, like her father's.

'I must look more like my father then.'

'Yes.' Lily held her breath. It must be so hard not knowing your birth parents. But as for the photos, she couldn't have wished for more. Josefine seemed receptive to them; it was as if seeing the images of her birth mother had made her real, made her someone with emotions, with thoughts and feelings, a woman pressurised to give up her daughter. Lily sensed for the first time that Josefine was beginning to want to understand.

Lily had added a few photos of herself when she was young – she hadn't included any happy family photos, though; that seemed too insensitive. In one, she was on a swing in a playground, going higher and higher, a look of pure delight on her face, blonde curls flying. In the other, she was a young teen, bent over a desk, frowning – doing her homework perhaps? Lily could vaguely remember her father taking the snap.

Josefine smiled as she looked at these two pictures. 'You were very cute,' she told Lily, and to Lily's relief, she couldn't detect any resentment behind her words.

Then came the final photo, which showed their mother at a family get-together when she was probably around Josefine's age now, glass of wine in hand, looking slightly tense as if she'd actually much rather be somewhere else – her studio probably, paintbrush in hand. Josefine examined this one too, her expression unreadable.

Lily hoped it hadn't been too difficult for her, seeing these images of the past. But it had seemed an important thing to do, to give her sister. And this portfolio was the best Lily could come up with. It hadn't been easy to find photos that might give Josefine an accurate flavour of the woman who had been her birth mother.

But at last, when Josefine looked up, Lily could see tears in her eyes and she could tell how affected she was by seeing this woman, her mother, for the very first time.

'She was beautiful,' Josefine said softly.

'Yes, she was.' Lily picked up all the photos, added the drawing of baby Josefine to the pile, put them in the folder and passed it across to Josefine. 'For you,' she said. And there were plenty more back at home if Josefine should want them.

'Oh.' Josefine hesitated. She looked up at Lily and, for a moment, Lily thought she would protest, say she didn't want them, push the folder of photographs and the drawing back towards her. But she did none of these things. 'Thank you, Lily,' she said.

Lily gave a little nod. 'And although you probably do look like your father,' she said, 'I must tell you something.'

'Yes?' Josefine stilled, watching her closely.

'You have our mother's eyes,' said Lily.

It was late by the time they arrived back in Perlarosa. Lily felt warm and fuzzy from the food and wine. The evening had gone better than she could ever have imagined. Josefine had let her guard down and Lily had been able to share lots of details about their mother, just as she'd wanted to. Lily knew that Josefine still had her reservations, and maybe she'd never fully connect emotionally with her past. How could she when she would never actually know their mother? But at least Lily felt that now she understood more of how it had been; the position their mother had been in when she'd been forced to give Josefine up for adoption. Would it also help her sister to feel less unwanted and abandoned? Perhaps. Lily knew it wasn't as easy or simple as that, but still, it was a start.

Just as they began walking down the road that led to Lily's B & B and then the Piazza Figoli, Josefine stiffened and grabbed Lily's arm. 'For the love of Madonna . . .' she muttered.

'What is it?' Lily couldn't see anything to be alarmed about.

'It is her – again. *Mio Dio*. My God, I do not believe it.'

And sure enough, there she was on the other side of the road up ahead talking to a woman Lily hadn't seen before. Carlotta. Lily knew that Perlarosa was a small place, but even so, this seemed more than a coincidence.

'She is haunting me.' Josefine's grip on Lily's arm was tight, too tight; Lily was sure there'd be a bruise tomorrow.

'Just ignore her.' She felt like a sister for the first time, giving advice. 'She can't hurt you any more.'

'You are wrong.' But Josefine loosened her hold. 'She shames me. How can I stay here when she is around every corner, humiliating me?'

They stood still for a moment in the shadows under the ilex tree, watching her. Lily was thoughtful – and worried. There was a solidity about Carlotta, and something about the way she was standing . . . She remembered how she had looked when she saw her on the rocks yesterday. She couldn't say for sure, but . . . Oh hell, she thought. What if . . . ?

Did she know she was being observed? Lily wasn't sure. But at that moment, Carlotta put her hand on her belly in a motion more like a caress. It was a protective gesture. It made Lily feel sick inside because suddenly she knew she was right.

'Lily.' In the moonlight, Josefine's face was ghostly pale.

Lily put an arm around her shoulders. Josefine seemed so vulnerable. Lily could feel how much this would hurt.

'No.' There was a lot of emotion packed in that one word. '*Merda*,' she swore softly. 'My God, Lily. She is not . . . pregnant, is she?'

'I don't know.' Lily squeezed her sister's shoulder. 'Let's go back to the *caffè*. I'll come with you.'

'There is no need.' From somewhere, Josefine seemed to summon strength. She straightened her back and pulled away. 'Goodnight, Lily, and thank you for a lovely evening.' She kissed her on the cheek. Once, twice.

'But are you all right?' Lily was worried. 'Are you upset?' Which were both stupid questions, Lily knew. Should Josefine even be alone, having just discovered that her ex-husband and his mistress were having a baby?

180

'Please.' Josefine held her head high. '*Non importa*. It does not matter. Life, it goes on, you see.' She gave a harsh little laugh. 'I am fine.'

'But . . .' Lily took a step forward. She hated to see her like this.

Josefine shook her head. 'It is best that I am alone. I need to think.' And with a thin smile and a brief final grip of Lily's arm, she swept off down the road towards the piazza.

Lily knew that it did matter and that Josefine was far from being all right. But what option did she have? She'd been dismissed and, for now, all she could do was watch her sister walk away.

CHAPTER 25

Italy, 2018

Today, he is looking after his grandson Tommaso; his daughter-in-law Adele has an appointment with her hairdresser which will apparently take up most of the afternoon. Eugh. He will never understand the needs of women; their desires too, come to think of it. Who can ever tell what they really are thinking? But she is a good wife to Stefano and a loving mother to Tommaso too, so there is nothing to complain about. Anyhow, he wants to spend the day with his grandson, this serious little lad with grey eyes and a slight but perpetual frown.

He is taking Tommaso to Zoagli on the train — let no one say he does not know how to show a child a good time . . . He chuckles to himself. It is a short journey and he likes the village. It is unpretentious and reminds him of simpler times, although, like everywhere, it is busier now; it has travelled some distance from its origins of silk-weaving and coral-fishing. Some places — like some people — have come further than others, he reminds himself.

From Zoagli train station, they walk along the platform and pass through a dank tunnel to the lungomare. *He loves this first sighting of the strip of blue, even after having lived by the sea his whole life, and from the way Tommaso's hand squeezes his, he guesses that his grandson feels the same. Perhaps, as his father has always maintained, such passions are carried in the bloodline . . .*

They pause reverentially at the tunnel exit, before descending the stone stairs, the inky water lapping onto the rocks beneath them. The narrow sea promenade uncurls towards the beaches and the village, as yet unseen around the rocky bend. It was built in the 1930s, before he was born, of course, almost a hundred years ago now, so it would mean still less to Tommaso. It had been strategically inset into this landscape of rocks and pine, following the pathway of the sea. And what had possessed the inhabitants of Zoagli to build it in the first place, hmm? He scratches his chin, as if the question has indeed been posed to him, and realises that he forgot to shave this morning. Allora, Zoagli was a fashionable resort, back in the day. And everyone loves a sea promenade.

He tells Tommaso what a popular place this village once was and the boy nods.

'Ah, si, si,' he goes on. 'There were many famous visitors to Zoagli. Ezra Pound, Kandinsky—'

'Who is Kandinsky, Nonno?' The boy's clear voice stumbles over the unfamiliar name.

'Who is Kandinsky? An amazing and innovative Russian artist, that is who.' He gropes in his pocket for his mobile. 'Maybe I can show you one of his pictures, hmm?'

They pause by the railings where tamarisks droop feathery branches over one of the little stone staircases. They are in sight of the beach now, the far watchtower, the hillside villas and churches, and the coastline stretching out from Rapallo, past Santa Margherita Ligure and even as far as Portofino on the tip of the peninsula.

'Let us sit for a moment, my boy.'

He eases the rucksack containing towels and a small picnic from his back and they sit on one of the seats carved into the granite facing the sea. Painstakingly, he types in the artist's name with his forefinger. He has to be sitting to do this, unlike young people who can text with both thumbs while standing on their heads. And they probably do as well — more fool them. Tommaso gives him a certain look but refrains from informing him that he is slow; Stefano must have had a word with the boy about respecting his elders.

'Here we are.' A picture appears on the screen. Geometric shapes — circles, triangles, something that looks like the sun in the bottom left corner and a wavy snake, though it is probably a mistake to try to relate the abstract to the concrete, he reminds himself. There are so many different kinds of art — this he knows, and much more, he remembers. 'He painted this, it is one of his most famous pictures.' Modern technology — it has its uses after all.

Tommaso pats his arm and leans closer to see, and he is gratified, uncaring that now he sometimes seems the younger one, the innocent, the one who needs someone to hold his hand, to guide him.

After a few minutes, they get to their feet. There is no big hurry. They walk down and settle on the stony beach.

'Can I go in now, Nonno? Can I swim?'

The boy is already pulling off his clothes; he is wearing his swimming trunks under his shorts.

'Certo. Of course.' He nods. 'I will come down to the water's edge.' From there he can paddle and see them both — the child swimming and playing in the sea and the view behind: the huge spanning bridge and the village, the two old Saracen watchtowers, the spires of churches on distant hills.

That bridge could be said to dominate the scene, he thinks. Or it could

184

be said to frame the picture. There are two ways of looking at it. A bit like the past really. He gives a little sigh. A frame or a domination. Are there not always at least two ways of looking at the past?

CHAPTER 26

Josefine

2018

The following morning, Josefine did not turn the 'closed' sign on the *caffè* to 'open'. She had taken the morning delivery from Angelo as she always did, because none of this was his fault, and why should he lose business? But she had no intention of serving coffee to anyone.

With Angelo, she did not indulge in any of the usual banter, and aside from asking her if she was okay (*Yes, fine, just busy*), Angelo accepted her mood without comment. Perhaps she was often like this and so he had grown accustomed? She had definitely had her dark hours in the days and weeks after Gianni's departure, but not so much lately, she hoped. Lately, she'd felt calmer, more accepting even. Until now.

When the church bells rang for eight a.m., she untied her blue and white apron, threw on a light jacket and walked out of the door. Now this, she never did. The *caffè* was her livelihood, her reason for existence. But what did any of that matter now?

At the junction, she took the narrow red-bricked alleyway that led uphill to Gianni's house. It was still early, but that was all to the good – he was more likely to be there. And if she was there too? Josefine realised she was grinding her teeth – not a good habit to get into. Then she'd have it out with her as well. Josefine was past caring.

Perlarosa was exactly the same as always – calm and beautiful – though Josefine wasn't usually out and about at this time of day and she was certainly feeling far from calm. The greengrocer called out a cheery greeting and she forced herself to call back as if nothing was amiss. Women of the neighbourhood were cleaning their front doorsteps, gossiping with one another or hanging washing on balcony lines, and she exchanged greetings with them too.

Would they speculate about where she was going, when normally she would be in the *caffè* serving breakfast? Perhaps. Josefine continued walking, head held high. The fragrances of coffee and *cornetti* were drifting in the air. It would turn out to be a warm spring day, but for now, the breeze remained a little chill and Josefine was glad she'd worn her jacket. She drew it closer as if it could make her safe.

She had enjoyed the evening with Lily, she thought as she walked on. She had relaxed, she had let herself go a bit, she had listened and she had even confided. Perhaps, then, this was her punishment. She had been lulled by Lily's presence, by her kind words, by the seductive fantasy she'd offered Josefine that the past had not been what Josefine had always imagined it to be. Lily had been both sympathetic and a good listener – perhaps that was why. Anyway, Josefine had found herself not just mildly curious, but really wanting to know more – about her elusive birth mother, about the reasons why.

She thrust her hands into her pockets, greeted another villager walking in the opposite direction from the church. *Buongiorno, buongiorno.* Managed to find a friendly smile. And she thought about those photos still tucked in the folder Lily had given her, waiting to be looked at again. Josefine knew that she would . . . Putting a face, a name, a body to that image of the birth mother she'd always held at such a distance had changed everything. It had made her think of that other's person's point of view. Josefine would examine and re-examine those photographs, searching for some resemblance, some clue, some sense of who she really was. She was discovering her identity. Now that she'd had a taste of it, she couldn't resist wanting more.

Josefine turned into a quieter alleyway off the main street. She had drunk it all in so desperately, she thought now, as she climbed the shallow steps. Not just what she'd seen in the photographs, but everything that Lily was telling her. Every nugget. Every last detail. The possibility that she had not been rejected, abandoned, unloved as she had always believed; the idea that in some way, after all, she might have been wanted.

But now this.

Josefine arrived at Gianni's door. The house was small, the door battered and ancient, its green paint flaking to reveal the bare wood beneath, the knocker tarnished and dull. The plants on the narrow balcony above were dying from lack of water, the windows were grubby. It had been his parents' house before they died and Josefine too had lived here for a while when they were first married, before she and Gianni moved into the apartment over the *caffè*.

They had been happy enough, but Josefine had never felt that she belonged in the house. His parents had still lived here;

188

she had felt like little more than a lodger and Gianni had been content to let them continue to run everything – he was always keen for an easy life, after all. After their death, she and Gianni decided to stay in the apartment above the *caffè* and it had been useful to rent this place out from time to time to bring a little extra money in.

She knocked on the door. Now Gianni's place looked as unloved as Josefine felt. And she sensed that the woman was not here; that Gianni was living here alone.

After a few moments, he came to the door, unshaven and sleepy-eyed. Well, it was almost the weekend and Gianni had always liked a lie-in.

'Fina.' He blinked at her as if she might be a figment of his imagination.

Josefine stood, back straight, fists curled, looking right at him. 'Gianni,' she said.

'Do you want to . . .' – he hesitated – 'come in?'

Ah. She had been right then, about Carlotta. Josefine shook her head. It was a quiet alley and there was no one around. But anyway, why should she worry about being overheard?

'This will not take long,' she told him.

She saw him take in her expression.

'You know,' he said.

'*Si*, I know.' Her fists curled tighter.

He spread his hands in that way he had, always pleading his innocence. 'I tried to tell you. The other night in the bar.' His voice trailed. He knew he had no defence.

'You did not try very hard.'

He sighed. 'Fina, it was the last thing I wanted . . .'

Josefine let out a harsh laugh. 'Really? Once, you let me believe that you wanted it more than the world itself.'

189

'That was when it was us.' His voice was low, intense. It reminded her sharply of when they were first together, those passionate encounters, that feeling of solidity Gianni had once given her. She had loved him then. Surely she had loved him then?

She shrugged. 'But you are the one who will have a child, Gianni. While for me, it is too late.' How cruel then was nature – especially, she thought, to women. For Gianni, already turned fifty himself, there was this chance with Carlotta – in her forties already, Josefine guessed. But still able to conceive.

'I am so sorry, Fina.' He pulled his fingers through his hair.

She believed him. But it made little difference. She understood now why he had stopped coming round, why he had stopped begging her to take him back. 'How long have you known?' He must have known since then, but she wanted him to say it.

'Does it matter?'

It mattered to Josefine. And yet, it was another example of Gianni's weakness, she supposed. All these months and Josefine had no idea that there was a woman right here in this village who was growing her husband's child in her belly – although Carlotta was not from here originally, of course, and Josefine could only suppose that she had come to Perlarosa because of the silversmith.

'I did not know how to tell you,' he confessed.

Josefine was not surprised at that. 'When is it due?' She folded her arms in front of herself now and that was how she felt – closed as a scallop shell.

He shrugged.

'For God's sake, Gianni . . .'

'She is five months gone, give or take.' He grabbed Josefine's arm. 'It was only the once, Fina,' he said. 'Before you . . . you know.'

Before she found him out. Only the once . . . And yet she and Gianni had tried for years. It made Josefine feel old; it made her feel useless. 'How could you?'

'I did not intend for it to happen. I did not intend for *her* to happen.'

And the way he said it, Josefine knew. He did not love Carlotta. He had not wanted this. And yet here he was. It was a bitter irony.

'I never wanted to hurt you, Fina,' Gianni said. 'You know that. I only ever wanted to love you.'

Ah, but she had not let him, had she? She had driven him into another woman's arms by keeping hers so tightly shut, by never allowing him to do or say anything right, by slipping out of love with him. 'So, what will you do?' Since Carlotta was not here in the house, perhaps they had not become a couple after all. It was beginning to seem that way.

His gaze met hers. 'I will stick by her, Fina. What else can I do?'

'She wants you?'

'Yes.' Even Gianni looked faintly surprised at this.

Well, he was older than Carlotta, for sure, but he was still an attractive man. Josefine guessed that after she'd thrown him out, Gianni had not immediately taken up with Carlotta as perhaps the other woman had wanted him to. Instead, he had continued pleading with Josefine to take him back. And who knows, maybe he would have continued to do that the rest of his life, if not for the child that was coming.

'I see.' And she almost felt sorry for him then – almost, but not quite.

He gazed beyond her now, towards the sea. 'It is what she wants,' he said. 'To have me. To have the child. To make a new life.'

'And what you want?'

He shot her a look, but he did not reply. Josefine interpreted that look to mean that he wanted everything to be as it was before Carlotta. But Josefine did not. As she had told Lily in the restaurant last night, it had been bad between them – very bad. She could not have continued like that and she doubted Gianni could have either. Perhaps he had forgotten the bad things already? She would not be surprised. In Josefine's experience, men tended to view the past through lenses of selective memory; they simply did not recall the bitter words spoken, the casual cruelties, the shadows that had shrouded every day. She sighed. They were fortunate then, in that respect and many others.

But . . . 'You cannot stay here in Perlarosa.' Her voice was urgent; she heard her own anger. 'Not with her. Not with a child.'

He blinked at her. She saw that although Gianni had been expecting Josefine to be angry and upset, he had not taken the situation he now found himself in through to any conclusion.

'Seeing you every day,' she said. 'Seeing her.' And then, her voice low. 'Seeing you with your son or daughter, Gianni.' Perlarosa was such a small hamlet. And everyone would know. The prospect was impossible.

'But this is where I live, Fina.' He was struggling even more now. 'This is where I work. This is—'

'Where I am,' she finished for him. 'And I cannot leave the *caffè*. It is all I have.' At last, her voice broke. Was she being so unreasonable? Carlotta had come from who knew where.

She was a stranger to Perlarosa still. Could Gianni really do this to Josefine?

'Yes, I know.' He frowned, his dark eyes troubled. 'But, Carlotta, she—'

Josefine turned on her heel. She could not stay here any longer. She could not listen to this any longer. 'You must deal with it, Gianni,' she said. 'Even if it is the last thing you do for me.'

'Fina, I still—'

'Carlotta is your responsibility now,' she reminded him. 'But please, Gianni. You have to tell her that you both must go.'

CHAPTER 27

Lily

2018

Lily was concerned when she walked through the piazza the following morning and saw that the *caffè* was closed. She'd got the impression that in daylight hours the *caffè* was never closed – which meant that something was very wrong with Josefine. She wasn't surprised after what had happened last night. But it was such a shame; it had all been going so well . . . Josefine had seemed open to hearing more about their mother, and her response when she looked at the photographs Lily had given her . . . That alone had made Lily's quest worthwhile.

She knocked on the door of the *caffè* – nothing. Had Josefine gone out? Lily decided to walk down to the Marina Bar for her coffee and *cornetto*, then she'd go for a stroll around the village and maybe try Josefine again. Perhaps her sister simply wanted some time to herself – Lily couldn't blame her for that. It must have been a horrible shock for her, especially after everything she'd already gone through.

As she passed the dusky facade of St Giorgio and approached the harbour, Lily spotted the silversmith sitting outside his workshop on an upturned crate, drinking an espresso, by the look of it, and gazing out to sea. It was the first time she'd recognised him from a distance – which gave her the chance to think of something half-intelligent to say when she passed by. Because, she realised, she needed to say something.

He must have heard her coming because he looked up the narrow street and watched her approach.

'*Buongiorno*,' she said breezily and inclined her head.

'*Buongiorno*.' His voice was low, almost wary.

'How are you?' she asked. And then, because that wasn't even half-intelligent and sounded far too bland to her own ears, 'I was wondering if you had started work on the pendant yet?' And then, because that sounded impatient, almost rude, she backtracked. 'Only I'm looking forward to seeing it – when it's finished, that is.'

Honestly. Why was she so worried about saying the wrong thing? What did it matter? Why was his opinion even remotely important to her? She hardly knew the man and in a few days' time, she'd be gone and would probably never see him again.

His expression didn't change. 'I have made a beginning,' he said. 'It takes time. These things always do.'

She nodded. 'Great.' In contrast, everything *he* said seemed imbued with added meaning.

'And as for me . . .' He almost smiled – but not quite. 'I am the same as always.'

'Ah.' Which told her absolutely nothing. Lily ploughed on. 'I found out that the stone is mined in Liguria,' she said. 'Anatase, that is.'

He made a small gesture – half-shrug, half-acknowledgement.

195

Did he know already? Probably. Was he wondering where she had obtained the gemstone from in the first place? Apparently not, since he didn't ask. Nor did he get to his feet and yet she had no sense that he wanted her to be gone. She decided not to mention what else she'd found out about anatase – that it was rare, that it signified the element of air and the heart chakra (that, she guessed, would be far too hippy-dippy for him) and that it signified good communication, hope and positivity, peace and trust. Lily didn't know about all that, but she did know it was special.

'Have you always lived here in Perlarosa?' she asked, trying another tack. 'It's so lovely.' Lovely. What an unimaginative word that was. Couldn't she have dredged around in the extensive vocabulary of the English language and found something a bit more, well, evocative?

'No.'

For a few moments she thought he was not going to elaborate. He still hadn't got up from the crate – not that she'd expected him to – and so she was left feeling a bit awkward, looming over him. She noticed the dark shadow of a day's stubble on his jaw and, as always, the unruliness of his raven hair. He, on the other hand, didn't seem to feel awkward in the least.

'I came here ten years ago,' he said at last. 'In a boat.' He looked out past the little harbour and the boats pulled up onto the slipway, to the sea beyond, which was greenish-grey this morning with waves frothing and frilling onto the concrete jetty.

'Oh, I see.' Though she didn't, and his remark had only left her more curious than ever. 'Where did you come from?' She wondered about his previous life. He spoke excellent English – might that be a clue?

196

He turned to glare at her. 'Does it matter where I came from?'

Hmm. She had obviously overstepped the mark. 'I suppose not.' She spoke evenly. 'I was just curious.' But you couldn't make ordinary conversation with this man, she reminded herself, because he was very far from ordinary. And it was definitely time to go. The man had issues and, whatever they were, they were not Lily's business. She shrugged. 'I'll let you get on.' And she took a step away.

'I am sorry.' He spoke in a rush. 'That was rude of me. Of course, *certo*, you are not to know.' He rose to his feet, she turned back and now she was sure that they both felt awkward.

'It's fine. No problem.' And she took another step away. It was his life after all and she was nothing to him, merely a stranger in Perlarosa.

The silversmith had left his coffee cup balanced on the side of the crate and now he plunged both hands deep into the pockets of his frayed denim shorts as if he didn't quite know what to do with them. He moved towards her. 'Sometimes, we need to escape,' he said.

'Yes, we do.' That was very true. Lily continued to hover, not sure whether to go or stay. She thought of how she had felt when her beloved father had died. It had been the biggest of blows. Her mother had needed her unflinching support but Lily had not been able to give it – or at least, not to the level that her mother required. It was as much as she could do to keep going herself and there simply wasn't enough space in her head or heart to do anything further. When she felt a little stronger – although the grief still pulsed inside her every day and she'd never get used to being without him – all she'd wanted to do was escape. From her mother's tears, her sentimental ramblings, her need. Lily had been so desperate to escape from her.

197

The silversmith was watching her intently. 'Do you want coffee?' he said.

'Oh.' Lily wasn't sure. Whether they were conversing or not, it was exhausting being with this man. 'Okay, yes. Thank you.' And equally compelling, she thought wryly.

He went inside and reappeared with another crate, on which he indicated she should sit, and then returned to the workshop again to fetch the coffee. He came back and handed it to her: a small white cup. The liquid inside was thick and black.

Lily smiled her thanks and took a sip. It was dense and tasted bitter, and yet also somehow delicious.

The silversmith sat down again and stretched out his legs. With the cut-offs, he wore a faded green T-shirt and a pair of worn trainers, and his bare arms and legs were strong, brown and weathered. What had he needed to escape from? she wondered. Grief, like her? It had certainly seemed that way when she'd come across him in the church that first time. Seldom had she seen anyone look so sad, but also . . . She struggled to recall the exact expression: guilt-stricken. But if that was the case, what had he done that he felt so very guilty about?

Their eyes met. 'Who are you?' he asked.

Lily had to smile. Theirs had been an unusual liaison so far, and they hadn't exchanged names. 'My name's Lily,' she said. 'Lily Knight.' She regarded him over the rim of her coffee cup. 'And you? Other than being the silversmith, I mean.'

He smiled then, a wide smile that reached his dark eyes, and to Lily, his face seemed transformed. 'Nico,' he said. 'Nico Ricci.'

She nodded. Nico . . . It suited him. 'Pleased to meet you, Nico.'

'The pleasure, it is mine.' He gave her a long look, but she couldn't interpret it, apart from not being sure whether he was being sincere or ironic. She could tell that he wasn't usually bothered with the social niceties of life, though.

'And what brings you to Perlarosa, Lily Knight?'

She liked the way he spoke her name; loved his accent and the slight raise of the dark eyebrows that accompanied his words.

Feeling a flush of heat rising, she looked away. 'I came looking for my sister,' she said. After all, it wasn't a secret.

'Your sister?' Clearly, he hadn't been expecting that. 'And did you find her?'

'Yes, I did.' She took another sip of the coffee. 'It's Josefine Parodi from the *caffè* in Piazza Figoli.' He would know her, of course. Everyone knew everybody here.

'Josefine?' He stared at her.

'Yes.' Once again, she couldn't read his expression but he seemed perturbed. Was there a connection between him and Josefine after all? Or was it to do with Carlotta? Or Gianni? She longed to ask him about Carlotta, but she didn't dare. This man was mercurial. If she said the wrong thing, he might shut down completely.

But now, he was nodding as if he understood. 'Gianni – he told me Josefine was adopted,' he said.

'That's right.' Lily was relieved that she hadn't spoken out of turn. The last thing she wanted was to betray any confidences but Josefine had told her that her adoption was no secret in Perlarosa.

He took a sip of his coffee. 'When the Parodis – her parents – left Perlarosa, I was surprised,' he told her. 'They went so . . .' – he made an abrupt gesture – 'suddenly and completely.

That is when Gianni told me they were not blood-related.' He sighed. 'I was sorry then – for Josefine.'

'Yes.' Lily was too. This was the longest speech she had heard him make. She liked the fact that he had felt sorry for Josefine. Only, she didn't want to talk about her sister right now. 'But what about you?'

'Me?' His face closed again, just a little. He looked slightly haughty with that Roman profile, slightly out of reach.

'What did you find when you came to Perlarosa?' That seemed safer. She kept her voice upbeat. 'Adventure?'

He laughed at that and she liked the sound. If this man were to lighten up a bit, she could see how appealing he might be.

'Not exactly.' He hesitated, as if unsure whether to go on. 'It was peace of mind I was searching for.'

Interesting . . . 'And did you find it?'

He sneaked a glance at her from under dark brows. 'To a degree. Sometimes, yes. Sometimes, no.' He gave a little shrug. 'I am still looking.'

'And what else did you find?' she asked. She wouldn't ask him more about his peace of mind – at least not for the moment – but they were getting somewhere.

'A friend,' he said. 'I made friends with an old silversmith who taught me all I know.'

'How romantic.' Lily lifted her face to the sun. 'What happened? How did you meet him?' She realised that she wanted to know a lot more about this man, even though she'd have to take it slowly. Not just about his past and his secret sadness, but an awful lot of other things besides. He fascinated her – the mystery of him. Who was he really? Had he ever been married? Was he married now? Did he have family? Who was he before he came to Perlarosa – and who was he now?

200

'I arrived in my boat at this tiny harbour.' He gestured towards the cobbled slipway. 'Drawn in here by that pink bell tower of St Giorgio there.'

'Yes?' Lily realised he was going to tell her the story and she felt a little thrill run through her. She guessed him to be the sort of man who didn't often release any personal details, especially to someone he hardly knew.

'I was exhausted. I had been through a bad time.' He paused but didn't elaborate. 'I looked up at this cliff, these rocks, these houses . . .'

Lily looked. The houses were so pretty – painted in pink, yellow and dark terracotta, with green shutters and orange slates, plants threaded through balconies and hanging to the ground. It was all so faded and elegant, so quiet and peaceful. He would have had a good view of the old Perlarosa wash-houses too where women once washed not only their clothes, but also the wool after sheep-shearing, according to the information plaque Lily had studied the first time she came down here. Next to the old washhouses was a fountain fed by fresh spring water; Lily imagined the women of the village walking down the alleyways with terracotta jars or copper pots balanced on their heads to collect the water from the fountain. She shook the thought from her mind. She was getting carried away. All that would, of course, have been way before his time.

'And I thought, what a beautiful place this is. Like a small piece of paradise.'

Lily nodded. She could see it all through his eyes, see Perlarosa as a haven, a place of potential tranquillity where he could make a new life for himself. Where no one knew him . . . The thought crept into her head once again. What exactly had he done?

'I jumped out and dragged the boat up the slipway here.' He pointed. 'And then I saw an old man, coming up the street, right here where we are now sitting. He had white hair, hanging thick around his shoulders like a snowdrift. He stooped as he walked and he was carrying two heavy bags of shopping.'

Lily too could see the man. She leant back against the wall of the workshop, enjoying the stony heat of it behind her and the warmth of the sun on her skin, her hair. It didn't feel at all strange to be sitting on an upturned crate outside a silversmith's workshop listening to this story told by a man who was virtually a stranger.

'As I watched him,' he went on, 'he stumbled, he tripped on an uneven cobblestone, although he knew the stones very well because he had lived here all his life.'

'Oh no.' Lily opened her eyes. His voice was so hypnotic that she had barely realised she had closed them. 'Was he all right?'

The silversmith smiled. 'Yes. Gabriele, he was very resilient. But the shopping . . .' He spread his hands. 'It shot out of the bags and went tumbling down the street towards the sea.'

'What did you do?' Though Lily could guess.

'I did what anyone would do – I helped him pick it all up.'

'That's nice.' Lily smiled.

'And so . . . he invited me inside for coffee.'

Lily heard the emotion in his voice now. They must have become good friends indeed.

'And he told me about his work.'

She shifted slightly on the crate. It wasn't the most comfortable of seats but it was precisely where she wanted to be at this moment. 'You were interested, I'm sure,' she said.

'I was.' He paused. 'I suppose apart from looking for peace of mind, I was also looking for something . . .' His voice drifted.

'Different?'

He gave her that intent look again. 'Different, *si*.' And then, as you can tell, as so often is the way, one thing leads to another, and the old silversmith, my friend Gabriele Oliveri, he repaid a small kindness a hundredfold.'

'He must have been a lovely man,' she said.

'He was.' He drained his coffee cup. 'But also, he was sad. He had lost his only son some years before and most of his family were dead and gone.'

'It sounds as if he treated you a bit like a son.' Lily hazarded a guess.

Another look. 'Yes, he did. He helped me find lodgings and he taught me all he knew about the art of being a silversmith.'

Lily wished she could have met this man, Gabriele Oliveri. He sounded very special.

'And then when he died, he left me his workshop,' he said. 'So I could continue his work. His work that had become my work, you see.'

'Yes.' She saw. 'It's a wonderful story,' she said. 'You must have given him great comfort.'

The silversmith (perhaps she should start calling him the young silversmith, Lily thought) got to his feet. 'He gave so much more than comfort to me,' he said. 'But if I gave him anything, then I am glad. Without him . . .' He gazed out beyond her, past the boats and the slipway towards the part of the ocean which was in the distance, where the water moved into a smooth turquoise edged with navy on the horizon, the peninsula of Portovenere and the smaller island with its national park standing proud against the spring-blue sky.

Was he looking towards his old home perhaps, wherever that might be? To his past?

'Without him,' he repeated, 'I was lost.'

The old silversmith had been his saviour then. Only, what had he been saving him from?

But Lily realised that since he had got up, this was her cue to leave. She'd finished her coffee and he had told his story, a special story. She was touched that he had trusted her enough to share it with her. 'Thank you for the coffee.' She handed him the little white cup and he took it in silence. 'And thank you for telling me the story of how you came here to Perlarosa.'

He acknowledged this with a small nod.

'It's so romantic to arrive in a boat,' she mused aloud. 'Most people would come in a car these days, I suppose.'

'I do not drive.' His brow clouded.

'Oh.' Was it her imagination or had the air suddenly grown a little colder? She smiled, to break the tension. 'I must let you get on with your day,' she added. 'And of course, I need to see Josefine.'

'Ah, yes, your sister.' He looked calmer again now. 'Well, *allora*, goodbye, Lily,' he said. 'And do not worry.'

'Worry?' She frowned. Was he aware then of what she and Josefine had witnessed last night?

He regarded her intently, but with no smile this time. 'Your pendant. It will be finished before you leave Perlarosa.'

CHAPTER 28

Josefine

2018

After she left Gianni, Josefine did not go straight home. She walked up the red-stepped alleyways into the upper reaches of the village, trying to stomp it out – the anger and humiliation she felt. *How could he? How could he?* was still drumming through her brain.

When she finally made it down to the piazza again, the first person she ran into was Lily, who was hovering around the *caffè*, peering in through the window.

'Lily, *ciao*.' She waved, went up and greeted her with the usual kiss on both cheeks.

'Are you okay?' Lily was scrutinising her closely. 'I was worried when I saw the *caffè* was closed . . .'

'Ah.' Josefine dismissed this with a shake of her hand. 'You know, I had to have it out with him. After what we saw last night.'

'Gianni?'

'*Si.*' Of course, Gianni. Josefine unlocked the door. 'Coffee?' But she kept the sign to 'closed'. She wasn't yet ready for people.

'And what did he say?' Lily followed her inside.

'You know Gianni.'

'Oh, but—'

'*Si, si* . . .' Josefine brushed her words away. She was aware, naturally, that Lily did not know Gianni, but she had told her enough about him for Lily to get the gist. 'He admitted it. He was sorry. He said he had tried to tell me.' She paused. 'He even said he did not want it – the child, I mean.'

Lily let out a little gasp. 'So, it's not serious between them then?' she asked.

Josefine snorted. She sat down at a table near the counter and Lily followed suit. 'Serious?' She shrugged. 'He may not have intended to be with her, but he will be with her now and he will look after her and their child. Gianni takes his responsibilities seriously, you can be sure.'

Lily reached forward to pat her arm and Josefine appreciated the gesture of support. 'It's hard for you,' Lily said. 'And it was a horrid way to find out.'

This was true enough. 'Gianni, he is a coward.' Josefine looked around the *caffè*, at the purple walls, the bulging bookcases, the mismatching tables and chairs and the piles of cakes and pastries on the counter. There were a couple of tourists loitering outside. But she really wasn't sure she had the emotional energy to open up today.

Certo, she had always known Gianni was not the bravest – look at how he had been dominated by his mother back in the day – but back then, Josefine had hoped she possessed enough strength for both of them. And if they'd had a child? If those months and years of trying so hard that they lost the sense

206

of themselves, of their marriage, had not turned out to have been for nothing and they'd had a child, what then? Would they have stayed together? Josefine guessed so. A child would have glued them, healed the cracks between them, given them something to stay together for. And perhaps they could have moved on from that as a couple and found even more . . .

Basta. That was enough thinking of the past. 'But you and I – we will have coffee,' she said to Lily.

Lily turned a little pale. 'Perhaps I'll have a hot chocolate if that's okay,' she said. 'I've just had coffee with someone, and it was . . .' – she waved her hand in front of her face – '. . . rather intense.'

Josefine laughed. 'Who was that?' And what, she wondered, was intense – the coffee or the encounter? Come to think of it, Lily did look a bit dazed. She was wearing a pale-yellow top and a blue denim skirt and her hair was tucked behind her ears. Her skin was beginning to acquire a golden-brown tan which suited her, but there was a delicate look about her too; with those big brown eyes she looked a bit like a startled faun. There was something else Josefine noticed this morning, though, now that she was inside and had taken off her sunglasses. She had a bit of a glow.

Lily hesitated. 'Um . . .'

'Lily?' Josefine had a sudden and black premonition. 'Not Angelo?' Because why else would Lily hesitate? Josefine remembered how keen Angelo had been to recommend Lily's accounting services the other day, the way they'd been talking, heads together in the *caffè*, almost like old friends. But he was too old for Lily, surely? He was only a few years younger than Josefine herself. Although Gianni . . . . *Mamma mia*. And look what had happened there. Everyone knew that men preferred

207

younger women. Perhaps they foolishly thought them more malleable? Perhaps they imagined those young looks would never fade? Perhaps they wanted to look after them? Perhaps – although she could not imagine this of Angelo – they made them feel more of a man? But Lily – she would not be interested, would she?

Josefine shook her head as if she could shake these thoughts away. But once the notion was there, it wriggled around like a worm and refused to disappear. Maybe Josefine was going crazy? She would not be surprised.

'Angelo?' Lily looked perplexed. 'Why would I be at Angelo's?' She backtracked. 'Though he's a very nice man, of course.'

'Sorry.' Josefine batted the notion away – with her hand this time. What was wrong with her? This business with Gianni and Carlotta was making her paranoid. 'Who then?'

A faint blush stole onto Lily's cheeks.

Aha, thought Josefine. She'd been right then, about the glow. Lily was so fair, she would always give herself away.

'Oh, just the silversmith, Nico Ricci. I got talking to him this morning.'

Josefine stared at her. 'And he made you coffee?'

'Yes, I . . .' It seemed as if Lily wanted to say something else, but she stopped.

'But he is practically a recluse.' Josefine hardly knew him, although, of course, he was a good friend of Gianni's. They used to go fishing together – probably still did – sitting for hours on the rocks hardly speaking. Though what the point was of that, Josefine could not imagine, especially when there was plenty of work to be done elsewhere. It was a strange sort of friendship, she'd always thought. Nico was such a loner, no one knew much about him since he'd turned up in the village ten years ago or so, but for some reason, he and Gianni had hit it off from the start.

'Yes,' Lily agreed. 'I had that impression too.'

Josefine narrowed her eyes at her. She was so naive. 'Be careful. He wants something from you perhaps.'

'Oh, no.' Lily re-tucked her hair more firmly behind her ears. 'No, no.'

She protested too much. Josefine arched an eyebrow.

'I don't think so, really. It's just . . .' Lily floundered. 'I was admiring some of his jewellery the other day, and—'

'My advice is to stay away from him.' Josefine decided it was time to tell it straight. 'He is bad news.'

'Why do you say that?' Lily paled.

'It is not just that he is Gianni's friend. It is not just Carlotta. There is something black here, you know?' She tapped her head. 'Maybe something in his past. Maybe something he has done. I do not know exactly what.' She had heard people speculate about it. People always would talk, of course, when someone kept himself to himself. People distrusted those who preferred privacy, who were unwilling to open up to all and sundry, who didn't spend their time gossiping about other people's lives. She had experienced some of that herself when it had first become known that she was adopted, and was not really a true Parodi at all. But it was different with Nico Ricci. Everyone knew there was something he was trying to hide.

Lily was staring at her. She looked upset. So . . . what? She liked Nico? Was that it?

'What about Carlotta?' Lily asked. 'Who is she?'

That woman . . . Under the table, Josefine clenched a fist. 'What do you mean?'

'I just wondered. What's Nico's connection to Carlotta?' Lily sighed and her slim shoulders drooped.

Immediately, Josefine felt protective – which was a new feeling. Was it because she was Lily's big sister? At least, they were half-sisters, which to Josefine had come to mean the same thing. Probably. Lily was, after all, the only true blood relative she had ever met, the only link to Josefine's past, the only person who might love her because they shared the same bloodline and, in a way, the same family history. It was a poignant feeling, a good feeling, and Josefine reached out and put her hand on Lily's shoulder, gave it a reassuring squeeze.

'I saw them arguing on the rocks the other day,' Lily continued. 'Nico and Carlotta.'

'Arguing? Huh!' Josefine took her hand away. 'They are as thick as thieves, those two.' She got to her feet. 'Carlotta Barbieri, she is Nico's sister-in-law. He is the reason she came to Perlarosa. It is through him that Gianni met her. Nico Ricci – he is at the root of it all.'

Lily was wide-eyed and open-mouthed now. *Madonna santa . . .* Josefine had saved her from a whole host of trouble, that much was obvious.

'His sister-in-law?' Lily echoed.

'*Si.*'

'And his wife?'

Josefine shrugged. 'No one knows. I suppose that when he came here, he must have left her behind.'

'Oh.' Lily flinched and Josefine felt a little guilty. She did not want to upset her sister, but equally, she did not want her to get hurt. Hopefully Josefine had nipped whatever it was in the bud, just in time.

210

'But who knows?' she added, just to be fair. Because really, she had no idea.

However, Josefine continued to feel irritated as she prepared the coffee and the hot chocolate. What was it with Nico Ricci? First, he disrupted Josefine's marriage by leading Gianni astray, and now he appeared to have designs on her sister. She loaded the espresso maker and turned the handle with a sharp twist. *Allora*, she thought. Just let him try.

'Do you have plans for the rest of the day?' she asked Lily when she returned to the table with their drinks and two pastries. There were a lot more on the counter, but some could go in the freezer and some might survive until tomorrow, she supposed. 'Because I wondered if you wanted to come with me to Lerici?'

'Really?' Lily brightened and even gave her a lopsided smile. 'But what about the—?'

'Forget the *caffè*. I am keeping it closed today,' Josefine told her. She drank her espresso in one shot and placed the cup firmly back on the table. 'You have come all this way to see me and so we should spend some more time together before you leave, do you not think?'

'Oh, yes, that would be great.' Lily sipped her hot chocolate more cautiously. 'And is there anything special you wanted to do in Lerici?'

'Mmm.' She was her sister and she seemed to be getting to know her rather well already. Josefine smiled, tore off a piece of croissant and chewed thoughtfully. 'Now that you mention it, Lily, I think I will buy a new dress,' she said. 'For the next time I am invited out to dinner, you know.' She winked.

'With Angelo?' Lily had already demolished her pastry and was wiping her mouth with the napkin.

'Ah, well, we will see.' Josefine toyed with her coffee spoon. 'Who am I?' she demanded.

Lily only blinked at her and did not reply, but that was fine because it was a rhetorical question. 'Some dowdy has-been of a woman who spends all her life wearing an apron and waiting on tables, eh?'

'No, I don't think that's who you are at all.' Lily sounded vehement. She drank some more of her hot chocolate.

'You are right,' said Josefine. 'I have been that woman and now I will be that woman no longer. So, *andiamo*.' She got to her feet. 'Drink up and let's go.'

CHAPTER 29

Lily

2018

Lily was glad to be on the bus with Josefine heading for Lerici. For one thing, she was delighted at the prospect of having some quality time with her sister. Josefine appeared to have taken the fact of Carlotta's pregnancy in her stride – although sneaking a glance at the woman beside her on the bus looking determinedly straight ahead, Lily wasn't entirely convinced. And the other reason . . .

Lily felt stupid. She'd let herself be affected by a few intense glances, a romantic story and a cup of very strong espresso. Maybe the story had been true – she hoped it was true – but what about the rest of it, the bits that Nico hadn't included? What about his past? What about his wife? What about the way in which he had colluded in Gianni's affair, the consequent breakdown of Lily's sister's marriage, and worse, the pregnancy that was – despite her brave face – no doubt secretly breaking Josefine's heart?

213

She gazed out of the window as the little bus wove its way along narrow roads and up and down the hilly countryside. They were passing by large gated villas, the road fringed by olive groves and the scrubland that led down to the sea, and to Lily's delight, they were occasionally rewarded with glimpses of blue, of the glorious Bay of Poets way below.

That was why she was quite glad to be leaving Perlarosa for the day. No more, Lily decided. She had come here for Josefine, and her loyalty was due to her sister, not to some bohemian artisan with dark soulful eyes who made bitter coffee and was prone to great waves of grief and guilt in churches. For the rest of her visit, she decided, she would keep well away.

After about ten minutes, they arrived at the outskirts of Lerici. Lily told Josefine that although she had stayed overnight in the town, she hadn't had the chance to explore.

'Then I will take you on a tour,' Josefine said as they arrived at the central piazza. They jumped down from the bus.

'Great.' Immediately, Lily could smell the sea air. She looked around, searching for the main landmark of Lerici that would give her the sense of direction she wanted – the grey-stone castle standing high on the cliff behind them. And there it was, surrounded by the red roofs and coloured houses of the old town, the harbour and the boats down below.

'But first, the dress.'

Josefine led the way through the busy Piazza Garibaldi to a row of sweet little boutiques and Indian-style shops situated under the arches of the colonnade opposite Lerici's wide promenade and seafront. The scent of incense filled the air, mingling with the fragrance of the fresh peaches outside the greengrocer's opposite and the rosemary *focaccia* from the baker on the corner. Lily was feeling hungry again already.

Josefine seemed very sure of what she wanted. 'No, no.' They swept past the first few boutiques with her sister barely sparing them a glance. 'No, no.' And then she paused.

They were standing outside a tiny shop crammed with dresses, saris, kaftans, silk dressing gowns and scarves in rich colours of purples, reds and blues, spilling from the interior out onto the pavement. They were hung on rails, draped over poles and mannequins, pegged on a makeshift line of rope. The inside of the shop was painted amber and pale gold with terracotta quarry tiles on the floor. Lily looked around her, in awe of the vividness, the sheer opulence of the place.

'Ah, but it is not expensive here,' Josefine whispered. She pointed to one of the rails where the dresses flowed in silky folds to the floor and, together, they went over and began flipping through the fabrics.

'How about this?' Lily pulled out a floaty dress in deep blue and grey with flecks of silver embroidery.

'Mmm.' Josefine put her head to one side, considering. 'It is very elegant.' *Too elegant for me*, she seemed to say.

Lily laughed. 'And so, you will be elegant,' she said.

'You are young,' Josefine said. 'Do you not think it is too young for me?' She frowned.

'No! Definitely not.' Why was she so worried? At fifty-two, her older sister was still a good-looking woman and the dress would look great on her, Lily was sure.

Josefine tried on several dresses and Lily was delighted when she chose the one in blue and grey.

'Not only elegant,' Lily told her, 'but it also goes perfectly with your eyes.'

Having made the purchase, they cut through to the Via Cavour and the Oratorio di San Rocco that stood on the corner.

215

It was a pretty building, with a simple facade of faded ochre and pale rust, a heavy wooden door and stuccoed plasterwork above. Its tower of pink and grey stone was tall and imposing.

'Here we start our tour.' Josefine peered at the information plaque which was written in both Italian and English. 'This oratory was built in 1287, it says here. And the tower was a defence fort.'

'Defence from what?' Lily put her fingertips to the pale stone. 'Or who?' The stone was dusty and crumbled at her touch. It seemed a miracle that the building had survived for so long.

'Oh . . .' Josefine shrugged. 'I suppose all land was for the taking back then. Come inside.'

The floor of the oratory was of black and white marble, the walls were pale green and here again was some exquisite carving, as well as some impressive religious paintings. This was one of the many things that Lily loved about Italy, she thought: the sense of history, the grand but faded architecture of the past.

As they left the church, Josefine's phone rang. She took the call.

Angelo, she mouthed to Lily. She spoke in rapid Italian. Lily caught the odd word and guessed Angelo was asking where she was and why the *caffè* was closed. '*Si, si.*' Josefine rolled her eyes at Lily, but Lily could tell from the tone of her voice that she was still upset and angry.

Continuing to talk at a rapid pace, she indicated to Lily that they should start walking up Via Cavour, which was full of shops and looked narrow and intriguing.

More Italian. Some fervent hand gestures, a sigh and a few of Josefine's expressive snorts of disbelief.

Lily examined her surroundings as they walked on. There

were more little boutiques here, jewellery and souvenir shops and a few restaurants and bars. There were quite a few tourists milling around and Lily found herself wondering what Lerici and Perlarosa were like in the winter. Lerici in particular must have a lot of holiday homes – when she'd booked her night's accommodation, there had been plenty to choose from. Did it become a ghost town then in the winter when all the tourists had gone home?

Josefine was still talking to Angelo, but eventually she said '*ciao, ciao,*' several times and finally ended the call.

She related the conversation to Lily as they walked further up the street. She had told Angelo, she said, about Gianni and Carlotta. And as for the *caffè* . . . 'I reminded him,' she said, 'it was he who told me the *caffè* should not be my entire life. It was he who said I should get out more. He who said I should welcome my sister too.'

'Oh, was it?' Lily gave her a nudge to show she was joking.

'Yes, yes, it was.' Josefine looked penitent. 'Look now.' She pointed to a tunnel on their left. 'Here is the Gallery Shelter – the Tunnel Padula. You must see this.' She led the way inside.

It was long and brightly lit. 'What's it used for?' Lily asked.

'Mainly exhibitions these days,' Josefine told her. 'But it is a piece of history for this town. It was a shelter, during the war. It could house entire families who had been made homeless.'

'Goodness.' Lily tried to imagine.

'It was a situation that continued well after the war too.' Josefine nodded. 'At least until new homes were built.' She glanced around. 'Although there were hygiene problems, as you can guess.'

Lily could. But she was aware that Italy had suffered greatly during the war. For the homeless, this place must have been a

217

godsend. At least it was shelter, and shelter was a basic human need.

They emerged onto the main road right opposite another church. This one too they visited – although it was more ornate and less atmospheric than some of the smaller churches, at least in Lily's opinion – and then they wound their way under crumbling archways and through the maze of narrow backstreets lined with tall colourful houses, their shutters flung open to the sunshine, their balconies hung with washing and trailing greenery, back to the Piazza Garibaldi.

'I am glad now, you know,' Josefine confided as they walked.

'Glad?'

'To have met you,' Josefine said. 'I thought you coming here, bringing in the past, that it would make things worse,' she said. 'But in fact, it has made me feel better – about everything, I mean.'

Lily felt the glow. After their first meeting, she hadn't expected to ever hear Josefine say those words.

'But before you came . . . I did not want it.'

'I understand,' Lily told her.

Josefine stopped walking for a moment and looked straight at her. 'I did not want the reminder,' she said.

Lily nodded. She was grateful that Josefine no longer felt like that; pleased that their relationship had moved on. 'I'm sorry for crashing into your life in the way I did,' she told her. Because she realised now how thoughtless she had been. All she had considered was her own desire to find her sister, her own excitement, her own sense of discovery. She had never fully considered Josefine's feelings, how reluctant she might have been to be found, to be reminded, as she said, of the time when her birth mother had given her away.

But now, of course, like Josefine, she was glad.

From Garibaldi and the magnificent magnolia tree, Josefine showed her a couple more historic piazzas and the legendary Carpaneta Road, which led up to the hills behind Lerici and eventually to Perlarosa, Josefine informed her, adding that they would not be going back that way. Then they went up in the lift to the leafy castle courtyard, which housed various bars and restaurants and which boasted, Josefine said, 'the best view in town'.

It was true. They ordered beer and a Ligurian version of the Sicilian caponata, an aubergine salad with *farinata*, a thin pancake made from chickpea flour, and as they waited for their food, Lily gazed down at the boats lined up in Lerici's harbour, the turquoise of the Adriatic Sea shimmering through the dark green of the pines, and gorgeous San Terenzo on the opposite side of the Bay of Poets. She was beginning to think that there was no ordinary view here in Liguria – every one was stunning.

She turned to Josefine. 'So did you tell Angelo you had bought a dress?'

'I did.'

'And?'

Josefine gave a little shrug. '"Where are you going?" he asked me.'

They paused as the waiter brought their food and drinks.

'*Grazie*,' said Josefine.

'And you said . . .' prompted Lily. She took a forkful of her aubergine, which was rich, silky and delicious.

'I said, "Out to dinner, Angelo. I am going to find myself a new life, you know. Just watch me."' She straightened her back and dug into her food.

'I bet he was impressed,' Lily said. She could tell how much effort Josefine was putting into remaining cheerful today, and her respect for her sister increased.

'You know, he was.' Josefine chewed thoughtfully. 'He said he could not wait to see it. He said, "Shall we make it tonight, or tomorrow?"'

CHAPTER 30

Italy

2018

One day, he rows with Stefano and Tommaso alongside the wooded mountain and grey-stratified granite cliff, over to Punta Chiappa. Boys' day out, Adele said and laughed her throaty laugh. Well now. His son chose a very different woman from his mother to be his wife. Where Caterina was quiet and steady, Adele is a thunderstorm; never still, always ready with a sharp retort or a joke she finds hilarious. He shakes his head, has to smile. But Stefano's choice was a free one and he respects that. This is the woman his son loves. And is love not everything?

Ahead of them, Punta Chiappa looks like a half-submerged crocodile, long and craggy, its mouth pointing out to sea.

There is a pleasure in the pathless woods,
There is a rapture on the lonely shore,
There is society, where none intrudes,
By the deep Sea, and music in its roar:
I love not Man the less, but Nature more.

He says the words in his head, but not out loud because Stefano will think he's lost his mind. He is not a boy for poetry and the words are English words, written by an English poet. Lord Byron, it was, who penned those lines back in the 1820s when he stayed with a local count and fell in love with Punta Chiappa and Liguria.

He, who struggles with the English language still, learnt and memorised them because they are special words and always will be.

They moor the little green and blue boat by the wooden jetty and walk past a grey cormorant drying its wings, up the steep steps to Punta Chiappa, Tommaso running ahead, him bringing up the rear.

Ouf . . . He is soon out of breath. Pausing, he gazes down through the oaks and pines at the boat, La Eugenia, his father's old boat, named after his mother of course, bobbing merrily in the turquoise sea. Every time he comes here, he thanks the gods above that he still can. It is rough and untamed, the Punta Chiappa, that is its charm, but also a potential downfall, at least for the older generations, for whom balance no longer comes so easy. He, certo, is now one of them.

They pass the Pozzo mosaic on the altar, dedicated to the Stella Maris, depicting the Madonna and child, Mary running to the aid of some fishermen caught by the storm. And he pauses for a moment to admire the work, and to pay his respects to those men of the sea who were not so fortunate, a few of his ancestors being among that number.

He and the other two know where the best places are for sitting and for swimming and so he settles himself on the natural rock bench that has fashioned itself over the years, through wind and storm. Stefano takes Tommaso down the ladder into the sea, while he watches the tiny natural waterfall, the slow motion of the waves lapping the base of the rock, splashing over the ledges like the best kind of music. The water here is clear as glass, the shadowy outlines of boulders visible below the oily surface. And there are fish – sea bream, grouper, amberjack. He knows about fish, if nothing else.

He stretches out his legs, leans back and gives a sigh of contentment.

Here, he has always felt free. He came here as a boy with his own father and then with friends, diving into the ocean for thrills, the shock coursing adrenaline through his body. Here, he once stood on a rocky ledge above the water and felt strong and unafraid. Just look at it — the world out there waiting for him . . . All he had to do was go and find it. All he had to do was grasp every opportunity, not allow himself to be held back, not hold himself back, because, allora, *you could be your own worst enemy.*

Si, si . . . Anything was possible. Everything was there for the taking. It was in the tang of the salt air, in the rhythm of the tide, in the ripple of the sun-speckled water as he looked out to sea. And what has he done with all those possibilities? Bene. *He has had his moments, he thinks now. Once, life was an adventure and adventure and freedom go hand in hand, is that not so?*

He thinks of that moment when, newly married, he stood outside the church at San Rocco. He glanced at the open sea with the briefest note of wistfulness, because he had chosen his future and it was Caterina. Did he mistreat her? he wonders now. Perhaps. He underestimated her, for sure.

Now, though, is a winding down. There is time now — almost too much time. Time to walk, to sit, to recall. He thinks of those old sea explorers, those men who achieved so much. Camogli has always been a town that men left — and some, certo, *did not return. Others . . . Once again, he sighs.*

He watches Stefano strike out into the waves. He watches his grandson clamber over the granite to stand on the rocky ledge where he also once stood, and he sees Tommaso reach out his arms as if to embrace the world.

And there it is, he thinks. He clenches his fist and holds it close to his heart, gnarled, brown, weathered by the sun and the rain and the sea. The exploring — it is up to others now.

CHAPTER 31

Lily

2018

After lunch, Josefine suggested they take a stroll along the promenade under the pine trees towards San Terenzo.

'This walk, it is called the Walk of Fame,' Josefine told Lily.

'Why is that?'

Josefine showed her the plaques placed at regular intervals along the way. 'They celebrate the poets honoured by the LericiPea *Golfo dei Poeti* poetry prize,' she told her. 'The competition began here after the war when Enrico Pea wanted to find a way to keep poetry in Italian hearts.'

'I see.' Lily was intrigued. 'Tell me more.'

'*Allora*, he partnered with a publisher at the time and they founded the LericiPea competition for unpublished poets,' she said. 'Since then, many of the winners have become famous in Italy. Giorgio Caproni and Maria Luisa Spaziani, for example. I am no expert in poetry . . .' Josefine gave a little shrug. 'But it is a beautiful tradition, I think.'

'Oh, yes,' Lily agreed. 'And isn't it the perfect place for it — the Bay of Poets.' She already knew that Byron and Shelley had lived and died here. And D. H. Lawrence had lived in Fiascherino, so the lady in the tourist information office had told her. Lily could certainly see the attraction, how those British writers must have been inspired by the landscape and why they had stayed. Who wouldn't be tempted?

'It is.' Josefine eyed her speculatively. 'Many of your British writers came to visit this area, you know. Henry James, E. M. Forster, Virginia Woolf . . .' Josefine was reeling off the names. 'And not just British writers, naturally. The *Golfo dei Poeti* — it has been a favourite residence of many Italian authors and artists too. Marinetti, the film director Mario Soldati . . . People you have probably not even heard of,' she said, not unkindly.

'Goodness,' murmured Lily. And she was quite right, Lily hadn't.

'Eugenio Montale even dedicated a poem to our little village.' Josefine was beaming. 'You see how it is?'

'Yes.' Lily saw.

Fascinating little market stalls lined Lerici's promenade, rocks and little ladders led down to the sea, and the dark pink houses of San Terenzo glowed invitingly in the distance. Turning back to face the castle, Lily showed Josefine where she had stayed among the jumble of orange rooftops and red alleyways of the old town. It had been less than a week ago, but it seemed so much longer. A lot had happened, she reminded herself. She had met and got to know her sister, for starters. And then, the silversmith . . . But she wouldn't think about Nico or the effect he'd had on her. She had read too much into it and now, after what Josefine had told her, she must let it go.

Josefine nodded approvingly. 'It is a nice town, Lerici,' she said, 'although of course, it is not Perlarosa.'

Lily had to agree. Lerici was charming. But Perlarosa – it had a way of drawing you into its heart.

Josefine showed Lily the dark orange and rather imposing Hotel Shelley and pointed out other grand villas and significant landmarks on the way.

'You are a very good guide,' Lily teased her.

Josefine kept a straight face. 'I missed my vocation,' she agreed.

After they passed the tamarisk trees and the Belvedere della Marineria, they reached a sandy beach. Although it was still early in the season, people were enjoying the afternoon sun and a few were swimming in the sea. 'Brr,' said Josefine. 'They are crazy, *no*?'

Lily laughed. The water was still chilly, agreed, but she herself had taken a few dips off the rocks beyond Perlarosa harbour – she'd been unable to resist the pull of the perfect turquoise water. 'It's positively balmy compared to the UK,' she told Josefine.

'Really?' Josefine shivered again.

'Really.'

They passed the Hotel Byron. 'Not to be outdone,' said Josefine. 'Byron, Shelley, they all live on.'

'Doing their bit for tourism,' Lily agreed.

Pretty soon they were in San Terenzo itself, which was as picturesque as it had promised to be from a distance. There were more elegant villas draped with bougainvillea to admire, tamarisks and pines to stroll under, and a constant view of the sea, where smart yachts were moored.

'And to continue in my role as tour guide,' Josefine said.

'This was the actual Shelley residence. He lived here with his wife Mary.' She pointed to a simple white villa on the waterfront with elegant arches and an exterior mosaic floor.

'Mary Shelley – she wrote *Frankenstein*,' Lily exclaimed, glad to finally add something to the literary discussion.

'*Si, si*, and here,' – Josefine gestured to more photographs and information plaques on the promenade – 'you can read about what the place meant to them both.'

Lily read the text. They were so young, only in their twenties, when they arrived here in 1822. She read about Shelley's sense of enchantment and amazement, his desire to 'heal the wounds of his soul' through the crystalline waters and clear skies of the bay. And then he came upon the Villa Magni on the waterfront, surrounded by a jungle of shrubs and lapped by the waves, and he made up his mind to live there. Lily was as transfixed as he too must have been. But sadly, he hadn't been healed by this place. He had recurring nightmares and hallucinations and when his boat got caught in a summer storm after a meeting with Byron in Livorno that same July, Percy Shelley died at sea in the bay he loved so much.

It was a sad story. But of course, many others had felt the magic before Lily. The bay was a poetic legacy. And San Terenzo was another village that had it all. A castle on a hill, ancient bell towers and churches, houses painted in ochre, terracotta and dusty pink, a picturesque harbour and the endless and tragic blue of the sea.

Later, as they strolled back under the pine trees to the Piazza Garibaldi, Josefine let out a sigh. 'I had such a nice time today, Lily,' she said. 'I had forgotten what it was like. To relax, to chat, to walk, to do something simple like buy a new dress.'

But her cheerful guard slipped for a moment and Lily noticed the sadness in her eyes.

'It's been lovely,' Lily agreed. 'But are you okay?' She touched her sister's arm. She wanted to tell Josefine that it was all right to be sad and angry, that it would take time before things got better, but who was she to assume that would be the case?

Josefine nodded. 'Why do you think our mother did not tell you about me?' she asked Lily. 'Was she ashamed?'

It was an abrupt change of subject, but Lily guessed that now that Josefine was processing things in her mind, more questions would surface that she must do her best to answer honestly. For so long Josefine hadn't let the past in, and now she had to take things one step at a time in order to still feel safe perhaps.

'She wasn't ashamed of you,' Lily assured her. She didn't know that for certain, of course, but she was confident she was right.

'But she was ashamed of being an unmarried mother perhaps?' Josefine shot her a sidelong glance.

'Maybe.' Lily had already told her they weren't close, so she wouldn't know the answer to that. 'But she never talked very much about the past.' No doubt she spent a lot of time thinking about it, though, which might account for that dreaminess Lily had seen so often in her mother's eyes.

'Like me then?' Josefine's laugh was hollow.

'You are a bit like her,' Lily ventured. 'But I think she was very good at keeping secrets. You had to be a secret – at first – because of the times she lived in. After that . . .' Lily shrugged. 'Perhaps the secret became so tightly locked inside her that it was almost unreachable. She wouldn't have talked about it then, I suppose.' And especially not to her second daughter, Lily thought. But Lily's father . . . he must have always known.

228

Josefine frowned. 'It makes sense,' she said. 'But by doing that, our mother almost denied you a sister, yes?'

'Almost, yes.' They smiled at one another.

And that made sense to Lily too. She doubted that their mother would ever have seen it from Lily's – or Josefine's – point of view. 'But she kept the drawing she'd made of you,' Lily reminded Josefine. 'She kept it close her entire life. That must mean a lot.'

Josefine considered. '*Certo*, it means a lot to me,' she admitted. And Lily was glad. It had been worth it then – if only for that.

They crossed the street onto the Piazza Garibaldi and Lily saw Josefine put on her determined face once again. But it was all good. Josefine had opened up and Lily thought she understood some of what her sister was going through.

'Time to go home,' said Josefine. She linked her arm into Lily's.

And they caught the bus back to Perlarosa.

CHAPTER 32

Lily

2018

Lily had some work to do that morning – a project that she'd almost completed but which still had a few loose ends that needed tying up. She had lunch at Parodi's, along with a snatched conversation with Josefine while she was cooking, and then made her way out to the rocks beyond the harbour to sit in the sun and read. Her trip was nearly at an end, but she had achieved far more than she'd hoped. She was beginning to feel a strong connection to Josefine. If only they didn't live so far apart . . .

She took a circuitous route to get to the rocks, wanting to avoid the silversmith's and yet hoping to catch a glimpse of him at the same time. Everything seemed so complicated. Lily had taken Josefine's words to heart and yet she still couldn't help feeling curious about him. And drawn to him too. She wasn't quite able to shake the thought of his dark and intense gaze from her mind.

As she made her way back towards her B & B late that afternoon, she realised that now would be a good time to collect the pendant – if the silversmith had finished it, that was. It didn't quite fit in with her plan to avoid him today, but Lily must give the gemstone to Josefine before she left Perlarosa, whether the pendant was finished or not. And besides . . .

But as she walked up the boat-lined street from the small harbour, she saw that the workshop was closed. Lily shook off the small dip of disappointment and instead continued up to the church and then out to the promontory where she had seen Nico arguing with Carlotta. From here, as she looked up, she could see the crumbling facade of the little chapel she'd noticed before high on the rocks above her and, on impulse, she decided to find it.

There were no signposts, but there were so few streets in Perlarosa that after wandering uphill through the winding alleyways in the right general direction for just ten minutes, she located the chapel on the top of the hill. Two olive trees in terracotta pots stood either side of the doorway, adding to the immediate sense of peace that seemed to Lily to hang over the ancient building. The pale stone of the little oratory was glowing pinkish golden in the late afternoon sun; the building was symmetrical with a small window above the wooden door, the plasterwork crumbling but still mostly intact. Lily was pleased to see that the wooden door was wide open, so she went inside.

The interior of the chapel was cool, simple and beautiful. There were few adornments, but Lily could make out the remnants of faded yellow and red frescos on the domed tunnel ceiling which was pale blue like the sky outside. She stood still on the black and white marble tiles for a few moments, absorbing the atmosphere, breathing in the peace.

231

When she emerged, Lily spotted the red-bricked belvedere area only a few metres away and made her way there to lean on the wall and look out towards the ruffled navy of the sea and Portovenere. She liked the look of Portovenere. There were boats that took day visitors over there, she knew; she'd seen them in Lerici and perhaps they departed from Perlarosa too?

'You should go there before you leave.' The voice was low, too close. She hadn't heard him coming. He had crept up on her.

Lily spun around. 'Hey . . .' For a split second she felt a jump of nerves and then he smiled, shrugged and took a step away, and she found herself smiling back at him. It seemed that it was hard to avoid people in Perlarosa.

'Portovenere?' she asked.

'*Si, si.*' Nico the silversmith stood beside her, leant on the wall and looked out, just as she was doing. The sun was still warm and it was an intoxicating view. She was conscious of his proximity, his arm resting on the stone only centimetres from her own.

'I was just thinking the same thing,' she admitted.

He half turned to face her. His dark hair was as messed up as usual, she noted, and he looked tired. 'I could take you in my boat, if you want?' he said carelessly.

Lily's heart skipped. 'The same boat you came to Perlarosa in?' She tried to keep her voice light.

'The very same.' He winced. 'Although she is not so good-looking – I repaired her several times since then.'

Lily longed to say 'yes', but then she thought of Josefine and what her sister had told her. She must stay strong. 'I don't think I'll have time,' she said warily. 'I'm leaving the day after tomorrow. And Josefine . . .' Her voice trailed. He would know

232

quite well that Josefine was busy in the *caffè*, that she did not claim so much of Lily's time. But presumably, he would also know that he wasn't Josefine's favourite man in Perlarosa.

Sure enough, he nodded. 'People – they have spoken to you about me,' he said.

'What do you mean?' she bluffed.

'There is no need to pretend.' He sounded matter-of-fact about it. 'Your sister – I am sure she is very angry with me right now. And I cannot blame her.'

Lily decided that with this man, honesty was the only policy. 'You're right,' she said. 'Josefine warned me about you.'

'And so yes, she should,' he agreed. 'Those who come into my life . . .' He bunched a fist. 'Bad things happen to them. Perhaps I am a curse, hmm?'

Into his life . . . The phrase performed a little dance inside her head. 'A curse?' Was he joking? But one glance at his set expression told her he was serious.

'Exactly,' he said.

'I'm sure that's not the case,' she said quickly. It was a horrible thought, and she hated that he might believe such a thing.

He shrugged.

But, 'What bad things?' She had to ask. Was this the darkness Josefine had hinted at? Was this something to do with the wife he had left behind?

'Never mind.' He closed his eyes as if the light of the day was suddenly too much for him. 'What has happened, it cannot be undone, it does not matter how much we want it.'

Lily was so tempted to ask him more. But did she really want to know? And whatever it was, the whole thing seemed so painful for him . . . She didn't need him to relive it just to satisfy her curiosity.

233

He would tell her when and if he was ready, Lily thought. She wouldn't press him. For a few moments they were quiet, both gazing out to sea.

'Do you often come up here?' she asked him. It was a delightful spot and she was sorry that she'd only just discovered it. It seemed a good place in which to think, to reflect. The little oratory stood proud, right at the very top and tip of the village. It was probably the first church of Perlarosa, she thought, built to provide a view of those who might be approaching as well as for worship.

'Often enough,' he said. 'I live just over there.' He pointed to a wooden door bleached pale brown and white by the elements. The house was small, originally painted pale terracotta perhaps, but like most of the houses here in Liguria, the paint was flaking, making the house look shabby but almost impossibly romantic. It was old and it was simple, but still, the house looked cared for. There was a black wrought-iron balcony, a thriving blue jasmine winding itself through the railings, a well-polished step and the dark green shutters that were characteristic of this village. And it was right next door to the Santa Maria Chapel.

'Oh.' She shook her head. In trying to avoid him, she'd walked right into his lair.

'It is tranquil, yes,' he said. 'But wherever you go, someone will find you.'

Was he talking about himself? He had wanted to escape, he had already told her so. Lily had a thought. Or was he referring to a person from his past? 'Are you talking about your sister-in-law Carlotta?' she asked. 'I saw you arguing down by the rocks the other day.'

For a moment she thought he wouldn't reply. Then, 'Carlotta,

234

si.' He swore softly. 'There has been no peace in Perlarosa since she came.'

This put things in a different light, Lily couldn't help thinking. At least as far as Nico was concerned. 'Why did she come?' she asked. Maybe she was about to find out something concrete about him at last.

He shot her a glance. 'Perhaps she wanted to make problems,' he said. 'Perhaps she wants to make me feel more guilty than I do already. With Carlotta, who knows?'

Guilty about what? Lily frowned. But she couldn't ask that question – it was far too direct and he'd clam up for ever. 'And Gianni?' she asked instead. 'You two are friends, aren't you?'

'Gianni is a good man.' He continued to gaze out to sea. 'But even a good man, when he is very unhappy, is open to taking the wrong path, *no*?'

'I suppose.' Though Lily wasn't sure that Josefine would see it quite like that.

'I warned him about her.' He let out a sigh. 'But men, they do not always listen. And Carlotta – she can be very persuasive.'

Hmm. Lily could see that his version of events fitted with what Josefine had told her – and yet it was also very different. 'And now?' she asked him. 'Now that Carlotta is pregnant?' Because he must know. Maybe that was even why they were arguing?

He looked taken aback by this. 'Josefine – she knows?' he said at last.

'She knows.'

Again, he muttered a low curse.

Once again, Lily turned to face him. 'Can't you persuade Gianni and Carlotta to leave Perlarosa?' That at least would make things less awful for her sister, she thought.

'It is a lot to ask,' he said.

'Yes.' Lily had to concede that this was true. 'But can't Gianni see what it would do to Josefine if they have the baby here? If they live here together as a family and she sees them every day?' Because it was, after all, such a small place.

He eyed her thoughtfully. 'You have not lived here in Perlarosa for many days, Lily,' he said. 'And yet you seem to know so much about many people.'

Lily took this as a criticism. She bristled. 'I don't know much about you,' she said pointedly.

'And you do not want to,' he returned. 'Rather, you would like to avoid me.'

Touché. She couldn't deny it.

He laughed.

Lily couldn't help smiling back at him – again. 'Yes and no,' she said.

'Ah,' he said. 'Yes and no. *Certo*, of course, that is exactly it.'

Lily absorbed this. The man seemed to have the ability to see into her head, which was unnerving to say the least. 'It's not just that people have been talking,' she said. 'I only have one full day left before I go back home, so I honestly don't think I can fit it in. Portovenere, I mean.'

'You need to go back to work?' he asked her.

'Not exactly.' Lily explained that she worked freelance and mostly from home. 'But I often need to visit businesses too,' she said. 'It's part of my remit.'

'Your remit?' He seemed interested so Lily explained what she did for a living.

'Your work – it sounds like a challenge.'

'Yes, it is,' she agreed. 'But I love it.'

'That is the important thing,' he said.

236

Nico had been nodding in all the right places and Lily sensed that although he was playing the part of village silversmith – and of course he was exactly that – he might also understand more about other kinds of businesses than she would have imagined. She wouldn't ask, though, she decided; anything about his past seemed strictly out of bounds. But it might explain why his English was so very good.

'I should be going.' Lily turned. But where was she going to? Josefine was out with Angelo tonight so she had no dinner companion. 'Oh, and . . .' *The pendant*, she thought. In the end, she'd seen him and yet she'd nearly forgotten to ask.

'It is almost complete.'

'Ah.' She would pick it up just before she left then. She would give it to Josefine as a parting gift.

Nico inclined his dark head. 'And if you change your mind . . .' he began.

'Change my mind?' Lily still had the pendant in her head.

'About Portovenere,' he said.

'Why?' She turned back to face him. Suddenly, she felt brave. After all, she was about to leave this place and who knew how long it would be before she returned? 'I mean, why me? Josefine said you don't have much time for people.'

He pulled a face. 'She is right again, of course,' he said. 'But you . . .'

Lily waited. She hoped he wouldn't think that she was fishing for compliments. It was just . . . she really wanted to know.

'You remind me of someone,' he said. 'I thought it the first time I saw you. An aura perhaps. A presence.' He shrugged. 'I do not know what.'

Lily waited for him to go on. An aura? A presence? She let his words sink into her.

237

'You shocked me into wanting to know you. And when I spoke with you . . .' He let his words hang.

Shocked him? It was a strange way of putting it. Lily was intrigued.

'Although for me too it was – it is – a matter of yes and no.'

Lily stared at him. There was nothing simple about this man. 'Who?' she whispered. 'Who do I remind you of?'

But already he had turned away. 'It was another life,' he said. 'Another place. Another time. And as for me, I was a different man.'

CHAPTER 33

Josefine

2018

That evening, Josefine put on the new dress and threw a wrap around her shoulders because it was only April after all, although warm for the time of year. Rather self-consciously, she headed out, making her way towards Angelo's place. She wished that Lily was here to spur her on, to make her feel that looking elegant was her right, rather than an impossible aspiration.

Lily, she realised, as she crossed the piazza under the ilex trees, had brought a new and unexpected perspective into her life, in more ways than one. And in less than a week . . . It was almost unbelievable.

Today, it had been back to the usual for Josefine. She'd spent the day in the *caffè*, making drinks, serving snacks, clearing tables – which would not suit everyone, she knew, but which held plenty of positives for Josefine. She liked the process of preparing food and drinks for an interesting mix of people; she relished giving them this short period of time in which to relax in a warm and welcoming atmosphere. She did not mind the small talk – as long as it did not go on for too long. And here, she was her own boss. She especially enjoyed the clearing up, creating a sense of order from chaos, putting things back in their proper places. It was soothing and gave her time to think.

As for that, all too often this week she had found herself thinking about her relationship with Lily. And now . . . She had let this new and un-looked-for sister of hers into her life much more fully than she'd first intended. Face it, she had not intended to let her in at all.

Josefine turned right at the end of the piazza and walked under the arches. Fortunately, there weren't too many people around to catch sight of her in this dress and speculate. Josefine loved Perlarosa, but it was a small village and people liked to talk.

Lily was so open, so refreshing, that Josefine couldn't help being drawn to her. And when she contemplated how much trouble Lily had gone to – in looking for her, by coming to Italy to find her – she was deeply touched. No one in Josefine's life had ever seemed to take so much trouble before.

The sun was already dipping in the west and Josefine paused to savour the early evening yellow light that added a golden glow to the red roofs and pink houses. In the past, when she'd thought about her birth parents, she had always felt angry. She didn't need them, she had got on just fine without them. Only . . . She had never imagined siblings – a girl or a boy out there who might share some of her DNA, who hadn't been responsible in any way for what had happened to Josefine and who therefore could not be blamed for any of it.

She turned left into another red alleyway. This one led up

240

to the little chapel on the cliff – Santa Maria, the first church of Perlarosa – if you followed it through, but she was heading left where Angelo's house was tucked behind it, with – like most of the houses in Perlarosa – its own slant of a sea view. She had thought she did not need blood relatives, but when her parents had turned around one day and said they wanted to talk to her, that they had decided to move to Australia, 'now that Dario has a family of his own', it had hit home. 'We do not want to miss out on being grandparents,' they had said. 'It is not that we do not care for you.'

Josefine had filled in the gaps. It was simply that they cared for Dario more.

And why not? It was natural. She had known it her whole life. If Dario had stayed nearby, made a home here, it would have been different, perhaps Josefine would not have felt it so starkly.

She paused to savour the sea breeze that she could feel up here. It was always fresher than down in the piazza; she could understand why Angelo still lived here, though it must be hard to go on with so many memories of his wife Ilaria all around.

Growing up, Josefine had always known that Dario was the favourite, the special one. And why wouldn't he be? She had always been very fond of him herself, especially when he was a baby and she had rocked him in his pram, made him giggle by tickling his tummy. But that was okay. She, Josefine, had been chosen. She had been wanted. That's what they had always told her. And they had been good parents. They had not mistreated her, they had looked after her, clothed and fed her. As for the rest . . . One could not always take that for granted, was that not so?

It was just that when it came to a choice . . . Josefine felt second best. When they left, they bequeathed her the *caffè* (they had not *had* to do that, she reasoned) and at first, they wrote and phoned regularly to check she was okay, to send photographs of 'the family' (which did not include Josefine, not any more). But lately, she heard from them much less often. It felt cruel. It felt almost as if they had swept her out of their lives. As if she had always been a replacement; never quite the real thing. Josefine knew quite well that this was not always the case for children who had been adopted – far from it. She knew that so many children were loved, wherever they had come from. And perhaps it was she, Josefine, who had not made enough effort to keep in touch, who was oversensitive on the whole subject. But . . .

As she walked on along the red alleyway between the skinny town houses, Josefine tried not to think about Gianni and Carlotta. Angelo had brought the subject up again this morning. 'Do not let it get to you,' he had said and then sworn under his breath so that Josefine knew it had certainly got to him. She hoped he wouldn't try and talk about it again tonight. Tonight, she wanted to pretend to be free of all worries. She would will Carlotta out of existence if she could, but since that was impossible, then pretence was the only way forward.

Josefine knocked on the battered wooden door and almost immediately it was flung open by Sienna. She was a sweet child with long dark curly hair and brown almond-shaped eyes just like her mother's. She must remind Angelo of Ilaria every day, Josefine found herself thinking.

'Sienna! *Ciao!*' Josefine shot her a big smile. Of course, Sienna had been deeply affected by her mother's illness and subsequent death. She had crept around the village like a mouse for a few weeks afterwards, but gradually the careful nurturing from her father, and from her schoolteacher – because Angelo had told Josefine how kind she had been – and close neighbours and friends like Paola, who lived next door to the two of them, had certainly helped in her recovery.

That had been two years ago. Now, Sienna gave the appearance of being a well-balanced and cheerful girl, though perhaps a little young for her years. No harm in that, though, Josefine thought. It was a shame that many children grew up too quickly.

'Josefine!' Sienna threw herself into her arms and Josefine held her close, relishing the life and the warmth of her. How she loved the trust and innocence of the young . . .

'How are you, *cara*?' Josefine asked. 'How was school today, darling?'

'Okay.' Sienna drew back from their embrace. 'Hey . . . I love your dress.' She touched it tentatively and then gazed up at Josefine and smiled. 'You look beautiful.'

'Well, thank you very much, little one.' Josefine was moved. She gave a twirl and immediately felt better about the dress. Lily had been quite right after all.

'Papa will be down in a minute. Come inside.' Sienna took her hand. 'I want to show you my dolls' house.'

She led the way into the small sitting room. The dolls' house had pride of place in the corner and Josefine had to smile. It was so typical of Angelo. He would not care about visitors and preserving any sense of adult space. It would be much more important that Sienna could have her dolls' house exactly where she wished.

It could be opened from the front with one large door, and Sienna knelt down and opened it now, revealing all the rooms simultaneously. Each one was complete with tiny sticks of furniture and in the kitchen there was even a fruit bowl with oranges and lemons as well as a saucepan and a fryer.

'It's amazing . . .' Josefine knelt down beside her to take a better look. 'Real furniture, pictures on the walls . . .' she marvelled.

'And people.' Carefully, Sienna took three miniature figures from the kitchen. 'A papa, a mama and a little girl.'

Josefine felt her chest tighten. Bless the child. 'So there are.' She ran her fingers along the roof of the house. 'Very skilful craftsmanship,' she murmured. But the dolls' house made her feel sad.

'Do you like it?' Sienna rocked back on her heels.

'Oh, yes, it is very fine.' Josefine peered in closer. The bed had a miniature purple coverlet and there was a dressing table with a gleaming mirror.

'Papa made it,' Sienna said proudly. 'He gave it to me for my birthday, you know.'

'Truly? Then isn't he the clever one?' Josefine had no idea that Angelo had either the time or the skill to create such a masterpiece. And she was surprised he hadn't mentioned it to her. She had known about Sienna's birthday, a few weeks ago, but she had been too busy to leave the *caffè* for the little girl's party and she regretted that now. She had given her a present, of course – a little bracelet that Sienna had seemed to love – but she wished she had gone to the party anyway and closed the *caffè* just as she had done yesterday. Angelo was right. The *caffè* had taken over. If she was not careful, there would be nothing else in her life at all.

'Yes, very clever,' Sienna agreed.

She was still at that age, Josefine found herself thinking,

244

when parents could be clever and admired, before children became teenagers and took another view entirely.

'This is me.' Sienna picked up the little girl doll.

'Ah, yes, she has your dark curly hair, I see.'

Sienna picked up the male doll. 'And this is Papa.'

'*Ciao*, Papa,' Josefine said. And then in a low, growly voice. '*Ciao*, Sienna.'

Sienna laughed. They both looked at the third doll, the mama doll. Josefine did not know what to say. It must have been hard for Angelo, she thought, when it came to the creation of the family of dolls. He had not discussed it with her, though – she hadn't even known he was making the dolls' house. Was that because he didn't want her advice? Or could it be that she was always so full of her own problems, her own concerns, that there was no time for Angelo to ever voice any of his?

'This is not my mama.' Sienna picked up the doll. 'Papa said it could be, if I wanted. But it cannot. Because my mama, she is in heaven.'

Josefine melted. The poor lamb, she thought. And how sensible of Angelo to give Sienna the choice in the matter. 'Yes, *cara*, she is.' She reached out and touched the child's warm cheek with her palm.

But the dolls' house, the perfect family with their perfect furniture, tugged at her heart and she could feel her eyes starting to fill.

'Josi.'

She looked up to see Angelo standing in the doorway. The way he was watching her, watching Sienna . . . She felt embarrassed, caught out somehow. Josefine fought for composure.

'Angelo, *ciao*.' He looked very smart in dark trousers and

245

jacket with a white open-necked shirt. Josefine struggled to get to her feet in the long dress she wasn't accustomed to wearing.

He moved forwards and reached out a hand to help her. 'You look amazing,' he told her.

'You do not look so bad yourself,' she returned and, thankfully, the moment of high emotion passed.

Sienna started complaining about having to go to bed and, right on cue, there was a knock on the door and Paola bustled in.

'Will you read me a story, Josefine?' Sienna begged.

'*Allora . . .*' Josefine hesitated. She would like to, but she also knew that Angelo had made a reservation.

'I will read you a story, little one.' Paola smiled. Her own children were grown up now and Josefine guessed that she enjoyed looking after Sienna and helping Angelo out – and he was lucky to have her.

Josefine and Angelo both kissed Sienna goodnight.

'Next time,' Josefine murmured in the little girl's ear. 'I promise.' And she watched as Paola took Sienna's hand and led her up the stairs.

Angelo glanced at his watch. 'Shall we?' he said.

'Yes,' said Josefine. She took a deep breath. She was used to being with Angelo, but somehow everything felt different tonight.

'Out of town this time,' Angelo told her as they left the house.

Which was, Josefine thought, given the dress and all, a blessed relief.

CHAPTER 34

Josefine

2018

The restaurant was simply furnished with low lighting and an intimate atmosphere and it was quiet tonight, as they sat opposite one another at a small table for two. They ordered a bottle of Vermentino and two pasta dishes — a *pansotti* with walnut sauce for Josefine and a *tocco de funzi*, a Genovese mushroom ragu, for Angelo. *Pansotti* was one of Josefine's favourite types of *ravioli*, stuffed with ricotta, fresh herbs and greens, and the crisp dry wine set the dish off to perfection. Anyhow, she thought, it was such a treat not having to cook for a change. Angelo was right: she should take more time out doing this kind of thing with her friends.

As they ate, they chatted comfortably about this and that, as they always did. It amazed Josefine that she never seemed to run out of conversation with Angelo. They could move from village life to world politics to a recipe for ragu in a nanosecond.

After they'd eaten their meal and almost finished the wine, Angelo put his hand on hers and Josefine knew he was about to say something serious. She tensed.

'Can I ask you, Josi?' he said. 'Do you still miss Gianni?'

So that was it. 'Not as much as I should do, no,' she said. Which said a lot.

In many ways it had been a relief not to have to worry where he was, what he was doing; not to nag him to help more in the *caffè*, not to cook dinner if she did not have the energy. And as for what went on in the bedroom . . . Since they stopped trying for a baby, since she had passed the age at which it was still possible to conceive, it had become just another one of those chores which she would avoid if she could.

Of course, she missed the companionship – they had been a team, even if a rather dysfunctional one – and now she was on her own for sure. But . . . 'It is not what you think,' she told Angelo. 'I am not jealous of Carlotta because of Gianni. I am jealous because she is carrying his child.'

Angelo nodded. 'I understand,' he said. He squeezed her hand before letting it go.

'The thought of seeing her belly grow as her time gets near . . .' Josefine shuddered. 'The thought of seeing them together as a family, pushing a pram through the streets of our village, having picnics on the rocks in the summertime . . .' She shook her head. She would be even more reluctant to go out than she was already. She would become a complete recluse, tied to the *caffè* by so much more than her apron strings. 'I cannot do it, Angelo.'

'And if they will not leave Perlarosa?' His voice was low. 'Because, *certo*, you cannot make them, Josi.'

'Then I will go myself,' she said.

He stared at her. 'What?'

For a moment, Josefine remained silent, as she took a sip of her wine. Had she shocked him, upset him even? His expression was giving nothing away. However, Josefine had been giving this matter a lot of consideration over the past two days. It was, she'd decided, the only way.

'You would leave the *caffè*?' He raised an eyebrow. But he was watching her very seriously.

Josefine shrugged. 'It was you who said it should not be everything to me. I can sell it. Why not? I can use the money to buy a different *caffè* somewhere else. It does not rule me. It does not own me.'

'Heaven forbid.' Angelo rolled his eyes.

'*Allora*, it could be part of my new beginning, who knows?' Angelo was frowning now.

'You know that the Caffè Parodi – it is not in a good position as far as running costs and finances are concerned.' Josefine had hinted at this to Angelo before. Accounting was not one of her strengths and it had not been a strength of her parents either.

'*Sì* . . .'

'And after all,' she continued. 'What is there in Perlarosa for me?' She waited for him to say something in answer to this but he did not. And it was true. Perlarosa was such a small hamlet and she knew everyone. Would it not be nice to go to some place where she knew no one for a change, to be anonymous and unobserved? That was the only real way she could make a fresh start, reimagine herself a little perhaps, present a new Josefine to the world. The new Josefine might even have fewer scars.

'I would miss you.' Angelo looked sad. 'And Sienna – she would miss you too.'

She shot him a warning look. *No using your daughter as a weapon for emotional blackmail*, it said. Angelo would get the message. She had known he would not like it, but that was below the belt.

'You are a good friend, Angelo,' was what she actually said. 'And of course, I would miss you too – both of you.' She offered him a weak smile. 'But maybe I will not be so very far away, hmm? We can still meet from time to time.' She gestured at their surroundings. 'Go out to dinner. Even to the cinema, huh?'

But Angelo still looked glum. 'It will not be the same,' he said.

'No, it will not.' Which was precisely the point – did he not see?

Later, after they had left the restaurant and taken a cab back to Perlarosa, they walked the short distance from the taxi rank towards the *caffè*. It was a balmy night, Josefine could smell the scent of spring flowers in the air, and she thought about how the season would soon be here in earnest, and her busiest time of the year would begin – in a matter of days now, she supposed. Already, she had noticed an increase in the number of visitors. Liguria, and especially the Bay of Poets, was a popular place in both spring and summer.

'Lily will be fast asleep by now.' Josefine looked up at the house, as they passed the B & B where she was staying. And very soon, she thought, her new sister would be gone.

'Will you two keep in touch?' Angelo asked her. 'After Lily returns to England?'

'Oh yes, of course.' They could exchange messages and photos, perhaps even chat on the phone from time to time.

250

'But Lily – she will not be a close part of my life.'

'Why not?' He sounded cross. 'Josi, why do you persist in pushing people away?'

'It is not that I am pushing her away,' she said, rather irritably, she knew. And she knew that he was not just talking about Lily.

Josefine was conscious that the atmosphere between them had changed since she'd told him that she might leave Perlarosa. She understood that he was upset about it – no one wants to lose the close and easy relationship with a friend who lives nearby, and probably that was all it was – but right now she was unable to see an alternative.

'It is because she lives so far away, that is all.' Though Josefine hoped that Lily would visit her again, wherever in Italy she happened to be.

Angelo sighed. 'You could go and see her in England,' he said. 'Would that not be something?'

'Oh yes.' Josefine felt wistful. Would she ever be able to do that? Would she be able to afford it, for one thing? And would she be brave enough? But he was right, it really would be something – to visit Lily in Dorset, to see all the places where their mother had lived, even to meet her aunt and the cousins Lily had told her about. Which was a weird and unexpected feeling, because only days ago she had not known that they all existed, not wanted to know and really not cared a fig. How things could change . . .

There was something else, though, that was preying on her mind, something niggling her, something that she wanted to do. She had never wanted to think about the past before, but now that she'd started, she wanted to find all the pieces of the jigsaw.

Josefine was just thinking this, and thinking that although this had been a difficult time, she could maybe now begin to see a way through it, when she missed her footing on the step. Perhaps it was the long dress that she wasn't accustomed to wearing. The moon was under the cover of cloud and it was very dark in the piazza. Perhaps that was why.

One moment, she was balanced and upright, the next she was tipping forwards, and although she tried to grab hold of Angelo's arm, he wasn't precisely where she had thought he was, and she fell, hard, on the bricked paving stones, her ankle twisting at the moment of impact.

'Josi!' Angelo began to help her to her feet. '*Va bene?* Are you okay? Have you hurt yourself?'

Oh, but she felt such a fool. And she wasn't sure she could get up – not straightaway anyhow. Because, ouch, her ankle was throbbing already. 'No,' she said. 'Yes, I am fine. No. Argh . . .' Somehow, he had got her up and now she leant her whole weight on him.

Thankfully he did not buckle. 'Do not put any weight on it, Josi,' he said sternly.

She could not, even if she wanted to.

Still supporting her, he reached down and touched her ankle gently.

'Ow.'

'We must get you home. We must put a cold compress on it. Hold tight.' And before she knew what he was doing, he had swept her up into his arms and was carrying her down the street.

'Angelo,' she protested, sure that she must be much too heavy for him. 'What are you doing? Put me down. I will be fine.'

'Shush,' he growled. 'I cannot talk. I need all my energy for this.'

Mio Dio . . . Josefine subsided. It hurt too much to argue. She had twisted her ankle for sure — a sprain perhaps? Or worse? And the *caffè* . . . She couldn't afford for it not to open. Especially now at the beginning of the holiday season. Josefine groaned. What in God's name was she going to do about that?

CHAPTER 35

Camogli, Italy, 2018

He sits on the bench he thinks of as his special bench since it is only a few metres from his house but conveniently tucked away in a place not many will find, and he watches the fishing boats coming and going. Fishing, it is in his family's blood, and so growing up there was supposedly no question of him not following in his father's footsteps. He was the only son after all.

At the harbourside, old Ernesto is in his boat La Contessa *(he has a sense of humour that one, for it is a simple craft) sorting his nets. The boat has two stainless-steel winches and two lifebelts and is crammed full of the equipment needed – tubs, nets, floats and markers, a big cool box in which to keep the catch. As far as he knows, Ernesto was never in any doubt about his life's path, and here he is, still following it.*

But, for him, there was once a question mark about which path he should follow. The old ways, they were not always the best and, back then, those times – they were changing.

He heard it on the radio and he heard it in the talk in the caffès *and* bars. *A new consumer society was flourishing, they said.* Allora, *not in Camogli, though, for sure. There is optimism, they said, after the horror of the war and what they called the crushing burden of fascism. Not that his father would have any of it.*

But as for him — he wanted to know about the world outside their village and so he made it his business to find out. Could reconstruction mean the end of poverty for their people? It was hard to imagine, but, certo, *many were migrating to the more urban north of the country. Even his father could not deny this, since a few from their own village were among that number. Would they be doomed, as Papa prophesied? Or would they find prosperity?*

He comes back to the present, sees Ernesto lift his hand in a wave and gives a wave back to his old friend.

'There could be something there for me too. Something good,' he said to his father back then. 'At least I have a choice.' *Fiat, Pirelli, Alfa Romeo . . . The names spun around in his head. He had heard there were big factories and they were all looking to hire. It was an opportunity at least. And there were other opportunities even further afield.*

'You think you are too good for this place,' *his father growled.* 'Too good for us.'

'No, Papa. It is not that.' *Why could he not understand?*

Because his father was steeped in the old traditions. He could see nothing beyond the fishing, the eking out of a meagre living, a life here in Camogli where his ancestors had also lived for ever and a day.

'What is it then?' *his father demanded.*

'It is only that there are other things.' *Because he did not want to live like his father. He did not intend to drown in the old ways. And they would drown him, he felt. They would suck the life out of him, for sure.*

'Other things?' *His father frowned.*

'Things other than fishing.'

He saw his father clench his fist. 'Such as?'

But he knew his father did not want an answer. Still, when word got around about those other possibilities, other jobs in other places, something snapped inside. He could do this. He would do this.

But in the end who can defy tradition? Now, he gets to his feet, his joints a bit stiff as always, and eases himself as upright as he will ever get. Slowly, he walks down to the harbour and along the promenade towards the museum. This place tells of the sailing traditions of Camogli, of the ships built in Genoa and Rapallo in the nineteenth century on which men, including his ancestors and others like them, traded all over the world and made the sea their life. It is a bit like visiting a graveyard, he always thinks. Necessary (he has to do his duty after all), nostalgic and not always a good thing.

The woman at the desk greets him in her usual friendly manner – well now, he is a frequent visitor after all. He walks around the exhibits. The ships painted by the Sea Painters, artists trusted by the shipmen of Camogli, are his favourites – accurate to the smallest detail, to the point of even using real silk in the sails. He walks on past the ships in bottles, the barometers and log books, the navigation instruments and maps, the stories.

This is the tradition, he reminds himself, and it is no small thing. Stories of men who fell from the top of the mast and yet somehow survived, lands of cannibals, the fiercest of storms. And never forget the fishing. He smiles. His great-great-grandfather had worked on the anchovies; his grandfather too. No wonder his father was proud. And most were sold to Britain. Funny that, he thinks.

Fishing got him in the end. He made that choice that seemed like no choice, followed the pathway that began to seem like the only road. It is as his father always said: there will always be fish in the sea.

CHAPTER 36

Josefine

2018

What an idiot. What a fool . . . Josefine shifted on her seat by the counter where Angelo had installed a comfortable chair and a footstool as if she was an invalid. *Allora*, she was an invalid. She felt helpless, pathetic, cross . . . and stupid.

Angelo had carried her down here this morning (having carried her upstairs last night), arriving early as usual with his bread and pastries. Arriving early and annoyingly jaunty – considering the situation. As if everything was the same. As if nothing had changed. As if she would be opening the *caffè*, for the love of Madonna.

'How can I open?' she had railed, though she was furious with herself, not him. 'I cannot get down there. I cannot walk. I can hardly stand.'

He had taken hold of her before she had even finished speaking, in a fireman's lift this time, and now here she was on ground level, like it or not.

'Where are you going?' she'd grumbled, the first time he disappeared, though at least he had made her a coffee and given her a pastry first.

'Deliveries,' he said. 'I will be back soon. Try not to get into any more mischief while I am gone.' And he had shot her a broad wink as if . . . well, as if he was enjoying this, damn him. It struck Josefine that the reason he might be enjoying it was because she was helpless and he was in control.

'But I cannot—'

'Do not try to open up yet.' He wagged an admonishing finger. 'I will come back and help you. I will bring Paola or Lily.'

'You cannot ask Lily.' Josefine couldn't imagine her younger sister helping in here, even for a minute. She wasn't used to this kind of work. And Josefine would not ask it of her.

'Oh, I think I can.' And he was gone.

Josefine had tried to struggle to her feet but the second she put any weight on that ankle, it was too painful and she collapsed back into the chair again. 'Fool,' she muttered. 'Idiot.' Speaking to herself, naturally.

Quite apart from the throbbing of her ankle – which thankfully had gone numb after Angelo plonked a big bag of frozen peas on it last night – it had been so embarrassing. To trip over the pavement like that, to fall (no doubt inelegantly; the dress had not helped her there) and then to suffer the indignity of being carried home like a sack of rice and taken upstairs . . . No doubt he would have put her to bed too if she'd given him half a chance.

When he returned, it was with Lily. Josefine sighed as she watched them crossing the piazza by the *tabacchi*, Angelo talking and gesticulating (probably describing to Lily in graphic detail

258

how it had happened) and Lily looking worried. What on earth had he told her? Josefine shook her head in despair.

They came into the *caffè*: Angelo whistling, Lily running to her side. 'Oh, Josefine,' she said. 'Look at you. Look at your poor ankle.'

Josefine grimaced. That was one thing she did not want to do. 'There was no need for you to come rushing over,' she said. 'I am perfectly fine.' Which was a ridiculous statement, given the way she was sitting with her foot raised in front of her, but never mind.

'Angelo said you needed some help.' Lily looked around. Angelo was turning the 'closed' sign to 'open'. 'What can I do?' she asked.

'How are you at making coffee and wiping tables?' Angelo asked her. He moved around, straightening chairs, putting things in order. He had already arranged the pastries and cakes behind the glass counter and now began getting food out of the fridge, clearly intent on making sandwiches.

Josefine clicked her tongue. Was no one going to consult her on what needed to be done?

'Good enough.' Lily was already reaching for Josefine's blue and white apron which was hanging on a hook by the counter.

What did they think they were doing? 'We cannot open the *caffè*,' Josefine grumbled. 'It is impossible. You two cannot cope on your own and I can hardly move.'

'But we must open the *caffè*, Josi.' Angelo stopped and looked at her. 'Is that not so?'

Josefine groaned. He was right. She couldn't afford not to open, but for the life of her, she could not imagine how this was going to work. '*Si*,' she conceded. 'But, Angelo, you will have to teach Lily how to work the coffee machine.' She wouldn't have a clue; she was English after all.

'*Va bene*,' he said. 'Okay. But this is a time when you must accept help, Josi.' And he was wagging his finger again, which was extremely annoying.

Josefine didn't relish his tone. But she supposed that, yet again, he was right.

Lily turned out to be surprisingly practical. Once she had mastered the coffee machine, she dealt with the rest pretty smoothly. She waited on the tables, brought over the snacks that Angelo was busy preparing according to Josefine's terse instructions, and if she couldn't understand someone, Josefine was on hand to yell out the translation. When the customer was ready to pay, Lily sent them to Josefine who was in charge of the till and the credit card machine and then Lily would wipe down the table again ready for the next customer. Most people seemed to find the whole thing hilarious, as if they were putting on some sort of dramatic performance for the entertainment of the customers.

Josefine sat on her chair like the Queen of Sheba, she found herself thinking. She knew she was being unreasonable, heard herself tutting and barking out orders – as if by behaving badly she could force them to stop helping her.

Angelo kept sending dark looks her way, clearly conveying the message that she was her own worst enemy, but Lily simply smiled and got on with it. *Mio Dio*, thought Josefine. She hoped she wasn't reminding her sister of their mother.

Marisa from the bar across the road came over for an hour to lend a hand, and when Angelo had to go, Paola came in to help. Meanwhile, Lily continued on, a real stalwart, barely even stopping for lunch. Other well-wishers appeared, helping themselves to coffee and leaving money on the counter . . .

Word had got around — but then it always did in Perlarosa. Josefine was beginning to feel a little overwhelmed.

And then the doctor popped in. 'Just to set Angelo's mind at rest,' he said.

Josefine rolled her eyes. 'I am fine,' she said. 'Or I will be. It is a sprained ankle, nothing more.'

'Kindly let me be the judge,' the doctor said as he examined the ankle.

'Well?' asked Josefine. Lily was hovering, looking concerned.

'It is a bad sprain,' he pronounced. 'You must rest. You must try to put as little weight on it as possible at first and then gradually test the strength. I will bring crutches.'

'Crutches!' *Mamma mia.* Josefine groaned. She couldn't wait to hear what Angelo would have to say about that . . .

The doctor gave her some painkillers. 'Sadly,' he said, 'you will not be going out on the town for a while.'

Nothing new there then, thought Josefine. Her time out on the town had been short indeed.

At four o'clock, Josefine had had enough. 'Let's close up,' she told Lily. 'There are no pastries left and you must be exhausted.'

'I'm okay.' But Lily did look tired as she pulled off the apron. 'Shall I help you upstairs?'

'Angelo will take me.' Lily would never be able to hold her weight and Angelo had said he would drop back at five o'clock. 'He likes playing the hero.' She knew it was mean. She knew she should not be behaving like this, but she didn't seem able to help herself.

'He's been amazing,' Lily said, and she gave Josefine a slightly disapproving look.

'I suppose he has.' Josefine was reluctant to admit it, but yes, it was true, he had.

'You have so many friends here. So many people care about you.'

Josefine gave her a suspicious glance. Had Angelo told Lily she was thinking of selling up and moving on? Perhaps . . . But she had to admit, she too had been affected by the level of support she'd received today. She hadn't realised she had so many friends here either.

'But you cannot come in every day,' she told Lily. 'You are about to go home. I will still be laid up and everyone else . . . Pah.' She made a forceful gesture with one hand. 'They will soon get bored of helping. What then?' And to her astonishment, she burst into tears.

It must be some sort of emotional build-up, she thought, as Lily rushed over and Josefine sobbed into her shoulder, once again. The strain of finding out that Gianni and Carlotta were about to have a child together . . . the fall, the worry about the *caffè*. Either that or it was Lily who brought it on. So far, she was the common denominator.

'Tell me, Josefine.' Lily had waited until Josefine's sobs had subsided. 'Is this just about the baby? Or . . . ?'

Josefine shook her head. There was too much to say.

'Is it the *caffè*? Angelo told me that it's not doing too well.'

Josefine hiccupped. 'He had no right to tell you anything,' she said.

'He cares about you, Josefine.' Lily's voice was gentle. 'And so do I. I'd like to help – if I can.'

'But . . .' Josefine did not want to think about Angelo, not in that way. It was too complicated and she did not want to lose him. He was the best friend she'd ever had. 'You already

262

helped me so much, Lily,' she said. How would she have managed today without her?

'I could stay longer.' Lily was speaking more quickly now. 'I'd like to. I could help out in the *caffè*, like today, even take a look at the books, see if there's anything—'

Josefine snorted. It would take more than a quick look at the books to sort out her financial problems. She wondered if her parents had any idea, when they left, just what a mess the business was in. Probably not. Her father hadn't been the best record-keeper and her mother wouldn't have had a clue.

'I could try at least.'

Josefine sneaked a look at her. It made her feel warm inside to think that Lily might stay for longer, but wouldn't that make it even harder to say goodbye?

'I'll change my flight tonight,' Lily said, as if it was decided. 'And then I'll come back and cook you dinner.'

'No,' said Josefine. 'It is too much.' And she almost started crying again. What was wrong with her? She did not deserve her, did she, this new sister of hers?

'Pizza then.' And Lily grinned.

Josefine felt something give, some tension lift. 'Pizza then,' she agreed. 'And Lily?'

'Mmm?' Clearly dead on her feet, Lily was already making her way to the door.

'Thank you. *Grazie mille.* I am very grateful. More than you could know.'

CHAPTER 37

Lily

2018

It had been a busy few weeks. It was still only the end of April but the season had begun in earnest. The bus brought day visitors to Perlarosa every hour and it seemed that Caffè Parodi was their first port of call as they walked to the piazza and then through to the pink bell tower of St Giorgio's, the little harbour and the sea.

Josefine's ankle was improving, though Lily couldn't say the same for her temper. Her sister's frustration emerged every day as she tutted and barked out her orders, as she struggled to her feet to help out during the busy periods. Lily knew that Josefine was grateful, but it was almost as if it hurt her to be grateful.

Angelo seemed oblivious to Josefine's moods and he dropped in to help for a couple of hours every day, despite being busy with the bakery and with looking after Sienna. Lily was always pleased to see him. Not just because he was so good at bantering with Josefine, trading verbal blow with verbal blow until he eventually made her sister laugh. And not just because he lightened the load. But because he was intelligent, he was caring, and he was fun.

For the rest, during this busy period, Josefine had conceded and now employed Loretta, a young girl from the village who was waiting to go to university in Milan in September and who was grateful to earn some cash to help her on her way.

After they closed, and for an hour or two during the day, Lily studied the *caffè*'s financial affairs. The books were a sorry mess. Josefine's attempts at bookkeeping were amateur at best and Lily could see that she'd inherited an out-of-date system from her parents. When was the last time anyone had considered how best to make money? It was a business, after all. And as she'd already noted, the *caffè* was in a prime position to catch visitors almost as soon as they arrived in Perlarosa.

Lily started from the beginning . . . She made a list of outgoings and examined each one, looking for ways of saving cash. She worked out where they were making the most money and where they were making the least. She looked at everything, from the way they displayed the snacks and drinks on offer, to the table arrangements, to the tubs of flowers outside. Could the *caffè* itself be presented better? Could Josefine make it more welcoming? How could they make the best of its natural assets and prime position?

Would the *caffè* make significantly larger profits if they stayed open a few hours longer a few nights a week? Lily believed so. The biggest profits came from alcohol and who didn't appreciate a sundowner while sitting at a table on a pretty Italian terrace with fairy lights all around and a splendid view of the Bay of Poets to boot? But for that, they needed a cocktail menu. And Lily also realised that they needed the menus throughout to be in English as well as Italian – and possibly in French and German too?

Josefine might scoff (and did) at Lily's ideas, but what was the point of catering only for Italians when most of the visitors were American, English, Australian and French? Yes, this was a traditional Italian *caffè*, and the locals were important. But the tourists were on holiday and, frankly, that was where the most money was being spent. No reason, thought Lily, that Caffè Parodi shouldn't have a share.

'I am tired enough already when I finish at six o'clock,' Josefine grumbled. 'And now you expect me to go on till nine and learn to make cocktails into the bargain? Pah! What sort of a place do you think this is anyhow?'

'If you carried on employing—'

'You know Loretta is going to Milan.'

'Yes. But when she goes, you could take on another young girl to replace her. To wait tables and serve, load the dishwasher, operate the coffee machine, whatever . . .'

'Then she takes all of my profits, *si*?'

Lily shook her head. 'I don't think so. Look.' And she started showing Josefine her spreadsheets and forecasts.

'Hmm.' She gave them only a cursory glance.

Did they mean anything to Josefine? Did she even care? Sometimes Lily wondered why she was bothering. Only, this was her job and she loved it. There was nothing she relished more than working out why a business was failing and then thinking of ways to turn it around until it was making a decent profit. And this was more important than any other job. This was her sister's livelihood.

'Just think about it,' she told Josefine. 'You'll never have more free time if you don't take on staff.' Because part of the new business plan had to include time off for Josefine. Without that, Josefine's life would remain exactly as it was now.

'I know you mean well,' Josefine told her. 'But I am not good with change. Sometimes . . .' – she sighed – 'it all seems too much to carry alone.'

Lily couldn't help her with that – not on any permanent basis anyway. Before very long, when Josefine was completely back on her feet, Lily would have to return to the UK, finish sorting out the sale of her parents' house, look for more work herself. She also had to go to London to retrieve the stuff that Cate was kindly storing for her. And after that . . . well, Lily wasn't sure where she would be.

'Are you sure there isn't a man involved?' Cate had asked her the last time they'd talked. 'Very sure,' Lily had told her. 'Even so,' Cate said. 'You are coming back to the UK, aren't you, Lily? It does sound as if you've fallen in love a little bit – with Perlarosa, I mean.'

But she laughed as she said it and Lily had to laugh too. 'I am coming back,' she assured Cate. But her friend wasn't entirely wrong. Perlarosa had certainly crept under her skin. And as for Nico . . .

Apart from dropping a note in at the workshop when she was sure he wouldn't be around, letting him know that she hadn't forgotten about the pendant and that she would be coming to collect it in a few weeks' time, she had stayed away. It wasn't exactly that she didn't trust herself. And she had, in truth, been tempted. But she was wary. And besides, she had been so busy helping Josefine that she'd hardly had a moment to herself to go anywhere.

She was definitely returning to the UK, though, just as soon as Josefine was up on her feet. Lily wasn't charging for her time (although her sister kept trying to pay her) and her funds were getting low – at least until the house sale went through.

And when it did . . . Lily was trying to work out how to send some of the proceeds Josefine's way. After all, why shouldn't her sister have a share? The only problem was that Josefine wouldn't see it like that, and she would very likely refuse. But . . . it was their mother's legacy after all, and so perhaps it was just a matter of how things were presented.

Lily was thinking about this as she walked back to the B & B later that evening. She was still there. Josefine had suggested she stay at the apartment for the rest of her visit, but Lily reckoned that they both needed a bit of their own space, and besides, the owner of the B & B had given her a good deal for a longer stay.

The night sky was cloudless and studded with stars, an almost full moon glimmering in the velvet sky. As always, a sense of peace seemed to hang over Perlarosa and it was a peace that Lily relished after such a busy day. Lily and Josefine had eaten dinner together as they often did, though tonight they had both been tired, and a frittata with salad was about all Lily had felt able to manage.

Lily passed under the shelter of the ilex trees. It was late. There was no one in the piazza – at least she couldn't see anyone – but nevertheless, she sensed another presence. She looked around. Nothing. Even the bar opposite was quiet as if everyone had gone home. She gave a little shrug and moved on.

As Lily left the piazza and headed up the road towards the B & B, she had the feeling that she was being followed. But that was ridiculous. She had never felt as safe anywhere as she did in Perlarosa. And after all, she was accustomed to Hackney and other parts of London where she was used to keeping her wits about her when walking home alone.

She half glanced behind her. Was that someone skulking in the shadows? Or was it her imagination? Or a trick of the moonlight? She walked more briskly up the street, conscious of the big stone church on the hill looming over her. And what else besides? She could definitely hear footsteps – heavy footsteps, a man's footsteps.

To test out her theory, she crossed over to the other side of the street. It was marginally brighter here and there was a security light glowing outside one of the houses.

A pause. And then the footsteps resumed on this side of the street. *Okay.* Lily tensed. She walked more quickly still, feeling for her keys in her bag, which she grasped in her right hand. With her left, she felt for her phone. No point calling Josefine. Her finger moved to the contact that read 'Angelo'.

She pressed, heard the phone ring and then go to voicemail. Damn it. '*Ciao*, Angelo,' she said loudly. Because even a pretend conversation might put a stalker off . . . 'I'm walking up the street to my B & B,' she said. 'Almost there. And I could be mistaken, but I think someone is following me.'

'Hello.' A voice in the darkness. 'Excuse me, please.'

For a moment, Lily imagined it was Nico, this tall dark shape that emerged in the haze of the moonlight in front of her, but she saw immediately that it wasn't. This man was older, slighter. And as she knew only too well, Nico rarely ventured to this end of town.

She was about to scream, when she realised that would-be attackers didn't usually say 'hello' or 'excuse me'. Plus, due to the fact that now that he had her attention, the man was keeping his distance.

'Hello?' she said cautiously.

'You are the sister of Josefine?' His voice was low but he didn't sound threatening in the least.

She ended the call to Angelo. 'Yes,' she said. And then she realised. 'Gianni?'

He nodded. 'Lily, is it?'

'Yes.' It was rather strange that he'd crept up on her like this, but she supposed he hadn't wanted to run into Josefine at the *caffè*.

'What do you want?' she asked. 'What is it?' She still felt slightly uncomfortable. It was dark and she didn't know this man.

He raised a hand as if to reassure her. 'I want to say – it is good, what you did. Coming to Perlarosa, helping Josefine with the *caffè*. I watch from a distance. I know.'

Lily shrugged. 'She's my sister.'

'Yes.' He smiled. 'Even so . . .'

Lily waited. Surely he hadn't waylaid her tonight just for that?

'I want you to tell her something – if you will,' he said.

Lily nodded, shifted her bag onto her other shoulder.

'Please tell her we leave Perlarosa soon. In a few weeks, in fact.'

'You and Carlotta?' Josefine would be pleased to hear that – and Angelo too. It might even persuade Josefine to stay.

'*Si*.' He frowned. 'I heard she was thinking about leaving herself – because of the child, I mean.'

Lily raised an eyebrow. Surely he couldn't have been surprised about that?

'And I . . . I cannot let her leave,' he went on. 'It is not fair.'

'No, it wouldn't be fair, you're right.' Lily had to agree. It

270

wasn't for her to judge, but this man's behaviour hadn't been the best.

Gianni fidgeted. 'I will not say goodbye. She does not want to talk to me.'

And then, as Lily was about to respond . . .

'I know. I do not blame her either.' He looked so woebegone at this that despite everything, Lily felt a rush of sympathy for him.

'You still care for Josefine?' she asked.

'*Si.*' He spoke as if this much was obvious. 'Always.' He hesitated. 'But Josefine, she is not easy.'

Lily repressed a smile. This was very true. 'And Carlotta?'

He shrugged. 'I am drawn to strong women perhaps,' he conceded. And she noted a glimmer of a smile. It showed Lily that Gianni had a sense of humour about him – perhaps it was this that had attracted the young Josefine? She hoped that he would get over the break-up of their marriage. She hoped that he and Carlotta would find some happiness together after all this.

'But what changed your mind?' she asked. 'About leaving, I mean?'

He sighed. '*Allora.* Carlotta, she has been through a lot and now that she has found Perlarosa, she does not want to leave.'

'And she has also found you,' Lily reminded him.

'*Si, si.*' Gianni held himself a little more upright at this. Lily guessed that whatever Carlotta's faults might be, she did at least make Gianni feel good about himself. 'But I told her that now we have no choice.'

'So, who persuaded you to go?' Lily guessed that it was Angelo. He was the one who would miss Josefine the most.

'A friend of mine,' he said. 'You know him, I think. Nico Ricci, the silversmith.'

Nico . . . Hearing his name on Gianni's lips sent a little shiver running through her. She thought again of what Cate had said. *Was* there a man involved? Just because Lily had not seen him in the past few weeks did not mean the thought of him hadn't crossed her mind. Quite a few times, actually. He wasn't the kind of man you could forget. And she would have to see him again, of course. She must collect the pendant he'd made for Josefine.

'Yes,' she said. 'I know him a little.'

They were silent as if they both knew this to be rather an understatement. On the surface, true enough, but not really covering the half of it.

'He is a decent man.' Gianni stood his ground, looking at her as if daring her to contradict him.

Lily said nothing.

'And he said what we were doing – staying here in Perlarosa, I mean – was not good for Josefine.'

She nodded. 'I see.'

'So will you tell her?'

'Yes,' she said. 'I will tell her.' She glanced at him. 'Good luck.'

He lifted his hand in a wave and disappeared back into the shadows.

Nico, she thought. She was surprised that it was he who had brought it about. Had she underestimated him? Perhaps. But the fact remained that he still had a dark secret he didn't want to share, and Lily reminded herself of this as she ran up the steps to the B & B and let herself in.

CHAPTER 38

Josefine

2018

The following day, Lily took Josefine by surprise when she suggested that the three of them have a meeting after the *caffè* closed in the afternoon.

Josefine wasn't sure she liked the sound of that. She opened her mouth to speak.

'*Va bene.* Okay.' Angelo got there first. 'Paola will watch Sienna for an hour.' He pulled out his phone and started to message her.

'Why the three of us?' Josefine asked. She was beginning to wonder who owned this *caffè*.

'I want to run some more ideas past you.' Lily remained unperturbed. 'But if Angelo is busy and you'd rather it was just the two of us . . .'

'No, no.' Josefine waved a hand. 'It is fine. Angelo deserves a say. Why not?' And she rolled her eyes to show she was joking – sort of.

When the time came, they sat around a table by the counter and Angelo brought over three bottles of beer from the fridge. 'To help the cogs go round,' he said.

Josefine had been thinking about what to say. She appreciated Lily's help, but . . . 'If I decide to sell the place and move on,' she said, 'then there is no reason to make changes, is that not so?'

Lily looked doubtful. 'But you will get more for the business if it's a good profit-making concern,' she pointed out.

'*Si, si*, she is right,' put in Angelo. 'It is obvious, I think.' He took a long swig of his beer.

Josefine glared at him. Obvious, was it?

'And so, the more we do now to turn things around, the better – whatever your decision.' Lily paused. 'And Josefine, I wanted to tell you earlier, but—'

'You have been in a terrible mood all day,' Angelo broke in. 'What is the matter, Josi?'

Josefine ignored him. She was in a bad mood, he was right, though she didn't care to admit it.

Last night, she had been sitting upstairs by the window looking down on the piazza, when to her astonishment she spotted Angelo charging up the street. He had his phone to his ear and he seemed to be talking urgently to someone. But who? Her next thought was that he was on his way to see her and for some strange reason her heart seemed to jump in anticipation. But, *certo*, she did not want him to come here. For goodness' sake. Why would he? He had only left a few hours ago. And besides . . .

But Josefine didn't go anywhere with that 'besides'. There was nowhere to go.

However, Angelo didn't even glance at the *caffè* or up at her

274

window as he strode by. Clearly his mind was on other things. But what things? And where was he going? Josefine waited. The road led to the top of town but he wouldn't be leaving town at this time of night. And apart from that, the road led only to Lily's B & B.

She sat and waited for him to reappear. She didn't feel tired in the least. She told herself she simply wanted to know. After an hour, he eventually came into view, looking far less urgent now, even smiling, though she wasn't at all sure about this since it was so dark and impossible to see.

Was it possible? What she was thinking? Of course, he and Lily had grown close, working together in such proximity these past weeks. It was only natural. Josefine had noticed how they chatted and laughed – did she not know what a good companion he was? He was a young-looking fifty-year-old, it had to be said, and having Sienna in his early forties had also kept him young at heart. And Lily – she was thirty-four, attractive, clever and kind, while Josefine was almost fifty-three years old, always grumpy and couldn't let anything go. Lily was, in fact, everything that Josefine was not, and yet they were sisters.

Josefine did not mind. Why should she? Really, it was quite lovely that her sister and her best friend got on so well, that they were perhaps even becoming attached to one another, despite the age difference between them. Only . . .

'What were you going to tell me?' Josefine asked Lily now. Was it some personal announcement perhaps? She was beginning to have mixed feelings about Lily's return to the UK. She had thought she was dreading it. But now . . . *allora*, things had been simpler by far before her sister came. Which was a horrible thing to say, given that Lily had been so wonderful, but . . .

'I saw Gianni,' Lily said.

275

'You saw Gianni?' Josefine hadn't even been aware that she knew Gianni. But Angelo was nodding as if he knew all this already.

Lily seemed to have got right into the heart of Perlarosa in the short time she had been here. She was even beginning to learn a little Italian from being in the *caffè*. She seemed to know everybody. How on earth had that happened? Josefine frowned. She wasn't sure how she felt about this either.

'And he asked me to give you a message,' Lily continued.

'*Si?*' Josefine tensed.

Lily beamed. Angelo was beaming too. Josefine looked from one to the other of them. She was beginning to feel distinctly excluded.

'He said that he and Carlotta are leaving Perlarosa. That he realises now that it would be wrong for them to stay.' Lily looked at him expectantly. 'That's good, isn't it?'

So, she would not have their child flung in her face every day. Which was what she had wanted. Josefine paused to let it sink in. 'Yes, that is good, yes, of course,' she said. And then, to be contrary, 'But I still might sell up. You know, there may be something more for me somewhere else, who knows?' She waved her hand airily, as if the world was her oyster indeed. Huh.

Angelo heaved a sigh and even Lily looked deflated.

'I do not know yet,' she added, to appease them.

'But you are glad they are going?' Angelo pushed. 'It was what you wanted?'

Josefine took a slug of beer. She glanced across at him. '*Si*, Angelo,' she said. 'I am glad they are going.'

It was, in fact, as if a weight had lifted from her chest and she could breathe more easily. It would not change the existence of the child, of course, but in time, if she did not see them every five minutes, perhaps Josefine could move on from the whole business and accept what she had. Despite everything, though, she could not help but feel a little sorry for Gianni.

'Okay.' Angelo put his palms on the table. 'Let's listen to your ideas then, Lily.'

For the next twenty minutes, they ran through various options for the *caffè*. No, Josefine did not want to sell *gelato*. A *gelateria* sold ice cream. Parodi's was a *caffè*. Then there were the cocktails and the salads, the planting and the solar lights. 'Parodi's could be a magical place,' Lily said. 'And a money-making place too.'

Predictably, Angelo seemed to agree with everything Lily suggested, but even Josefine had to concede that there were a few good ideas in there. She realised that when she had taken over the *caffè* from her parents, she hadn't even thought to consider how she could change things. Even so . . .

'I agree,' Angelo kept saying. 'Yes, you are right.' It was beginning to annoy her.

'Yes, of course you agree,' she snapped at him at last. 'Of course Lily is right.'

Angelo and Lily exchanged a look.

They had no idea how frustrating these past few weeks had been for Josefine – sitting around, unable to do anything, feeling her world shift beneath her until she was breathless, with nothing left to hold on to. And now this new bombshell. When were they going to tell her what was really going on between them?

'You could sound a little more enthusiastic, Josi,' Angelo said. 'Lily has been working very hard on your behalf.'

'But Lily does not know our town.' She tried to explain a

277

bit of how she was feeling. 'She does not know the business, the people.' She turned to her sister. 'That is the thing, Lily. Parodi's is a local *caffè* serving the people who live here. I do not want them to think I am selling out.'

'Sometimes it is easier for an outsider to see how it really is,' Angelo countered, quite reasonably.

'It's up to you, Josefine,' Lily said. 'In the end, you must do what you're happy with, what you think is right for you.' And Josefine could see that she'd hurt her. 'These are only suggestions. It's your *caffè*. It always will be.'

'Yes,' said Josefine. 'I know.'

'But it won't be long now before I go home,' Lily said. 'So, if you want me to give you a hand with putting any of these ideas into practice . . .'

Josefine felt awful. She knew she had behaved badly. Lily was only trying to help and she had thrown it back in her face – as good as.

One glance at Angelo's expression confirmed what she was already feeling. He was disappointed in her, she could tell, and she hated that feeling too. Anyway, she was disappointed in herself.

'Thank you, Lily,' she said humbly. 'You have been so good, and I am a crotchety old madam who does not deserve you – no, not in the least.'

Lily's eyes filled and Josefine reached out to her. She put a hand on hers. 'I appreciate everything. I really do. I am sorry. I will miss you so much when you are gone.'

And the worst thing was, that whatever was happening with Angelo and Lily, whatever challenges Lily had brought into her life, however things might change for Josefine, she knew without a shadow of doubt that this was true.

CHAPTER 39

Camogli, Italy, 2018

He waits on the quay, feeling the breeze ruffle his hair. He is wearing a T-shirt and shorts because it is a warm summer's day, warm enough even for him to shed his usual fisherman's sweater and denim jeans. Around him, the tourists cluster, eager for the best seat on the boat, but it is he who will have the best spot – right at the front next to the helm – and he won't even have to queue for it.

His son has the dream job – or so he always says. He navigates the ferry-boat over to Portofino and he never tires of it, he tells his father.

'Do you not get bored?' he asks Michele. 'Going to the same place all the time?' There and back, there and back . . . He remembers how he felt when he was young.

His son shakes his head. 'Not really, Papa,' he says. 'It gives me the chance to think.'

And that is something, he has to agree. Space, freedom, the chance to stare out at the blue . . . And think.

Some days, like today, he goes with Michele – partly for companionship and partly for a chance to be on the sea, because he never tires of that. They chat desultorily on the way over, Michele steering with one hand, casual, giving only an occasional glance to the tourists behind. So long as no one jumps overboard, there is not much that can go wrong.

Once, Michele told him, a young lad dived off the top deck into the sea. After they threw the lifebelt and brought him up to safety, the boy shaking himself like a seal and grinning as if he had won a bet, Michele clipped his ear. People seemed more shocked by that than the jumping, Michele told him, but the boy slunk off and hopefully would not try the stunt again. It provided a moment of drama, Michele told his father, but one that he could have done without.

He thought about this a lot. Mio Dio . . . About the current and how close the boy must have been to the boat. It made a shiver run right through him. Life, he thinks. It is full of these kinds of narrow escapes.

But mostly the tourists are docile; like sheep in a pen, he thinks. Once, he too was a tourist but in a different place. Once, he too was looking for something unfamiliar, unknown. His hand clenches into a fist and he uncurls it slowly.

As they cruise, he gazes out to sea, rippling slate-green, to the mountains hazy in the distance, and old forts and watchtowers, mostly ruined now, standing on rocky promontories, relics of the times when danger came in other forms . . . and he finds himself searching for that elusive sense of peace. Is that what is still missing from his life? He holds on to the rail in front of them. It is here in this landscape somewhere. It has to be.

They approach the tall, slender houses of Portofino, an arc of pink, ochre and pale ginger in the morning light, and draw into a harbour cluttered with boats. The promenade too is thick with people; the land up and beyond densely wooded, as it all was in the old days.

The tourists are herded off and in seconds they are gone from sight — disappearing along the caruggi, *the narrow alleyways of Liguria, to find somewhere for coffee, taking the pathway to the old church, or the steep steps that lead to the sixteenth-century Castello Brown, the Punta del Capo lighthouse and the little rocky beach. He knows these places; ah, si, si, he has been here many times before, walked the sun-dappled path through olives, jasmine and pine as tiny lizards darted across the paving ahead, yellow butterflies fluttering through fronds of bamboo.*

But he will not be doing that today.

He looks around, taking it all in. This place is not for him. Eugh, no. It is too sleek, too sure of itself, too expensive; rather like the rich men's motor cruisers that lurk shark-like on the outer reaches of the bay. Portofino has changed. Once, it was a small fishing village. Early settlers would have been attracted by its sheltered and strategic position; people always fought over it — but then people have always craved power . . . Allora, now, it is all designer shops and swanky ristorantes. There is nothing for him here.

The boat rocks gently on the diamond-sparked waves, waiting. His son passes him a bottle of water and he drinks thirstily. Alongside, a small motorboat churns the waves, a ribbon of silver streaming behind. The ferry begins to fill again. He hears the dull, ancient clang of a church bell on the hour.

His son gives a little nod and switches on the engine. It thrums softly. There is no peace to be found here, although the companionship of his son and being on the sea again — those things are a tonic. But now . . . It is time to go home, he thinks.

CHAPTER 40

Lily

2018

The following day, Lily told Josefine she was going out for an hour and she set off to walk down towards the little harbour. The time had definitely come. She must thank Nico for his intervention with Gianni; she must collect the pendant. She was sure it would be finished by now.

Lily wasn't upset that Josefine had been less than enthusiastic about her suggestions for the *caffè*, though she was gratified that Angelo at least had seen the value in them. She'd experienced it before. People were often unwilling to accept change. She supposed that sometimes it felt a bit too much like admitting defeat.

In Josefine's case, the *caffè* wasn't only her business. It was an important part of her childhood; it was the inheritance her adoptive parents had given her. The *caffè* meant a lot to Josefine and it must feel like a betrayal to change anything about it. But Lily's job was to lay out the figures, the evidence, the possible solutions and the predictions, and then it was up to the client – in this case Josefine, although strictly speaking she was not a client, since she hadn't exactly asked Lily to take on the work – to mull it over and decide what action, if any, to take. Patterns, she thought. Numbers didn't lie. And the number patterns she'd seen when she looked at the books of the Caffè Parodi – well, they told a clear story of lack of efficiency and care, of opportunities missed. Josefine was brilliant at her job, but in Lily's experience there were other parts of running a business that were just as important, though much more behind the scenes.

As she walked down the red-bricked alleyways, drinking in the perfumes of the flowers blossoming in tubs outside the tall houses and dripping from the wrought-iron balconies, Lily waved and greeted a few people she had got to know since she'd been here. There was the gardener who delivered plants in his blue van parked at the top of the town, Antonio the fruit-seller, Marisa from the bar on the other side of the piazza. She had become almost a part of this town in the short time she'd been here, Lily realised. And she knew that she would miss it – the easy camaraderie, the blue skies, the captivating landscape, the crumbling buildings . . . And that wasn't even to mention the food.

When Lily reached the belvedere by St Giorgio, she looked out across the glistening sea to the harbour. Although she hadn't been down to this end of the village for a while, nothing had changed. The boats were still pulled up on the slipway, greenery still overflowed from the planters on the balcony of the pink house by the harbour's mouth, and the peninsula of Portovenere with the smaller green mound of the island of Palmaria still crouched in the middle of the smooth blue ocean, seeming to beckon her closer. Perhaps the blue of the sky was deeper now that summer was not so far away; perhaps the sea was darker too, moving from turquoise into a denser green and blue, bleeding into navy in the distance. Lily watched a speedboat skim through the water, a channel of white frothing in its wake. The whole scene was so beautiful that it brought a lump to her throat.

She turned her attention to the narrow street where the boats were parked on one side and the silversmith's workshop stood further down, closer to the harbour. Nico wasn't sitting outside this time but she hoped he'd be there. Lily was conscious of a thrill of anticipation. She couldn't wait to see the pendant. She hoped it was beautiful. It was Josefine's birthday next week and Lily planned to give it to her then. Lily and Angelo had arranged a dinner party at the seafood restaurant in Fiascherino where Lily had gone with Josefine before, and they were trying to keep it a secret – although that wasn't easy with Josefine's eagle eye on them the whole time. It would be the three of them, Paola, Sienna and a couple of Josefine's other friends.

After that . . . well, Lily supposed that she would be gone. Once Josefine got back fully on her feet, there would be no reason to stay.

She turned and walked down the street, feeling a little nervous. Every one of her encounters with Nico had left her feeling . . . what was the right word? Discombobulated. How did he do that?

The workshop door was ajar, and Nico – dressed in his usual blue boilersuit; a speck or two of glitter caught her eye – was sitting on the high stool, hunched over the counter, focused on whatever it was he was making or mending, a long pair of tweezers in one hand, the magnifying eye-glass inserted over one eye.

Lily took a breath. '*Ciao.*' She stepped inside the cool interior.

He looked up, raised an eyebrow, took out the eye-glass and got languidly to his feet. He hadn't taken his eyes off her and, as usual, Lily fidgeted under his penetrating gaze.

'So, you are still here,' he said.

Lily smiled. It wasn't much of a welcome but it seemed typical of the man. 'You didn't think I'd leave without the pendant?' She looked around the workshop as if it might be lying on the counter among the pots full of tools or hanging on the wall next to the plyers and saws. Anyhow, it was safer than looking at him.

'Ah, the pendant. Well, no.' He continued to stare at her and Lily felt more uncomfortable than ever. Was it obvious? Did he know what effect he had on people?

She shifted her weight onto the other foot and waited. Presumably, he would show it to her eventually.

'I hear you are helping Josefine with the *caffè*.' He put his head to one side enquiringly. As usual, his dark hair was awry and standing up in thick tufts as if he'd been tearing his fingers through it all morning.

'You hear right,' she said. Not so much of a recluse then, though he'd probably heard it from Gianni. News travelled fast in Perlarosa.

'That must have been . . .' – he hesitated – 'different for you.' His dark eyes gleamed.

'It was.' Lily couldn't help but chuckle. Very different. And certainly not what she'd expected to be doing when she'd first come to this village to look for her long-lost sister.

He continued to eye her appraisingly. 'And do you think Josefine will now leave Perlarosa?'

'I don't know.' Lily had done all she could. Partly for Josefine,

285

because her sister seemed to belong here, and partly for Angelo, because he certainly didn't want Josefine to go.

Lily had grown very fond of Angelo since she'd been working in the Caffè Parodi. He was a kind man and funny too. She wasn't sure how she would have coped with Josefine's moods without Angelo there to diffuse things. And when she recalled how he'd rushed over when he'd picked up that garbled voicemail she'd left on the night she'd encountered Gianni . . . She'd really appreciated that.

'I was worried,' he'd said when he arrived breathless at her B & B. '*Mi Dio*. I thought you had been mugged or something.'

'I was scared,' she admitted. 'But it was only Gianni.'

Although it was late, she'd invited Angelo in and made hot chocolate for them both in the kitchen of the B & B. She'd told him what Gianni had said and he'd cheered up considerably. 'You coming to Perlarosa,' he'd said, 'it has been such a good thing. Not only for Josefine. But an amazing thing for us all.' And to her surprise and pleasure he had enveloped her in a bear hug, before saying that he must rush back so that Paola could return to her own house from his, where she was watching out for Sienna.

Lily wasn't sure that Josefine saw her arrival in Perlarosa as being quite so amazing, but she was grateful to Angelo nonetheless.

'I hope she stays,' Nico said.

'Really?' It seemed that Nico thought more of Josefine than her sister did of him.

He shrugged. 'Josefine – she belongs here,' he said. 'She has lived here her whole life.'

Well, almost . . . But Lily nodded. He was echoing her own thoughts exactly. 'I hope she stays too,' she said. 'And thank you.'

'What for?' He was eying her quizzically now.

'For persuading Gianni and Carlotta to leave Perlarosa.'

The eyebrow went up again.

'Gianni told me,' she explained. 'And it means a lot.'

'I did only what anyone would do,' he said. 'Carlotta – she may not have meant to do it, but she has caused enough trouble in Perlarosa already. And she does not belong here, any more than I do.' He looked out, beyond her now, towards the harbour and the sea.

Was he thinking of that time he'd arrived here in his boat? And once again, Lily found herself wondering, what had happened in that past life of his – and how had he become the man he was now? Gianni had told her that Carlotta had been through a lot. Had Nico had anything to do with that?

But he was wrong about one thing, of that she was sure. Nico, creative and enigmatic as he was, did belong here in Perlarosa. He might not have lived here his whole life, but she was convinced Perlarosa had become an integral part of him.

'But Gianni was born here, wasn't he?' she asked. 'It must be hard for him to go.'

'Pah.' Nico frowned. 'It is his fault for taking up with Carlotta in the first place. He is a good man, but he is also an idiot. He did not appreciate the wife he already had.'

Again, Lily was surprised. 'I thought it was you who introduced them,' she said, before she could stop herself. He would wonder how she knew this, and come to the correct conclusion that she'd been talking about him. And that, she guessed, would not go down well.

But he was shaking his head. 'It was not exactly like that, no,' he drawled. 'If you want to know how it was . . .'

Lily nodded. She did.

'I was in the bar down there.' He pointed to the Marina Bar by the harbour, 'having a quiet drink with Gianni one night – trying to pacify him, in fact – when Carlotta . . . she just walked in.' He muttered a low curse. 'How she found me, I do not know.'

Lily tried to work this out. 'So you're saying that she turned up out of the blue in this place which you thought you had escaped to?' Because he'd said as much to her before.

'Carlotta – she would never let me escape. She cannot.' He sat back down on his stool and gestured to Lily to take the other one. 'You have not met her, I think?'

Lily sat down. 'No.' Though she'd heard so much about her that she almost felt she had. And if Carlotta was Nico's sister-in-law, then who was her sister – Nico's wife? And where was she? Presumably, they had separated, but there must be more to it than that, surely? 'But why?' she asked him. Did Carlotta hate him so very much?

He gave one of his little shrugs. 'She still suffers,' he said. 'I understand that. But she is a damaged woman. And she thinks she holds something over me.'

'Does she?'

That look again . . . 'Whatever it is,' he said, in that obtuse way he had, 'it is not so heavy as the thing I hold over myself. Coffee?'

Lily blinked at him. How was it that whenever she saw him, they ended up getting into such intense discussions? 'I'd love one.' It was an instinctive decision. She glanced at her watch. 'Just a quick one, though, and then I must get back.' Josefine was now on her feet and able to work, but she still needed to rest that ankle from time to time. Yesterday, Angelo had threatened to tie her to the chair if she kept jumping up to do things, and that hadn't gone down at all well.

'Ah, yes.' He got up and went over to the stove. 'To the Caffè Parodi.'

'But I was thinking . . .' Lily felt emboldened by his story of how Gianni had met Carlotta. Josefine had been wrong in her assumption that Nico had introduced them and encouraged the relationship. It seemed the opposite was true.

'*Si?*' He turned around from preparing the coffee and she was treated to another of his dark looks.

'Before I go home, I would like to visit Portovenere,' she said. 'If your offer still stands, that is.'

After all, once she explained to Josefine, her sister would understand that she'd done Nico a disservice and that he had played no part in what had happened between Carlotta and Gianni. It was simply bad luck. And what harm would it do? Josefine didn't much like the man, but wasn't Lily her own person? Couldn't she make up her own mind? Besides, it was only a day trip . . .

Nevertheless, as she waited for his reply, she licked her dry lips and felt that same nervousness fluttering in her belly. Only a day trip maybe, but this man was out of the ordinary to say the least and unlike anyone she'd ever met before. Just half an hour in his company made her feel both drained and invigorated at the same time. So why on earth was she asking him to take her to Portovenere?

'*Allora*,' he said, after a lifetime. 'The offer still stands.' He brought over two steaming cups of espresso. 'When do you want to go?'

'Any day next week?' Josefine would be pretty much okay by then, and . . .

'After that, you will be gone.'

289

Lily blew on the liquid and took a wary sip of the strong, bitter coffee. 'After that I will be gone,' she echoed.

They were both silent for a few moments as if digesting this thought. Was the time right to ask him about his wife? Lily wondered. She decided not. Perhaps there never would be a right time. And wherever she was, whatever had happened between them, what business was it of Lily's anyway?

'And the pendant?' she asked him instead after the second sip. She could get used to this kind of coffee, she decided. It was harsh but invigorating. After the rich flavour touched your tongue, it hit you deep in the throat, ran through in a bitter stream to your belly, where it gripped hard and then let go. But in a good way . . . She looked at him over the rim of the coffee cup. 'Is it finished?'

He nodded, looked thoughtful. 'It was a challenge,' he said. 'The stone, the lines, the pyramid . . .'

Another sip. 'Can I see it?'

'Of course.' But he waited until he'd drained his cup, before swinging to his feet. He opened one of the glass drawers under the counter and removed something, held it tenderly in the palm of his hand.

Lily could hardly breathe. Suddenly, this felt like a very important moment.

He came across to her, held out his hand in a fist and slowly uncurled his fingers. The pendant lay in the palm of his hand, the anatase glowing deep amber and the silver setting shining pure and true.

'Wow.' Lily stared at it. He had turned the gemstone upside down and cleverly encased the bottom half in a hammered thin silver cage shaped to mirror the lines and elongated point of the pyramid in an art deco style. The little kite-shaped deco cage

290

was attached to the silver chain Lily had chosen. And inside it, the gemstone looked, she decided, entirely at home. He had polished the stone too – the orange light seemed to shimmer from it like a flame, reaching down from the silver mounting to its pinnacle. The overall effect was stunning.

'It's beautiful,' Lily said.

'It is,' he agreed.

She smiled. He was not a man for false modesty. And why should he be? He had done an amazing job. She held out her hand. 'May I?'

He held her gaze. 'It is yours.'

As she took it carefully from where it lay in the warmth of his palm, she felt a frisson, a jolt, as if the pendant had acquired some magical property while in his hands.

'Thank you.' Lily let the chain trail slowly through her fingers. She knew then that her instinctive decision to ask this man to make the anatase gemstone into a pendant for her sister had been the correct one. Because it was Josefine's birth right. Nico had more than done it justice and Lily knew that Josefine would love it.

CHAPTER 41

Josefine

2018

'*Happy birthday to you* . . .' Rather shyly, Lily sang the English version and then the rest of them sang '*Tanti Auguri a Te*', the Italian equivalent, and much more boisterously.

Josefine beamed at them; her favourite people sitting together around the table in the restaurant. It was all a bit of a fuss, granted. But how lucky she was . . . Her ankle was better, she was now practically back to normal and Angelo and Lily had organised this wonderful birthday treat. It had been a surprise. They had let her imagine that they had forgotten her birthday and then just as she was becoming grouchy about it, they sprang it on her. Really, she did not deserve them.

'*Grazie.* Thank you all.'

The lights dimmed, the people at the other tables hushed, and the waiter brought through a cake: a wonderful confection – chocolate, which was Josefine's favourite – complete with dark morello cherries and a frosted icing. On the top, seven candles burned, their little flames flickering.

They started the song again, even the other diners joined in, and the waitress placed the cake carefully in front of Josefine.

'Close your eyes,' said Angelo.

'Make a wish,' said Lily.

Josefine closed her eyes, wished for the elusive sense of contentment she longed for and something else she could hardly even admit to herself. And she blew.

Everyone clapped and Josefine smiled and looked around, slightly self-conscious at all the attention, she had to admit.

'Now you must cut the cake.' Angelo handed her a knife.

'Did you make it?' she asked him.

'*Si.*'

She smiled at him. 'It is a splendid cake.' And he was such a good friend. She was fortunate to have him in her life, she knew. But for how long? She paused for just a moment and then winked at him. 'Let us hope it tastes as good as it looks, eh?'

Lily whispered to the waitress and, in moments, champagne arrived in an ice bucket – two bottles and six flutes.

'May I try some, Papa?' Sienna asked Angelo.

'*Certo.*' Josefine handed the first flute to the girl. 'Of course you may. It is my birthday and so I get to decide. Right, Angelo?'

'Whatever you say, Josi.' Angelo rolled his eyes and they all laughed.

Angelo poured the wine, Josefine cut the cake and they toasted her birthday, then the *caffè*, then Lily and her journey home and, finally, Josefine's ankle.

'Thank you,' Josefine said again. 'I could not have asked for a better evening. It has been perfect.' She sat back, sipped her wine and looked around at them.

On her left was Lily, wearing a green dress that showed off perfectly her blonde hair and the golden tan she'd acquired since being here. Perlarosa suited her, thought Josefine. On her right was her old school friend Teresa, who Josefine had lost touch with over the years but who had come to see her when she was laid up, thus reigniting their old friendship. Opposite Josefine sat Angelo, Marisa on his right, Sienna on his left, and Paola at the head of the table between Teresa and Sienna. Everyone had dressed up in their best things. Angelo looked super smart in dark jacket and trousers with his trademark white linen open-necked shirt. And Josefine? She was wearing the dress she'd bought with Lily, of course. Perhaps elegance was something that came with practice after all, and hopefully she would not fall over again . . .

For the first time in ages, she felt . . . almost happy, she realised. She had come to two decisions in the past few days and she was looking forward to telling these friends – and family, she thought, looking at Lily – what she was planning to do.

'And now, presents!' Sienna exclaimed. 'Mine first, Papa?'

He nodded gravely. 'Yours first.'

'There is more?' Josefine could hardly believe it.

'There must be presents on a birthday,' Sienna informed her. And she handed Josefine a flat package, gift-wrapped in purple tissue paper.

'Beautifully wrapped,' Josefine commented, as she carefully ran a finger under the tape.

Sienna was so excited, she was jumping up and down in her seat, dark curls flying.

It was a painting – framed – of a *caffè*. Josefine's *caffè*. There was the name – Caffè Parodi – there was the terrazzo mosaic terrace and there was a small figure in a blue and white apron standing outside. 'That is you,' Sienna told her.

'Sienna . . .' Josefine was trying not to cry.

'I painted it myself,' Sienna said proudly.

'*Grazie mille*. Thank you so much, *cara*. It is a wonderful gift.' And it was.

But Josefine couldn't resist glancing at Angelo, looking so innocent, so unaware. Had he used his influence on his daughter to choose her subject matter perhaps? He seemed so determined that she should stay at the *caffè* after all.

Angelo knew her too well and he immediately raised his hands in denial. 'It was entirely Sienna's idea,' he said. 'But a good choice, I think.'

Josefine smiled. She remembered what he'd said about his daughter and how much she would miss Josefine if she went away. Over the past weeks it hadn't only been Lily and Angelo who were growing closer, she thought. It was also herself and Sienna. Sienna had got into the habit of coming to the *caffè* after school where she would sit and do her homework – aided and abetted by Josefine – while her father waited on tables and made snacks for the customers. Josefine thought of the dolls' house Sienna loved so much. There was safety, she supposed, in the miniature. It was something the girl could control, unlike the tragedy that had befallen their family when Sienna's mother had become ill. Unlike the huge loss when her mother had died.

Across the table, she put her hand on Sienna's. 'It is beautifully painted, *cara*,' she said. 'It is perfect and I love it.'

Was this the time to tell them? Josefine thought so. 'An announcement.' She dinged her spoon on her glass and everyone stopped chatting. She cleared her throat. 'As you know, things have not been so easy lately, what with my ankle and everything.'

There were murmurs of agreement. Everyone knew that 'everything' encompassed the situation with Gianni and Carlotta and the break-up of Josefine's marriage, and the fact that Josefine's ex-husband would be having the child that Josefine had longed for.

'I did think that it might be time to start again,' she said. 'Somewhere new. Reinvent myself, maybe.'

'But we like you as you are,' Angelo intervened.

There were sounds of agreement.

'But, Lily' – she turned to her sister – 'has made me see that I can make changes to the Caffè Parodi, that I can manage, that I can stay in Perlarosa with my friends.' She looked around the table. She hadn't realised what a wonderful support group they all were until she had needed them. But she would never undervalue them again. 'And that is what I have decided to do.'

'Wonderful!' Angelo was grinning.

'Bravo.' Lily gave a little clap.

'Yay!' shouted Sienna, getting in the mood.

And the others all echoed the sentiment.

'More presents now,' said Sienna and they all laughed.

Paola had bought her some perfume 'for when you go on nights out in your new life,' she added with a wink.

'You are joking,' Josefine said. 'I will wear it every day.'

Teresa bought her some bath oil. 'For when you are getting ready for those nights out . . .' and Marisa a bottle of Prosecco, 'to drink before you leave.'

Angelo and Lily exchanged a look. *What now?* Josefine wondered, because she might not be the only one making announcements tonight. But before she could spend any time brooding about this, Angelo brought out his gift.

Josefine unwrapped it eagerly. It was a shoulder bag, made from the softest, most exquisite leather the colour of pale turmeric, and tucked inside was a delicate silk wrap of dark aubergine fringed with gold.

'Angelo,' she breathed, as she took out the scarf and wrapped it around her shoulders. It was much too much.

He brushed away her thanks. 'For this new Josefine you keep talking of,' he said. 'But please leave most of her exactly as she is now.' And again, they all laughed.

'And this is from me.' Lily passed her a small package. 'At least, it's from someone else and me . . .'

Whatever did she mean? Josefine opened it slowly. It was in a small box; she lifted the clasped lid. *Mamma mia.* 'Lily,' she breathed. 'This is so beautiful.' It was a silver pendant, set with a stone the colour of dark amber, shone through with a filament of light; its sides serrated, forming a pyramid which had been captured in the delicate hammered silver cage.

Lily blushed. 'It has a story.' She leant closer. 'It's about your birth parents – do you want me to tell it now or later, when it's just the two of us?'

Josefine hesitated. She looked around at the faces, each one belonging to a good friend. 'Now, please,' she said, and she turned so that Lily could fix the clasp around her neck. The pendant hung perfectly, pointing towards her heart, warm and comforting as sunlight.

'When your father met our mother, he gave her this gem-stone,' Lily said.

Everyone at the table was quiet, listening. Josefine frowned.

That didn't seem like the action of a man who planned to walk away and never return.

'My Auntie Glenda recalls our mother showing it to her,' Lily went on. 'And our mother kept it – I guess because it was something to remember him by.'

'It looks old.' Josefine picked up the stone to examine it once more.

'It is rare,' Lily told her. 'It is linked to the element of air and the heart chakra and it signifies hope and positivity.'

'*Mamma mia.*' Josefine said it aloud this time. 'It has come to the right person then. I need positivity, for sure.' She looked up. 'Where did you find it, Lily? Our mother – she gave it to you?'

'No. But when she died . . .' Lily's eyes filled. 'I found the drawing she'd made of you when you were a baby, Josefine, just as I told you. And with it, I found this gemstone wrapped in a little fabric pouch.'

There were *ahs* and *ohs* from around the table. Sienna's dark eyes were like saucers.

'But now it is not just a gemstone. It is a pendant,' Angelo pointed out. He was smiling.

Lily smiled back at him. 'Yes. I had this idea . . . I hope you don't mind, Josefine?'

Josefine shook her head. Mind? She was delighted.

'And I asked Nico – the silversmith – to make it into a pendant,' Lily went on. 'He has done a good job, I think.'

'An excellent job,' Josefine had to admit. She'd often cursed the man in recent months, but he was good at what he did, no question.

'And the stone?' Paola asked. 'It's so pretty. What gem is it, Lily?'

'Anatase,' Lily told them. 'It gets created from two different

298

minerals and titanium dioxide is its core element.' She shrugged. 'I looked it up.'

'What else did you find out?' Josefine asked. More information might give her some clue.

'It's associated with good communication.' Lily frowned. 'And trust.'

'Trust,' Josefine murmured. She ran her fingertip over the striated edges of the gemstone. Had there been trust between her birth parents? Had there been hope, positivity and good communication? It did not seem to fit with the story somehow — at least, how she understood it.

'Oh yes, and it's mined in Liguria, among other places,' Lily said. 'In the mountains behind Genoa, in fact.'

Josefine drew a sharp breath. 'Do you think this means my father came from Liguria?' she whispered.

'I don't know.' Lily frowned. 'I suppose it's possible.'

Josefine took Lily's hand. 'You could not have given me anything more precious,' she said. 'And I must tell you. I made another decision this week.'

Angelo groaned and laughed at the same time. 'So many decisions,' he said. 'What is happening to you, Josi?'

She ignored him. 'You see, I want to try and find my father,' she told Lily. 'Or find out who he was, at least.'

'Really?'

Josefine could see she was surprised, and this was understandable, given that before Lily had come here, Josefine had not wanted to know any details whatsoever about her birth family. But she had already changed, she realised. Lily had shown her that her roots, her family — they mattered. This was a part of her history, her very identity, and she needed to understand it in order to be herself, in order to grow.

But there was another thing. 'And I want to try and find out why he did not go back to her.'

Lily's eyes were shining. 'Yes,' she said. 'I get it. Of course, I get it.'

Josefine had known that she would. Had she not made this journey herself to find Josefine? 'You are my sister,' she said. 'So, will you help me?'

CHAPTER 42

Lily

2018

Several times, Lily had been tempted to cancel her planned trip to Portovenere with Nico. Whyever had she asked him to take her? She was still busy helping Josefine in the *caffè*, and she knew her sister wouldn't be best pleased since Josefine – despite conceding that he was a skilled craftsman – continued to hold a rather low opinion of him. And besides, what on earth would they talk about all day? Lily hated awkward silences, while this man seemed to thrive on them.

Was she scared of spending time alone with him? Perhaps. But why this should be . . . Now that, she didn't dwell on.

But Josefine merely shrugged when Lily told her she was going to Portovenere and with whom.

'You don't mind?' Lily asked.

'Why should I mind?' Josefine flipped a tea towel onto the oven handle. 'And Angelo?'

'Angelo?' Lily was confused.

'Is he going too?'

'No . . .' Though perhaps she should ask him – he'd make a perfect chaperone.

'Hmm.'

Lily couldn't read her sister's expression. 'What?' she asked.

'Just that if it were me . . .' – Josefine shuddered dramatically – 'I would not trust that boat.'

The boat, Lily wondered, or the man?

Josefine gave her a dark look. 'I told you about your poet Shelley, did I not?' she said.

'You did.' In graphic detail.

'And if you go to Portovenere with Nico Ricci, you will also learn about your Lord Byron.' And with that, Josefine moved purposefully away from the counter with a swish of her apron and a damp cloth in her hand.

In the end, Lily told herself that she had no way of getting hold of Nico to put him off as they hadn't even swapped numbers – despite the undeniable fact that she knew where he worked and she knew where he lived – and so Lily turned up at the harbour at ten on the appointed day where she found him and the boat apparently ready to go.

Nico turned his attention from the faded blue and white boat he was in the process of untying and regarded her intently. 'You came,' he said. 'I wondered if you would.'

You and me both, she thought. 'Yes. Here I am,' she said brightly.

He held out his hand to help her into the boat. His skin was warm and her hand nestled briefly inside his palm. A good fit, she found herself thinking. For a moment, the boat seemed to rock precariously and Lily gripped his hand more fiercely. She didn't want to end up in the water at this early stage. Josefine would split her sides laughing.

He chuckled. 'She may not be the prettiest star to look at,' he said. 'But she is reliable and she will get us to Portovenere.' He rested his hand lightly on the stern.

Lily was glad to hear it. She could see the peninsula of Portovenere and the green island of Palmaria glimmering invitingly in the distance, but there was an awful lot of ocean in between.

'Life vest.' He handed it to her.

Definitely a good sign, she told herself. Not the fact that she might need it . . . But it showed that he was responsible, at least. Lily put it over her head and he helped her do up the straps. She was conscious of his proximity as she breathed in the scent of him – dry and slightly metallic, it seemed to mingle with the light breeze and the saltiness of the sea. As always, his dark hair was sticking up at all angles and, as usual, he was wearing a faded T-shirt, cut-offs and old trainers. He wasn't the smartest but somehow, she conceded, this went with his territory and was part of his appeal.

He saw her scrutinising him and raised an eyebrow.

Lily didn't care; he'd done the same to her on more than one occasion. 'You're not wearing a life jacket?' she asked.

He shrugged. 'I never bother. Though there is one under the seat for emergencies.' He pointed.

'Then if we capsize, I suppose I shall have to save you,' Lily said tartly. Because perhaps he wasn't so responsible when it came to health and safety after all.

He tipped an imaginary cap at her. 'Very kind of you, *signorina*. Ready?'

As ready as she would ever be. Lily nodded.

He pushed the boat off from the slipway and jumped in,

303

making it rock violently again so that she grabbed the sides to steady herself. He sat down opposite her and started the motor. The boat felt very small to be out in the open sea and if Lily stretched out her legs, they would come into contact with his, so she kept them half-folded under her – uncomfortable but definitely safer.

After a while, though, Lily relaxed and started to enjoy the sensation of the rocking waves, and the sound of the gently chugging engine, as they carved a slow and steady pathway through the sea, the frothing water streaming behind them. Thankfully, it was a calm day, and Nico seemed as confident and focused in charge of the tiller as he did when he was in his workshop, leaning back, observing the roll of the blue-green waves as the boat took them forward and Portovenere became clearer and bigger and closer.

For a while they didn't speak and Lily was surprised to find that the silence wasn't an awkward one after all. Being here felt so peaceful after so many frenetic days in the *caffè*. She closed her eyes for a moment, lulled by the boat's movement, her face warmed by the sun, her hair ruffled by the breeze, her senses soothed. But when she opened them again, he was watching her.

'And Josefine?' he asked softly. 'Did she like the pendant?'

'She loved it.' Lily met his gaze and abruptly looked down at his hands instead. Capable and brown-skinned, they were practical hands, attractive hands. She found herself wondering again, what had he done for work before he came to Perlarosa?

'I am glad,' he said simply. 'But tell me, why did you choose that particular gemstone to give to your sister?'

They were alone in the middle of the ocean. And why

shouldn't she confide in him? Josefine had made it clear that it didn't have to be a secret. So Lily told him the story.

'That is a lovely thing,' he said when she'd finished.

'Her father giving our mother the gemstone?'

He shook his head. 'That *should* have been a lovely thing,' he said. 'But if he did not return?' He shrugged. 'Not so lovely then perhaps?'

'No.' She had to agree. Privately, she couldn't help wondering if Josefine's father had given their mother the stone because he wanted something from her in return. Was that very cynical of her? She supposed so. But he wouldn't be the first man to try and buy love or a sexual favour. And the more she thought about it, the more it worried her. What other reason could there be for him not coming back?

Even so, Lily couldn't help preferring a more romantic view. Perhaps he'd intended to return and hadn't been able to? Perhaps he'd had some sort of tragic accident, for example? *Heaven forbid* . . . Or less dramatically and rather more likely, maybe he'd been persuaded by his family not to return for an English girl he hardly knew? In whichever case, the chances of Josefine discovering her birth father's identity were slim indeed. And even if she found out who he was, would he still be alive after all these years? It seemed unlikely.

Nevertheless, it was important to Josefine and so Lily had agreed to help her – she just had to work out how. Auntie Glenda, she decided, would be her first port of call. Glenda had already recalled several details from that time. What other nuggets might she have up her sleeve?

'The lovely thing, Lily . . .' – and his voice seemed to caress her name as he brought her thoughts back to the here and now and the man beside her – 'was what you did.'

'Hmm?' They were slowing now, getting closer to their destination, and Lily put her hand in the water, enjoying the silky feel on her skin. She could see the brightly coloured houses on the promenade and the grey church right on the tip of the peninsula.

'Choosing to have the stone placed into a pendant for your sister, caring about her, coming to find her in the first place, helping her in the *caffè* . . .'

Lily looked down at her hand, trailing in the water. 'I always wanted a sister,' she confessed.

He laughed. 'Only you can make an unselfish act sound selfish.'

'Oh.' She was taken aback by that. Embarrassed too. It was the way he said *only you* that touched her. As if he knew her somehow . . .

CHAPTER 43

Camogli, Italy, 2018

He takes the bus from Camogli to Ruta and walks from there to the hamlet of San Rocca. He used to take a different route. He used to practically skip up the mountain track from Camogli, past figs, olive groves and derelict villas with overgrown vines. Past tall bamboo, lime trees and horse chestnuts, with cockerels crowing and donkeys braying, the scent of citrus, olive and thyme in the air. But it is a steep trail from Camogli uphill to San Rocca and he cannot manage it now — there are far too many steps. Now, from Ruta, he does the much shorter and level walk instead.

Next to the old villa with the faded fresco on the side, at number sixteen, there is a bride-to-be, or just married perhaps, evident from the shiny white rosettes tied to the gate and railings, the white hydrangeas in white-tissued vases. He leans against the green railings and stares out to sea. From here, the views of the coast, down to Genoa and beyond, are the best views you can get.

Marriage, he thinks . . . That is why he is here. A pilgrimage, you might say, to the church of San Rocco, because this was where they married all those years ago.

His wife Caterina lived in San Rocco with her family, and so it was that they married here, following tradition. Following tradition in other ways too by way of the bridal gown she wore of white lace, her demure veil, the church full of family, friends and flowers.

Ah . . . He walks on, more slowly now, his head full of memories; a heavy load. He misses her — the quiet companionship of their life together; the family life with their two sons; the life they made.

A cacophony of church bells breaks into his reverie, ringing one after the other from hilltop to valley to hilltop, sounding the silence, clanging out the hours. Three, he notes, as he breathes in the scent of sweet resin from the pines.

Living together for so many years meant that their days fell into patterns and rituals which they both understood, because they had created them together, like a dance; one step forward, two back, three forward and so on. Demand and compromise. He probably did more of the demanding, she the compromise — and here, they had been traditional too.

The railings transition into a low wall and still the pines frame the village of Camogli, the bell tower and dome of Santa Maria Assunta and the Castello della Dragonara on the promontory. He turns as an Ape truck trundles down the street belching fumes. But the green dome of the church of San Rocco is in his sight now, surrounded by the bright Ligurian houses, the hamlet perching uncertainly on the cliff as if contemplating the dive in.

Some marriages might be about diving in, he thinks, but not his and Caterina's. Their marriage was more of a gentle swim across the bay, easing themselves over lightly rolling waves, riding the crest, coasting through. There were always ripples, but in their case, no tidal storms.

So many trees . . . He walks on. The woodland cloaking these

308

mountains is sufficiently thick to lend a soft thermal tranquillity to the air. He breathes in, savouring the musty smell of damp soil and rich leafiness, very different from the air at sea level below. Here, he feels immersed in the inner earth. Is this what it would feel like to be buried alive? Now that is something he does not want to find out, however old he gets. He chuckles.

He takes the boardwalk path, the woodland dropping steeply down to his right before the houses begin again, signalling the entrance to the hamlet. He stops at Pippi's bar for an espresso and a slice of focaccia. Even this walk is more tiring than he remembers and he supposes it will become more tiring with every year that passes, until he can no longer do it at all.

Eugh. He swallows the coffee, bitter on his tongue, bites into the salty focaccia. What is he complaining about? He still has two sons, one grandchild and most aspects of his health remaining. And he can still eat, for God's sake – and enjoy it too. He can still linger outside a caffè and enjoy the afternoon sunshine. But is he putting it off – even now? He pays the bill, rises unsteadily to his feet. Perhaps.

He is paying homage to her, to their marriage. She rescued him from a bad experience. And she remained constant. This pilgrimage seems the least he can do to atone.

He enters the pale-yellow church and stands on the patterned marble floor in front of the altarpiece, where he stood before. As then, he looks around him – at the stained-glass windows, the frescos, the gilt decorations and the dome of cherubs above. He knew even then and he knows now . . . But how can anything ever be perfect? This is a truth of life that he has had to learn.

He turns and walks back, out of the door, standing at the top of the marble steps, contemplating the view before him. To his left, the everlasting sea, the coastline to Genoa and beyond sparkles as seductively as the future he once had; to his right, the wooded hillside reminds him of home. In front of him, the two umbrella pines form a guard of honour.

Their friends and families cheered, cried, threw rice at them. They had photographs taken standing by the railings with the view of the future, the sea a beautiful backdrop behind them – nothing more.

Now, he sits on a bench on the Via Morelli beside the church, by the old water fountain, and gazes out to that same sea. 'I am sorry,' he whispers.

He misses the quiet companionship of their life together, this is true. He misses the patterns, the rituals, the way they mastered the steps of the dance. What he does not miss and will never miss . . . Ah, well, that is the thing, is it not? He will never miss the sadness that always remained half buried somewhere in Caterina's eyes.

CHAPTER 44

Lily

2018

'Are you an only child?' Lily asked Nico. 'Do you have any brothers or sisters?'

They were on their way back to Perlarosa in the boat and she was reflecting on her search for Josefine, wondering if it had been prompted partly by her not having any siblings. Plus, they had spent the whole day together and yet she knew so little about him still.

It had been a good day. But not exactly what she had expected. They had begun by wandering past the market stalls by Portovenere's harbour and strolling down a narrow strip of a street that ran parallel to the promenade. Like the other towns Lily had visited here in Liguria, the houses were narrow and tall, casting their shadows over the street, filling it with fragrances of tomatoes, garlic, *focaccia* and flowery perfumes emanating from kitchens, windows and wrought-iron balconies.

311

'Remember that this – it is a tourist trap,' Nico warned her, but Lily couldn't help but be charmed by the tiny independent shops selling jars of olives, green pesto and pasta, bottles of the local wine, *focaccia* and fried fish.

Every so often, a sweet and sunny little walled piazza with a fountain and an olive tree came into view, and she caught frequent glimpses of the sea down past narrow-stepped alleyways. Lily wanted to dip into every shop, see everything there was to see, and he watched her, smiling, seeming to enjoy her enthusiasm.

'Everyone walks this way, up to the church,' Nico informed her, when they came to the end of the busy street, 'and it means that we will pass Cala dell'Arpaia, Byron's Grotto.'

'Ah, yes.' Lily remembered what Josefine had told her and so she was not surprised to learn from Nico that Byron had drowned in the waters between Lerici and Portovenere. What with him and his mate Shelley . . .The Romantic Poets, she thought, had done far too much swimming for their own good.

In the grotto – a truly magical place, Lily felt – they sat on the rocks and relaxed for a while. From here, there was a good view of the coastline opening up towards Genoa, and also of the nearby castle and cemetery on the hill. The turquoise water was so clear that Lily could see right down to the fish swimming just above the sea bed.

Lily had thought ahead, and was wearing her bikini under her sundress, but now, she hesitated. 'Aren't you going to swim?' she asked Nico. She wasn't sure about stripping off in front of him, but the water was very tempting.

'Not right now. Look.'

Lily followed the direction of his gaze. She could see

something black-blue and filmy just below the surface, some jelly-like substances trailing in the sea.

'Jellyfish,' he told her.

'Oh.' She could see them now and there were rather a lot of them. What a shame . . .

Nico pointed along the coastline. 'Have you visited the Cinque Terre region?' he asked her.

Lily shook her head. 'It's my first time in Italy,' she said. 'Tell me about it?'

And so, he described the five little villages situated on the clifftops, the past hardships that the people had endured, the enterprising way in which they had built their terraced olive groves and vineyards on the slopes and how their unique beauty had attracted visitors from all round the world.

'Has that spoilt the five villages?' Lily asked. She guessed so, although perhaps tourism had helped keep them going, since the landscape hadn't made it easy to survive.

He shrugged. 'The truth is, they are too small to take the vast numbers,' he said. 'So many people crowd onto the tiny platform at Vernazza station at once that it is hard for them to get off. And when they come into the village . . . pff.'

'Pff?' She glanced across at him. He seemed so much more relaxed today, leaning back against the rocks, taking in the sunshine. There was a stillness about this man that appealed to her. It seemed like self-confidence — self-knowledge perhaps. But he was not always like that, she reminded herself.

'It is like an invasion of locusts,' he said gloomily.

'Perhaps I'll give it a miss then,' Lily said.

'But it is such a glorious area, Lily.' Lightly, he touched her shoulder. 'Perhaps instead, come back to us out of season. Liguria — she is so much more beautiful then.'

'Yes, I can imagine.' And Lily very much expected that she would return. Was it Italy that had crept into her soul? Was it Liguria, this very special part of the Italian Riviera? She could still feel the sensation of his warm hand on her shoulder. Or was it the people who lived here? A combination of everything, she suspected.

She thought of the gemstone, the anatase that could have been first mined in the mountains behind Genoa and which signified hope, trust and the heart chakra. Was there a story to that? One that meant something to Josefine's birth father perhaps? For Josefine's sake, she hoped they could find out, but they had less than a week in which to do it. Lily had already booked her flight back to the UK. In seven days' time, she would be gone.

From the grotto, they walked up the steps made up of pink, white and grey paving slabs to the building that Nico introduced as the Gothic church of San Pietro. It was very striking, she thought; in particular, its filigree green bronze door with miniature sculpted biblical figurines. The door was worn with time and from the elements it had to face night and day in its position right on the tip of the rocky peninsula, but it remained very impressive.

After exploring the interior of the church and admiring the view of the Bay of Poets at the rear, Nico suggested that they visit the cemetery.

'The cemetery?' That hadn't been quite what Lily had envisaged seeing.

'It is very fine, and a necessary place to see,' he confirmed solemnly.

'Okay then.' She shrugged and they walked up some granite steps, and down the cobbled walkway under spreading conifer trees.

It was, however, unlike any cemetery Lily had ever seen. 'What an amazing burial ground,' she said. 'If you had to die, could there even be a lovelier final resting place?' There were so many gravestones and plaques and the most spectacular views of the church of San Pietro on the rocks and out to sea.

But Nico had gone very quiet, and he made no response as he led the way out and towards the castle ramparts and another more ancient church in Piazza Lorenzo. Lily examined the crumbling barley-twist pillars and pale tangerine chapel, and took more photos than she needed, just to fill the silence. Something was wrong, but she had no idea what it was or what to do about it. Was it the cemetery? Had he lost someone dear to him – a parent perhaps? She wouldn't ask him, though, she decided. Let him speak in his own time.

They had a very late lunch down at the waterfront watching the people and the boats go by and Lily felt sad that she didn't have more time here in Portovenere. She'd return, she decided, on her next visit. Would it be with Nico? She simply had no idea. Sometimes she felt as if she was getting close to him, sometimes they felt miles apart.

He remained quiet for the rest of the afternoon, but Lily sensed that his change of mood had nothing to do with her personally. It was more about this secret sadness that he seemed to hold inside him, she guessed.

Nevertheless, she had enjoyed his company and quite liked the more relaxed side of Nico that had emerged today and which was almost a relief from the intensity she'd experienced before. She was still curious to find out more about him, though, so when she sensed his mood was lifting as they were coming home on the boat, she risked a personal question.

'I am an only child, yes,' he told her now. 'And like you, I

315

always wanted a brother or a sister.' He stared out to sea, back to Portovenere this time, and she caught a glimmer of a smile as he turned to face her. 'Is it not always the way? We want what we do not have?'

'Perhaps you're right.' Lily too was watching Portovenere disappear in the distance: the grey and white striped church, the rocky peninsula, the castle on the hill . . .

'And at times . . .' – he grinned – 'it is nice to have all the attention of our parents, no?'

'I suppose so.' Lily thought of her own parents. 'My father gave me a lot of attention,' she admitted.

'And your mother?' He was watching her closely.

Lily considered. Sometimes it had seemed as though her mother was more like a sibling, competing with Lily for attention, rather than a parent with attention of her own to give. 'Not so much,' she said. 'But I'm learning now that she had a lot of disappointments in her life. So perhaps she wasn't so capable of giving me her time, her love?'

'Ah,' he said. 'The family story.'

She smiled back at him. 'The family story.' And it was a story that she was sure wasn't quite over yet.

'But also, the only child – he or she must shoulder all the expectations.' Nico looked thoughtful, his grip light on the tiller of the boat as they cut a pathway through the water. 'My father, he only wanted me to be successful, in business, or in whatever profession I chose.'

'And were you successful?' Lily knew she was sliding close to the edge of dangerous ground. After their day together in Portovenere, just how much was the silversmith willing to confide?

He eyed her seriously, as if he knew exactly where her

316

thoughts had taken her. 'I suppose I was, up to a point,' he said. 'I worked hard, the company did well, I made some money.'

Ahead, in the harbour of Perlarosa, she saw a small fishing boat coming in, gulls flocking above it, shrieking into the wind. 'But?' she suggested. From his tone, there seemed to be one.

'But there is always a price to pay, is there not?' His voice was so low now that she had to lean forwards in order to hear him over the sound of the engine and the rush of the sea.

'A price?'

'Stress,' he said. 'Long days working instead of being with those you love. Worry. It eats into you, you know?'

'Yes.' She did know. She worked with people who were nine times out of ten suffering from stress – otherwise they might not have called her in. Her job could be stressful too, and living in London, that hectic pace had compounded it. Lily could cope with it, but sometimes she wondered if she should consider going back to live in Dorset or somewhere a bit quieter where she could at least hear herself think.

What would it be like to live here in Italy? The thought drifted into her mind and for some reason it seemed hard to dispel. But what was to stop her? She could do her work here, her sister was here and she was already more than half in love with Perlarosa. Hadn't she been looking for a fresh start?

She sneaked a look at Nico. 'Is there a man involved?' Cate had asked. Yes and no, she thought.

Lily was lucky – she didn't have to go into an office every day. Working freelance was edgy – you never had that sense of stability that you got from having a steady and permanent job – but it was far more interesting and Lily valued the variety. If she didn't work freelance, she wouldn't have been able to stay

317

over here for as long as she had, she wouldn't have been able to get to know Josefine in the way she had. And she wouldn't be on this boat with Nico the silversmith right now.

Lily waited for Nico to say more. But the door was still closed, she realised. Perhaps it always would be.

'Whereas being a silversmith . . .' she said, instead of asking the question she wanted to ask, 'that is not stressful in the least, I imagine?'

He came out of his reverie, his gaze brightened. 'Only when customers require beautiful pendants to be made in less than a week,' he teased.

That was better. Lily was relieved. If he didn't want to go there, then she wasn't about to push. She looked towards Perlarosa. The late afternoon light was slanting over the pink and red houses, making the entire village glow.

'I suppose you don't get many of those sorts of clients.' Once again, as the boat slowed, she trailed her hand in the water. It was delicious and irresistible.

'Very few.' He looked at her with an expression that seemed at once thoughtful, amused and . . . tender?

She frowned. This man was a mass of contradictions. One minute he was so intense she could feel herself going into some sort of meltdown, the next he was brusque. He could be funny, he could be serious, and he certainly could be sad . . . Did he like her? She had no idea. Did she like him? She wasn't sure about that either. Not that there was any point in becoming involved with a man who lived so far away. But . . . There was something.

When they arrived back at Perlarosa harbour, Lily realised that she didn't want the day to end. She ought to get back to Josefine and yet the *caffè* would have closed by now and she could see her sister tomorrow. She needed to phone Glenda too, but . . .

'And now, a drink perhaps?' He touched the side of the boat as if he was thanking her for bringing them safely home. Lily smiled. She liked that.

'Okay,' she agreed. 'Thank you so much for taking me to Portovenere, Nico.'

'It was a pleasure,' he said. And he certainly sounded sincere.

Lily struggled to get out of the life jacket and he came to her aid, standing very close as he undid the straps and helped pull it over her head.

'Thank you.' She always seemed to be thanking him. He was standing close – very close – and although he'd freed her of the life jacket, he didn't move away. Lily looked up at him, into those dark eyes that held so many secrets. *Who are you?* she wondered.

'It was a perfect day. I thought . . .' He sighed.

'What?' she whispered.

'I thought that I would never have such a day again, and yet . . .' One of his little shrugs. 'Here we are.'

Here they were indeed. 'But still, you were sad?' She had said it before she could stop herself from saying it. She needed to know.

'But still, I was sad.'

She felt the pull of him, drank in the scent of him, that mix of the metallic with dry saltiness. Instinctively, she lifted her face and he bent so that his lips were so close to hers that she was sure he would kiss her. Gently, he reached out and brushed her hair from her face. It was just the faintest touch and yet the jolt ran right through her. *Oh my*, she thought.

He must have felt it too. He didn't kiss her. He stared at her, stepped back and abruptly the spell was broken. '*Andiamo*,' he said. 'Let us go for that drink.'

'Yes.' Though she was so shell-shocked she was finding it hard to speak.

All of a sudden, across the piazza, she sensed that someone was watching them. A figure was standing outside the Marina Bar and as Lily watched, she slipped inside. Carlotta, she realised. Was she here with Gianni?

'And then,' said Nico. 'I will let you go.'

But did she want him to let her go? Lily wondered. That was indeed the question.

CHAPTER 45

Lily

2018

Inside the busy Marina Bar, they chatted – but not about anything too personal this time. Among people, the atmosphere between them had changed.

Lily asked him about his work. Did he get much business tucked away in Perlarosa? Was the silversmith's workshop too off the beaten track, or were there enough tourists looking at his jewellery and silverware?

She thought it was a safe topic, but he gave her a searching look. 'You are asking me if I earn a decent enough living, yes?'

'No!' She was horrified. He made it sound as though she was interviewing him as a potential marriage partner, for heaven's sake. When this thought occurred to her, she blushed; she could feel the heat of it creeping right up to the top of her head. 'Of course not,' she said. 'I just meant . . .'

But he was smiling, so Lily smiled too. 'It's kind of the business I'm in, remember?'

'Yes,' he said. 'I remember.'

But Lily was cross with herself for asking the question – especially after what he'd told her on the boat about his father putting pressure on him to be successful. It had been insensitive of her, she felt.

They continued chatting about this and that, but they had, Lily sensed, both taken a step back. Two steps forward, one step back. Was this how it was going to pan out? It seemed so. But maybe without as many steps forward as she would like.

They didn't linger in the bar for very long and they were both quiet as they walked up the little street towards their respective homes – or in Lily's case, the B & B, she reminded herself, which was beginning to feel like home, since she had been there for so long. But it was a comfortable silence, she felt, and she was enjoying the walk. The tall and narrow stone houses which had absorbed the warmth of the day were so close that they seemed to wrap themselves like a blanket around Lily and Nico as they strolled between them. Lily smelt the fragrances of jasmine and warm stone and felt a slow sense of tranquillity wash over her.

'Thanks for today,' she said, when they came to the crossroads of narrow alleys which was their parting of the ways. 'It was lovely.'

'I am glad you enjoyed the trip.'

In the darkness, his expression was hard to read. Lily was aware that they were resorting to politeness – which was perhaps a bad sign. 'Portovenere is a very special place,' she added. And Nico? She had to admit that he was a special man. He was complicated, yes. But would she like to get to know him better? She knew that she would.

Lily waited, half hoping that he might suggest a final coffee

322

together before they said goodnight, and half hoping that he would not. It was all rather confusing – not least her own emotions.

'Shall I walk you back to your place?' he asked. 'It is no trouble.'

She hesitated. But suddenly, she wanted to be alone, she realised. She wanted to think and replay the day to herself. And he was, clearly, just being polite.

'I'm fine,' she told him. 'But thanks, anyway.'

He gave a little nod. 'Goodnight then, Lily.' His voice was as soft as the darkness surrounding them.

'Goodnight, Nico.'

He came a step closer. Kissed her on the cheek once, twice. Did his hand linger on her shoulder a few seconds longer than necessary? Did he look at her once again with that same note of tenderness? Did he hesitate – as if he might kiss her on the lips?

Lily wasn't sure. It could just be her imagination and the close proximity of the man. At any rate, the moment passed and all she could do was walk away.

She was deep in her own thoughts by the time she reached the Piazza Figoli. Being an analytical person was certainly doing her no favours right now. What did that word really mean? How could she interpret that gesture? It was impossible to know.

In the square on the bench under the ilex trees, a figure stirred.

Lily jumped. She had not forgotten that encounter with Gianni and although she was confident that Perlarosa was one of the safest places on earth . . . who really knew?

'Oh.' In the next second she realised that it was Carlotta. She'd seen her earlier outside the Marina Bar. And now? This couldn't be a coincidence. She slowed.

Sure enough, as she saw Lily approaching, Carlotta put a hand to her belly and got to her feet. Her pregnancy was much more visible now, Lily noted.

'*Buona sera.*' Lily nodded, but Carlotta wasn't going to let her get away with that.

Out it came, a torrent of fast Italian that Lily had no hope of comprehending. She could only stand and listen. 'I'm sorry, I don't understand. *Mi dispiace. Non capisco,*' she said, because thankfully, she had learnt some Italian phrases while she was here, and perhaps the most useful one was how to say she did not understand.

But Carlotta continued unabated. She looked close to tears. She was wringing her hands. And Lily thought she heard the word '*sorella*' which she knew meant 'sister'.

'*Mi dispiace,*' Lily said again. Because if Carlotta was concerned about her sister . . . Lily certainly knew how that felt. Nico had told her that Carlotta was still suffering, and it looked as if he'd been right.

Carlotta barely stopped for breath before continuing again.

Lily shrugged helplessly. She caught the name *Nico Ricci*. Carlotta's sister must be Nico's wife – or ex-wife, she supposed. Was Carlotta warning her off? She guessed so.

Lily wasn't scared. In fact, she felt sorry for the woman. Carlotta seemed so distressed. What could Lily do? Perhaps she was simply berating Lily for asking Nico to help to persuade Gianni and Carlotta to leave Perlarosa? It was possible, but Lily was sure it was more than that.

She wished she was fluent in Italian. And she wished she knew what had made Nico leave his home town and his wife and what had upset Carlotta so much about it all. Whatever it was, Carlotta seemed determined not to let him forget it, not

324

to allow him to move on. But then, Lily didn't know the full story. What she did know was that when it came to Gianni and Carlotta's affair, it felt as if Carlotta was being punished more than Gianni had been.

At last, with a final stream of rapid Italian, Carlotta turned and walked away. Lily watched her go. She felt terrible about all this, but what could she do when she didn't know the facts or speak the language?

But Lily gave herself a stern talking-to on the way back to her B & B. A relationship with Nico Ricci was not a good idea for so many reasons, quite apart from whatever Carlotta might have been trying to tell her. Everything seemed to be much too complicated.

She knew that there had been a charged moment between them. When they'd arrived back at the little harbour and he'd helped her out of the life jacket, she knew that he had felt something too.

But perhaps he had then regretted that charged moment? And perhaps . . . Lily sighed. Perhaps that was a good thing.

CHAPTER 46

Josefine

2018

The next morning, Josefine was expecting to see Lily first thing – she was hoping her sister might have come up with an idea as to how they might go about searching for Josefine's birth father. Surely there must be a way . . .

But there was no sign of her. As she rearranged the snacks under the counter, Josefine wondered how it had gone in Portovenere with Nico the silversmith. A strange choice of companion . . . But she supposed that soon Lily would come by and then Josefine would find out. The man was unusual and somewhat of a recluse, but Josefine guessed that Lily had a bit of a thing about lame ducks. She had helped Josefine, had she not?

But in the event, it was only Angelo who turned up at eleven o'clock, ready for his espresso and chat.

'What can I do to help, Josi?' he asked, as he had been asking every morning since that stupid fall.

Why was it, Josefine wondered, that when you were young

you fell over and that as you got older you 'had a fall'? She didn't mind getting older – what choice did one have, after all? – but she was not completely past it yet, was she? There was still time . . . for something.

'*Basta*,' she said. 'Enough, Angelo. You have helped me more than enough.'

'It is no problem,' he said. 'You know the doctor said you should continue to rest that ankle. "Do not go crazy," those were his exact words, I think.'

'I am not going crazy,' she said through gritted teeth. Though she would if Angelo kept on about it. 'But I can cope on my own now. I am grateful to you and Lily for all you have done, but that time – it is now finished. Okay?'

He held up his hands in mock surrender. 'Okay,' he agreed. 'But if you change your mind . . .'

She nodded as she whisked past him. '*Si*. You will be the first to know. Coffee?'

'Please.'

Josefine was conscious of his eyes on her as she bustled around behind the counter. He meant well, of course. After her wonderful birthday meal, Josefine was determined not to be grumpy.

She took the coffee over, and sat down for a few moments. It was good to take the weight off. In truth, that ankle was still aching from time to time but neither Angelo nor Lily needed to know that.

Angelo was eyeing her over his coffee cup now. 'It is good to see you two getting along so well,' he remarked.

Oh, but he looked so innocent . . . 'We two?' Though she knew who he was referring to, naturally. And it was quite true. Her sprained ankle and the enforced rest had been a trigger for Josefine to let someone in – and that someone had ended up being the younger sister she had not even known existed. It was funny how things turned out.

He only grinned. 'She has not come over this morning?'

'Not yet.' Josefine was determined not to mind that once again Lily was the main topic of conversation. Still, she sighed.

'What is it?' He frowned.

'Is there something you want to tell me, Angelo?' She braced herself.

'Hmm? No . . .'

'Are you sure?'

'*Si*, I am sure.' But he did look a little shifty.

Josefine moved the small basket containing the olive oil and balsamic over to the other side of the table. 'I am your friend, yes?'

'It would seem that way, yes.' He winked at her.

'And you confide in your friends, is that not so?'

'Yes,' he agreed. 'Perhaps. Sometimes.'

Allora . . . He was tricky. Was he playing some sort of game with her?

'Never mind,' she said. It would all come out eventually, she supposed.

'And you are wearing the pendant, I see.'

He stared at a point just above her breasts and Josefine fidgeted in her seat, picked the gemstone up between her fingers and let the touch of it soothe her. 'But of course,' she said. Since Lily had given it to her, she had been doing this exact thing quite a lot.

What had this gemstone meant to her birth father? she wondered. If the stone had indeed been mined here in Liguria, why had he ever taken it over to England in the first place? It was a

328

curious choice to make. And if it had been important enough to be taken, then why had he given the stone to Josefine's birth mother, if it was only a casual encounter and he had no intention of going back to her? Unless he *had* really cared for her and *had* fully intended to go back. Trust and hope, she thought. It was a mystery, and one that Josefine would love to solve.

'Such a special gift,' Angelo mused.

'Indeed.' Josefine smoothed her fingertips over the tabletop.

'Lily – she is quite something.' His eyes grew dreamy.

Oh, *mio Dio*. Abruptly, Josefine got to her feet, pushing the chair away with a clatter.

'Josi?'

'*Si, si*, excuse me, Angelo, I have to . . .' She pointed vaguely at some customers who had just come in and were now perusing the menu.

'Oh, *va bene*, okay, off you go then.'

He simply had no idea.

Josefine served the customers, who predictably took an age to decide what they wanted, and then fetched someone else's bill. When she looked around, Loretta, the girl she'd employed to help out, was coming in the door, ready for the busy lunchtime shift. Josefine gave her a list of things to do and then forced herself to sit down opposite Angelo once more. He was taking his time over his coffee today. Perhaps he was waiting for Lily to arrive?

He put down his newspaper. 'And now you want to find your birth father, you say? I am surprised, Josi.'

'Why is that?' She had to stop herself from snapping at him.

'*Allora*, because he left your birth mother, no? Had a fling with her and then left her to cope with the consequences . . .' He gave her a pointed look. 'Alone.'

329

'Mmm.' Josefine did not care to comment on that right now.

'And so . . .' He spread his hands. 'You never wanted to know your mother – the woman who gave birth to you, who was forced to give you up for adoption because she was young and alone and had no one to support her . . .'

It sounded as though he had been talking to Lily. 'Yes, Angelo, and what is your point exactly?'

'In which case, why would you want to know your father?'

Josefine tried to remain calm. It wasn't his fault that he did not understand. 'Things change,' she told him. And she knew she had changed. 'People – they can change their minds. You do not know how it is, Angelo, when you know nothing of your family, your background.'

He grew more thoughtful. 'I suppose not.'

'It is different for you,' she said. 'You know where you come from, how your parents got together, why you came into this world, *si*?' Josefine was conscious that her voice was rising.

'*Si*, yes, maybe.'

'But of course, yes,' she snapped. 'So how can you hope to understand how it feels when you do not?' By now, she was glaring at him. She supposed she was overreacting; he was having that effect on her a lot lately.

'You want to know exactly what happened between them?' Angelo's eyes were calm. Calm and, yes, trying to understand, she had to admit.

She nodded. There was a lump in her throat and she felt as though she couldn't speak.

'I see.' Angelo reached across the table and put his hand on hers. 'Yes, I see.'

Josefine left her hand there. She appreciated the gesture of friendship and support. And besides, under his palm, her hand felt warm and safe and she liked the sensation. She closed her eyes, for a moment oblivious to the sounds around them, the bustling *caffè*, customers chatting, the gurgle and hiss of the coffee machine.

'Josi?' Angelo sounded concerned.

She opened her eyes. 'In fact, it is you who inspired me to look for him,' she said.

'Me?' He arched an eyebrow. 'How do you mean?'

'You and Sienna,' she explained. 'You two are so close, you have such a special relationship . . .' To her surprise, her voice broke. 'Father and daughter . . .' *Mamma mia*. Any moment and she would be crying again. 'And so, what of my father? Who is he? He may be alive somewhere still. It is possible, *no*? I may be able to meet him and find out everything I need to know. Can you imagine?'

Angelo had got to his feet. He led her out behind the counter to the back kitchen and Josefine did not resist.

'Yes, Josi, I can imagine,' he said softly when they got there. 'And I am sorry. For upsetting you. For not trying hard enough to understand.' He took her in his arms and he held her.

Josefine found herself leaning into him, relaxing against him, as if he was relieving her of some of the burden she carried, a burden she had carried for as long as she could remember. Their bodies folded together; a natural fit and a comfortable one. And how wonderful it was to feel comfortable, safe and secure. Angelo's arms were wrapped around her, and it felt good. It felt . . . Josefine tensed. She felt something else then, something she had not felt for a long, long time.

But this was Angelo. And Angelo was . . . *For the love of Madonna* . . . She pulled away, barely registering the hurt expression in his eyes. It would be wrong. She took another

331

step away from him. Why was it that life or fate or God brought you something good – in this case in the shape of her brand-new sister – only then to take something else away?

CHAPTER 47

Lily

2018

Lily bumped into Angelo in the piazza on her way to the *caffè*.

'Angelo, *ciao*.' They exchanged kisses on the cheek.

'*Ciao*, Lily, *ciao*.' He wasn't quite his usual cheerful self today; he seemed distracted. As for Lily, she felt distracted too after the events of yesterday.

'How is Josefine this morning?' She glanced warily towards Parodi's. They had fallen into the habit of discussing Josefine's moods as well as her ankle. Perhaps it was wrong of them, but it had proved necessary over the past few weeks and now it was hard to break the habit.

Lily was sure that Josefine was no longer as happy as she had been the day they'd bunked off to go to Lerici. Of course, her sister hadn't known about Carlotta's pregnancy then, but now, at least some of Josefine's problems had been solved. Gianni and Carlotta were leaving Perlarosa, Josefine could start again, and Lily had given her some ideas of how the *caffè* could turn

333

over a better profit and give Josefine more time off as well. Her ankle was better too. Was there something else troubling her? Lily hoped it wasn't her fault. Josefine had told her once that she didn't want her past to intrude into her present, and yet, here she was now, wanting to find her father.

'Feeling vulnerable, I think.' Angelo frowned. 'And not able to admit it.'

Lily nodded. She appreciated the warning. Angelo had known Josefine most of his life – he knew her better than anyone.

'She seems angry with me,' Angelo went on. 'I do not know why. At least . . .'

Lily touched his arm in a gesture of support. 'Maybe I can find out,' she whispered. Angelo had helped her – she'd love to return the favour.

He smiled. '*Grazie*. Thank you, Lily.' He took her hand and squeezed it.

Lily glanced across the square and saw Josefine in the *caffè*, wiping down a window table, staring at them, brow creased into a frown. Oh dear. What now? She waved.

'Bye, Angelo,' she said. 'See you later.' And she made her way inside.

It was another fifteen minutes before Josefine had time to sit down with her.

'So, how was Portovenere?' she asked.

'Beautiful. I loved it.'

'Hmm,' said Josefine. 'All the tourists do.' But her smile softened her words. 'And how was the silversmith? A bundle of laughs, I bet?'

Lily smiled back at her. 'Actually, he was pretty good company,' she said. 'You know, he may like to spend a lot of time alone – a lot of creative people do, don't you think? – but he's not a recluse. I think he's a nice man.' She didn't want Josefine to think badly of him, she realised. Despite Carlotta's warning last night, and even if nothing further was going to happen between Nico and Lily, she wanted her sister to give him a chance.

'Maybe you are right,' Josefine conceded, rather to Lily's surprise. 'Gianni certainly liked to spend time with the guy.' She paused, looking around the *caffè* to make sure no one was waiting.

'But Lily' – she leant closer – 'what about the thing we talked about? Have you thought of a way?'

Lily knew what she was referring to. Now that she'd had the idea, Josefine was clearly determined to take it further. But Lily suspected she would be disappointed. 'I could phone my Auntie Glenda,' she said cautiously. 'Our Auntie Glenda, that is.'

'You think she might know something?' Josefine's voice was eager. But she also sounded tired, Lily thought. She recalled what Angelo had told her. *Josefine is feeling vulnerable*. Would it be a good idea then for her sister to meet her birth father? To face what might be yet another rejection? Lily shrugged the thought away. It was unlikely to happen. And it wasn't for her to decide, after all.

'Glenda was around when they met,' she told Josefine. 'Our mother confided in her quite a bit, I think. But . . .'

'And she would remember?'

Lily thought of Glenda's razor-sharp mind. 'It's possible,' she said. 'If, that is, there is anything to remember.'

'*Va bene.*' Josefine nodded. 'Okay then, let us try.'

'Now?' Lily looked around the *caffè*. She was faintly surprised that Josefine hadn't wanted to wait until closing time, but waiting clearly wasn't an option for her sister.

'No time like the present.'

'Okay.' Lily pulled out her mobile. She supposed they had nothing to lose. She walked over towards the open doors that led to the terrace. There was better reception here and it also boasted the most amazing view. The colours of Perlarosa – pink church, pale green olives, ochre houses and red roofs – had a way of lifting her spirits and making her smile, especially when outlined against a deep blue sky. Lily sighed. There was a big part of her that really did not want to leave this town.

Josefine followed her towards the terrace, taking someone's order and shouting instructions to Loretta on the way.

'Auntie Glenda?' Lily had got through.

'Lily? You're still in Italy?'

'Yes, I am.' Lily smiled at Josefine. 'I've been helping out in the *caffè*. Josefine sprained her ankle. It's a long story . . .'

'Oh dear. Please send her my regards.'

'I will.'

'But you're coming home soon?'

'At the end of the week,' Lily told her. 'But in the meantime . . .'

'Yes?' Her aunt's voice sharpened with interest.

'Josefine wants to find out more about her birth parents.' Lily glanced at Josefine, who was hovering by the open doors.

'Ah, that's good,' her aunt said. 'It sounds as if the two of you are getting on swimmingly.'

Lily smiled across at Josefine. 'We are.' And it was a huge source of pleasure for Lily. Josefine could be tricky – this was undeniable. She continued to remind Lily of her mother, but she was helping Lily to understand her mother too. And the pure pleasure of getting to know Josefine was greater, far greater than Lily had ever dreamt.

336

'So how can I help?' Glenda became practical. 'What do you want to know?'

'Well, for starters, do you know Josefine's father's name?' Josefine took a step closer, eyes wide.

'Yes, I do. His name was Bruno.'

'Bruno,' Lily said aloud.

'Bruno,' Josefine repeated.

But there must be an awful lot of Brunos in Italy. 'Bruno . . . ?'

'Hmm, let me think.' Lily could imagine her aunt frowning. 'Something like a Ferris wheel?'

'Something like a Ferris wheel,' Lily whispered to Josefine. Josefine looked baffled. 'What is . . . ?'

'Ferrus? Feristo?' Lily wracked her brains.

'Fernando!' Glenda sounded triumphant. 'That's it, I'm sure. I never forget a name. Not for long anyway.'

Lily could believe it. 'Bruno Fernando,' she repeated for Josefine's benefit. But again, there must be an awful lot of Bruno Fernandos in Italy. If it was a bona fide Italian surname, that was. To Lily, it only sounded like part of the title of an Abba track.

'Bruno Fernando,' Josefine echoed. '*Va bene.*'

'I don't suppose you know what part of Italy he was from?' Though this was expecting rather a lot, even from her aunt. Her mother might not have known either, although even if she had, it would have been impossible to trace him back in the 1960s.

'No, my dear, I'm sorry. I'm not sure I ever knew . . .' Lily could hear the cogs whirring. 'But . . .'

'But?'

'I know where he was lodging. When he was here in Dorset, I mean.'

'Oh?' Though Lily couldn't see how that could possibly help. It was, after all, so long ago.

'Old Mrs Briggs's B & B.' Glenda lowered her voice as if Mrs Briggs was actually in the room.

Lily remembered her. But she had been at least fifty when Lily was a child. So, she'd be an old lady now. 'Surely she wouldn't remember?' she said doubtfully. That's if he even told her.

'Hardly.' Glenda tutted. 'She passed on over six months ago, Lily.'

'Then . . . ?' She would be of even less help presumably.

'But Helen still lives there. She took over the B & B years ago.'

'Helen?'

'Her daughter.' Glenda's tone suggested that Lily was being slow on the uptake. Perhaps she was. She gazed down at the spectacular sea view. Beyond the red-roofed houses, the sea glittered in the sun, and at the bottom of the village, she could see the dusky pink and grey bell tower of St Giorgio, outlined against the blue and cloudless sky.

'Helen. Ah, yes,' she said. She remembered her too, although she was only a passing acquaintance. And you think that Helen . . . ?' Lily let the sentence hang. She wasn't sure where Glenda was going with this.

Lily knew how hard it was to locate someone. People trawled through birth and death certificates for days, months even, just to find a small nugget of information about their family history. People contacted television companies and went on programmes like *Long Lost Family*, where experts did the trawling and had access to many more records than the amateur would have at their disposal. For Josefine, even finding out that

338

her birth father's name was Bruno Fernando might be as far as she would get. Back in the 1960s, biological fathers weren't named on the birth certificate if the mother was unmarried, or so Auntie Glenda had told her, and so any further detail would have to come from the mother herself. In this case: Marilyn. And she was no longer around to ask.

'In those days people kept records,' Glenda said. 'It's possible those records still exist. At the B & B, I mean.'

'You think?' Lily was sceptical. Records might have been kept there originally, but she doubted they'd be kept for so long. And even if they had, how would that help? Apart from confirming Bruno's surname, of course. But she supposed even that would be useful.

'In those days,' Glenda said again, and this time her tone was reproving as if it were Lily's fault that this was no longer the norm, 'people were more thorough.'

'I'm sure you're right,' Lily said meekly. She glanced across at Josefine, who was clearly straining to hear the other side of the conversation.

'I'll go round there.' Glenda was decisive, Lily would give her that.

'Really? Would you?'

'Of course. It's no trouble. It's only round the corner. I'll call in to see Helen and I'll ask her what happened to the old books. Because the name . . .'

'The name?'

'Bruno's name. Now, was it Fernando? I'm starting to doubt myself.'

Lily repressed a sigh. It wasn't Glenda's fault. It would be nothing short of a miracle if she remembered his full name after forty years. Should she mention the Abba track? Best not, she decided. 'Thanks, Auntie,' she said.

'Ooh, it's terribly exciting,' Glenda said. 'I always wanted to be a private detective when I was a girl. You know, following people and taking pictures. Catching them in the act.' She chuckled.

Lily laughed too. 'Well, let me know if you discover anything.' She didn't hold out much hope, but this was the only lead they had. Their only certainty was the name of Bruno and that on its own was next to useless.

'Leave it with me,' Glenda said. 'How old is Josefine again?'

Lily frowned. 'Josefine?'

'Yes.' Glenda tutted. 'We need to work backwards, Lily.'

'Oh, I see.' Lily got it. 'To find out the date they met, you mean?'

'Yes, yes, of course.' Glenda sighed. 'I need to look in the records, don't I? If they exist, that is. You can't expect me to remember which summer it was. Although Jane was, how old? Maybe three or four, maybe even five, so . . .'

'Fifty-three a few days ago.' Josefine had told her. Again, Lily glanced across at her sister, who nodded. 'So, they must have met in the summer of 1965.' How romantic that must have been. The summer of free love and all that hippy stuff. Had her mother been part of all that? She guessed so. Lily recalled a picture of her from around that time, where she was wearing a flouncy maxi skirt, a white cheesecloth shirt and love beads. She must find that one and give Josefine a copy, she thought. With her long blonde hair their mother had certainly looked the part at least. And then there was the free love, she couldn't help thinking.

'Good. Yes, that fits. Oh yes, and of course my David was

340

born the following year, and oh . . .' She paused and Lily could hear the emotion in her voice, guessed that her aunt was remembering that time and how difficult it had been for Lily's mother. She had said, hadn't she, that she had fallen pregnant herself while Marilyn had been in the mother and baby home.

'Thanks, Auntie Glenda,' she said again. 'I appreciate it.'

'No problem. I'll give you a ring later and let you know how it goes.'

Lily thanked her again and ended the call.

'Well?' Josefine's expression was eager.

'Don't get your hopes up,' Lily warned her. 'It's very unlikely we'll even be able to confirm his surname.' She decided not to mention the Abba track to Josefine either. But at least she'd tried. And even if they found out nothing more, it would be hard for her, but it might help Josefine to somehow put the matter of her birth father to rest.

Later that day, when Josefine and Lily were having a quiet drink together after the *caffè* closed, Lily's mobile rang. She checked the caller display. 'Auntie Glenda,' she told Josefine, and answered it. 'How's my favourite amateur sleuth doing?' she teased.

'You may mock.' Glenda chuckled. 'But . . .'

'But?'

'I had tea with Helen. And it turns out that her mother did keep records from when she first started running the B & B – exactly as I suspected.'

'Well, that's something, certainly.' Lily looked at Josefine, who was sitting in her seat, leaning forwards, trying to make out what was being said. Lily was reluctant to put her aunt on speaker phone though as the connection wasn't great and she wanted to have a filter in case Glenda said something unintentionally that might upset her sister. 'And does Helen still have these records?'

'She keeps meaning to sort through them and get rid,' Glenda told her. 'But luckily for us, she hasn't got round to it yet.'

'So, did you find him? Was he on record?' Lily was amazed.

'Yes! We trawled through that summer, checking all the names, and there he was.' She paused for dramatic effect. 'Bruno Ferrando. Not Fernando,' she added.

'Wow, you were so close!' Lily gave Josefine the thumbs up. 'It's Bruno Ferrando. Confirmed.'

'Incredible.' Josefine beamed. 'Please thank your aunt for me. Our aunt, that is.'

Lily nodded. 'Josefine says thanks,' she told Glenda.

'You're both very welcome.' Glenda paused. 'It was actually very interesting, seeing all those names from the past, reminiscing with Helen.'

'And how long did he stay in Dorset?' Lily asked.

'Three weeks.'

Wow . . . It hadn't taken their mother long to fall in love.

'And that's not all, my dear.'

'You found out some more?' Lily wondered if Helen's mother had spoken to her daughter about Bruno? It seemed unlikely. But could that be it?

'Well, yes. Rather a lot more, as it turns out.'

'Go on.' Lily knew that Josefine would be grateful for any information at all, anything that could help her piece together her roots.

'Mrs B had one of those old-fashioned visitors' books. That was the norm then, as well, in case you're wondering.'

'Right?' Though Lily wasn't entirely sure what she meant.

'Yes, and that was what we found. Name, signature, and . . .' Another pause. Once again, Lily thought, Glenda was savouring her moment. 'And home address,' she said.

'Home address?' Lily could hardly believe it. 'So, you know whereabouts in Italy he came from?' Opposite her, she heard Josefine give a little gasp. And it was incredible. This was supposed to be so difficult. How could one visit to a B & B in Dorset provide information that all the trawling of records in the world would probably have failed to produce? It was so weird, that something you would expect to be so complicated and out of reach could turn out to be relatively simple, dependent only on an old lady and her meticulous record-keeping.

Lily registered the excitement in Josefine's blue-grey eyes.

'Not only the region, my dear. I have an entire address. Town, street name, house number, the lot.'

'Wow.' Lily was lost for words.

'Of course, it's possible – probable even – that he no longer lives there,' Glenda said. 'You must remind Josefine of that.'

'Oh, I will.'

'And if you go looking for him, it might well end in disappointment.'

'I know.'

'He could be dead. Or . . .'

'Yes.' Lily had thought of that too.

'Well then, here you go. Have you got a pen?' And she read out the address, which Lily wrote down on a napkin, handed to her by Josefine, who was saying, '*Mamma mia*. I cannot believe it. *Mamma mia*,' over and over.

'Okay,' Lily told Glenda. 'I've got that.'

343

'And you'll go there?'

Lily glanced at Josefine, who was still shaking her head, a look of incredulity on her face. 'We'll go there,' she said. It couldn't even be far. The address was of a town in Liguria, the same region as Perlarosa, for goodness' sake. Which didn't surprise Lily as much as it might have done, if she hadn't found that gemstone, the anatase, known to be mined in the mountains behind Genoa. Josefine's father had once lived in Liguria. The question was, did he live here still?

'Good luck then, my dear,' said Glenda.

'Thanks, Auntie,' said Lily. 'You're a star.' She ended the call.

Lily looked at Josefine and Josefine caught hold of her hands. 'It is further up the coast,' she said. 'A couple of hours, no more.' Her voice was low.

Lily guessed she was holding a lot of emotion inside. But, yes, of course they would go there because Josefine wanted it. And together, they would deal with whatever they found.

CHAPTER 48

Josefine

2018

They set off for the town two days later, Josefine in a high state of nerves. Angelo had given them a lift to the busy station at La Spezia and now she and Lily were on the train heading for their destination. What would they find there? Or who? Josefine could not still the thoughts and feelings fluttering through her mind.

Why was she even trying to locate this man? she asked herself. After all, she had never wanted to know him before. But she had so many questions. The biggest one being, why had he abandoned her birth mother after giving her this precious gemstone? She touched the pendant lying just above her breastbone. It made no sense to her.

Josefine had wanted them to leave straightaway, as soon as they discovered Bruno Ferrando's old address, but she also knew she had to make arrangements for the *caffè*. It was decided that she would open as usual today: set up, do the early breakfasts

345

and then Loretta would come in to take over. Angelo would drop by to help with the lunchtime shift and then they would close earlier than usual. This plan gave Josefine and Lily most of the day for their quest.

They were fortunate, Josefine realised, that the return journey could easily be done in a day. She shifted in her seat and gazed out of the window at the Ligurian countryside as the train sped by. Though she hardly registered the landscape. One day . . . It seemed nowhere near long enough for such a momentous task.

'How are you feeling?' Lily asked her.

'Terrified,' Josefine admitted. 'Do you think he will be there, Lily? Do you think we will find him?' Though of course, her sister couldn't possibly know.

Lily didn't answer immediately. 'Perhaps not,' she said after a few moments had passed. She put her hand on Josefine's and Josefine was reminded of Angelo doing the exact same thing in the *caffè* the other day. But she did not want to think of that now. 'People move on,' Lily added.

'Though some people do not.' Josefine knew that her sister was keen to keep her expectations realistic, but she felt it only fair to point this out. 'Especially Italians. They often do not move on. In fact, they might stay in the same town their whole lives, even the same house sometimes, and then their children, they do the same.'

'Maybe.' Clearly, Lily was not convinced. And perhaps she was right. Perhaps Josefine was fooling herself.

Josefine let out a sigh. 'That is what I am hoping anyway,' she told her. There was no harm, was there, in hoping? 'Or even if he is not there, even if he is no longer with us . . .' She swallowed a lump that had appeared in her throat from nowhere. 'Or if he has, as you say, moved on, then someone else might be there, someone who knows.' Because Josefine so wanted to find out more. Wasn't knowledge power? She did not want to have this pathway whisked away from under her nose now that she had embarked on it.

'Yes, perhaps,' Lily conceded. 'But just don't hope too hard.' Her expression softened. 'I don't want you to be disappointed, that's all.'

Josefine shrugged. Was she not accustomed to disappointment? She glanced outside as the train pulled up at Sestri Levante. People descended from the carriage and walked briskly down the platform; others lingered to say a fond hello or goodbye to a loved one; cases and bags were hauled off and then onto the train. The doors closed. And off they went again. 'I will be disappointed however little I hope,' Josefine said, almost to herself. 'And without hope, what is there?'

Lily was still watching her thoughtfully. 'What will you say to him?' she asked. 'If he's there, I mean.'

That was easy. 'I will ask him what happened. How they met, how they parted, why he never returned to her, everything.' Did she not deserve to know the story?

Lily nodded. 'I'd love to know too,' she said wistfully.

Of course she would. Because it was Lily's story too. It was part of what had happened to their mother, part of what had made Marilyn who she was.

Josefine leant back in her seat. She stared out of the window again. They hadn't travelled so far and yet even this journey was new to her. What a sheltered life she had lived. Angelo was right. From a young age the *caffè* had become her life. Wasn't it indeed time for Josefine to get out and about a bit more, to travel, to see more of her own country, even the world? And

347

this was what she would do, she decided. She would aim to make the *caffè* more successful – if Lily's predictions were correct, this was a distinct possibility. And she would take time off to travel. She glanced at Lily. Even to England, maybe.

'It will be a shock,' Lily said after a few moments. 'For him, I mean. If he's there.'

'I know.' Josefine considered this. 'He might not even know about me.' She straightened up and shot Lily a look of trepidation. How strange that she hadn't considered this before. Wasn't it obvious? He might not know of her existence . . . Or – and this seemed worse still – what if he had known about her, and that was one of the reasons he hadn't gone back? *Mamma mia* . . . She was feeling more nervous than ever now. 'What do you think, Lily?' She leant forwards. 'Do you think Marilyn ever told him about me?'

'I don't know.' Lily seemed upset now. She was frowning and fiddling with the strap on her bag. She looked as if she'd quite like to catch the first train going in the opposite direction back to La Spezia. 'Wouldn't Mum have written to him? When she found out she was pregnant, I mean? That's what I've been thinking. Wouldn't that be the obvious thing to do?'

'Of course she would.' Especially if she was feeling as unsupported and alone as Lily had said. Especially if they were in love. Especially if she thought he might be able to come and rescue her, marry her, give her baby a father and a future. 'Why would she not? She was on her own. She was vulnerable. Why would you not turn to the man you love?'

'I never found any letters,' Lily said doubtfully.

'Maybe he did not write back to her.' Josefine was getting a bad feeling about all this now. What kind of man must he be to have put a woman in this position and then not stand by her?

They stared at each other, digesting this.

'I suppose it depends on how they left things when they parted,' Lily said slowly. 'Glenda seemed sure that Mum thought he was coming back . . .'

'And yet he did not.' That fact could not be doubted.

'But what if she didn't know his address?' Lily said. 'What if she had no way of contacting him and telling him about you?'

'Pff.' Josefine shook her head. 'She could have found it out, couldn't she? Just like Glenda did? It was written in the land-lady's visitors' book.'

'Yes, she could.' Lily frowned. 'And she worked on the reception in a hotel nearby, so she must have known how these things operated and that the landlady would have it . . .'

They exchanged another glance.

The guard came walking down the carriage and Josefine and Lily scrabbled for their tickets. '*Grazie, grazie*,' he said.

They waited for him to be out of earshot. Fortunately, they were practically the only ones in this compartment of the train.

'Unless they'd had a row?' Lily suggested. 'Or she didn't want him to know? Or . . . ?'

Josefine shrugged. She leant back once more in her seat. It was all speculation. Perhaps it would always remain specula-tion. But by the end of today, *allora*, they might at least know a little more of the story.

Lily was biting her lip and her shoulders were hunched practically up to her ears. Josefine touched her shoulder. 'Lily? What is it?'

'I'm worried for you, that's all. We don't know what we're going to find, and it might be . . .' – she hesitated – 'difficult to hear.'

Josefine gave her shoulder a quick squeeze. 'Do not worry,'

she said. 'I am not some innocent young girl who is expecting to throw myself into this man's arms just because he happens to be my biological father. I do not know him. I may hate him.'

Lily laughed. 'You might.' She sighed. 'But I started you off on this pathway and I can't help feeling responsible.'

Josefine raised an eyebrow. 'You are not responsible, Lily. It was my choice, remember?'

'Mmm.' But Lily regarded her appraisingly. 'Be honest, though. Didn't you want Angelo here with you today?'

Josefine glanced at her in surprise. So that's what she was thinking. 'Why? Did you?' She heard the edge in her own voice.

'No, I mean instead of me.'

Oh. 'No,' she said. 'I did not.' And she put her arm around Lily once again. Josefine was the big sister after all and she needed to reassure her. 'This is our journey, Lily,' she said. 'One that we must do together.'

CHAPTER 49

Camogli, Italy, 2018

*The church bell emits its dull clang as he wanders past. Wandering . . .
Now that's a word that says a lot, he thinks. When a man is young,
he strides around his territory (allora, and that of others sometimes).
But when he is old, he wanders.*

*Nearby, the tourists mingle around the entrance to the church,
admiring the grey-white statues of the saints in the niches of the facade,
looking down at the bright jickety-jackety houses lining the promenade.
The sun is glittering on the sea and it almost makes his eyes hurt, the
sheer brightness of it.*

*Meanwhile, the talk goes on . . . There are different languages.
Sometimes he allows them to wash over him unheard, but now, he pauses
to listen. He identifies Italian (too easy), Spanish, German and then
English. Sometimes this makes his breath catch, sometimes he cannot
resist glancing over . . . That is why it is safer not to hear at all.*

*The language of the church bell — that, though, is a language everyone
can understand. The bells call people to attention, to worship, to prayer.*

They proclaim the hour, they mark an occasion; they are a reminder of what needs to be done. But for him, now, there is nothing left to be done, surely? There is no one to answer to. His life — what is left of it — is certainly his own.

He walks more slowly across the fine, pebbled mosaic outside the church, which can be slippery and catch a person by surprise. 'Scusi . . .' From time to time, he has to wait for people to see him and move out of his way, for with age comes invisibility, as he has also discovered.

Language . . . This was his undoing once upon a time. If only . . . There are many if onlys still in his head; they fill it sometimes. He pauses by the church doors. These doors are also a proclamation of sorts, he thinks: signifying a holy place, a consecrated entrance, peace. And they are indeed a glorification. He stares at the wooden carving, follows the curve of the folds of a robe with his fingertip and wonders at man's patience.

Most of the tourists, though, give the magnificent doorway a cursory glance and then move away. Well now, he gives a little shrug — there is so much to see, there are so many things to grasp the attention, and the poor brain only has so much spare space for new observations. Even he does not know the significance of all the carved figures and flowers. He knows the church was built in the twelfth century, on a rock, and that is about it. Still, he gives it his full attention. He does not want to be one of those who look but never see.

He takes the steps up to the castle even more slowly. He always takes them, though, at least most days. It is his way of making sure he still can. He grits his teeth, wonders if crossing himself first would be overdoing it. Routine. Practice. That is the trick.

What use is poetry? he thought once. What use are pretty words and flowery sentences when they will not be understood? Better perhaps, he thought, to wait and say his words face to face. Give them meaning with his hands, his expression, the look in his eyes. Then, he thought, then he could make her understand. There are ways of making someone understand. But not when you are so far apart. And in this case, it was he who did not understand. It was another culture, another time, another way of seeing.

The Romantic Poets, they called them, those Englishmen who chose to exile themselves in Liguria. He had been a Romantic too. But what if romantic words make a man a fool? What then? Perhaps it was a lucky escape after all.

He walks down the steps to the narrow alleyway which leads to the artists' quarter. These alleyways – damp and silent and holding their secrets deep within – are the most ancient of Camogli. He looks up to a top balcony where a sheet and a pillowcase billow in the faint sea breeze. Some of these skinny houses are six floors high and all of them crouch in the shadow of the church and the castle.

There is a fish art gallery of all things . . . He gives a little snort of laughter. Paintings on stones from the beach, jewellery made of sea glass. The things men and women think of . . . It is hard for him to imagine making a living from such random pastimes, but long gone are the days when fishing was all.

He could not write that letter, could he? And under the circumstances perhaps that was a good thing. What he saw, what cut through him . . . now that will stay with him, no matter how many years pass. Like this town and its fishermen. Like history. Like the tolling of this ancient church bell.

CHAPTER 50

Lily

2018

From the railway station, they crossed the main road and took the *scalinata*, the steep steps by some green railings, down to Via Garibaldi. The long promenade of the town stretched out in front of them, lined with restaurants, bars and tall narrow buildings of ochre and rust, following the gentle curve of the bay and ending with a church and a castle built on higher ground. The water was turquoise, smooth and inviting – a few swimmers and paddle-boarders were already in – and the town was, Lily thought, almost as charming as Perlarosa.

Josefine too was gazing around her. Perhaps she was imagining what it must have been like for her father – growing up here, coming back here after he'd met their mother, choosing to stay here rather than return to Dorset. Lily just hoped that what Josefine found here wasn't going to be too upsetting.

'Oh, look.' Lily's attention was caught by a huge frying pan nailed onto the wall – she'd never seen *that* before.

They moved closer and she read the sign out loud. 'Left over from *la Sagra del Pesce* . . .'

Josefine nodded. 'The local fish festival – it is world famous,' she informed Lily.

They paused to take a closer look. Inside the pan were information and pictures, which showed the festival in full flow from 1952 – when apparently Camogli hoped to attract more visitors to the town, Lily read – through to 1982, by which time so many people attended that the frying pans had become as big as this huge specimen in order to accommodate all the fish they had to cook. She chuckled.

'*Mamma mia.*' Josefine was scrutinising all the old photographs.

Was she wondering if her birth father was pictured there? They could almost be just two of the many tourists flocking here today, Lily found herself thinking. Almost . . . but not quite.

On impulse, Lily reached out and took her sister's arm. Angelo was right. Josefine was vulnerable – even now, Lily could see it in her eyes. Josefine must have felt rejected and unloved, first by her birth mother, then by her adopted parents who had gone to live overseas, then by her husband Gianni. But she was also good at hiding it behind that veneer of self-assurance. More than that, when she felt herself under attack, Josefine didn't crumble; she fought back. This was why she so often seemed brusque and bad-tempered, Lily supposed. The question was, though, if they found Josefine's birth father, would his reaction make her feel better – or worse?

Josefine gave Lily's arm an answering squeeze before relinquishing it in order to check the directions on her phone. Lily waited for her to decide which way they were heading. She frowned. When she came to think of it, Angelo was the main one who had to put up with Josefine's bad temper. But why? Had he done something to upset her? Or . . . was it what he hadn't done that was the problem?

When she first arrived in Perlarosa, Lily had assumed that Josefine and Angelo were a couple. They had both told her they were close friends, but Lily was sure it was more than that – or that it could be. Look at how upset Angelo had been when he thought Josefine was leaving Perlarosa . . . Look at how he had helped her in the *caffè*, tirelessly, giving up so much of his free time for her. And there was more – there had been the new dress (Lily was convinced it had been for Angelo) and the dinner date that had ended so disastrously. Josefine always denied it, but surely they were destined to be more than friends?

'On to the harbour then.' Josefine tucked her phone in her pocket.

They made their way down a narrow shady passageway with tall buildings looming on either side, but already, Lily could glimpse the glittering sea beyond. Should she intervene between Angelo and Josefine? she wondered. She had promised Angelo to try and find out why Josefine might be angry with him. But if she did, surely no good would come of it? She didn't even know for certain how either of them felt about the other. Perhaps Angelo didn't want to commit to another woman again? Perhaps Josefine didn't want to commit to another man? Was Josefine not allowing Angelo to get close because she was scared of being rejected again? No. She wouldn't interfere, Lily decided. They would have to sort it out for themselves.

They emerged into sunlight and the dazzle of the sea, onto the wide paved promenade where steps led down to a public beach of grey stone. Lily looked from left to right taking in the sights and sounds. The promenade was busy and there was a holiday atmosphere about the place, as if the season was already in full swing. As they passed a *focacceria* she sniffed appreciatively. A coffee and a snack would be nice, but now Josefine seemed to have a new spring to her step and Lily guessed she wanted to get straight on. She was on a mission after all. They both were.

Ahead, Lily could make out the domes of the old town: the pink bell tower slightly reminiscent of the bell tower in Perlarosa, and the grey-stone castle on the promontory. The houses lining the promenade were traditional, but all different heights, with shutters of dark green and ochre.

Josefine pulled her phone out of her pocket once again and checked the map.

'This is a lovely town,' Lily ventured. Though the old *Bagni Lido* on their left had been converted into a pizzeria, and the town was crammed with shops, bars and restaurants with outside tables and parasols clearly aimed at the visiting tourist, each place looked individual and interesting. Lily felt her stomach rumble. Her fault. She should have eaten more breakfast this morning.

'Mmm.' Josefine was non-committal. She was becoming more focused by the second.

'How much further?' Lily asked.

'Just beyond the church. Not far.' Josefine shot her a quick glance and Lily's heart went out to her sister. Her nerves must be positively jangling by now . . .

They walked through the tunnelled archway under a building painted vivid tangerine, and to her delight got briefly tangled up with a wedding party having reception drinks and photographs taken there. It was a colourful affair. The bride was adorned with spring flowers, and female guests were dressed to kill in shades of royal blue and fuchsia with plenty of bling and stiletto heels. People were chatting and laughing, posing for photos against a massive sundial positioned on the wall by the Via al Porto. It was a sweet little square with an intricately mosaiced stone floor, and once again the scents of coffee, *focaccia* and tomatoes assaulted Lily's nostrils. But already, Josefine was striding on towards the harbour and Lily had to almost run to catch up with her.

The harbour was lined with rows of coloured houses and bars and cafés, all looking out over the clutter of ropes, pulleys and winches on the harbour-side, and fishing boats, trawlers and pleasure craft crowded wing to wing in the water. Lily spotted a diving boat on its way out to sea, another fishing vessel approaching the harbour mouth with shrieking gulls clustering overhead and even a family of ducks paddling safely close to the harbour wall.

Josefine meanwhile was scanning the houses. 'Which one is it?' she muttered. She peered at her phone and Lily looked over her shoulder.

'Up there?' she suggested. There was a terrace of mis-matching skinny houses in terracotta, pale browns and pinks, some very much the worse for wear.

'Umm . . .' Josefine hesitated, looking from her phone to the houses and back again.

Throughout the journey she'd been full of nerves, but now, as they gazed up at the row of houses, which might hold some clue to Josefine's background, Lily saw her straighten her shoulders, take a deep breath, almost become more steely

358

right in front of her eyes. Nevertheless, Lily took her sister's arm in silent support and received a flash of a smile in return.

They took a few steps closer. They could make out the numbers now . . . It was the terracotta house. There was nothing distinctive about it. It looked tired but not unloved. Like many of the houses around here, the paint was flaking from the walls, but the green shutters were flung open and a line of washing fluttered cheerily above the balcony. The house looked lived in, at least.

Josefine nodded at Lily. 'No turning back now,' she said. She walked up the steps and lifted the door knocker, letting it fall once, twice. She looked back at Lily, who gave her a smile of reassurance.

They waited for a minute or two, but no one answered. Josefine turned towards Lily again, disappointment etched on her face. She shrugged.

'Try again?' Lily suggested. She turned to look back at the view. From this house, to the left, she could see the pretty pink and cream bell tower, the ivory-coloured church and statues, the harbour wall like a bridge with deep arches. To the right, red and turquoise rowing boats were moored on the nearby harbour wall and above them were the brightly painted houses, shops and bars that hugged the promenade, many of them with wooden benches perched outside. A glorious sight to see every day of your life, she found herself thinking. If Josefine's father had stayed here all of his life, that was . . .

Josefine knocked again – louder this time – but still no one came to the door. She walked back down the steps. 'What now?'

'Maybe go and get a coffee? Come back later and try again?' Lily suggested.

'Yes. Or . . .' Josefine's face brightened. 'We could try next door? Everyone knows everyone in this kind of town.'

'Okay, go for it.' Josefine would know. Camogli was a bit bigger than Perlarosa, but very similar in many ways.

Lily waited while Josefine went back up to knock on the neighbour's door. For a brief moment, she thought of Nico, the silversmith. She would never be able to think of Perlarosa without thinking of him, she realised.

After a minute or two, the door was slowly drawn open to reveal a tiny, stooped elderly lady dressed entirely in black. Josefine spoke to her in rapid Italian that Lily had no hope of following and the old lady said something back. The conversation continued for several minutes. At one point, Josefine clutched onto the wall and Lily took a step towards her in alarm. What had happened? What had she discovered?

Finally, Josefine thanked the elderly lady and with many nods and smiles, the woman shut the door and Josefine turned to face Lily. She was beaming.

'What did she say?' Lily was starting to feel nervous now.

'He still lives here,' Josefine said.

'No! In this town, do you mean?'

'But, yes. Not just in this town but in this actual house. Bruno Ferrando. She knows him well. They are friends. He is still alive. He still lives here, Lily.'

'Oh my goodness.'

They stared at one another, almost in disbelief.

'Does he live here alone?' Lily realised that they had given little thought as to whether or not Bruno was married or had a family. Perhaps they should have done, but it was a bit late now.

'Yes,' Josefine said. 'I asked her. He lives alone.'

'And what else did she tell you?' Like, where might he be now, for instance?

'He was married,' Josefine told her. 'His wife – she died some years back.'

That was sad – but on the other hand, it might make things a bit easier for Josefine, Lily thought, if that wasn't being too insensitive. 'So what now?' she asked her sister. 'Did she have any idea where he might be?'

'There are a few possibilities.' Josefine's eyes were gleaming. She led the way back to the promenade. 'He is a creature of habit, she says.'

'And the possibilities are?'

Josefine pointed. 'Back there, under the arches. He meets his friends there sometimes.'

Lily shivered. 'So he could have been there when we walked by just now?'

'He could, yes.'

They were both silent, digesting this.

'Or he could be up there.' She pointed up the street. 'There is a certain bench around that corner. She described it to me.'

'Okay . . .'

'Or over by the church and the castle.' She gestured towards them.

'So which shall we try first?'

For a moment Josefine looked as if she couldn't possibly decide. Then she gave a little shrug and indicated the way they had come.

They retraced their steps. In the arched passageway under the tangerine house, a few men of around the right age sat next to a roughly hewn window looking out onto the quayside and chatting.

Lily and Josefine exchanged a glance.

'Will you be able to tell if it's him?' Lily muttered.

'I do not know,' Josefine whispered back.

They hung around for a few minutes, listening to what Lily supposed was idle chat. But then Josefine did that steely thing again and walked right up to them. Once again, she spoke in Italian of course, but Lily caught the name Bruno Ferrando and none of the men put up a hand or got to his feet. There was a general shaking of heads and then one of the group talked to Josefine for a few minutes, pointing and gesticulating back the way they had just come. Josefine thanked him.

'Any luck?' Lily asked her.

'They know him.' Josefine led the way back along the promenade. 'The old man with the beard said he might be up by the castle and church or he might be sitting on that bench the old woman told me about.' Once again, she shrugged.

He was a creature of habit indeed, thought Lily.

They tried the church and castle, observing the people rather than the buildings, the mosaics and the statues, but there were no likely looking candidates, just tourists milling around the piazza. And then they ducked down into the maze of narrow shady alleyways below.

'Perhaps he's gone somewhere else today,' Josefine said. 'Or . . . ?'

Lily looked at her sister. 'The bench?' she suggested.

They weren't exactly sure where the bench was located, but they walked back up to the narrow terracotta house by the harbour and then up the road in the direction the neighbour had indicated.

As they turned a corner, they came across a little belvedere, a lookout point with an olive tree, a scooter parked by an old

362

green water pump and, yes, a small grey bench. Was this the one? Perhaps. Lily could see immediately why anyone would want to spend time there; the view from the bench was perfect since it looked out over the harbour, the pretty coloured houses on the quayside, the church and the open sea beyond. And . . . Lily blinked.

Josefine had been just behind her, but now, she let out a little gasp and they shared a quick conspiratorial glance. Because sitting on the bench was a man, in his late seventies, she guessed, with a shock of white hair. He sat very still, staring out to sea.

'It is him,' Josefine whispered. She clutched Lily's arm. 'I know it. It is him.'

Lily wasn't sure how she could tell – from here, they couldn't even see his profile – but she seemed very sure.

'I will go and talk to him,' Josefine said.

'Okay. I'll wait here.' On hand, Lily thought. In case it wasn't him. In case he upset her. In case . . . well, whatever.

She watched Josefine as she walked over, as she sat on the bench beside him. He gave a polite little nod, but otherwise barely registered her presence. Lily guessed that he came here to be alone.

For a few moments, the two of them both sat looking out to sea. Was it her imagination? Lily wasn't sure, and they had their backs to her, but she thought she could see a resemblance – in the shape of their heads, the set of their shoulders.

The little square was surrounded by buildings of pink, orange and brown and in the tiny patio gardens in front, the oleanders were in full bloom. Lily could hear the sounds coming from the busy harbourside below – conversation, laughter, a boat's horn, the thrum of an engine starting up and a gentle splash.

And then Josefine turned and spoke to him.

363

Lily could see her expression – soft, gentle, curious.

They chatted for a few moments. He seemed approachable, he looked friendly, though of course you never could tell for certain.

And then Lily saw him turn towards her, a look of incredulity on his face. And in that moment, Lily knew that everything would be all right.

CHAPTER 51

Bruno

Camogli, Italy, 2018

He was sitting quietly on his special bench watching the fishing boat come in and letting his mind drift as it so often did. And where did it drift to? Usually into the past – remembering, reimagining, reliving and, yes, sometimes doing things differently this time around. He couldn't say he had no regrets. He hated to leave things unfinished and unresolved, and that business in England was both.

Over the years, though, he had been able to let it go – sometimes for short periods, sometimes for longer; distracted by Caterina, by his fishing, by his sons or grandchild. Always, though, it lurked in the back room of his mind. Should he have sent one of those letters he'd tried to write? Earlier, when he first got back to Italy? Because she wouldn't have known, would she, why he did not?

He frowned. Or perhaps he should have written later, when he returned the second time? What would it achieve, though?

he had wondered back then. Hadn't he seen how things were? What point would there have been in drawing it out, what point in recriminations? Wouldn't it have been just another way to linger in the past when what he should be doing was moving forward – and in a different direction now that he knew the truth? But as time went by, he realised that it might indeed have achieved something. It might have achieved some sort of resolution. He would know the reason why. And that might have allowed him to let go.

A young woman came and sat next to him on the bench. When he said 'young', this wasn't exactly the case perhaps, but once you passed seventy, everyone seemed young. He gave a slight nod, which acknowledged her presence but should make it clear he had no wish to engage. *Allora* . . . It was unusual – people generally left him alone when he sat here; they sensed he didn't want company. He sat almost in the centre of the bench for one thing, and this, he had found, gave him claim to the whole seat. Besides, this little square was not on the tourist route; it was half hidden and away from the promenade, the historic sights, the *gelato* and the restaurants. Most people who visited Camogli would not venture here. As for the residents – they knew him and they let him be.

He glanced at the woman from the corner of his eye and liked what he saw – strong features, an unsmiling mouth, but one which could smile in an honest way, he sensed; a deep intelligent brow and dark hair pinned up in an untidy but somehow appealing way.

Like him, she was gazing out to sea as if it could give her some peace, and he liked that too. Perhaps it didn't matter that a person like her should share his special bench. Why not, if she was *simpatica*? Maybe she too had things on her mind, maybe she too needed space in which to think.

But then she turned to him. 'Excuse me for interrupting you,' she said in a soft voice, 'but may I ask, are you Bruno Ferrando?'

This surprised him. He had been sought out – but why and by whom? 'Yes,' he said. 'That is I.' And then when she continued to gaze at him. 'Can I help you with something, *signorina*?'

She pushed her sunglasses up onto her head. 'Yes,' she said. 'I think you can. My name is Josefine. Josefine Parodi.'

He looked into her eyes. He was confused. Did he know a Josefine? He thought not. Did he know a Parodi? No, he was sure he did not. He nodded politely. 'I am afraid I do not quite see . . .' He let this hang. What he *could* see was that her eyes were very lovely. And, in fact, they were familiar, since they were a particular shade of blue-grey that reminded him of . . .

'My birth mother was Marilyn Bennet,' she said. And then as he sat there, frozen somehow by her words, 'I am sorry if that is a shock to you.'

He stared at her. Her words reverberated through his brain. 'Marilyn?' he whispered. Hearing her name, after so many years, when for so long it had existed only in his head . . . This was the shock. Seeing her eyes and trying to make sense of what this young woman was telling him. *Birth mother?* What was she telling him? That she was Marilyn's daughter, yes? Only . . . 'Birth mother, you say?'

'I was adopted,' she explained, quite matter-of-factly. 'By a couple living in England who then moved here to Liguria.'

'Liguria,' he echoed. This was getting stranger and stranger. His brain had no hope of keeping up. She was Marilyn's daughter, yes? Marilyn would have married, of course, he almost knew that much already. And had a child – he knew that too. But why would Marilyn's daughter have been adopted? And why Liguria?

'I believe that you may be my biological father,' she said.

He blinked at her. His mind seemed to turn to mush. 'Your . . . father?' Marilyn's daughter? His daughter? What was she saying? But as he stared at her, a feeling of incredulity creeping through his body, his mind . . . he noticed other things. The look of her – those strong features and wide mouth reminded him of his own mother. There was indeed a familiarity about her, and it wasn't just those eyes. Was it possible? He lifted his hand, saw that it was trembling, and reached out to her.

She took his hand and held it in hers. Her touch seemed to warm somewhere deep in the core of him and he wanted to take her in his arms. His daughter? But no, it could not be. He was seeing things he wanted to see as he so often did, that was all. 'I do not understand,' he said. He knew what he knew. 'How can this be true?'

'But, yes.' She smiled. 'I think it can be true. I am sorry for simply turning up like this, but . . .'

'How can this possibly be?' Although she was still holding his hand and he would not pull away. 'I saw with my own eyes . . .'

Her face softened. 'What did you see?'

'Marilyn.' Again, he said her name. He bent his head, just for a moment, remembering. He had thought he would never say her name out loud to another human being.

There was a man and there was a kiss and that kiss was seared into his memory like a firebrand. After everything that had happened . . . That kiss had broken him. And there was more. There was a baby – a very young baby.

'What about Marilyn?' she asked him. 'What did you see?'

'She was pushing a pram,' he said. 'And . . . the baby was much too young to be mine, you understand.' For a moment, now that he had met Josefine, something felt wrong with this account but for now, it eluded him.

'You went back to England to see her again?' she asked him.

'But, yes.' How could he not have gone back?

Josefine seemed to be considering his words and he appreciated that. She had her head held slightly to one side and she was still holding his hand. She was a serious type and he liked that too. 'Do you speak English?' she asked him.

It was not the question Bruno had been expecting. 'Yes,' he said. Although back then, his English had not been good at all.

When he first met Marilyn on the beach, there had been such a spark between them, he had never known the like. She had looked so beautiful with her golden hair and grey-blue eyes, slim legs stretched out on the shingle as she sketched the scene in front of her. He was mesmerised.

She had hardly noticed him at first, so caught up had she been in her work. And then . . . he had plucked up his courage, walked up to her, asked to look at her drawing. He had looked first at the sketch and then into her eyes and that was it. He was lost as if to the sea. All thoughts of his life in Italy disappeared. He was lost and drowning.

Yes, his English had been poor, almost non-existent, in fact. But somehow, in a language other than words, they had understood one another. And that spark had taken him to places he'd never even dreamt of.

'Because my sister is here,' Josefine told him. 'That is her.'

She pointed, he turned round, and this time Bruno did a complete double-take. For a moment, it could be Marilyn standing there.

'Your sister? *Mio Dio*,' he muttered.

'She is my half-sister, in fact. She came to Liguria to find me.'

So, yes, Marilyn had married, as he had assumed, and had children too. 'And you?' He had to find out more about her. She had been adopted, she had said.

'I do not think that I was the baby you saw,' she told him. 'I was not with my birth mother for very long. And she did not have a partner then – at least, as far as I know.' She seemed very calm about it all. But in her eyes he could see a positive torrent of emotion. She felt it then. He could see that she felt it.

But now, he was at even more of a loss. No, she could not have been that baby, he already knew that fact. Who was she then? Could what she was telling him possibly be true? She had discovered his name. She had come to find him. Could she indeed be his daughter?

'It is hard to take it all in,' she said. 'I understand.'

Her sister had come to find her too, she had just said. So she too must have experienced quite a shock. And still, she was holding his hand. But how could Bruno not have known about any of this? Was it possible that Marilyn . . . ? The awful thought struck him. If this was true, then he and Marilyn had together conceived a child who had grown into this woman sitting beside him now. And if that was the case, then he had abandoned them.

He pulled his hand away from her and stood up. Josefine stood up too and he put his hands on her shoulders. It felt natural. It felt the right thing to do. 'You really are my daughter?'

370

he whispered. He was shaking. There were so many emotions fighting for priority that he couldn't work out what to feel.

'I think so, yes.'

'Marilyn's daughter?'

'Yes.'

He hung his head. How could he not have known? How could he have left Marilyn alone to cope with such a thing? 'But the baby I saw . . .' It made no sense. '*Mio Dio,*' he said again. 'And your mother? Marilyn?' He had the most awful feeling. Her words came back to him. *Marilyn was my birth mother . . .* He knew what that meant. 'Is she . . . ?' He could not say the words.

'I am sorry,' Josefine said. Her eyes filled with tears. 'I never met her. But I am so sorry.'

He swallowed back the pain. 'It was a long time ago,' he managed to say. He had lost her such a long time ago. And this brave young woman had never known her at all.

'Yes.'

They were both silent for a few moments. He let out a long sigh. Life, he thought, was full of such losses. So, he would never see Marilyn again – but of course, he had always known this. It felt like a new pain, but after all, it was very like the old.

As he glanced behind them, he saw that the other young woman was shifting her weight from side to side and looking rather anxious.

'Lily is English,' Josefine explained. 'She does not speak Italian. But she knows the story and she will help us understand.'

'The story?' He was still struggling. Understanding anything seemed beyond him.

'Our story.'

'*Mio Dio.*' But she was here right in front of him and she seemed so familiar that perhaps it was true. In his head, he could not work it out but in his heart he knew. And at last, he held out his arms to this beautiful young woman, this miracle, this Josefine, who was apparently his daughter, his and Marilyn's daughter, and he held her very, very tight.

CHAPTER 52

Josefine

2018

Josefine beckoned Lily over. 'This is Bruno,' she said. And to him, 'Meet Lily.'

They embraced politely, warily. He still looked shell-shocked, poor man. Josefine too felt shell-shocked. She had been expecting to feel angry; she had been prepared to fire questions at him, to demand of him why he had left their mother and, in so doing, Josefine herself. But he was an old man. When she saw his expression of bafflement, when she heard his confusion, when it was clear that he had no knowledge of her existence . . . what then could she possibly blame him for?

'Bruno did not know about me,' she confirmed to Lily. And she gave his arm a reassuring squeeze. Because they had rather thrust themselves upon him. And he was her father . . .

Lily's mouth made a small 'o' of surprise. She turned to him. 'But you remember our mother?' she said. 'You remember Marilyn?'

'Marilyn . . .' As Josefine had noted before, his voice took on a dreamy quality, one that sounded tinged with pain. He had certainly been upset when she'd told him Marilyn was no longer alive. He couldn't be that good an actor, surely? Which only left more questions as far as Josefine could see.

'I never forget Marilyn,' he said in English. 'Of that, you can be sure.'

Josefine and Lily shared a look. If he had never forgotten her, then why did he ever leave her? Josefine's entire life had taken its course because her birth mother had been vulnerable, alone and unmarried. And now, Josefine had to know the reason why.

'Do you mind talking about it?' Lily asked him. She perched on the railings opposite the bench, apparently oblivious to the drop below, and Josefine and Bruno both sat down on the bench once again. 'To us, I mean?' She glanced at Josefine. 'There are so many things we'd like to know.'

That was true enough. Josefine smiled grimly. Lily was so much more diplomatic . . . But then, she'd had some practice. She'd already come all the way to Italy to look for Josefine; no wonder she was an expert by now.

Bruno was smiling sadly, as if Lily had offered him some gift. '*Si, si,*' he said. 'I speak of that time, yes. For me . . .' – he spread his hands – 'it is wonderful to do.'

Josefine raised an eyebrow at this unexpected development. 'What made you go to Dorset in the first place?' she asked him. 'You were a builder, *si*?'

He nodded. 'My parents – they want me to settle down here in Camogli, to fish for my living as my father does. Me – I want to see the world for a while. I go to Bristol, I work on a building contract, but . . .' He shrugged. 'There is

374

an accident – on the scaffolding, you know? – and some of the men . . .' He frowned.

'They were laid off?' Lily guessed.

'Yes,' he said. 'Yes, exactly right, I think. Taken off the work. And some of the other men – not Italian, you understand – they want the work, so . . .' Again, he let the words hang.

Josefine was getting the gist. Her adoptive father had told her that there was racism directed against the Italians in the UK back then, perhaps harking back to the war years, perhaps due to so many Italians emigrating to the UK in the decade before she was born. Her adoptive father had been one of them and if it hadn't been for Caffè Parodi, he might have stayed there too, especially having married an Englishwoman. Josefine guessed that the British company wouldn't want the work going to Italian builders when Englishmen needed it for themselves.

'You must have felt very disillusioned,' Lily said.

Again, he frowned in confusion.

'Annoyed,' Josefine clarified. 'Disappointed too?'

Another shrug. 'I understand the way it is,' he said. 'But I decide to go home as my mother is begging me to.' He rolled his eyes and Josefine and Lily both laughed. 'But before I go, I visit Dorset.' He grinned broadly.

'Where you met our mother,' said Lily.

'*Si, si*. Where I meet Marilyn.' His expression grew sad again.

'But after a while, you had to come back to Italy,' Josefine said.

'*Certo*. I have to explain – to my mother, to my father, to Caterina.'

375

'Caterina.' Josefine thought she knew what he was saying. 'Your parents – they wanted you to marry someone else?' She knew how things had worked in Italy back then. And these were her grandparents, she realised with a pang of wistfulness.

'*Si, si*,' he agreed. 'I have to explain what happens to me in Dorset,' he said.

Their mother had happened to him in Dorset, thought Josefine.

'Explain also,' he said, 'that I am to return to England. To Marilyn.'

Mamma mia, thought Josefine. So that was the way it was. She raised an eyebrow at Lily, who gave a surprised little nod.

'I suppose they weren't happy about that?' Lily put in.

'You are right.' He nodded sadly. 'When I come back to Italy, we argue, my family and I. Many times, we argue. But I give it all up for Marilyn, oh, yes.'

There was a short silence as they took this in.

'So our mother never wrote to you?' Lily asked. 'To tell you she was pregnant, I mean?'

This was what they had been discussing on the train, and it really made no sense.

'No.' He shrugged. 'I do not give her my address.'

Lily and Josefine exchanged another glance. They had found his address easily enough and surely Marilyn could have done the same? Had she tried?

But Bruno seemed unaware.

'Can I ask . . .' Josefine pulled the pendant from under her shirt and held the orange pyramid stone carefully between her fingers. The sun lit it like a flame.

Bruno gasped.

'Did you give this stone to my mother?' Though now,

376

Josefine hardly needed to ask. She could see the recognition in his eyes.

'Yes.' He gazed at it with longing. 'I do.'

'And can you tell us why?' Josefine knew she was being rather direct, but she needed to know the real truth, not some sanitised guilt-free version. He had said he came back for Marilyn, so what exactly had happened between them?

Bruno looked from the stone to Josefine, then back again. She could barely imagine how it felt – to have the past resurrected like this; to meet a new daughter, to hear that the woman he had loved was dead.

'The stone, it is mined by my grandfather,' he said. 'He give it to me when I am a young boy. It is my – how do you say?'

'Good luck charm?' Lily suggested.

'Yes,' he said. 'Exactly right. Good luck charm. I carry it wherever I go always.'

'And so you took it with you to England?' Josefine asked.

'Yes.' He was still staring at the pendant, so Josefine unclasped it and handed it to him.

'Here.'

He turned it slowly around in his hand as if it represented some sort of miracle. And in a way, she supposed that it did. The Italian flame, she found herself thinking. It held the truth of the story in its ancient heart.

'It looks good.' He indicated the chain and the setting. 'Marilyn. Does she . . . ?'

Josefine smiled at her sister. 'Lily had it made into a pendant by a skilled craftsman in Perlarosa,' she told him. 'She gave it to me on my birthday just a week or so ago.'

He looked at her and then at Lily. 'Your mother – she give the gemstone to you, yes?'

377

And Josefine realised something that she hadn't realised before. Bruno too wanted to know what had happened. There were gaps in the story for him as well, and talking like this, the three of them, was the only way to fill in all the missing pieces.

Lily shook her head. 'I found it.' She glanced at Josefine, who gave a little nod.

'He knows,' she said. And she could rely on her sister to tell the story sensitively.

'After she died,' Lily continued, 'I found it hidden under my mother's mattress in a little pouch, along with a drawing she had made of Josefine as a baby.'

'A drawing . . .' He caught his breath. He kept looking at Josefine in wonder as if he still could not believe it. 'So, Lily, you also did not know?' he said. 'About Josefine?'

'I didn't, no.'

Once again, they all remained silent while he took in this information.

'She kept it then,' he whispered after a moment or two had passed. He turned the pendant over in his hand. And there was a note of reverence in his voice that made tears spring to Josefine's eyes. 'All these years.'

'All these years,' Josefine agreed. Because it was rather amazing. And it meant – did it not? – that Marilyn had loved Bruno. He seemed to have felt the same way too. Her biological parents had loved one another . . . This was quite something. But it made her feel the sadness even more keenly. They had wanted so very badly to be together. So, what in the name of Madonna had gone wrong?

'It is yours.' Bruno handed her back the pendant and then as she hesitated . . . 'Let me,' he said. And he put the pendant around her neck, did up the clasp.

'Thank you.' She tucked it inside her shirt where she liked to wear it next to her skin, and leant back on the bench, taking a few moments to reflect, to absorb the view of the harbour, the boats, the coloured houses on the quayside. This was her father's town. He had lived here all his life. He had been so close to her geographically, and yet Josefine had never known; never wanted to know, if the truth were told.

She retraced the story a little. 'So when you first went to Dorset in the summer of 1965 – that is when you gave Marilyn the gemstone?' she said. That much seemed indisputable.

'*Si.*' He too was looking out towards the ocean. Perhaps he was thinking of that first journey from Italy. 'I meet your mother. I fall in love. Pff . . .' He raised both hands in the air. 'I never see love before, you know?'

They both nodded. Though privately, Josefine wondered if she did know. In the past six months, so many things she had taken for granted had changed. There were so many new emotions darting around, filling her with longing, with affection, with regret, that she hardly knew where she was – or who.

Bruno – her father, though she hadn't quite come to terms with this yet – reached out and held her hands. 'You have love?' His dark eyes seemed to burn into her. 'You have husband? Children?'

She shook her head. 'I was married,' she said carefully. 'But there are no children.' Which would probably disappoint him, since they would be his grandchildren after all.

'Pff,' he said again. 'I have a grandson, and maybe more to come – we share.' And he laughed, a laugh that was contagious, so that Josefine found herself chuckling too. He was an unusual man, her father. And already she was beginning to feel some kind of affection, some fragile bond.

379

'And then what happened?' Lily asked. 'In Dorset. With Marilyn?'

He let go of Josefine's hands. 'We spend three weeks together,' he said.

Three short weeks, thought Josefine. And yet so much had happened as a result.

'I hate to leave her,' he said. 'I promise to write. I say I return when I have money. I give her the gemstone to keep her safe.'

Josefine considered this as she stared out to sea again. The sun was warm overhead and the water was glistening with shards of light clear as diamonds. So, she had been right. He had loved her. He had really loved her. 'You wrote to Marilyn when you got back then?' she asked. Because perhaps after all, it had been Marilyn who did not want *him*.

To her surprise, he hung his head. 'No, I do not. At least,' he said. 'I write – but I do not send.'

'But why not?' She could see that Lily looked as surprised as she. In those days, they wouldn't have phoned each other, she supposed, and there wasn't any other way of getting a message across. It was all about letters back then, was that not so?

'I have not the words.' He gave a little shrug and looked back up at her. She saw the sadness and the pain, and maybe a sense of embarrassment too. 'I try. Over and over, I try. So many times. But I feel ashamed. I feel stupid.' He wrung his hands. 'How to explain in English how I feel? How to tell her what I plan for us?'

Josefine caught her breath. Plans? He had made plans for them? Once again it forcibly struck her how different her life could have been.

'You did not speak much English back then,' she suggested. 'Was that it? You found it too difficult to write to her?'

380

'Yes, yes.' He was clearly upset. 'Now, yes, I learn. I speak to the tourists, I have the words, the English words. I want to learn. Always, I want to learn. But then . . .'

Josefine felt so sad for him. And she was beginning to understand. He must have been so afraid he'd say the wrong thing; at the very least, he must have felt inadequate. She wondered how many letters he had started and not finished. 'But how would Marilyn have known how you felt?' she asked him. It seemed so obvious. No matter how strong their love had seemed to be, they'd known each other only three weeks. In the overall scheme of things, it was not very long.

Lily too was nodding agreement. 'When she didn't hear from you, she might have assumed you didn't care,' she pointed out gently.

'She know I care. She know I love her,' Bruno burst out.

Josefine took his arm. 'Perhaps she began to doubt it,' she said. 'She was young. She was vulnerable. She'd known you for such a short time.' Although she still couldn't understand why Marilyn had not at least written to tell him that she was expecting his baby. She would have done, would she not? If she could.

A look of comprehension seemed to touch his eyes. Josefine guessed that this had never occurred to him before. 'You are right,' he said sadly. 'It is my fault, I know this.'

'And you didn't go back to England?' Lily asked him. 'You didn't go back to tell her how you felt?'

'He did go back,' Josefine told her. And that was when he had seen the baby he had mentioned. She definitely needed to know more about that.

'I gather money,' said Bruno. 'I save money, I mean.' He sighed, and some long-ago emotion flickered in his eyes. 'It is a long time, yes, a year and a half. But I think she wait for me, yes? I think she know. Our love – it is no ordinary thing.' He shook his head mournfully. 'And I send her the postcard that first February after I leave, *si si*, so she knows I am coming some day.'

'Postcard?' Josefine looked from Bruno to Lily. So, he *had* written to her? 'What postcard?'

'Of this village.' He flung out his arm towards the scene in front of them.

Josefine looked down – at the line of houses, at the church and castle on the hill, at the blue-sapphire sea. 'What did you write on the postcard?' she asked him. That first February? That must have been not long before she was born, surely?

He frowned. 'I come. Please wait.'

'And you sent it to the house?' Lily put in.

He shook his head. 'Not the house, no. I think maybe her parents – they do not like it.'

'So . . . ?' Josefine was confused.

'I send it to the hotel,' said Bruno. 'Where she work. You know?'

Lily nodded. 'The Cliff Hotel.'

'Yes.'

Josefine sighed. 'Perhaps she never received it.'

'Because she did not wait for me?'

'Oh, I think she did wait for you,' Lily said softly. 'I think she might not have got the card – it would have been easy for that to go astray – but I think she did know that your love was no ordinary thing and I think that she did care. I'm sure she cared very much.'

Josefine agreed. There was the gemstone. Why would their mother have kept it otherwise, if not to remember him by?

And perhaps she wasn't even working at the hotel when the postcard arrived? Perhaps it was too close to her due date and she was somewhere else entirely?

'No.' He squared his shoulders, and for a moment, he appeared to Josefine like the man he must once have been. And she did bear some resemblance, she felt. He looked like family.

'I go back. I go to her house where she live with her parents. I see her with a small baby, a new-born. I see her push the pram. I see her with a man. I see them kiss.'

Josefine reached out and touched his arm. Poor man. He seemed to be tortured by what he had seen. She could make no sense of it either but perhaps Lily would.

'But who was the other man?' Lily frowned and Josefine knew her sister was trying to work it out.

Yes, thought Josefine. Who was the other man? She leant back once more to consider the conundrum. The sounds and smells of the harbour-side were still drifting up to the belvedere where they sat. And who was the baby?

CHAPTER 53

Josefine

2018

Once again, they were all quiet for a few moments. Josefine suspected they each needed time to digest the facts they were discovering. Not to mention the speculations they were making . . .

Bruno, her father – and once again, she felt a twinge of recognition, of warmth – looked stricken. He surely hadn't reckoned on this when he sat down on his special bench this morning and gazed contentedly out to sea . . .

'I do not know,' he said.

'Didn't you ask her?' Lily leant closer towards him. 'You'd come all the way from Italy to see her again. Didn't you even speak to her?' She sounded as if she couldn't believe it. She looked as if she couldn't believe it.

Josefine was tempted to tell her to give the poor man a break, but she couldn't help but feel the same way herself. Why in the name of Madonna would he just have walked away?

Bruno hit himself on the chest. 'I cannot,' he said. And he seemed to sit up straighter. 'I am a young man,' he said.

'Was a young man.' Josefine couldn't resist correcting him.

'Was a young man,' he said. 'I have pride, yes? I have the ego, yes? Stupid perhaps. Stupid, yes, for sure. But I cannot stand for her to laugh at me for being a fool.'

The three of them fell silent yet again. It made sense to Josefine now, though. She'd come across other young men who probably would have done the same thing. Naive and arrogant, they expected their girl to wait for them unquestioningly; they rarely had the empathy to understand how it would feel to be left alone in the way that Marilyn had been left. And then to see that girl with another man . . . It would have been quite a blow to the ego as well as to the heart. And as for the pregnancy . . . no doubt the possibility hadn't even entered his mind.

Josefine did not doubt Bruno's account of what he thought he had seen. But it didn't fit, not at all. Josefine had certainly not been that baby – obviously, she would have been born around nine months after Bruno and Marilyn first met and so she'd have been far older than a new-born, even if she had still been with her birth mother. But perhaps he had made a mistake. How many men would even recognise a new-born baby? *Could* she have been that baby?

'Not you.' He seemed to read her mind. 'The man, he pick up the baby, he kiss it again and again, and they both laugh. He loves that baby, you see? The baby, he is the man's child.'

'He?' Lily put her head to one side.

'The baby, he wears blue,' Bruno said solemnly. 'I think he is a boy.'

'A boy?' That certainly seemed to settle the matter.

'Their baby,' said Bruno. 'I know it.'

Josefine exchanged a glance with Lily. 'Do not tell me that we have an unknown brother?' she said.

But Lily was looking sceptical. She got to her feet and took a few paces away from the bench, before walking back again. 'Something doesn't add up,' she said.

Allora, Lily should know – she was the numbers magician after all.

'That baby couldn't have been our mother's child,' Lily went on. 'It's impossible.' Off she went, pacing away from the bench again.

'I see it,' Bruno insisted. 'I see it with my own eyes.' Though in those eyes Josefine was sure that she could recognise a glimmer of doubt. For all these years . . . had he been telling himself the wrong story?

Lily was shaking her head. She seemed very sure. 'The timeline doesn't fit.' Back she came to the bench again.

Josefine was getting dizzy. She tried to do the calculation, but maths had never been her forte. And Bruno too was frowning in confusion.

'You and our mother met in July, right?' Lily paused in her pacing and looked to Bruno for confirmation.

'Right.'

'And Josefine was born at the beginning of May.' Off she walked.

'As I was,' Josefine contributed. 'The fourth of May to be precise. As you know.'

'And Bruno, you came back to England when? You said one and a half years later. So, was it December nineteen sixty-six? January nineteen sixty-seven?' Back she came to the bench.

'January,' he said. 'At the end of the month.'

Lily looked triumphant. 'By which time, Josefine would have been just over eight and a half months old.' She spread her hands, clearly expecting them to get it.

'So . . . ?' Josefine was still all at sea. 'What are you saying, Lily?' She frowned. 'And please stay still for a minute, will you?'

'Sorry. Well, clearly there wouldn't have been time for our mother to have had another baby after giving birth to you,' she explained. 'Like I said, you were less than nine months old.'

'Oh . . .' Josefine got it and when she looked at Bruno, she saw that he had got it too. He put out a hand as if to steady himself, although he was still sitting down.

'And the baby couldn't have been Josefine because a) she wasn't young enough, b) she'd already been adopted and, c) you're saying it was probably a boy.'

'So, it was someone else's baby,' Josefine breathed.

'Exactly.'

They all considered this.

'And your father?' Bruno addressed Lily. 'Who is your father, my dear?'

Josefine knew he was on the wrong track if that was what he was thinking.

'His name was Tom,' Lily told him. 'He and my mother were friends before they got together.'

'Tom.' Bruno considered. 'Marilyn – she tell me about a friend called Tom, yes.' He frowned. 'I think, yes, I meet him.'

'Was it him you saw?' asked Josefine.

He shook his head. 'No, I not see this man before, no.'

'It wouldn't have been my father,' Lily agreed. 'It was some time later they got together – in the early nineteen seventies, he told me.' Lily half turned to gaze out to sea. 'She was unhappy. I think he saved her in a way.'

Josefine wasn't sure this was the most sensitive thing to say under the circumstances, but . . .

'Saved her,' Bruno echoed. He still looked confused, Josefine thought, which was hardly surprising, but also a little angry. Was he angry with a man named Tom who had saved Marilyn? Or was he angry with himself?

'What did he look like – the man you saw?' Lily asked.

'Dark hair. Thick-set. Short in height.' It sounded as if Bruno had been holding a visual image of the man he'd seen kissing Marilyn for many years.

Lily was still looking thoughtful. 'And how did they kiss?' she asked.

Josefine had to admire her sister. She was like a dog with a bone. If anyone could discover the truth, it was Lily.

'What?'

'Was it a kiss on the cheek like this?' She leant towards Josefine and planted a kiss on her cheek. 'Or . . .' She hesitated.

Josefine took over. 'Or was it full-on mouth to mouth?' And she added the Italian translation just to be clear. She could see where Lily was going with this.

Bruno blushed. Really, he was quite a sweetie – though Josefine was still having trouble truly believing he could be her father. Just think . . . a couple of months ago, she had no blood relatives – at least none that she knew of. And now, she had two . . . And plenty of others who she hadn't yet met in both England and Italy. She could share his grandson, he had told her.

It was a nice feeling, she realised. She had family – a family who seemed already to care for her, if Lily was anything to go by. And it had subtly changed the way Josefine thought about herself. It was as if now, she had some sense of background, some personal story. She had learnt who she really was and where she came from, she supposed.

Bruno pointed to his cheek. 'Cheek, yes, not mouth. But they are in a public place, so . . . you understand? And this is not Italy, no, no.'

Josefine nodded. In England, kisses on the cheek were not the norm for more casual acquaintances. She understood all right. Or at least, she was beginning to.

'And did they hug?' asked Lily.

'Hug?'

Josefine translated.

'*Si, si.*' He seemed sure on that. 'They hug.' He sighed and shrugged as if the hug had only made it so much worse.

Lily sat bolt upright. 'Hah!' she said.

'Hah?' Had she worked something out? It seemed so.

'I think it was my uncle,' said Lily.

'Your uncle?' Bruno was staring at her.

'*Mamma mia,*' Josefine whispered under her breath. Things were indeed becoming much clearer. But could Lily be right? Bruno had seemed very sure it was a rival lover and surely his intuition was to be trusted?

'My Auntie Glenda's husband. Marilyn's brother-in-law.'

'What makes you say that?' Josefine asked.

'He was short, dark and a bit overweight.' Lily spoke hesitantly, obviously aware of the bombshell she was creating. 'But not just that. My Auntie Glenda had to go out to work . . .' Now, she glanced at Josefine as if unsure that she should continue. 'And she told me that Marilyn often helped out with the kids in those days.'

No one spoke.

'Mum worked shifts at the hotel,' Lily explained. 'So sometimes she was free during the day.'

Josefine held her breath. What had their mother felt back then? If Lily was right, then how hard it must have been for Marilyn to have given up her own baby and then have to look after her sister's instead? Or had it been some consolation? Josefine hoped that this was the case.

'Did you ever meet Marilyn's brother-in-law?' Josefine asked Bruno. 'When you were in Dorset the first time, I mean?'

'No.' Bruno was deep in thought. 'Our love – we keep it a secret. Not everyone is . . .' – he hesitated – '*simpatico*, you understand?'

Josefine and Lily both nodded.

'But, the kiss . . .' Clearly, Bruno was not yet convinced. It would be hard, Josefine could see, when he had believed something different for so many years. Even harder, when it meant that he need not have given up on the woman he loved.

'If it was just a hug and a kiss on the cheek,' Lily ventured, 'then perhaps she was just saying goodbye to him before she took the baby out for a walk in the pram.'

It sounded so innocuous the way she explained it, Josefine thought. And also rather probable.

'Sorry.' Lily looked down.

'But does Glenda even have a boy of the right age?' Josefine asked her. That would decide the matter, surely?

'I can check the dates with my cousins' birthdates.' Again, Lily hesitated. 'But, yes. Their son David is just a bit younger than you.'

Once again, they were all silent. What else could they say? Bruno looked devastated – so much so that Josefine reached out to him again and this time took his hand. She guessed what he was thinking. And whatever outcome she and Lily had expected from this meeting, this had certainly not been one of them.

'Her sister's husband,' Bruno muttered. 'Her sister's baby. Can it be true?'

Josefine thought it probably could. 'I am sorry,' she said.

He turned to her. 'So, Marilyn – she is having my baby. And I do not know. I do not help. I do nothing . . .'

'It was not your fault,' she told him. Because what else could she say?

'I leave her, I abandon her.'

He was desolate, Josefine was in no doubt. 'You did not know she was pregnant,' she reminded him.

'And I leave you,' he whispered. 'I abandon you, my daughter.'

Josefine shook her head, but she didn't trust herself to speak. There would be time, she hoped, for them to talk about all this again, time in which she would try to help him come to terms with the consequences. As for Josefine, she did not blame him. Indeed, she hoped that he had found happiness in life. What was the point in looking back at these pathways in life and berating yourself for taking the wrong one? Each pathway, you must view it in context. Because perhaps everything happened for a reason . . .

'What did you do afterwards?' Lily asked Bruno. 'You had spent so long saving so that you could come back to England for our mother. When you saw her outside the house and you felt so betrayed, what did you do?'

It seemed that they were all holding their breath.

391

Bruno bent his head and did not answer for a long time. At last, he raised it and met Josefine's gaze. 'I go back to Italy again,' he said. 'I do not speak to Marilyn. I do not write. I think she forgets me. I go back to Italy. And I grieve.'

CHAPTER 54

Bruno

2018

What might have been . . .

After the women had left, Bruno walked slowly back to the house he had grown up in. There was something he needed to see, needed to hold.

It was tucked in the top drawer of the walnut chest in his bedroom; he knew its location exactly, although he had not looked at it for a while. Too many sad memories. And yet, he had never been able to throw it out, not quite.

For a moment, he scrutinised the drawing; for a moment, he held it to his heart. Then he tucked it carefully into his rucksack and left the house. This house was full of Caterina and their life together. He needed to leave it in order to think of Marilyn. *Marilyn . . .*

How could he reconcile himself to what he now knew to be the truth?

Bruno walked back towards the shadowy arches where the

orange paint was flaking, the grey stone crumbling and where a man could close his eyes and hear the waves pounding the rocks night and day. He must let it sink in; if he were not to go half-crazy with the guilt and the grief, he must somehow come to terms.

But this was not the right place. He looked around him. The promenade was too busy, so instead, he turned back, heading for the church and the maze of alleyways beneath. He needed a few minutes of solitude.

He took the steps down to the dim alleys. Here, it was quieter always – tourists wanted sights and sunshine – and it was still the Camogli he had grown up in; it had not changed. There was light here, but it was the kind of slanted light that darted down between high buildings, hardly reaching the stone cobbles – this was all that was needed in the heat of summertime. This village was his life, and yet he would have left it for Marilyn.

He thought of the drawing tucked in his rucksack. How had she felt back then, imagining that he had abandoned her? How had she felt, pregnant and alone? And how could Bruno reconcile himself to the fact that he had done this thing to the woman he loved?

He did not know how it was possible. He could not think . . .

The houses on opposite sides of the alley squatted so close together that facing neighbours might reach out from their balconies to shake hands if they were so inclined. It was brighter on the top storey; people hung out their washing, grew plants on the roof gardens and balconies. Bruno sighed.

He should have written. One postcard was not enough. So, he had not known how to express all those deep and poetic feelings in a language he did not speak or understand. So, what?

What kind of flimsy excuse was that? And even that one post-card . . . He had thought himself so clever for sending it to the hotel where he knew she sorted the post every day, rather than to her home where it might be seen or intercepted and cause her a problem when she tried to explain. It had never occurred to him that she would not see it because she would not be there.

And why was she not there? She was not there because she had been sent away − to give birth to their baby.

Bruno swore softly. He took a left and then a narrow right. He wished he might get lost in these alleyways, but like a cat, he would always know his way in this town; he had lived here so long. He stopped abruptly by a door once painted an oily blue, now stripped back almost to bare wood by sun, wind and rain. He had kissed a girl once on this very doorstep. He had been fourteen, he supposed, or thereabouts; she was a year older, and he had responded to her black wheedling eyes without a second thought. Even then, the confining arms of the town had seemed to offer not so much an embrace as a straitjacket. He had wanted something different.

And someone . . .

But now this. Bruno had always thought that Marilyn had broken his heart. But, in fact, the opposite was true. Because it was his fault, all his fault. He had let her down, he had abandoned her, and now he must somehow live with the knowledge of that.

Bruno walked on. There were more doors, always more doors; different colours, in various states of disrepair. More doors, more houses, more shadowy alleyways.

When he first came back to Italy, determined to return to Dorset just as soon as he was able, he had told Caterina and his parents about Marilyn. Despite his parents' prodding, Bruno had never spoken to Caterina officially about marriage, but even he could not deny the understanding between the families. An understanding which, according to his parents, was embedded in the very rocks of this town upon which their family's house had been built.

'You have been foolish,' his mother informed him. 'You have let yourself be swayed by a pretty face. But you are wrong to do this. Why, you do not even speak the same language. You would be making a big mistake.'

Bruno shrugged. He had known they would react like this. He was not surprised.

'Have you heard about English girls?' his father asked darkly. 'They have no faith, no shame.' And he crossed himself. 'This girl, she will not be true to you, you can be sure of that. No. You must stay here and do your duty, my son.'

'But I love her. I love her.' Bruno said the words over and over, hoping by repetition to make them see.

'Pff. In three weeks? You cannot love a woman in three weeks,' his father retorted.

'You do not know her,' his mother agreed. 'Do you know her family, her parents, her grandparents, her roots?'

No, of course he did not. Marilyn had not wanted him to meet any of them. And who could blame her if they were anything like his family?

'We have not even met her,' his mother said. 'And Caterina . . .' She shook her head sadly. 'That girl will be broken,' she said. 'We will all be broken. Bruno, it hardly seems that you are our son at all.'

Bruno paused, remembering even now the dull feeling that his mother's words had left in his belly. He knew that he had disappointed them all. But they were living life in the old way.

He was young. He had his life ahead of him and, now, his life meant Marilyn.

It was harder telling Caterina – she was so sweet and dear and unlike his parents, she had never put any pressure on him.

'I have met someone,' he told her. 'A girl, an English girl.'

She had nodded and smiled sadly at him as if she already knew. 'You have fallen in love, Bruno?'

'Yes,' he said. 'I am sorry.'

'Thank you for telling me.' She had been accepting, practical even. 'You must not worry. We were chosen for one another by our parents, were we not? We hardly had a chance to make our own voices heard.'

This was true enough. The two couples must have been overjoyed when each produced a girl child and a boy child respectively within a few years of one other. It would cement the friendship; it would be an important alliance. Their children would belong to all four grandparents and they would thus all be safe and secure. Bruno had heard the story often enough; it was imprinted in the map of his family.

Bruno and Caterina had grown up together. No doubt that was why Bruno always thought of Caterina more as a beloved sister than a potential wife. For Caterina, though, it was different. She loved Bruno; she had always loved him, he knew that. For Caterina, it was simple and pure.

Bruno shivered. It was growing chilly down here in the shadows and he had a yearning to be closer to a sight of the sea, to feel the evening sun on his skin. He climbed the steps that he knew would lead him back to the harbour, back to the boats, back to the house in which he had grown up.

Bruno had worked, he had saved his money, not going out with his friends as he used to; squirrelling away every last cent.

Because it was her face that filled his head at night. Marilyn's. Her face that haunted his dreams.

By the time Bruno arrived back in Dorset, he was exhausted . . . by the guilt, by the family bickering. He was desperate to see Marilyn; he needed to be reassured that it was the same for her as it was for him; that she too was waiting. His father's words had become a worm in his brain, wriggling and twisting and trying to change something that was good and true into something darker, something to be feared.

Now, suddenly, Bruno could hardly breathe, but he did not rest until he had climbed the steps, until the harbour was there in front of him, inky blue and slick in the light of the evening sun.

When he reached Marilyn's house, which was also her parents' house – how he wanted to surprise her, how he longed to see her face – he was wrung out with anticipation, tired desperation, anxiety.

He was still some metres away, when her front door opened. He stood stock still.

The dark-haired man came out first, carrying a pram that hardly fit through the doorway. Then, Marilyn emerged, blonde and beautiful but with a baby in her arms. Marilyn . . . Bruno was confused by the baby. But he took a step forwards, then he waited, doubt creeping in. He watched the man take the baby from Marilyn, saw him smother the child with kisses as she – Marilyn – laughed and looked on. He watched the man as he tucked the baby into the pram. He watched as the man turned to Marilyn and he watched as they embraced.

Bruno froze. It was such an unmistakeable tableau. A young couple with their beloved new-born . . . So, she had not even waited a year.

Now, Bruno stood still and watched the water. The sheen of it in the evening light had always fascinated him. Best of all, he had loved the time when he brought the boat back into harbour in the gentle twilight, the oars melting through the soft yellowing blue, the lap and surge of the water on the bow.

Bruno had stumbled as he walked away. *Allora*. He had thought she understood. He had thought she knew.

At first, he could not think what to do, where to go. He was devastated. He was furious. He felt so stupid. He sat in a quiet corner of a nearby park and he ran it through his mind. Marilyn, what he had just seen, what his parents had said to him. And so . . . They had been right after all. He had been ready to give up everything for her, but she had made a fool out of him. What kind of a woman must she be?

And he knew then what he must do. He had too much pride to approach Marilyn; he would not give her that satisfaction. He must return to Italy, his tail between his legs, he must apologise to his parents, he must fall at Caterina's feet and hope that she could forgive him. He had been an idiot to think, to imagine . . .

He had thought he would forget her, his pale English rose. But he never had. Yes, he had married Caterina and he had loved her – in a different way. Not all-consuming perhaps, but in a way that should have been enough. Who wanted, anyhow, to be consumed by love? He had lived the life he had been destined to live – but he had never fully accepted it, he saw now. Always, he had carried that first love in a small corner of his heart and it had touched everything that followed.

Now, Bruno shook his head, almost in disbelief. There was no time in the past when he had ever considered he could have been wrong about what he saw in Dorset the day he returned to find Marilyn. But today the veil had been lifted and Bruno could see the truth. Marilyn had loved him; she really had loved him. In fact, Bruno had been loved by two good women. It could be said then that he was a fortunate man indeed.

He walked along the harbour-side, absorbing the sights and sounds that were as familiar to him as the very air he breathed. Now, Bruno could see that he had indeed been the fool – for not speaking to her at least, for allowing his pride to rule him, for not giving Marilyn a chance to explain. And now he had discovered the real truth – that he had left the woman he loved all alone to have his child, believing that he, Bruno Ferrando, had abandoned her.

It broke his heart.

And yet in some ways, was it not better to discover the truth? Was it not preferable to learn that he had not been wrong, that Marilyn had indeed loved him, and that she had waited too? Bruno watched the tired old sun, the amber globe that reminded him so vividly of the *anatase*, the ancient orange gemstone he had given Marilyn, to give her hope, to keep her safe, which now hung around the neck of his only daughter, of Josefine.

Because, yes, he had a daughter and she had come here to find him. When he had woken up this morning there had been no possibility of this. And yet now . . . As the sun sank lower, Bruno realised that he was smiling. He had a daughter – a daughter who, if he was not mistaken, seemed to need him. A daughter who was part of Marilyn too, who wanted to get to know him. Which showed – did it not? – that some good could come out of this whole thing?

Bruno sat down on the bench by the harbour edge. From the envelope in his rucksack, he took out the drawing that

Marilyn had made of him on that first day. Sentimental old fool to keep it . . . But now, he was glad. He had destroyed the rest when he returned to Italy that final time. But this one drawing – this he had been unable to destroy.

Bruno studied the sketch once again. The thick pencil lines of his face were more blurred than they once were, but the heart-stone of the drawing remained. It showed a young man with dark, hopeful eyes, untroubled and smiling, meeting the girl for the first time, the girl who was to become his true love. She had died not knowing that he had come back for her. She had died not knowing the truth. 'Please forgive me,' he whispered.

He watched the evening sun as it dipped into the horizon, as the sky streaked with yellow, with red, as the clouds turned pink and slowly darkened.

And so. He could mourn his lost love, the love he might have had for so much longer, but he could not regret his life with Caterina, the children, young Tommaso too. A thought occurred to him. How would his family react when he told them he had a daughter? He must be careful and sensitive, he realised. He must not upset them. He must do his best by all of them.

He had not been there for Marilyn. He had let her down. But he would not let their daughter down, he was sure of that much. He would be there for Josefine in the future – as he would for his sons and their families too. And perhaps this was how he could find that elusive sense of peace?

He tucked the drawing back into the envelope. He would show it to Josefine and she would show him the other drawing that had brought Lily, her half-sister, to Liguria; the drawing of his baby daughter. He wanted to see that so much.

Sí, sí, he thought. He must not look back – enough of his life had been wasted already by looking back. Because he had been given another chance – and this was the good that could come from it all. The truth, a daughter, the chance to atone – and the knowledge that he had been wrong all these years and that love after all did not lie.

CHAPTER 55

Lily

2018

When they got back to Perlarosa that night, Lily took her leave of Josefine at the piazza and continued walking down towards the pink church, the silversmith's workshop and the little harbour. She was tired, but not yet ready to go to bed. It had been quite a day and she could still feel the adrenaline racing.

The streets were quiet and her footsteps echoed as she meandered through the alleyways between the tall houses, their elongated shadows looming in the velvety darkness with only a pale-yellow gauzy moon and the occasional lamp from a window lighting the way. Nico would not still be at the workshop, she was sure, but even so, she felt drawn to this part of the village, wanting to stand on the little slipway, looking across the inky water. It seemed to hold so many secrets.

She was still going over the events of the day. It was amazing that they had found Bruno Ferrando and even more amazing that he seemed delighted to have acquired a daughter. Lily was so relieved; she had been concerned for Josefine. Lily had started this family search and she didn't want to be responsible for it all going horribly wrong. But Bruno Ferrando seemed like a good man, and Lily was confident that he'd be good for Josefine too.

On the way back, on the train, she and Josefine had spent some time piecing together the stories — from what Glenda had told Lily, from what Bruno had told them today, and from everything else they'd discovered. Lily had struggled at first to match the mother she knew with the Marilyn that Bruno had spoken of, but she was beginning to understand her more.

Lily's mother must have been heartbroken when Bruno didn't come back for her as promised, and when she found out that she was pregnant and would have to deal with the responsibility, the shame, alone . . . Lily could barely imagine how difficult it must have been. Had she tried to find out her lover's address from Mrs Briggs, his landlady? It was very likely. But perhaps Mrs Briggs had refused to give it to her? Perhaps she was just one more person who disapproved of Marilyn and Bruno and their love, and who would not have lifted a finger to help them? If Lily was right, then Mrs Briggs' refusal to give Marilyn the information she needed had changed so many lives.

Lily's mother had never been strong and, in Lily's experience, she had never been maternal. Having been forced to give up one baby, Marilyn had apparently been unable to fully love or care for a second . . . Or so it seemed. What was she so afraid of? Of loving too much? Of having another child taken away from her? Had her thoughts, her sadnesses and losses, made her so restless, so unable to settle? Certainly, her view of the world must have been affected by having her child taken away

404

from her. And certainly her ability to bond with her second daughter had been impaired.

Lily would never know it all. What she had discovered . . . It didn't give her a sense of resolution, exactly. And she wasn't sure she could entirely forgive her mother either for not being there when Lily needed her, for not being present during so much of Lily's growing up. But . . . She thought of her mother's frailty when she knew she was dying, the way she had looked at Lily, as if trying to tell her something that Lily needed to know. *Darling.* Her mother had called her 'darling'. And a sense of understanding was something. It was important; it almost felt like love.

The pink church stood strong and silent in the darkness and Lily brushed the cool stone lightly with her fingertips. These Italian buildings seemed to breathe in and out – the stone absorbed and reflected the sun, the warmth, the damp – and so many years of history were buried deep within.

She walked across to the belvedere, stood there for a few moments looking out over the sea. The moon was casting a filmy spotlight on the water and in the distance, Portovenere squatted, silently waiting for its next round of day-trippers. Lily put her hands on the railings and let out a sigh. Families . . . They could be complicated. And as for love . . .

But at least her father had been there. He had provided the stability her mother needed, Lily guessed – or at least, he had tried to. But there was still so much Lily could only speculate on. Had her mother loved him? Lily thought so. Fervently, she hoped so – for both their sakes. Perhaps, though, for her mother, in the same way as for Bruno, first love had never entirely been forgotten, never died. Which was another sadness, she supposed; a waste.

But at least Lily had been able to make this journey to Italy that her mother had been unable to make. At least she had found out the truth.

Lily turned from the sea and made her way down the street that led to the silversmith's workshop and the harbour. In contrast to the quietness of the rest of the village, at the end of this road, the Marina Bar was still busy, by the look of it, and she could already hear the buzz of conversation and laughter. But she had no desire to go in. She wanted to get closer to the inky water. She wanted to think.

Lily felt for Bruno. As the three of them had worked out what had really happened when he had returned to Dorset and to Marilyn that second time, she had watched his face and seen comprehension dawn – and horror, at what he had done.

Poor man. His life would have panned out very differently if he had chosen another moment to pitch up at the family house. In another world, would Bruno and Marilyn have stayed together? Would they have been happy? Who could say? Lily didn't know him well enough to even hazard a guess, and besides . . .

'Hey, Lily.'

Lily emerged from her moonlight reverie with a start. It was Nico, walking up the street towards her. He must have only just left the workshop, she realised.

'Nico.' Lily supposed that somewhere inside, despite that confrontation with Carlotta, she had been half hoping . . .

'How did it go?' He kissed her on both cheeks; once, twice. Friendly enough, but nothing more. He smelt of the workshop, of flames, of salt, of metal. Lily drank it in. It was a male scent quite unlike any she'd ever encountered before – but then again, how many silversmiths had she met? He was very definitely the first.

'Good.'

'Shall we?' He took her arm, turned her around and they walked back up the way she'd just come. Where were they going? she wondered. Did he assume that she had been coming to find him? But she didn't protest. His presence was comforting after the dramatic events of the day.

'So what happened?' he asked.

She took a deep breath and told him – an abridged version at least. It was easy to confide in this man, especially in the soft darkness of these alleyways, amidst the stone houses that had heard so many secrets in their time.

Nico listened in silence and when she'd finished, he let out a low whistle. They had arrived at the street that led up to the little chapel on the cliff with Nico's place right opposite and here, they paused. It was a crossroads, because to go back to the B & B, Lily should turn left and to go home, he must turn right. So . . . what next?

'It is an incredible story,' he said. 'I imagine if this Bruno had gone over to them, said something . . . *Allora*. His whole life would have taken a different course.' He looked thoughtful. 'And perhaps Josefine's life too, hmm?'

'And mine,' Lily added. 'In fact, I probably wouldn't have been born at all.' Which was a distinctly weird feeling.

He chuckled, then to her surprise, moved closer, tilted her chin with his fingertips. 'That,' he said, 'would be very sad.'

Lily tensed. Here they were, in almost exactly the same position as they had been the other day when they returned from Portovenere. Yet again, his proximity was having a strange effect on her. She felt on edge, breathless . . . and yet again, it seemed as if he might kiss her. What was going on with this man? Every time she felt they were getting closer, he took a step away, and every time she kept her distance, he moved closer.

'Can I offer you a small drink, Lily?' he murmured. 'Perhaps we can talk a little more before we say goodnight?'

In a bar? Lily wondered. Where would be open at this hour, apart from the Marina Bar back in the direction they'd just come? At his place? She repressed a shiver. She supposed that was what he meant. *Keep it light, Lily*, she reminded herself. Because there had been no kiss. Perhaps there would never be. And perhaps there shouldn't be either.

'Okay,' she said. 'Why not?' Though that was a question she hardly dared contemplate. Even so, she was curious about the man and curious to see a different part of his life: where Nico lived, the way he lived . . . There were bound to be a few clues.

'And Josefine?' he asked her as they walked up the slope of the alleyway to the right. 'Is she happy to have discovered yet another member of her family? Is she pleased to have found her father?'

'Oh, yes.' And all the more pleased, since she'd discovered that he hadn't abandoned their mother and he hadn't abandoned her. 'She now has two half-brothers she knew nothing about, as well as a nephew. Her family has expanded well beyond her expectations.' She hadn't met any of them yet, of course, but Lily sensed that it would happen before too long and that Bruno Ferrando and his family would enrich Josefine's life and she theirs.

'You have reunited a family,' Nico said. 'Which can only be a good thing.'

Lily liked the sound of that. 'And I have found more family for myself,' she said.

'Things – how they can change,' Nico murmured.

And this, thought Lily, was very true.

CHAPTER 56

Lily

2018

They arrived at the pale chapel which stood serene in the moonlight near what must be the highest belvedere in the village, and Nico lifted a stone outside his door to retrieve a key. Lily raised an eyebrow. He was trusting. But, despite the tourists, this was very different from London after all. The villagers were part of a community; presumably they all watched out for one other.

Nico led the way inside.

Lily followed. She wasn't surprised to see that the place was furnished minimally. The sitting room was tiny; there was a small threadbare couch and a rocking chair in the corner. Simple tastes, she thought. Perhaps he was unable to afford more. Or was this all he thought he deserved? The worn wooden dining table was also small and had two chairs tucked under it. A dark blue cotton rug was laid on the floor and a little television sat in another corner.

'It is not much,' he said.

But, perhaps because of its very simplicity, it was charming. The walls had been painted a warm and earthy sage-green and the place was homely. 'I like it,' she said truthfully. 'It has a good feel.'

He gave a little nod and disappeared through a door on the far side into a small, square kitchen. Lily could see a stove, a sink and a few old-fashioned cupboards.

He rummaged around in the fridge and came back to stand in the doorway. 'I have beer,' he said. 'Or red wine?'

'Wine, please.' Lily looked around a bit more. There was a newspaper on the arm of the couch, but otherwise, little evidence that he really lived here. No ornaments, no books, no personal possessions.

Nico came back into the room, bottle and glasses in hand. 'I do not spend much time here,' he said, following her gaze. 'The workshop – that is as much my home.'

She got that. But how had he lived before he came here? She couldn't help wondering. 'Though you have been living here for some time.' He hadn't accumulated any of the stuff that most people accumulated. But then again, she reminded herself, he wasn't like most people.

He nodded. 'It is the place I found when I first arrived in Perlarosa,' he said. 'With the old silversmith Gabriele's help, I mean.'

He poured two generous glasses and handed one to Lily. 'We can take these to the belvedere,' he suggested. 'It is a beautiful night.'

'Why not?' Lily said again. This was Italy. A moonlit night, a glass of red wine, an attractive but inscrutable silversmith . . . It wasn't exactly what she'd come to Italy for, but . . .

411

They left the house and strolled to the belvedere, looking out across the water at the shadowy outlines of Portovenere and the island of Palmaria, just as Lily had been doing at a lower level earlier on. The sea gently rolled beneath them, lapping onto the rocks below; otherwise the belvedere was still and silent. It was as if no one else lived here or ventured up this way. Lily and Nico had the place entirely to themselves.

He put his wine glass down on the ledge beside them. 'Although I do not want to spoil a beautiful moment . . .'

Then don't, was Lily's first thought. She watched his hand clench into a fist over the railings and she felt the sudden tension in the air.

'I also know that I owe you an explanation.'

'You don't.' Lily continued to stare out to sea. She thought of Carlotta. 'You owe me nothing.' She felt his gaze on her, but she didn't look around. He had been right the first time. He shouldn't spoil a beautiful moment. She took a sip of the wine, which was deep and rich and tasted of blackberries and warm summer nights. She wanted to remember this when she was back in the UK. How she had stood with this man, glass of wine in hand on a moonlit evening, how she had listened and watched the waves rolling and tumbling under a dark starry sky.

He sighed. 'Lily, Lily, I never thought I would meet anyone like you.'

Still, she did not turn around to face him. But his words seemed to creep softly into her heart. 'I never thought I would meet anyone like you,' she whispered.

He let out a harsh laugh that seemed to echo from the stone, too loud in the stillness of the evening. 'But you do not know me.'

And you do not know me, she thought. *Even so . . .* She too put her wine glass down on the ledge beside the railings. She moved her hand so that her little finger was just touching his. 'In some ways, you're right, I don't. But in another way, yes, I do.' She couldn't explain. It was just that in some small inner part of her, he felt familiar; he felt known.

She heard him sigh. 'It is the same for me,' he admitted. 'I did not intend to have feelings for you. For anyone.'

Feelings? The word hung between them. Lily looked down at their hands, fingers just touching.

'I assumed at first you were only a tourist,' he said, 'and that soon you would be gone. I knew I did not deserve . . .' – he hesitated – 'to meet someone. To move on.'

'And now?' she asked. What did he think now? And what had he done that made him believe he didn't deserve a chance of meeting someone new?

As if in reply, he moved his hand so that it rested on hers. 'Will you ever come back to Italy?' he asked her.

At last, she turned to face him. 'Yes.' She knew that she would. Not only for Nico, but for her sister, for Josefine.

His face was in the shadows, but she could make out the pain in his dark eyes and in the twist of his mouth as he spoke. 'I told only one man why I came here to Perlarosa,' he said.

'Gabriele?'

'Yes.' Nico shrugged, picked up his glass, took a deep slug of the wine and put it back on the ledge. 'He recognised the sadness in me. I could not hide it. He saw a tragedy and the heaviness of the burden I carry.' He took a deep breath. 'He asked me what had happened and I told him. He had been good to me and it was the least I could do. I trusted him.'

'And what did he say to you?' Lily asked gently.

413

'That the work would be restful, that this place . . .' – he gestured towards the nearby houses, the sea, the tiny chapel – 'it was tranquil. That here, I might find peace and, in time, I might even heal, if I was prepared to stay a while.'

But Lily knew that Nico had not healed. Not yet.

'And more,' he said. 'Gabriele – he told me I was the kind of son he would have wanted.' Nico shook his dark head angrily. 'How could he say that, when he knew what I had done?'

But what had he done? Carlotta must know, of course. Had she told anyone else in the village? Or did she hold the knowledge over him? Lily realised that she needed to hear it, whatever it might be. And she needed to hear it from Nico Ricci himself. 'And do you trust me?' she asked.

He did not reply at first – which was perhaps answer enough. Then he took her hand in his.

'I was not looking for a woman,' he said sadly.

'Because you have a wife?'

'Had a wife,' he corrected. 'She died.'

'Oh. I'm sorry . . .' Lily winced. She hadn't been expecting that.

His shoulders drooped and he let go of her hand, half turning away to face the sea once again.

Lily waited for him to go on. Because there must be more.

'She died in a traffic accident,' he said. 'I was driving. It was my fault.'

'But . . .' It was an accident, he'd said.

Again, he shook his head. 'My phone rang. She told me to leave it, but I did not want to. That call – I thought it was important, but it was not. Not compared with what happened next.'

Lily stared at him. Now, she was beginning to understand.

414

'She grabbed the phone. I grabbed it back. I was angry. A car was coming the other way. I lost control of the steering wheel . . .'

Lily realised that he was shaking. She held his arm. 'Nico, you don't have to tell me.'

'But I do.' Even in the moonlight, she could see what he was going through – it was written on his face.

Lily waited for him to go on.

He let out a low groan. 'The two cars, they collided. I survived. The two people in the other car also – although they had to go to hospital for their injuries. But in the end, they were okay too. Alyssia – she was killed outright.' For a moment he looked as if he could say no more.

But again, Lily waited for him to finish. She could see how much this was costing him.

'There was no prosecution. But I have never forgiven myself.' He shrugged. 'Of course, I have never forgiven myself. I should have died with her. She should not have died at all.'

'I see.' It was a terrible thing. Lily remembered how he had looked the first time she saw him in the church. She thought of the stressful job he'd told her about before and the fact that he did not drive and that he seemed unwilling to enter arguments – she had witnessed him doing this with Carlotta. She could imagine the scenario of the car crash all too vividly. And she could feel the force of his guilt, his grief, the burden he had spoken of.

Once again, he gripped the railings. Once again, she was conscious of the force of him, the tension he carried. 'So now you know.'

'Carlotta . . .' she began.

'She will not leave me alone.' He looked haunted. 'She

415

followed me here, she found me, she threw it in my face. Always she throws it in my face. I cannot escape it.'

'But she lost her sister,' Lily reminded him gently. No wonder Carlotta was so angry with him. No wonder she did not want him to move on.

'Yes.' He bowed his head. 'You are right, of course. I do not want to be reminded. I do not need to be reminded. But Carlotta . . .'

'She cannot let it go,' said Lily. She thought of Josefine. A sister was a precious thing indeed.

He nodded sadly. 'I wanted to get away from people who knew, but now . . .' He shrugged.

'But Nico, have you ever talked to Carlotta about what happened, about how she feels?' Lily asked him. 'Have you asked her forgiveness?'

He lifted his head and met her gaze. 'I tried.'

'Perhaps you should try again,' Lily whispered. So much more time had passed since the tragedy. But Carlotta clearly needed help in order to move on herself. She had come here to Perlarosa to find Nico, but she had ended up getting involved with Gianni – a married man – and having a whole village turn against her. Whatever her faults, the poor woman could certainly do with a friend.

He nodded. 'You are right,' he said.

They were quiet for a few moments. It was an awful thing. Lily knew that nothing she said could ever lessen the tragedy – nor should it. But . . . 'You have been punishing yourself ever since.' It wasn't a question.

Still, he nodded. 'I gave up that job. I vowed to live life differently. But yes, I punish myself. I always will.'

Lily studied the dark outline of his strong features, the lines

416

of his nose, his jaw, his mouth; the wildness of his soft black hair. 'And you think you don't deserve any happiness.'

'It is true. I do not.' His arms on the railings tensed once more.

How could she get through to him? Gently, Lily put one hand on his shoulder, the other on his arm. She got him to turn around and she drew him closer, both hands on his shoulders now. 'Would Alyssia want that?' she asked.

He glanced at her and then quickly away. 'Perhaps not. But it makes no difference.'

'It's up to you.' This time she pulled him closer still, only wanting to comfort him. 'If she has forgiven you, then perhaps in time you need to forgive yourself.'

They stayed like that for several minutes, holding one another, his head bowed toward hers. Lily felt a sadness wash over her. She had found Josefine, but Carlotta had lost her sister and she still held this man responsible. It had been a tragic accident, but Carlotta could not forgive him any more than Nico could forgive himself.

There would be more he might tell her, Lily was sure. But for now, this was enough.

CHAPTER 57

Josefine

2018

The following morning, Angelo was there in the *caffè* as usual and as they were quiet, Josefine told him the story of what had happened in Camogli, in between serving the few customers who came in. There were not many people, but there were still too many people, she thought.

'Maybe I will come back this evening for a drink?' Angelo seemed to have read her mind. His eyes searched her face. 'Would that be okay?'

Still, Josefine hesitated. They had not spent so much time together lately and of course there was Lily to think of, Lily who was returning to the UK tomorrow. But, given the situation . . . 'Okay,' she said. 'I will invite Lily too.' Which should please them both.

'Yes, good idea, Josi.' And was it her imagination, or did his expression change?

As the *caffè* got even busier, Josefine spent the day moving from table to table, trying to remain calm and capable, but in truth, in a bit of a daze. It was a lot to take on board, now that she had not only a sister, but a father too – and more besides.

She found herself smiling every now and then as she thought of Bruno. She would invite him over soon, she decided. Show him the *caffè*, tell him more about her life and hopefully find out more about his. She would show him the photographs Lily had given her too – she was sure he would like that, although it might make him sad. Maybe later in the summer she would take a day off and go and meet some of his family? They would be astounded at what he had to say, he had told her, but pleased for him, he was sure, that he had a daughter he had never known of. He would talk to them, he would pave the way. He was proud of her, he'd said. And that was a new and very pleasant feeling for Josefine.

Angelo turned up early that evening, and when the last customers had drifted away, she closed the *caffè* and they took their drinks out onto the terrace.

'Early bird,' she told him. She was still wearing her apron and hadn't even had time to freshen up, though she had prepared the risotto for supper.

He shrugged. 'It is the only way I can be alone with you these days, Josi.'

She smiled. 'Good to be busy, though, you know.'

He stretched out long limbs. 'But you must be tired. Yesterday was quite a day, hmm?' He seemed to be watching her closely.

'Yes, indeed.'

'And now? How are you feeling now?'

'Better,' she said. Better and better, in fact. 'I feel as if I belong somewhere. And maybe it is the first time in my life I have felt that way.' She smiled at him, feeling strangely shy. Perhaps that sense of belonging was what families brought you more than anything. You could get on or not get on, but with family you had an identity and you had roots. You had somewhere you belonged, someone you belonged to. Her adoptive parents had tried their best, she was sure, and for many people, adoption was a wonderful thing. But perhaps for them, and therefore for her, something had always been missing.

'I hope that does not mean you will reconsider your decision?' Angelo seemed very serious, his dark eyes hooded, his expression closed.

'Reconsider what?'

'Selling the *caffè*. You will not think about moving to Camogli to be near your father, I mean?' He frowned.

'Oh, I do not think so.' She brushed this away. 'It is early days, you know, Angelo. He is not far from here, is he, after all? But I am looking forward to getting to know him.'

'And Lily?' he asked.

'What about her?' Josefine helped herself to more wine and topped up his glass. Lily was special. She had instigated everything. She had searched out Josefine and in so doing had somehow given Josefine a new sense of self-worth that she treasured.

'Will she come back to Perlarosa?' He seemed wistful today; not quite himself. She supposed it was the thought of being parted from Lily.

'You will have to ask her yourself,' she retorted crisply.

He raised an eyebrow, fiddled with the stem of his wine glass. 'Josi, can I ask you something?'

She sipped her wine. 'Go ahead.' But she hoped he wasn't

going to ask her how Lily felt about him. How would she know? Lily had not confided in her. This morning she had come into the *caffè* with a blush on her cheeks and a strange excitement in her eyes. But Josefine had not asked what it was all about. She supposed Lily might have met up with Angelo when they returned last night; she hadn't gone straight back to her B & B – she had gone off into the village purposefully, almost as if she had an important date. Josefine swallowed the lump in her throat. So . . .

'Are you angry with me about something?' he asked.

Josefine took another swig of her wine. She realised she was drinking quite fast. Angelo – he was making her nervous. 'Why would I be angry?'

He spread his hands. 'I do not know. But . . .'

'But what?'

He sighed. 'Something has changed.'

'I do not know what you mean.' Although she did, of course. Josefine shifted uncomfortably in her seat. And how could she help it? He was right. Everything had changed. The only mystery was that he could not see.

'I thought . . .' Yet again, his voice trailed. Angelo was usually so much more self-assured. He sighed. 'We are friends, are we not, Josi?'

'*Certo.* Of course we are.' Josefine heard her voice break. *Mamma mia*, she thought. This was hard.

'Then talk to me.' His voice was urgent. 'Tell me what it is. Tell me what I have done.'

Okay then, she would. Because apart from any feelings she might have about Angelo – which she was not willing to give headspace to right now – Josefine was annoyed. Yes, they were supposed to be friends and, yes, Lily was her sister. And yet neither of them had shown the good manners or the grace to inform her that something was happening between the two of them. It simply wasn't fair. It made Josefine feel a fool. She took a breath. '*Allora*—'

'Hey, you two!'

It was Lily. Josefine turned around, waved her over. 'Come and join us,' she said. She was conscious of Angelo giving another little sigh at the interruption, but as for Josefine, she was relieved. She had never liked being interrogated.

'Great.' Lily still had that look about her. A sort of pent-up excitement but mingled with something else – maybe a sort of sadness. Josefine felt aggrieved yet again. Why hadn't she confided in Josefine? She was her sister. Why all the cloak and dagger? Did sisters not share?

Josefine sloshed some wine into the third glass. 'I have made some risotto for our last meal together,' she said. 'I must go and check it is not drying up.'

Lily smiled. 'That reminds me of the very first dinner you cooked for me, Josefine. Asparagus risotto. When I turned up and gave you the shock of your life.'

Josefine touched her shoulder as she passed, on her way to *la cucina*. Lily had done so much. She might like her secrets, but Josefine would be sad to see her go.

The dinner went well enough. They chatted some more about their day in Camogli and even about some of Josefine's future plans for the *caffè*. But Angelo was quiet, and to Josefine there remained a strong sense of something left unsaid. Which was probably where that something should stay . . .

At the end of the evening, Josefine was half expecting the two of them to leave together. But it was Lily who began yawning at nine o'clock, who made her excuses about tomorrow's early start. 'I need to get a good night's sleep,' she said.

'I will take you to the airport, of course,' Angelo said. 'Josi, will you come too?'

Josefine thought of the prospective goodbyes. 'Maybe not,' she said. 'The *caffè* . . .' She pulled a face at Lily, knowing she would understand. 'And I have never been good at goodbyes.'

'See you in the morning then. I'll have to leave by seven thirty, Angelo, if that's okay?'

Angelo said that it was, and Lily gave Josefine a hug and then embraced Angelo too. One kiss, two; no hint of more. 'And thanks, Angelo. I appreciate that.'

Josefine watched her walk away. She looked across at Angelo. He leant forwards intently. *Mamma mia.* Hastily, she got to her feet and began clearing the plates. 'I am tired too,' she said. 'An early night is a good idea, I think.'

Angelo got up too. He took hold of her wrist, gently, but she stopped what she was doing. 'In a moment,' he said. 'I want to talk to you first.'

'*Si?*' She had known, had she not, that he would not allow her to get away with it?

'Be honest with me, Josefine.'

She looked at him in surprise. He so rarely used her full name. And as she looked, she got caught in his gaze. A gaze that said a lot. A gaze that was very confusing.

He pulled her towards him and he kissed her. It was not the kiss of a friend, definitely not, but the kiss of a lover, the kiss of a man who wanted more.

'Angelo!' she gasped when she came up for air. The kiss had made her feel she was somewhere quite different. But surprisingly, here she was still. 'What are you doing?'

423

'What I should have done weeks ago,' he said. He still had his hands on her shoulders. 'I thought I must give you more time after you and Gianni broke up. But . . .' He moved closer. And he kissed her again.

'But what about Lily?' she asked, when she came up for air the second time. This kiss had been even better. Not only had it tasted good, but it had taken all the air from her lungs, all the energy from her limbs. All that was left was the kiss and the hunger she saw in his eyes.

'What about Lily?' With his fingertips, he brushed her cheek, so gently.

What could she say? 'I thought that you and she . . . that maybe something . . .'

'What?' He was looking at her as if she was a crazy person. And now she felt like a crazy person. She also had the feeling that he was about to kiss her again, and that this was what she wanted more than anything.

'You seemed to like her.' Josefine floundered.

'Yes, I like her. *Certo*. Of course I like her.' His lips were close again now. 'But not in the same way I like you.'

Mamma mia.

This time, when she surfaced, Josefine was struggling to even think. She wasn't sure she could form words any more either. It was as if her whole life — all the work, all the rejection, even her time with Gianni — had all somehow been building to this moment.

'Why would you imagine such a thing?' Angelo whispered in her ear. Josefine shivered. She was liquid, she thought. All liquid.

'I do not know,' she admitted. Because it hardly mattered now.

'It is you, Josi. It has always been you.'

'But, that night . . .' she heard herself saying. Just to be clear. 'I saw you running up the street to Lily's B & B. And then you came back. And . . .' Suddenly it all sounded rather flimsy.

He laughed, low and soft. 'That was the night Lily thought someone was following her,' he said. 'She was scared and she called me. And she was right, someone was following her. But it was only Gianni.'

'Gianni . . .' Josefine was fitting the new pieces together in her mind. And funnily, they were forming a quite different picture from the one she had visualised before.

'She asked me in for a hot chocolate,' Angelo went on. 'She told me what he had said.'

'Ah.' Josefine wished he would stop talking and kiss her again.

'But that was all it was, Josi.'

'Mmm.' And now, strangely, it did not seem to matter at all.

'We are friends. Nothing more. I promise. And I rather think . . .'

'What do you think?' That she was stupid perhaps? Stupid and jealous and crazy as hell?

'That Lily is interested in someone else,' he said. 'A certain tall, dark silversmith. I saw them walk past the house last night. And I have seen them together before.'

'Silversmith,' she echoed. But of course. The trip to Porto-venere. How could she have got it so wrong?

'Let us go inside,' Anglo suggested. 'I think we have a lot of time to make up, you and I . . .'

'Sienna?' she whispered.

'She is staying at Paola's tonight.'

'Oh.' Then there was nothing to stop them, she supposed.

She let the thought hang, enjoying it – that delicious anticipation.

'I have a proposition I want to run by you,' Angelo said.
He took her hand.

'Proposition?' Josefine was beginning to think she might
agree to anything.

'Come inside,' he murmured. 'Come upstairs. And I will
tell you all about it.'

CHAPTER 58

Lily

2018

The following morning, Lily set off for the *caffè* with a heavy heart. So much had happened in these six weeks since she'd first arrived here. And now it almost felt like home.

She had spent much of the day before with Nico, down at his workshop, drinking coffee with him at the harbour, walking the narrow streets of Perlarosa. And they had talked.

Not just about Nico's past. Lily told him about her childhood, her work, her love of numbers.

'Numbers?' He had smiled. 'And is there any reason why you have this love?'

'I like the patterns they make.' Lily never grew bored with that. 'Numbers help me to understand the world in a different way.' Plus, they had given her a career, of course. 'I like the safety of them. The predictability. The beauty.'

'Ah, the beauty, yes, I see that.' He seemed interested. 'And which number do you find the most beautiful, hmm?' The look he gave her was quite unnerving.

And it wasn't an easy question. 'Maybe eight.' She frowned. 'It kind of represents everything. And it's a feminine number, of course.'

'Of course.'

But she decided not to elaborate on Pythagoras's number gender theory – at least for now. Instead, they talked about mystical numbers such as the 'magic' three, the 'lucky' seven and the 'unlucky' thirteen – which was actually one of Lily's personal favourites.

He held up his hands in surprise at this. 'But thirteen – it is a lucky number in Italy,' he said.

'Oh, really?' Lily was inexplicably pleased about this.

'But, yes. Something to do with fertility and the lunar cycles, I believe.' He raised a quirky eyebrow and Lily was forced to look away.

Lily even told him about the dreams she'd had as a child, and the fear of the never-ending numbers.

'Like Pi?' he asked.

Lily was pleasantly surprised. 'Like Pi,' she confirmed. 'Its decimal representation never ends. It's a transcendental number.'

Nico gave a little frown.

'Don't worry,' she told him. 'I've embraced infinity now.'

He was, he told her, very relieved to hear it.

Nico was a good listener. As for his past, it seemed that telling Lily why he had left his home town in northern Italy and come to Perlarosa had opened the floodgates. Maybe it had been so long since he'd talked of it that now he couldn't stop. Or maybe (and she hoped this was the case) he wanted to talk to her because she understood, because he trusted her, because he felt the time might be right to at least try and move on.

It was a lot for Lily to absorb. And a lot too late, because here she was, one day later, preparing to leave Perlarosa. When would she even see him again? Nothing had happened between them – at least nothing physical. And yet everything had happened. He was so different from the man she'd imagined him to be at first – taciturn, difficult, bad-tempered. Things, she now realised, went deep for Nico. He had been through a lot. He might be moody, but he could also make her laugh. He was good company and he was interesting. He was attractive too and she was only too aware of the sparks flying between them.

He had told her that he planned to talk to Carlotta properly – to discuss what she was feeling, to bring it all out in the open between them, however painful that might be. And that, Lily felt, could only be a good thing. He had also told her that despite the way they had got together, Carlotta and Gianni were determined to make a go of it, to make a fresh start somewhere new.

'Carlotta – she always wanted a child,' Nico said.

Lily thought of Josefine. How that was what her sister had always wanted too.

'But her ex-husband – he had no wish for a family. And so now, with Gianni . . .' – he shrugged – 'she has a chance for what she has always dreamt of.'

Lily nodded. She understood. Fortunately for Carlotta, she had met Gianni when there was still time. And Nico? What might Nico be like if he ever managed to forgive himself? If he ever managed to come to terms with the awful tragedy that still burdened him? Lily wanted to be around to find out. But that was in the future, and right now, she didn't even know if he would come and say goodbye.

Lily wheeled her case the short distance down to the *caffè* to say her final farewell to Josefine. They hugged and Josefine forced on her some lunch for the journey.

'You will get hungry,' she told her.

'Thank you.'

'Have a good journey. Tell me when you are home safely.' There were tears in her eyes. She looked sad, but also happy, as if the emotion was almost too much for her. Lily was touched. Coming here to Italy had brought her so much more than she'd dared hope for.

It wasn't only Josefine who had found a family. Josefine was the first person Lily had found in Perlarosa, Lily reflected, but not the last. And she didn't want to let any of them go.

Angelo arrived soon after. He embraced Lily and then flung an arm around Josefine's shoulders. '*Cara*,' he murmured and she lifted her face for a kiss.

Lily blinked at them both in surprise. 'Uh . . . ?'

'*Sì?*' Josefine looked like innocence personified. And also like the cat who had got the cream. She was practically purring.

'Have I missed something here?' Lily looked from one to the other of them. 'What's going on?' Last night, they had been cool with one another, if anything; she'd had the distinct impression Josefine hadn't even wanted to be left alone with the man who was supposed to be her best friend.

'Ah,' said Josefine. 'Yes.'

'You could say . . .' – Angelo was looking at Josefine and there was little doubt in Lily's mind of what must have happened between them last night after she left – 'that we have come to an understanding.'

430

'Well, it's about time.' Lily grinned.

'You are right,' Angelo agreed. 'She is a tricky one, as you know. But the truth is that I have been in love with this woman for a long while.'

Lily laughed. 'So, what took you so long?'

'Fear,' said Josefine.

'Pride,' said Angelo.

Josefine smiled. 'And a bit of jealousy, of course.'

'*Certo.*' And he kissed her again.

Lily was mystified. But whatever had happened, it had clearly been a good thing that she'd left so early last night. There was a softness about her sister that was new – and it suited her.

'Shall we tell her?' Angelo asked Josefine.

'Of course,' Josefine replied.

'Tell me what?'

'We have decided to join forces,' Angelo said. He squeezed Josefine's shoulder.

'Join forces?' Lily had thought that was obvious. 'Get together, you mean?'

'But yes, get together,' Angelo said. 'Not only on a personal level – because, why not? My daughter already loves your sister and we know that we get along . . .'

A daughter for Josefine . . . Lily couldn't help but smile. Josefine's family was increasing by the day.

'And when we fight . . .' – Josefine gave a little shrug – 'it will be good to make up, *si*?'

'I am looking forward to it already, *cara*.' Angelo remained straight-faced.

'But also, we plan to get together professionally,' Josefine continued. 'What do you think of that? A *caffè* – it needs a bakery, *no*?'

'*Sì, sì*. And a bakery ...' – he spread his hands – 'it might find a *caffè* most useful, I think.'

'Oh, I'm with you.' Lily clapped her hands. 'What a brilliant idea.'

Angelo nodded modestly. 'It was mine,' he said.

Josefine gave him one of her looks. 'I am glad you approve,' she told Lily.

'And now.' Angelo took her case. 'I must get you to the airport, I think.' He pointed. 'My car is just up here.'

'Thanks.' Lily looked back down the street as they left the piazza, but there was no sign of Nico. She couldn't blame him. It was never easy to say goodbye.

Lily hugged Josefine once more while Angelo put her case in the boot. She looked again. Nothing. She had told him what time she was leaving and she had hoped ...

Lily got in the car and opened the window. 'Goodbye, Josefine,' she said sadly. It was hard, much harder to leave than she had ever thought it would be.

'*Momento*.' Josefine stood back. She looked down the street. Someone was running towards them.

Nico. He got to the car, out of breath, raven hair sticking out at all angles. 'Lily,' he said.

'Hello, Nico.' She smiled. It meant the world to her that he had come to say goodbye.

He thrust a hand through the open window and dropped a small package onto Lily's lap.

'What's this?'

'Open it,' he said, 'and you will see.'

She slipped a finger under the tape and pulled the paper

432

apart. It was a small box. She looked at Nico. He nodded. She opened it.

Nestling on a gauzy cushion was a silver pendant. Lily picked it up. The pendant was the symbol of Pi and the delicate chain was the very same chain he had shown her the first time she'd entered the workshop and chosen the chain for Josefine. *This chain for you*, he had said.

'You made this for me?' She traced the little symbol with her fingertip. *Infinity* . . .

He gave a shrug. 'For the woman who loves numbers,' he said. 'Especially numbers of the never-ending kind.'

When on earth had he made it? She'd only told him about her love of numbers yesterday. Last night then? She'd half hoped to see him but instead he must have been in his workshop until late, making this, for her.

'It's beautiful,' she said.

'You are beautiful.'

Lily was dimly conscious of Josefine pulling Angelo away from the car, to give them a bit of space, she supposed. 'Thank you.' She held it tightly in her palm. She loved it. She would wear it always.

He nodded. 'I could not let you go without . . .'

'Without?'

He leant in the window. His gaze was as intense as ever. He smelt of silver and the sea.

When he kissed her, Lily thought that she was drowning. She closed her eyes. She was in very deep.

Finally, he broke away. 'Goodbye, Lily.' His voice was low. 'And thank *you*.'

'For what?'

'For making me see what might be possible . . .'

'Goodbye, Nico,' she whispered. She looked into his eyes once again, that dark gaze that held so much wrapped within. But she was leaving. Perlarosa was not her home.

'Will you come back soon?' he asked her.

She nodded, hardly trusting herself to speak. There was so much more she wanted from him. It might not be easy, but . . . She would be back, she realised, just as soon as she was able. And she couldn't help thinking of Bruno Ferrando, her mother's lover. He had asked her mother to wait. And she had. Lily hoped it had been some consolation for Bruno to know that.

By coming here, she hadn't only found Josefine, Lily realised. She had discovered her mother's story.

'Will you wait for me?' she asked Nico.

'I will wait for you,' he said. 'I will wait for as long as it takes you to come back to me.'

Lily smiled, held the little silver pendant of Pi between her forefinger and thumb. 'I will count the days,' she said.

ACKNOWLEDGEMENTS

My first big thank you goes to my fabulous team at Quercus, without whom this book would never have been born. Special love to the best editor, Stefanie Bierwerth, and grateful thanks also to Jon Butler, Kat Burdon, Emily Patience, David Murphy and the rest of the team who have done so much over the years to support my writing. Thanks also to my brilliant copy-editor, Lorraine Green, who always understands what I am trying to do.

Thanks to all at MBA Literary Agency for their hard work over recent years, especially my lovely agent, Laura Longrigg, who has now retired, and Louisa Pritchard of LPA who worked with my overseas publishers. I am now delighted to be represented by Broo Doherty at DHH Literary Agency and I'd like to thank Broo for her careful reading of this novel, for her helpful comments and for all the exciting work we are now doing together for the future.

This is the second time I have written about adoption. The first was in the novel *Bay of Secrets* when I was drawn in to the subject partly by my horror at the travesties that occurred during the Spanish Civil War and beyond, in terms of adoption practices, which have now been well-documented. This time it was rather different. I was watching the TV programme *Long Lost Family* and having a good cry, like you do – because it's rather wonderful when birth family members meet each other for the first time. Then I started thinking about all the stories that never get aired. What might happen, for example, if someone who had been adopted simply did not want to be found?

I did a lot of reading of personal stories of women who had their babies adopted, often against their wishes and because circumstances gave them very little choice. Often, this sad and traumatic parting affected them for the rest of their lives. As a woman who grew up in the later 1960s and 70s, I and my peers had a lot more say when it came to birth control and choices. But in 1965, many of these choices were not available to girls like Marilyn, as they had not been for many girls and women in the years preceding. There was also a great deal more disapproval and shame. This must have led to so many heart-breaking situations and decisions, also impacting those who had been adopted. Adoptive parents (unlike Josefine's parents, who did their best but who couldn't quite love her enough) are usually amazing, but many adoptees also feel the need to understand why they were given away in the first place. They often want to find out more about their birth families.

This led to me thinking about sisters . . . I don't have a sister, though I always wished I did (I do love having a brother, though, Alan!). But I do have two daughters and I know that the relationship between sisters is a very special one. These two strands then came together to create *The Italian Flame*.

The book is set in an imaginary village named Perlarosa which is very much based on a small town in the famous Bay of Poets on the Italian Riviera. As I have mentioned in the text of the novel, the Bay of Poets (or Gulf of Poets) is so named because it attracted many writers to the area (not to mention the

436

fact that some of them died here) and these writers found the landscape inspirational. They include Filippo Tommaso Marinetti, Eugenio Montale, writer and director Mario Soldati, writer and painter George Sand, Henry James, E. M. Forster, Lord Byron, Mary and Percy Shelley, Virginia Woolf and my own literary hero D. H. Lawrence, who came to visit Shelley and subsequently lived for some years in Fiascherino. By all accounts, it was the playwright Sem Benelli who baptised the gulf with the name *il Golfo dei Poeti* (or *la Baia dei Poeti*) on 30th August 1910 while living in a beautiful villa overlooking the sea in San Terenzo and working on his masterpiece *La cena delle beffe*. Nice.

This novel is a work of fiction and any resemblance to inhabitants of any of these villages is purely accidental. As always, my research trip to this beautiful area of Italy was a complete joy and I hope I have managed to convey my love and passion for the place in this story. And once again, I hope that some readers will be inspired to visit this unique part of Italy after reading the book! (You will not be disappointed.)

My research partner was, as always, my husband Grey, who did a great job taking photographs, accompanying me on the walks, helping me find the right houses and churches – and in this case the right blue and grey dress, which Josefine too happened to find in Lerici. (He is also good at listening to me as I drone on about plot problems.)

As far as jewellery and silversmithing is concerned, I should like to thank Linda Child for welcoming me into her silversmithing workshop in Bothenhampton, Dorset, for showing me her lovely jewellery and for answering my questions and checking the text – any mistakes are all my own work. Linda was also one of my early readers – thanks again, Linda – and thank you to my other early readers, Meriel Powell and Sue Browne, for their valuable feedback and for giving their time (and timeline, Sue!) so generously.

As I have mentioned before, we are very fortunate to have made the county of West Dorset our home and I love to write about it. I wasn't born here but I think of this place as my soul home and certainly a place of inspiration. I have walked many a cliff in an attempt to iron out a bumpy plot, but for this book I am also thanking the Canary Island of Fuerteventura since a lot of the original writing took place there. Sitting on a beach with a notebook is my favourite way of writing and as far as I'm concerned, that's the perfect place to do it.

Love and thanks to my friends and family for their continuing love and support. Especially Wendy Tomlins – you are always amazing. And thanks to all those who have helped me with publicity, who have tracked down my books in bookshops and elsewhere, taken pictures to put on social media and given me such positive feedback. Too many to mention individually, but you're all great and I appreciate everything you do.

Thank you to the stunning Finca el Cerrillo and the writers I have taken there. Sue, Gordon and Alison are the most welcoming hosts and they have a great team who continue to offer the best possible venue for a writing group such as ours. I love these writing holidays and would like to thank everyone who has joined me there over the past fifteen years.

I have dedicated this novel to my writing buddy Maria Donovan, who has helped me so much during the writing of it. It's not easy to find a good, working writer with whom you can have a successful editing relationship and who can be a good friend too – and Maria is that person. She is a thoughtful and perceptive writer and editor and I value our meetings and discussions so very highly. Thank you for everything, Maria.

Last, but not least, thanks to the writing and reading community at large. That's all of you ... But especially those supportive librarians, readers, bloggers and writers and everyone who has got in touch to tell me they have enjoyed a book. As I have said before, it is humbling, it is wonderful, and it is very much appreciated. Thank you.

Rosanna

www.rosannaley.com
X @RosannaLey
@rosannaleyauthor
@RosannaLeyNovels